T0375720

Murder, Suicide
or
Natural Causes?

Murder, Suicide

or

Natural Causes?

Dr. Richard E. Reason II

Inspired by real events and genuine cases, however, any resemblance
to actual people living or dead is purely coincidental and,
extremely convenient.

iUniverse, Inc.
Bloomington

Murder, Suicide or Natural Causes?

Copyright © 2012 by Dr. Richard E. Reason II.

All rights reserved. No part of this book may be used or reproduced by any means, graphic, electronic, or mechanical, including photocopying, recording, taping or by any information storage retrieval system without the written permission of the publisher except in the case of brief quotations embodied in critical articles and reviews.

This is a work of fiction. All of the characters, names, incidents, organizations, and dialogue in this novel are either the products of the author's imagination or are used fictitiously.

iUniverse books may be ordered through booksellers or by contacting:

iUniverse
1663 Liberty Drive
Bloomington, IN 47403
www.iuniverse.com
1-800-Authors (1-800-288-4677)

Because of the dynamic nature of the Internet, any web addresses or links contained in this book may have changed since publication and may no longer be valid. The views expressed in this work are solely those of the author and do not necessarily reflect the views of the publisher, and the publisher hereby disclaims any responsibility for them.

Any people depicted in stock imagery provided by Thinkstock are models, and such images are being used for illustrative purposes only.
Certain stock imagery © Thinkstock.

ISBN: 978-1-4620-3652-3 (sc)
ISBN: 978-1-4620-3653-0 (ebk)

Printed in the United States of America

iUniverse rev. date: 01/10/2012

CONTENTS

Dedication

I dedicate this book to my beautiful wife Cindy.
My best friend and the smartest woman I know.

(A good husband knows how to dedicate a book!)

Dedication

Iced in a Jacuzzi

They were floating a' la natural, in a bubbling mixture of chlorine, water, and their own hemoglobin; you know, the red stuff. The monstrous Jacuzzi was placed in a corner of the flagstone deck below the big copper clad roof hanging two stories overhead. Behind the spa, stretching toward the roof, were two large cut crystal and stained glass windows.

Experience has taught me that depending on the volume of drugs, alcohol, and/or moral values, Jacuzzi jumpers often end up exposed at some point in the evening. Bare I understand, dead I don't. Knowing the victims as I did, I doubted ending the evening as human stew had ever entered their minds.

Larry and Judy Schulman were nice people who supported local charities and attended church every Sunday. Their two boys, Todd and Winthrop, were neighborhood football stars, the pride and joy of their parents. Larry owned the local bank, grocery store, mini mall, and two gas stations. Money was no object when it came to toys in the Schulman household. This explained the ornate design and unbelievable size of the hot tub that dominated the back deck of their palace.

As with most bankers, Larry wasn't the most loved person in town. With each repossession or foreclosure the list grew of people wishing some misfortune would befall him. After nearly twenty years in the business, Larry's list of potential assassins was quite extensive.

Judy, on the other hand, was adored by most of the community. People wondered how a nice lady like her could be married to such a hard-ass.

The two other occupants of this unsavory stew were Dan and Bethany Fitzsimmons, the owners of a casino in Broken Creek. As one might expect, many of those who lost their butts at the Golden Ass were more than willing to take it out on those who prospered from their misfortune. Thus, the stage was set for a horrendous murder.

On the other hand, was it murder? As county coroner, the decision would be mine alone to make. Staring at the carnage before me, I wondered who could have committed such a grisly act.

Four well-known local figures indelicately iced in a Jacuzzi was a scandal I really didn't want any part of. The only thing to do was gather the evidence to make a ruling as quickly as possible and get these people off to the morgue. If I worked fast enough, I could accomplish the task before any reporters arrived on the scene.

As a death investigator, I've been trained to photograph a scene before touching anything. Through painful experience, I've found that using a Polaroid avoids finding out later you forgot to put film in the camera. Once bodies have been moved, there really isn't any way to put them back for a second try, although I've known people who've tried.

I photographed the pool these people called a hot tub and its occupants from every possible angle. Getting the entire scene in a single shot was difficult without hanging over the railing and risking serious injury, something I'm never willing to do.

Glamour shots done, I began inspecting the victims. It was totally baffling. The entire group had been bludgeoned to death, yet there were no wounds on the palms of the hands or forearms that might indicate an attempt at self-defense. Gash wounds and depression fractures were clearly visible on the head and shoulders of one of the male victims. It looked as though he had been hit from behind with an ax or hatchet.

I also examined the drift of snow that came to the lip of the tub and stretched as deep to the edge of the deck fifteen feet away. There were no footprints or signs that anyone had been outside the tub for many hours. Staring at the bloody water, I thought this was the most bizarre murder-suicide I'd ever seen! Bludgeoning yourself to death; now that takes commitment.

As I stood near the remains bobbing in the tub, a voice startled me from behind. "Hey, Doc. Ed and Patty are coming . . ."

"Damn, Deputy! Don't sneak up behind me when I'm surrounded by corpses. I could have wet my pants!"

People sneak up behind me deliberately. Make the coroner jump out of his skin; it's a game people like to play. Trust me, it works.

"Have you tried Depends?" the Deputy asked. "Are you ready for the mortuary people?"

"Sure, tell Ed and Patty to bring four body bags and hip waders".

"No need to shout," Ed said. "I'm here. I should tell Patty to bring a gaff and net," Ed added as he peered into the pottage in front of us. "I hope they didn't want an open casket ceremony. What the hell happened to them?"

"I just don't get it," I said. "There's no sign of an intruder."

Patty arrived, took one look, and promptly got in my face. "I'm not going in there, no matter what you say."

For the next ten minutes we stood thinking of ways to remove the Schulman's and Fitzsimmons from their current predicament. Actually, we were thinking of how the other guy could do it, alone. Patty volunteered to hold the bags open on the snow. Whoopee! Ed and I decided just to glove up and do the best we could. Slippery wet corpses on snow; now that's an experience. Once we had a body on the edge of the Jacuzzi it just slid down into the bag. Ed coerced the patrolman into helping him load the bodies into the big white hearse. I had no idea what to do with ten thousand gallons of pool water that no one wanted to swim in anymore, so I seized the opportunity to bug out on the cleanup.

Within a few hours the bodies were ready for autopsy. I arrived at the morgue early enough to fill Betty, our dispatcher, in on the facts of the case as I always do.

My dramatic story was interrupted by the sound of my name echoing through the hallway, "Rex Reedman . . . paging Rex Reedman . . . people are waiting for you." It was Dr. Steve Bilmarian, the pathologist.

Dr. Bilmarian stands five-foot-three in boots, with shoulder-length jet-black hair and a big bushy mustache. His arms sport three colorful tattoos: an eagle, the Harley Davidson logo, and a naked woman that moves when he flexes his arm. His wallet is chained to his belt and he always wears thick, heavy, motorcycle boots. This is not the kind of man I'd want to meet in a dark alley, or so I thought the first time I met him.

In reality, he's one of the greatest guys I've ever known. His loud laugh can be heard for blocks and the only thing bigger than his laugh is his generosity. There was a time shortly after we moved here when I was really struggling to make ends meet. No one knew it, or so I thought.

Suddenly, there was a loud knock, no, banging on my office door. It was Dr. Bilmarian hollering at the top of his lungs, "What's the matter with you? Are you nuts?" In his hand he was waving an envelope with my name on it. "How could you leave this just laying outside your door?"

When I opened the parcel, there was Dr. Bilmarian's check for three thousand dollars. "Keep the faith," he said. "I promise God will take care of you."

As I entered the autopsy suite, Dr. Bilmarian flashed a big grin.

"So nice of you to join us, Doctor. I hope we aren't disturbing your sleep."

"Yeah, you missed his off-key rendition of 'bob-bob-bobbin along' in honor of our guests here," the autopsy tech teased.

"Okay, Rex. I know I can always count on you to bring me some strange cases, but this one's too weird. I've read your report about the scene and seen your attempt at photography. Have you had a close look at these bodies?" he asked as he unzipped one of the bags.

"Of course, my dear Watson, but let's test your skills of deduction." I wasn't about to admit that I didn't have a clue as to who or what killed these people.

"Watson, eh? Well, Sheer-luck bones, there's only one way to do that," he quipped. "Todd, who's our first guest today?"

"Well, Doc, coming to us today from lovely Pine Park is our first contestant, Larry Schulman," he continued, reading from the toe tag. "He's a well-respected banker and all around good guy."

"Never mind his civic achievements; he turned down my motorcycle loan. Todd, wheel that jerk over here and let's see if he had a heart after all," Dr. Bilmarian ordered with a wry smile.

Dictation began with examination of the wounds to the head and chest areas. "Thirteen slice type wounds are noted on the patient's head and scalp region. There is a deep puncture wound noted above the left clavicle extending into the plural space beneath." Doc looked up from the body. "He had a punctured lung. There's your bleeder."

Dr. Bilmarian and Todd measured and sketched the dimensions of every cut, bruise, or abrasion, noting the location of each on a small chart, and then photographing them for the record. As the morning progressed, they repeated the same careful notations for each of the four bodies. Internal examinations were unremarkable for any signs of disease, tumor, or pathology of any kind.

"They're as healthy as horses; they'll live a hundred years," Dr. Bilmarian pronounced jokingly. "I'm sorry bud, but other than massive blood loss, punctured lungs, and multiple skull fractures, I can't tell you what killed these folks".

"That sounds like a cause of death to me," I protested.

"Moron! You know what I mean. If I believe my own examination, all the blows were from different angles. Whoever sent these people to meet their Maker used about ten different knives and clubs and was both right and left handed. Oh, and they didn't struggle. You tell me how someone did that."

"And they didn't leave any tracks in the snow," I added. "Can you at least confirm a time of death?"

"They died last night."

"Liver core temperatures and stage of rigor mortis are pretty much useless due to the fact they were submerged in hot water most of the night. Biggest moron! The best I can say is that they all died at about the same time, less than twenty-four hours ago," Dr. Bilmarian grinned.

"Brilliant, I have four corpses and all you can tell me is they died together at the hands of an ambidextrous killer who leaves no footprints. My dear Watson, you're a rectal genius!"

Still clueless, I returned to the scene at the Schulman's mansion, now empty of residents since relatives had taken the boys home with them. I crunched around on the ice and snow trying to capture the view the victims had at the time of their deaths. How could someone sneak up behind them and not be seen? Does this mean they trusted whomever it was, not suspecting them? Did that mean it could have been their loving, now grief-stricken children? Oh, shit.

I thumbed through the Polaroid's of the scene and was struck by several things, like the fact that there were no splatter marks. If you hit someone with an object more than once, each time it's drawn back to strike again, a small amount of blood flings off the end of the weapon. This leaves a splatter pattern on any surrounding objects. Red blood on fresh white snow and ice would show up on any photos and clearly be seen even now. Yet, there was no splatter anywhere. How could the facts be lying to me?

Then I had an epiphany and knew I had the answer. They were killed somewhere else and then placed in the pool! Sure, that would explain it.

No, it didn't. The crime team had checked the entire house and there wasn't blood anywhere. So much for my epiphany, I was back to feeling like the village idiot.

I knew the answer was right in front of me and if I could just open my eyes I'd see it. I stayed until sunset, still clueless when I finally decided to call it a day. Part way down the drive, I paused to look back at the house one more time. The sight of the large copper roof partially snow covered and floating in the treetops struck me; it was gleaming like gold and the snow looked like diamonds.

It was about three o'clock in the morning when it suddenly hit me. I could hardly wait to tell my solution to Dr. Bilmarian.

*   *   *

For as long as I can remember everyone called me "the wrecking ball." The name made me sound like some pro wrestler. My parents say my grandmother gave me the name. Apparently when I was two, I disassembled grandma's favorite antique music box to "see where the little men were." Grandma says it's a good thing I was so cute or she'd have killed me.

As a boy I was the kind of kid people just weren't sure about. My mom's friends were certain I'd either win a Nobel Prize or spend my life in prison. Bets were on the prison term. Don't get me wrong, I didn't have criminal tendencies. It's just I was an inquisitive child who took apart anything I could get my hands on. During a single week in the third grade, I reverse-engineered my dad's stereo, my mom's toaster, and my brother's alarm clock. Taking things apart wasn't what got me into trouble. It was my total lack of interest in reassembling them once I'd figured out how they worked. My dad always said I'd grow out of it. "It's just a stage Rex is going through," he would calmly tell my mother when she saw her Maytag in pieces, *again*. However, he didn't seem as understanding when my experiments involved the occasional destruction of *his* prized possessions.

Like the time I removed the gas regulator from my dad's barbecue. The idea was to cook dinner faster with a hotter fire. The result was the fastest haircut and beard trimming my father had received in his life. To this day I can still see the look on his face. Eyes wide open, screaming, "REX! What the hell did you do to my new barbecue?" Today, he takes great delight in telling my children there is a place on his chin he still doesn't need to shave due to the famous barbecue re-design.

When I arrived at college, I became friends with my biology professor. We hit it off on the first day of anatomy lab. I think it was my ability with a scalpel and the fact that nothing he did could gross me out. Whether it was dissecting a frog or skinning a cat, he said I had natural ability. In dissection class my team actually found the cause of our fetal pig's death: heart failure. It probably occurred about the time he discovered he was to be pickled and sent to our class.

I guess it was inevitable, a career doing autopsies. In retrospect, it was the perfect job. I moved from taking apart mechanical things to taking apart people. I really liked it and I didn't have to put them back together.

Okay, I'll admit I was a little naïve. I had no idea what a pathologist was, much less what they did. I never even questioned why such a person needed an assistant. I thought, how bad could it be?

I found out on my first day when a friend introduced me to a pathologist, Dr. Hollister, out at his ranch. He was a tall man, very thin, clad from head to foot in white paper overalls and wearing a breathing apparatus that made him sound like Darth Vader.

The doctor beckoned me to come join him. "Oh, sorry," he said as he removed the apparatus from his face and stripped off his blue rubber gloves with a pop. "Welcome to my blue-sky lab. I keep this old operating table here for cases like this one. Today's feature is a floater."

We stood alone behind the barn in two inches of mud. Oh God, I hoped it was mud. I quickly learned the body on the table had been in a lake for three days. The skin was really loose. Fluids below the skin begin to pool soon after death. "Skin slippage," I was told. At this point, if you touch the skin, it slides off leaving the deeper tissues exposed. The body was green and bloated, like an overripe watermelon. He called it a stinker.

Dr. Hollister made a 'Y' shaped incision from the top of the shoulder area to the center of the chest then down to the pubic bone. The smell engulfed my virgin nose. One Happy-Man burger lunch coming up! Then he began to pull organs from that body like a magician pulls rabbits from a hat.

In an attempt to draw my face closer, Dr. Hollister removed a rotting hunk of flesh, pushed it into my face and asked, "What do you think this could be? Isn't it amazing what three days under water will do?" The body's juices dripped from his glove onto my leg and shoe. Time to burn those jeans and loafers.

It didn't take long for me to figure out his game. My brother played it with me when we were kids. It's called "gross out." Only my brother used his own bodily fluids.

In reality, once I focused on one small area, it wasn't so bad. The colors were incredible: the beautiful nutmeg appearance of the liver, the blues and violets of the heart, the yellow of the fat layer, the ten shades of green of the internal organs. It almost took my mind off that God-awful smell. I did say *almost*, didn't I? Some people say death smells like fresh mowed hay, but this reminded me of the time my family went on vacation for a month and forgot to close the freezer door.

That day I made a lifelong friend; the doctor, not the corpse. With subsequent autopsies, he would tutor me in the fine details of anatomy and physiology. During the first post of the day he would cover a new subject: cardiology, neurology, nephrology, etc. Then, during the afternoon procedure, he'd drill me on it. Thus began my career in death investigation.

That kind of treatment is probably what led me over the years to enjoy quizzing friends and relatives about some of my cases. They especially enjoy those involving celebrities.

Now, it's your turn. In the following chapters I will take you with me on some of my more bizarre and challenging cases. At the end of each case, instead of telling you the answer, I will ask, "Is it Murder, Suicide, or Natural Causes?" Of course, occasionally the cause may be accidental. You decide, and then I'll reveal my findings that solved the case.

Let's go back to our floating foursome. Have you solved it yet?

*   *   *

Doughnuts are the way to the heart of just about every pathologist I know. So, I drove to the office early, pastries in hand.

When Dr. Bilmarian finally arrived, he immediately surmised, "This means one of two things. Either you want a favor or you're here to gloat. Which one is it?" he asked, as he opened the box.

"I think I have the answer to our floating foursome," I crowed. "Want to hear a bedtime story?"

"Okay, I've got to hear this one. I'll just have a bear claw and you can enlighten me," he stated as he propped his feet on the desk and continued to eat his pastry.

"Remember each one of the victims had a variety of wounds, no two of them were the same, and yet they all died together? I kept thinking about how deep the snow on the deck was and how there weren't any splatter marks of blood on the walls. It had been driving me nuts."

"Drive? It's only a short walk for you, Sherlock." Powdered sugar puffed into the air as he spoke.

"As I was saying, I also remembered looking back at that beautiful house with its shiny copper roof. Bang! It hit me, just like it did them."

"What hit you?" he asked, now sampling a jelly-filled.

"*Ice.* It was the ice and snow from the roof that killed them. Their roof is made of metal; snow piled up and formed ice. It had been a warm day and when they turned on the Jacuzzi, heat from the rising steam warmed the eaves of the roof, allowing tons of snow and ice to come crashing down on them from two stories up! It would explain the differing wounds and why there were no footprints. The beauty of it is, the evidence melted."

"You know, as crazy as that sounds, I think you're right," he said as he saluted me with his doughnut and then walked off with the box.

The Case of the Frozen Guest

It had been snowing non-stop for two days with temperatures well below zero. My wife and I had been house bound for the past twenty-four hours. Being trapped in the house during a snowstorm is something like being shipwrecked; the scenery is lovely but you go island happy quick.

So, when there was a break in the storm, I locked the hubs on the "Beast" into four-wheel drive and we took off for the local service club's quail omelet and elk sausage breakfast. Hey, I was desperate.

The plaid-suited club president began his welcoming speech, "Good morning ladies and germs!"

"Ladies and germs, is he kidding?" I whispered to Lori. "I haven't used that joke since the third grade."

"Be nice," she said, giving me "The Look."

I couldn't help myself. "How long do you think he's owned that suit"?

"Shhh, I want to hear this. If you can't behave you won't come next year."

"Promise?"

Oh God, get me out of this, I prayed.

Five minutes into the mind-numbing speech, my faith in a compassionate God was affirmed. I could hear a faint 'beep-beep' coming from my breast pocket. I excused myself to call Betty, the dispatcher.

"Rex. How's the sexiest Coroner in Colorado? You know I miss you when nobody dies."

"You tease. I'm sure you didn't page just to flirt with me. What's up?"

"Spoilsport. If you're not going to flirt back I'll just make you go to work. You're needed at 1255 East Fifth Street. Get your butt in gear, the police are waiting, darling."

You've gotta love poor, warped Betty. She sits alone all day in a dark room, her only companions the giant phone recorders taping every incoming call. I think the constant hum of the electronics has affected her mind.

I returned to the banquet room and quietly explained to Lori that she would need to find a ride home, again.

"You're a liar!" she hissed. "I didn't hear your pager."

"I swear on my sainted mother's grave. I'll take the whole day off for the turkey egg and moose horn soup next month," I pleaded.

"Your mother isn't dead and I'm going to tell her what you said." Lori was clearly annoyed. "Go on, get out of here. I want to hear about stuffing sausage."

I tried not to laugh, kissed her cheek and made for the door.

The tires on the Beast qualified as bald some time ago. Now they would best be described as almost round rubber things. It was only two or three miles across town to the scene, and in good weather I'd have arrived within a few minutes. Once the beast was moving, the idea of controlling it was out of the question. It was more a matter of pointing it in the general direction I wanted to go and praying I wouldn't meet another car. All it required was nerves of steel and several pair of adult undergarments.

I arrived on the scene with clean underwear, barely.

"About damn time, I thought *you* died," said Ted McDonald, Pine Park's finest.

14

"Good to see you, too, Ted."

"Looks like we've got a humanoid Popsicle, the only thing missing is the stick," Ted smirked.

"Are you sure? I mean, did you really check?" Knowing him, it was a distinct possibility.

He ignored my comment and explained, "The paperboy found him this morning sitting against the mailbox frostbitten and frozen stiff."

I saw what appeared to be a Hollywood prop—a waxy blue man with snow piled up in his lap and small icicles falling from his nose and ears. His eyes stared blankly into space. His head leaned against the post of the mailbox, legs stretched out in front of him. It was as if he was trying to catch a quick tan.

"You mean hypothermia, don't you?" I said, as I knelt down for a closer look. Ted knelt down next to me. "Looks relaxed, doesn't he?"

"Almost too relaxed," I commented. "There aren't any signs of a struggle. It looks as though he was just sitting here having a good 'old time, along came a storm and froze him in place."

"That theory might work, but did you notice his left hand?" Ted said, pointing to the far side of the body. A blood-soaked cloth concealed the limb. "It looks like he bled to death to me."

I could tell he was pleased I had missed the injured left hand.

I stared at the bloody rag wrapped around the man's hand, then back to his face wondering how he could look so content with an obviously painful wound while at the same time freezing his ass off!

"There's a trail of bloody footprints," Ted said, as he pointed to a three-story Victorian mansion. In the heydays of mining this had probably been one of the finer houses in town. Now it was only a cheap rental with bare wood showing through and a three-story icefall coating the north face of the building.

As I stood on the lawn taking this all in, it occurred to me. "Think about it, Ted. It was ten below last night. Wouldn't it be kind of hard to bleed to death in temperatures that low? Hypothermia would cause the blood vessels to constrict. If anything, that might have saved his life or at least allowed him to live long enough to freeze to death."

The police photographer, Bob Newman interrupted my discussion. "Want any special shots?" he asked.

"No, as long as you get these blood stains and wherever they lead in the house, I'll be happy. Oh, and don't forget to get a few close up shots of the victim's left hand."

"Oh, right away, Mr. Spielberg."

"When will prints be ready?" I asked. "Ted here would like a couple of wallet size."

"And people say photographers have a sick sense of humor."

I turned to Ted, "Do you know if the victim lived here?"

"Just before you arrived I spoke to the resident. He told me the stiff was a friend of his who was here last night celebrating the New Year."

"Did he elaborate on the term celebrate? Was it just alcohol or were there drugs involved?" I inquired.

"Funny you should mention that. The guy in the house admitted they did a 'couple of lines and were smoking."

"How much did he consider a couple of lines, more than a gram, less than a kilo?" I asked. "Did he know what it was cut with?" I continued.

"Well, if you'll let me answer," Ted interrupted. "The guy in the house says the deceased mostly drank. Seems they began at about six o'clock and the victim left about one in the morning. His friend claims they split about a quarter of a gram between them."

"You believe him?" I laughed. "You know as well as I do users and alcoholics are liars when it comes to the extent of their habit. How did he explain the blood on the walkway and the body by the mailbox?"

"Oh, he can't. He can't explain the body or the blood and it gets even better than that. There's blood all over the house. Beside the dining room table is a pool big enough to swim in, and the sofa cushions in the living room are covered. It's no wonder he's blue, there can't be any blood left in him. Want to go in and look?"

"Oh Ted, you know it's what I live for".

Inside the house, the floor had a definite list to the left. I felt like a drunken sailor as I crossed the living room to greet David Cronshaw, a forty-six-year old sheet metal worker.

He looked like hell and it was clear he hadn't slept. We sat down at the dining room table, careful not to slip in the now sticky pond of blood. He lit his second cigarette from the burning butt of the first and began to babble nervously.

"Me and Bruce were celebrating the New Year, drinking and partying. We do it every year, well, since his divorce anyway. By about nine he was really drunk and began to get angry. We started to argue; out of nowhere he hit me. Then he turned and put his fist through the glass in my gun cabinet."

The cabinet was a beautiful dark walnut with leaded cut glass panels. It looked like a temple to his collection of antique shotguns and Chinese imports. There was a bloody six-inch diameter hole in the left side.

Cronshaw continued, "He settled down in a hurry when the blood started pouring from his hand."

"Why didn't you call an ambulance?"

"Well, we didn't want the hassle, so I put a towel on it to stop the bleeding".

"Of course that makes sense. Who had the drugs?" I asked.

"Um, I did. Well, he gave me the money and I got the stuff." He was looking at the floor, a sure sign of a lie—or at least someone who's trying to cover his butt.

"So, when did you say your friend left last night?"

"Bruce left at about one or one-thirty."

"And when did you two do your last line?" Ted asked.

"Around nine o'clock," he answered, sounding agitated.

"Then what happened?"

"At about one, Bruce said he wanted to go home. He went out to his car and that was the last I saw of him. I fell asleep on the couch and didn't wake up until you banged on the door," he said, pointing to Ted.

I could tell he was wearing thin, and despite what you see in the movies or read in cheap detective novels, it's not a good idea to push a witness too far. Better to keep them as comfortable and cooperative as possible until you have enough evidence to hang them. Anyway, I had all the information I needed for now and something in my gut told me that party animal Cronshaw wasn't being totally honest.

What I really wanted to do was get back to the morgue and do the autopsy while this guy was still frozen. Popsicles don't smell.

*   *   *

Few people ever want to spend much time in the morgue but I think the autopsy suite is beautiful. Ours is large, clean, and always cold. It's nothing like Dr. Frankenstein's lab, despite what most people think. The walls and floors are pale blue tile with bright white grout. Eight neatly stacked refrigerators for cadaver storage, complete with shiny stainless steel doors and slide out trays, line one end of the room. Clocks hang on the wall to the left and right of the autopsy table. This way no matter which side of the table the doctor works from, he or she has a clear view of the time for his dictation.

Cut into the wall directly across from the left side of the table is a set of wire-reinforced windows for a viewing audience. It's for those who are afraid of the sounds of the saws, chisels and hammers, or the smell of burning tissue as the cutting blade vibrates through bone. They have a wonderful view of the deceased's head as well as the pathologist's butt. This is a favorite spot of paramedic and nursing instructors who will bring their classes for a field trip.

At the front of the room sits a stainless steel table with slats to support a body above the sink section, which runs the full length of the table. The sound of running water can be heard coming from under the slats. It runs from a sprayer at the top of the table into a drain in the base. Above the foot of the table is a large and extremely accurate produce-type scale for weighing body parts.

A bank of surgical lights and a large exhaust fan hang overhead. The fan draws aromas from our subject right past our noses. If anyone were to ask me, the fan should be in the floor under the table, sucking the stench away from my face. You can tell a pathologist didn't invent that piece of equipment.

We began the post at 10:30 a.m. Those attending the procedure were a reluctant Ted McDonald, detective, Dr. Bilmarian, pathologist, Jim Simmons, autopsy assistant, and Rex Reedman, coroner.

Jim dimmed the lights in the main room and everyone moved closer to the table, except Ted.

"Let's start at the top," Dr. Bilmarian chuckled looking in Ted's direction. Ted swallowed hard and looked at the floor. I smiled behind my mask.

Dr. Bilmarian began his dictation. "The deceased is a slightly obese forty-eight-year old man weighing 290 pounds, sixty-five inches in height. His skin appears somewhat cyanotic (blue, due to lack of oxygen); areas of frostbite on his nose, ears, and fingertips are noted. He is cold to the touch; pupils are fixed and dilated, and marked rigor mortis is observed . . ."

Rigor mortis is the stiffness that can help to establish the time of death. Initially, a body will be warm but not stiff. Within three to eight hours, it will be warm and stiff. From eight to thirty six hours the body becomes cold and stiff. Anything beyond thirty-six hours, the body will most likely be cold and flaccid. In this case, the frozen state of the cadaver makes that determination useless.

Dictation continued, ". . . Several large lacerations appear on the anterior aspect of the left hand and distal wrist. These injuries appear to be consistent with the reported injury or might possibly be defensive-type knife wounds. The deceased is clothed in blue jeans, a red patterned flannel shirt, white athletic socks, and gnarly looking tennis shoes. He has no coat, gloves, or hat. A blood soaked rag accompanies the body. The body is devoid of tattoos, scars, or other distinguishing marks. The pattern of lividity . . ."

Lividity is the bluish-violet blood that settles to the lowest points of the body. After bodies remain in one position for a short period of time, gravity pulls blood from the tissues to the lowest points. This creates a pattern similar to a deep purple bruise. Pressure points, however, blanch to a bright white. The resulting pattern makes it easy to determine the position at the time of death. Even if the body is moved later, the original pattern remains.

". . . The pattern is consistent with that of an individual in a seated position," Dr. Bilmarian continued as he began the Y shaped incision. Jim peeled back the overlying tissues, which revealed several small areas of ecchymosis. Ecchymosis is the medical term for bruising. Recent bruises were noted over the sixth through eighth ribs on both sides. Using large pruning shears, Jim removed the ribs.

". . . The connective tissue is separated revealing the organs of the thoracic cavity. The lungs are those of an apparent smoker. Cardiac blood is drawn for toxicological study, as is the vitreous humor of the eyes."

We use the eye because the fluid from the eyes holds toxins longer than the blood due to its slow circulation.

". . . The organs are removed for closer examination. Dissection of the cardiac tissue reveals the presence of multiple foci of atherosclerotic plaque formation."

Atherosclerotic plaque is a buildup of calcium in the artery. You might call it hardening of the arteries.

". . . There is a large area of recent necrosis (dead cells) within the cardiac musculature. This might be indicative of a recent heart attack. Vessels are saved along with representative sections for microscopic examination. The liver appears to be somewhat fatty and infiltrated which is consistent with early cirrhosis or hepatitis, most likely due to alcohol abuse. The brain appears normal with no signs of edema, stroke or tumor, as do all other organs and systems of the body."

The post concluded at 12:00 p.m.

Two days later, I was given the toxicological studies.

The deceased's blood alcohol level was elevated. Not lethally so, but party animal number two definitely wasn't walking a straight line with his feet or his mind when he left Cronshaw's house.

The tests also revealed a high level of cocaine in the blood. However, the metabolite benzoylecgonine was almost nonexistent. This was not going to be happy news for Mr. Cronshaw.

Let me explain. Within thirty to forty minutes of entering the bloodstream, cocaine is broken down leaving no evidence of the cocaine molecule, only the metabolite. So, if it was true the deceased had done a line at nine p.m. and left at one a.m., why was there cocaine still present in his blood?

This new information put a definite wrinkle in Cronshaw's version of what happened. Surprise! So I went back to the Boy Scout's house to tutor him about a little thing called honesty and maybe give him a hint or two on first aid.

"It happened like I told you, I swear!" Cronshaw said, defensively.

"Well, you said you did your last line at nine o'clock and he left at one, but our toxicological reports say your friend had enough in him to kill an elephant when he died. That means either he left here at nine or he used the drugs just before one. Which is it?"

Cronshaw looked panicked, which could make him dangerous.

"Relax, I'm not here to arrest you. I just need to know exactly what happened so I can close this case." He relaxed a little. I smiled. His shoulders relaxed even more. "Mind if I grab a beer? Want one?" He was mine.

"Well, we were doing our third gram at about 1:00 a.m. when suddenly Bruce began to bitch about chest pain. So, I gave him a beer."

"Makes sense," I said.

"Next thing I know he slumped over on the couch and stopped breathing. He was dead! So, I decided to carry him outside and let people think he died there. Hell, I didn't think it would matter."

"How did you plan on explaining the trail of bright red blood leading directly to your front door?" I could not believe what I was hearing.

"Hey man, I didn't know there was any blood; it was dark."

"Oh yeah, I forgot," I replied as I thought, this man is as dumb as a box of hair.

You now have the evidence in this case. You decide how to sign Bruce's death certificate. Is it *Murder, Suicide, or Natural Causes?*

REX'S REVIEW

This was a very interesting case to rule on. The findings lead in different directions at the same time.

Consider the severe blood loss caused by his hand injury. He could have bled to death or, low blood volume might have resulted in cardiac arrest. In these scenarios, the cause would be accidental.

Or, possibly he suffered a drug overdose due to the combination of alcohol and cocaine; another accidental cause.

If we consider the narrowed arteries and necrotic (dead) heart tissue, one could reasonably conclude this man a suffered heart attack. This would be considered a death due to natural causes.

Then again, if David were aware of his friend's heart condition and provided the drugs anyway, it could be argued as a form of homicide.

It seemed clear from David's rendition of the evening that if he had summoned help, Bruce may have survived the heart attack with proper medical attention. The same holds true for the possible drug overdose. He may also have lived through the blood loss, had he received prompt medical attention.

But none of those are what killed him. Remember David hauled Bruce outside? Bruce wasn't dead; he was only unconscious. How do I know Bruce was only unconscious?

Dead people don't frostbite, they just freeze.

I signed the cause of death as: Cardiac arrest complicated by hypothermia, cocaine use and severe blood loss.

The manner of death: Death at the hands of another.

The District Attorney would have to decide what degree.

Ding, Dong, a Witch Is Dead

I hate crowds. Well, that's not completely true. I hate being required to be polite around strangers. I'm concerned I'll say something uncouth. I've always described myself as rude, crude, lewd, and socially unacceptable. It's just my nature to say whatever is on my mind, whenever it's on my mind, usually without editing. It's why I work with dead people. My close friends are used to it and my family learned to just ignore me long ago.

It was late on Friday night as I arrived home and found my driveway filled with cars. I entered the living room and was confronted with a house full of Lori's friends. They'd decided to come over for a night of cocktails and cards.

With a house full of strangers, all I wanted to do was escape to my den unnoticed and watch TV. No such luck. I hadn't been home five minutes when a small group of inebriated poker players cornered me in the kitchen to ask about the witch.

"Lori said it was a funny story," Tracy pleaded. Tracy is about forty-three, stands five-foot-two and will tell you just how the cow ate the cabbage. She put her arm around my neck, squeezed tightly and looked directly into my eyes, "Come on, be a buddy."

"Tell us or I'll rip your arms off," Tracy's husband, Glenn, ordered with a wink. He was accustomed to giving orders. Glenn had been an Air Force Colonel for thirty years and didn't mind telling everyone he met about the fact.

"Okay, grab a drink. We can go into my den. I'll tell you the story of the witch. You decide for yourself who or what killed her."

I should begin with 'once upon a time' to protect the deceased's confidentially and keep myself out of jail for telling you this.

It was the morning after Halloween. Lori and I rose early for breakfast on the patio. The aspens had begun turning yellow and the scrub oak bright red, a sure sign that winter was just around the corner. It's also the season when tourists, busy looking at this beautiful sight, drive into each other, over road embankments and into trees. So when the phone rang and my daughter Tina said, "It's Betty from the Sheriff's office," I immediately assumed another crazy flat-lander had driven off into oblivion.

"Rex, you cutie, did I interrupt your bath?" Betty asked.

"For your information, I'm a shower man. What's up? Are you lonely with nothing to do, so, you decided to make a few dirty phone calls to innocent citizens?"

"You are the only citizen I call and I'd hardly call you innocent. If you don't want to talk filth with me I have no choice but to send you to work. The owner of the Piney Pines campground called and wants you to come right over. He sounds shaken; it's something about a witch."

"You're kidding, right? If this is a Halloween joke, you're late. When was the last time you went outside for a little air?"

"This sounds too weird to be a prank, and I'll have you know, there is a vent right over my desk. How soon can I tell him you'll be there?" she chuckled.

"I'm on my way, but if this is one of your Halloween tricks, I'll get even."

Bart, who owns Piney Park, has an extremely sick sense of humor. Even as I drove the two miles to the campground, I still wasn't sure if this was a real call or his way of getting even with me for my water-balloon attack last Labor Day.

As I pulled into the parking area, Bart came scurrying out. The look on his face made it obvious, this was no joke. It takes a lot to upset him and he was visibly shaken.

"Okay, Bart, what's this about a dead witch?" I asked hesitantly.

"Oh man, Rex, get her out of here quick. This is terrible for business."

"Okay. Show me where she is and I'll do what I can."

Strangely, there were no police cars in the area. Bart said he'd asked dispatch not to send any marked cars, just to call me. For some reason, people on vacation don't want to be reminded that death can come to such a beautiful place. He didn't want to upset any of the kids in the campground, especially the day after Halloween.

He led me to a new, shiny, twenty-eight foot trailer near the back of the campground. No one was around; the only sounds were those of crunching twigs beneath our feet and of birds in the trees.

As we walked, Bart told me he rented this space about eight weeks ago on a long-term lease. He didn't know much about the owner, just that she lived alone with her rat dog and had just gone through a messy divorce. "She thought this might be the perfect place to begin again."

As we approached the camper, I noticed candy wrappers on the ground and a skillfully carved pumpkin left over from the night before. Bart opened the door using a handkerchief so as not to 'destroy any fingerprints.' Of course, I won't mention that he probably didn't have the foresight to do the same thing when he found her earlier. Nevertheless, let's not make the guy feel bad.

We entered. Directly across from the door there was indeed a lady dressed as a witch sitting at one of those fold out dinettes. On the table in front of her was a large bowl filled with what looked like water and an ashtray with the butt ends of several cigars. The trailer was very neat and clean. The only other occupant was a small terrier sitting on the bed in the rear of the unit. Bart said the dog's name was Jackson and to be careful around him.

"Why, does he bite?" I asked looking at what to me was obviously a well-pampered little ankle-nipping grandma's dog. (Sorry Grandma.)

"No," Bart said. "The little monster will sneak up behind you like the snake he is and pee all over your leg. Then he runs away and hides. I've had several run-ins with the little stealth pisser."

As we stood there talking, the dog just sat on the bed in the back of the trailer, looking at us with sad little eyes. I'm sure he's just waiting to seize the moment and christen me.

"Okay, at the risk of sounding 'Jack Webbish,' who found her and when?" I began my interrogation.

"I did, at about six o'clock this morning," Bart replied.

"What made you check on this space so early in the morning?" I asked.

"I was doing my morning rounds, cleaning up from last night. Through the trees, I could hear the dog whimpering. When I came to see why, I saw him scratching on the door to get in. Her car was here, so I knocked and knocked. There was no answer. I opened the door to see if everything was all right. There she was, slumped on the table. She looked like she was asleep. I tried to wake her, but couldn't. When I touched her, she was cold. Then, I knew somebody killed her. I closed the door and hauled ass."

"Well, it doesn't smell like she's been dead long," I noted.

The smell of death is distinct, to say the least. Actually, the aroma depends on conditions such as room temperature, length of time since death, and some weird ones like if the deceased smoked, or had a strange diet. But, most times it is sweet smelling like fresh mowed hay.

"Dressed like she is, she must have been alive yesterday. Unless that's the way she always dressed." Bart wasn't laughing. "Did she go out last night?" I inquired.

"No, she was here. The kids in the park did some trick-or-treating. She had scary music, spooky noises and fog. I think my girls came by to see her twice, because she was giving out big candy bars."

Every kid's favorite, I mused. "Was she alone?" Now I was thinking about the cigar butts. Did they belong to a guest or perhaps her killer?

"I don't know. I can check the parking register to see if there were any cars in her space yesterday," Bart offered.

While Bart went to check, I radioed Betty requesting Detective Ted McDonald and Dr. Hank Boren, the toxicologist, join us.

"Is it really a witch?" Betty asked.

"Yes, warts and all," I quipped. "Be sure to tell them it's a dead witch. That should pique their interest."

Hank arrived about ten minutes later. He slammed the car door and skeptically asked, "Okay Rex, give me a break. A witch? How gullible do you think I am?"

"Hank, would I do that to you?"

Last April Fool's day I had sent Hank and Ted on a wild goose chase—something about a reported alien body. It turned out to be a decomposing cow. I tried to hide my smile.

"Just open the door and take a look," I challenged.

Hank slowly opened the door and peeked inside. I think he was still expecting Ted or something to jump out at him. He closed the door, turned around, and smiled at me. "This is a joke, right?"

"Not to me," Bart grumbled. He had just returned from the front office, reporting that 'Margaret,' the victim, had not had a visitor for the past week.

As Ted arrived, Hank turned to me and said, "Let me show him, please." Hank hurried to meet him.

Ted could see from Hank's face that something was going on. "All right what's up?"

Hank escorted him to the witch's door. "Just look and tell me what you think."

Peering in the door, Ted chuckled, "He's at it again isn't he? Sure it's not a cow?"

I turned to Bart, who was now pacing like a caged tiger. "Who was the last person to see her alive?"

"I don't know," Bart answered. "The last I saw her was around nine-thirty when I brought the girls here for the second time. They loved her special effects. They were great."

"Special effects?" I asked. "You said before that she had music and noises. What other kind of effects were there?"

"Oh, you know lights that went out when you reached the door, screaming and fog, the kids loved it."

"Are you sure it was fog and not smoke?" I asked.

"Yeah, when she opened the door it was all around her feet and would come rolling out. She scared the kids to death."

An interesting choice of words, I thought.

Hank and Ted had begun to poke around outside the trailer. Hank claimed they were looking for footprints. Oh yeah, well known trackers, these two. They reported nothing out of the ordinary. Hank suggested we check the heater for a carbon monoxide leak.

"Good idea," Ted agreed and began pulling on the tank hard enough to rock the entire trailer. "The propane tanks seem okay, no signs of a leak here."

We moved the investigation inside. Actually, we stood at the door thinking of good ideas for the other guy. No one wanted to be the first in the door for some reason. Perhaps we've all known each other long enough that no one really trusts anyone else, with good reason. Everything seemed all right; no smell of gas and nothing really looked out of place.

"Ted, since Bob isn't here yet why don't you take a few pictures before we disturb anything," I suggested.

Just then, Hank in his best Mae West voice said, "Oh, boys, I think you've forgotten something." He was holding up two pair of limp, latex gloves.

The rubber gloves were not only to protect us from contaminating a possible crime scene, potentially ruining a prosecution (Hello, O.J.), but they also protect us from all of those nasty little things that might be crawling around. After all, this lady's dead and most likely something in here killed her. I sure didn't want it on me.

"Where's the police photographer? Shouldn't Bob be here by now?" Ted whined.

"Ted just hates to take pictures," Hank observed.

"Well, if you look at his family photo album, you'll know why," I teased.

Once the portrait session was complete, we began to go through the trailer from one end to the other. I checked the desk, nightstand, and outgoing mail for a suicide note or last farewell to a friend or relative. Nothing. Then I checked the incoming mail for any bad news. Still nothing, not even a postcard. Ted looked in the refrigerator and kitchen cabinets, as well as the trash, for liquor or anything else that might provide an answer to this puzzle.

"She doesn't even have cooking sherry," Ted observed. "The only things in the trash are a frozen chicken dinner container and a piece of brown paper with the Mountain Market's logo on it. There's a receipt for some aspirin, dry ice, and candy. There are also fifty-seven candy wrappers."

"Maybe she was diabetic and ate all the candy. She could have died of a coma," he hypothesized.

"People don't die of comas you moron. A coma is just a term for deep sleep. You know, like you most of the day," Hank quipped.

While Ted thought of a brilliant retort, Hank checked for medicine bottles in the bath and bedroom. Bottles of prescription medication would have her doctor's name as well as the pharmacy that dispensed it. The type of medication would give us a clue as to any medical condition she might have had. Investigators really do like to find the answers the easy way. Nevertheless, the search yielded nothing.

"Well, nothing left to do but check out the body," Ted said with a groan.

Moving the witch to the floor, Hank checked her stage of rigor. "She's cold as ice and in full rigor mortis. She's been dead for more than eight hours, right?"

"That's what the manual says," Ted answered.

"All right, its 8:45, that means she died around midnight," Hank offered.

"He's a mathematical genius!" Ted jibed. "How did you do that in your head?"

I love having these two around; it reminds me of the way brother's act. As they continued to exchange insults, I noticed "the little pisser" sneaking up behind Ted.

Ted continued kneeling over the witch, not noticing he was being stalked. I nudged Hank in the side. He gave me a funny look. He knew that something was up, but he wasn't sure what it was. At that moment Ted screamed. He leaped up, hopping toward us and shaking his foot. Hank about jumped out of his skin, screaming in response to Ted's yelling. The entire trailer rocked like there was an earthquake. The race for the door was on. I'm certain Hank thought the body had come to life or Ted had found a rat in her clothes. In any case, he was not about to stay around and find out. As I stood there laughing hysterically, I was almost killed by the two-man stampede for the exit.

"What the hell did you scream for?" Hank demanded.

"That dog peed on me!" Ted exclaimed as he pulled off his shoe and tried to wring out his sock.

"You almost trampled me over dog pee?" Hank said.

I stood in the door laughing, the little dog between my legs watching the two crazy men dance. They both looked at me at the same moment.

"You did this on purpose," Ted said.

"I knew he'd pull something," Hank responded. "He just can't resist. He probably hired the dog."

"Yea and the witch is a rubber dummy," I added.

"Want me to tie up the rat?" Bart offered, his voice coming from behind the open trailer door. He had almost been trampled in the panic as well.

"Please," Ted said, wringing his sock on the ground.

"I'll restrain the rat if you clowns will stop playing and get that stiff out of here before the other guests get suspicious," Bart quietly pleaded.

"Okay, he's right," Hank said. "Let's get this over with."

We returned to the body leaving Ted to his laundry task. Our inspection revealed no wounds, signs of bruising, or vampire bites. She appeared to have just stopped breathing.

Hank began to bag her hands and seal them with evidence tape. He signed his name as well as the time and date on the seal. This is done to protect any evidence on her hands or under the fingernails, assuring it will still be there when the autopsy begins. In addition, it prevents foreign matter from contaminating existing evidence on the hands.

"Well, I guess we'd better get her down to the workshop," Hank suggested. "I'll call for Ed and Patty to transport her."

"She's sure not riding with me," Ted grumbled as he put his shoe on, minus a sock.

"What are you going to do now?" Bart asked with a hint of unsteadiness in his voice.

"Don't worry. Ed and Patty will come in the back way. No one will even see them," I tried to reassure him.

"That's not what's bothering me." Bart scratched his head. "I just want to know what to do with the trailer and her belongings. Her rent is paid until the end of January and the last thing I need is another dog."

Give a refund to her next-of-kin, you cold-hearted cheapskate, I thought. "Detective McDonald will send someone out to inventory the contents of her trailer and car. Animal control will take the dog. Just lock it all up until then."

Hank came slowly strolling back from his car phone. "Hey Rex, transportation is arranged. It will take about forty-five minutes for them to get her down to the morgue. Wanna go eat?" he asked.

"Sure, do you think we can get Ted to join us?"

Ted, of course, was nowhere to be found. He could see the food thing coming. Like me, Hank didn't mind eating prior to an autopsy or, for that matter during the autopsy. Following a high fat, low fiber breakfast of bacon, sausage, and eggs sunny side up, we headed for the office.

As we pulled into the parking lot, I almost ran over a beautiful black Harley Cruiser parked in the handicapped spot. That meant only one thing; it was Dr. Steve Bilmarian's turn to be on duty.

Once a cadaver is placed on the autopsy table, it belongs to the pathologist not the coroner. Unable to do any further examination without Dr. Bilmarian, I just stood next to the sheet-clad body of the witch trying to make sense of it all. Suddenly, the suite door slammed open and in charged Dr Bilmarian with his usual exuberance.

"Ta da! Okay boys and girls, let's play doctor," he attempted a bad Groucho Marx impression.

As he began his gross inspection of the body, checking for outward signs of injury, he tested the dictation equipment by telling a bad joke.

"All right, what do you get when you have a room full of men from Mt. Centennial?" Mt. Centennial is a really, really small mining town nearby without a dentist.

"Give up a full set of teeth," he laughed hysterically as he delivered the punch line and pulled the false teeth from the dead witch's mouth, waving them over his head. There was suppressed laughter from those assembled. After all, we really didn't want to encourage this lunatic.

Then he began to dictate, "Case number 2259 is that of a Caucasian female with a stated age of fifty-two. She stands five feet six inches and weighs one hundred and forty three pounds with shoulder length black hair. The deceased arrived clothed in the Halloween costume of a classic witch. The garment's label identifies it as being made in Taiwan for the HA-HA Novelty Company, size medium."

Moving his attention to the body Dr. Bilmarian continued, "The body is devoid of petechial hemorrhages . . ."

These are tiny blood vessels that burst when someone is choked. They are usually found under the eyelids and on the inner lip.

". . . cuts, abrasions, puncture marks or signs of blunt force trauma," Dr. Bilmarian continued, his dictation like a Latin auctioneer. "The pupils are fixed and dilated equally, measuring three millimeters in diameter. A small well-healed incision measuring 3.75 centimeters in the lower right quadrant between the iliac crest and umbilicus is noted and is consistent with an appendectomy. Over the insertion of the deltoid musculature on the left arm, a small circular scar is observed apparently caused by smallpox inoculation".

Br. Bilmarian made the initial "Y" incision into the chest asking his assistant, Jim, to remove the ribs. "Now we can see in there. Let's do some digging."

Hank leaned over to me and whispered quietly, "Sometimes I just don't know how to take him."

"I find a good sense of humor helps and keep two things in mind: one, we're not the patient, and two, we're not from Mt. Centennial."

Everyone I know who practices this kind of medicine has an extremely sick sense of humor. It's the easiest way to deal with the stress created by a constant flow of dead bodies. Most people become doctors to heal. In forensic medicine there is no chance to save those who come through your office.

Pretending he didn't hear us, Dr. Bilmarian persisted with his dictation. "Upon gross examination of the exposed thoracic cavity, all organs appear to be present and normal in appearance and orientation. Examination of the lung tissue reveals the normal number of lobes. There is no sign of tumor, infarct (clot), or pyogenic (pus) material. Dissection of the bronchi shows the deceased had a history of tobacco use. There appear to be no signs of infarction or arteriosclerosis. The heart weighs 1800 grams. Upon dissection the bi—and tricuspid valves appear to be within normal limits; there are no signs of prolonged hypertension (high blood pressure). The cardiac vessels appear patent (fully open) and devoid of plaque or signs of endothelial (lining) damage".

Reaching up with his not so clean scalpel, Dr. Bilmarian turned off the Dictaphone and turned toward

Hank. "She's healthy as a horse. Want to bet we don't find anything?"

"Oh, no, you don't. I don't need that kind of pressure. You find the cause. Besides, last time we bet, you lost and never paid me," Hank laughed as he left for his lab down the hall.

"He's such a chicken-shit. The only reason he left is because he knew the head was next and he doesn't like the smell," Jim murmured under his mask.

"Good idea, Jim. Let's take a look under the hood," Dr. Bilmarian suggested.

As Jim began to open the head (this is done with a bone saw—the same kind of saw doctors use to cut off a cast), Dr. Bilmarian asked, "Rex, I know you. You must have figured this one out already. What do you honestly think brought her here?"

Even though I knew he was being sarcastic about my abilities, I ran the scene through my mind again and kept thinking how orderly her trailer was, everything in its place. No dust, no trash no nothing. She just didn't strike me as the type of person who would be careless in any way.

"I have no idea," I admitted. "It looked to me like her batteries died and she just stopped functioning."

"Well, I think someone or something might have suffocated her. Did you guys check the furnace and oven for leaks?"

"Hank and Ted vigorously checked the propane tanks. No leaks. Since she's not discolored I assumed we could rule out carbon monoxide poisoning."

Typically, when someone is exposed to CO_2, his or her body turns cherry red, caused by gas binding to the red blood cells.

"There are other poisonous gasses you know. Ever consider cyanide or mustard gas? We'll draw blood gasses just to check for anything out of the ordinary," Dr Bilmarian continued. "I had a professor who'd say she left her body for a little too long or just dreamed a little too deep. I think sometimes we forget that people just die. Not everyone lives to be ninety, although I plan to live to at least 150."

"Oh, wonderful, I'll just list the cause of death as 'dreamed a little too deep.' That will insure my reelection."

The balance of the autopsy was uneventful. The microscopic and toxicological findings were negative; blood gasses showed nothing out of the ordinary; no sign of carbon monoxide, cyanide, or for that matter, mustard gas. There was absolutely no indication of foul play or any apparent reason for the witch's death.

This was not good news for Ted and his team of investigators. No answer at the post-mortem meant he had to pound the pavement to find some solution to this puzzle.

After several days, the investigators interviewed everyone in the campground who had anything to do with the witch in the last few days of her life. This pretty much ruined poor Bart's plan to keep the witch's death a secret from his guests.

Very little knowledge was gained. The witch apparently led a solitary life. However, as in any small town, gossip is a favorite sport. Thank God for the phrases, 'I don't want to say anything, but' and, 'if you think it will help.' These statements are always followed by something juicy, true or not.

A woman from Kansas staying in the next campsite offered her valuable tip, "She was a really nice lady who loved to bake."

Wow, big clue, case solved. Bart told investigators campground records revealed the witch had no next of kin and she didn't work or leave the park very much. God save me from such helpful tidbits. Did no visitors mean that the cigars belonged to someone in the campground? Someone who could have just dropped by unnoticed? The only useful clue came from an eight-year-old girl on vacation with her parents.

"The witch was a bad lady," she stated flatly.

Kneeling, I hesitatingly asked the sweet-faced little girl, "What did she do that made her a bad lady?"

"I saw her smoking big cigarettes. Smoking kills you and is bad."

A woman who smokes cigars? Well, so much for the theory they belonged to her killer.

While poking around in the trailer one more time, I sat down at the dinette, thinking about what could have killed this lady. There were no signs of a struggle. Whatever killed her didn't harm her dog. Suddenly, it dawned on me. The answer to the witch's demise had been sitting right in front of me all along.

Finishing my story, I looked up and my audience had been taking notes on their paper plates. Strange people, I thought.

"That's everything we could find. Do you think you know what happened?"

Was it *Murder, Suicide, Natural Causes*?

"I know!" Tracy blurted out. "Probably the food she bought at the market. Maybe she bought something tainted and died of food poisoning."

"That's stupid!" Glenn interrupted. "If she had food poisoning there'd be signs that she had been throwing up. He didn't mention any puke. I think somebody in the campground dropped by at about midnight after the kids were gone. Then they held their hand over her mouth until she was dead."

"Well, the only thing to prove you wrong was the lack of petechial hemorrhages around her lips and eyes. As for food poisoning, I can't deny it could be a possibility, but people rarely die of food poisoning. They just think they are going to die, and chances are if she were that sick, she'd have called a doctor."

"Okay, I give up. What killed her?" Tracy asked.

REX'S REVELATIONS

When the nice witch went to Mountain Market, one of the things she purchased was dry ice. The bowl of water on the table originally contained a combination of dry ice and water, generating fog and discharging CO_2. Remember the receipt?

Dry ice will slowly release carbon dioxide (CO_2), an odorless gas that is deadly when used in a confined space, like a trailer. As with CO (carbon monoxide) poisoning, the victim is never aware of the danger, they just stop breathing and simply go to sleep, forever!

Unlike carbon monoxide (CO), carbon dioxide (CO_2) does not cause the body to become cherry red or discolored, other than the normal lividity found on any cadaver.

To further complicate the issue, carbon dioxide occurs naturally in the human body. It's what you breathe out! After death, high levels of carbon dioxide findings would be considered normal.

I ruled the cause of death: Asphyxiation due to carbon dioxide poisoning.

Manner of death: Accidental.

You Can Have Another

When I was ten, my three-year-old cousin, Monett, died. Her death, due to pneumonia, was something I did not understand.

To comfort me, my grandmother said, "The only time a baby dies is when God needs an angel. Only the purity of a child can make an angel."

On August twenty-first, God must have found himself in need of an angel because he took one and her name was Sarah.

We were at church that Sunday morning. The minister was leading the Lord's Prayer and my pager began to beep. It began quietly at first, then louder and louder with each passing second.

I could feel every eye in the place look at me in silence as I fumbled for the off switch. Everyone realized what the piercing sound meant. As I rose to leave, no slink, from the sanctuary, hands reached from the pews to comfort me as I passed.

Now, my minister teases me saying she thinks I will do anything to get out of going to church. After all, this was the third Sunday in a row my pager had disrupted her service. By now, Lori knows to bring her own car or risk being left at the altar, so to speak.

Using the phone in the minister's office, I called the dispatcher. "Okay, Betty, if this keeps up I'll need a note from you, excusing me from church."

"Would you like it perfumed and on letterhead?" I could sense her smile as she spoke. "You know I hate to call you on the weekend, but we've received a report about the death of a newborn baby. The person who called said it had just happened."

"Oh, damn. Oops."

A child is the most difficult kind of case to handle. Not only are the parent's weirded-out and unpredictable, but also it's the pits emotionally for me. Any parent will confirm their worst nightmare is of something happening to their child. Here I go again being reminded how precious my own children are to me. Each time I return from a call like this I hug my wife and kids, just to make sure they're okay.

"Betty, tell me it's not someone I know," I pleaded.

"Do you know Harry and Lena Ford?" she asked hesitantly.

"No. Thank God. What is the address?"

"Two, Two, Twain Trail. Get it? Two, Two train?" she laughed loudly. Betty had obviously seen the movie 'Murder by Death.'

"You need a break. You've been alone in that dark room way too long. Have you considered a dog?"

"I promise it is a real address," still giggling.

"I've never seen that name. Can it be one of the ten thousand recently renamed Aspen streets?"

*   *   *

Up here in the mountains it's best to know *exactly* where you are going. Sometimes directions consist of 'Turn right at the big boulder and left at the fork in the road.' That's real fun at night with only starlight to illuminate the landscape.

45

*   *   *

"On the map it looks like its two miles past Manly Lake, turn right on County Road Two. From there you're on your own. Good luck".

"Of course, two-two twain just off route two. Someone has a sick sense of humor".

Manly Lake is about five miles northeast of town and about a thousand feet higher in elevation. Great fishing if there's ever a chance. The drive is one I love. The road is lined on both sides with huge pine trees. In the afternoon, sunlight streams through the branches lighting small patches of highway. I found the turn-off. About four miles up the heavily rutted dirt road I found a hand painted wooden sign in the shape of a pointing finger reading "Twain Way." The street went almost straight up with deep ruts meandering to and fro. I stopped at the bottom of the drive and put the Beast into four-wheel drive. After grinding up what was left of my first gear, I went to work on second. I ascended the goat path these people used as a driveway. Each time the trail turned, I could get a glimpse of a house through the towering Ponderosa Pines. It was a custom log home with light honey-colored stain and a beautiful deep green metal roof.

Arriving in a cloud of dust, I parked behind the Sheriff's white Bronco and walked toward the house. The covered porch wrapped around three sides of the house extending twelve feet toward the forest. Two handmade aspen rocking chairs sat in the shade of the verandah, creaking as they rocked in the morning breeze.

Deputy Pat Kelley met me at the door. He was a thirty-something academy graduate and had only two months on the job.

His hands were shaking, "Thank God you're here. Let's step out on the porch where we can talk."

"What is wrong? Are you feeling okay?" the doctor in me had to ask.

"I'm fine, but I don't know quite what to do."

"Sit down in the rocker and breathe deeply a few times. Everything will be all right. Unless you killed the kid," I jibed, trying to get him to lighten up a little.

"I've never seen a dead person before, much less a little baby," he explained.

"I understand. How are the parents doing?" I inquired.

"You won't believe it; they're as calm as can be. The mother is holding the baby and they are praying."

"Is anyone else in the house?"

"There is a man and two ladies. Their older kids are visiting grandparents in Durango."

"Is there a doctor or midwife present?"

"The short, fat woman says she's a doctor. She chased me out here to wait for you."

Leaving poor Deputy Kelley on the porch, I introduced myself to the 'short, fat lady.' We will refer to her only as Dr. Yahoo for reasons that will become obvious shortly.

"The baby died at birth," she flatly informed me, hands firmly planted on her hips blocking the hallway.

"It had Down's syndrome and I didn't expect it to survive long. Anyway, it's a blessing that it happened now," she whispered in my direction, as if it were some kind of secret I'd understand.

If she's right and the infant had been diagnosed as a Trisomy 21, statistically it might be at risk for a higher mortality rate. Genetic abnormalities such as cardiac defects might lead to complications at the time of delivery.

Turning to Dr. Yahoo, who was still blocking my way, I asked, "If you knew this baby was a Down's, why isn't the mother in the hospital?"

Whispering even lower and with her hand covering her mouth, she explained, "They can't afford to go to the hospital. They have five other children to feed."

Here in the mountains, it is not uncommon to find large families who cannot afford basic health care. Therefore, this explanation did not seem out of the ordinary to me.

"Where's the placenta and cord?" I asked wanting to make certain it had not been disposed of.

"It's in the bathroom sink. I was getting ready to wrap it up for my flower bed," she said as she led me in the direction of the bathroom.

Due to their high mineral content, placentas make fantastic fertilizer. The placenta was complete with the umbilical cord intact. This would be important. When a baby dies at birth there is as much information about the possible cause found in the placenta and umbilical cord as in the body itself. I stood there looking at the organ lying in the sink.

From behind me a man's voice said, "Hi, I'm Harry Ford. You must be the coroner, Reedman."

"Yes, I am. Are you the father?"

"Yeah, would you like to see my littlest angel?" A smile rose over his face and his eyes sparkled.

I followed him down the hall to the master bedroom. Lying in the huge, king-size bed was an obviously tired and grieving mother. In her arms, a small bundle. A tiny pink receiving blanket wrapped the baby like a cocoon. As I entered the room the mother forced a smile and tried to be polite. The pain in her face ripped at my heart. I had to concentrate to keep from bawling.

"Her name is Sarah," she said, folding back the blanket so I could see the tiny face. The baby's nose appeared more flattened than normal for a newborn. Newborn babies naturally have a flattened nose to make breathing easier while nursing.

"Isn't she beautiful?" the mother prompted, sensing my discomfort.

It is always easier on me if I try to forget the human aspect of situations like this, and here the mother was pointing it out to me. I could have gone all day without knowing that this little bundle was named Sarah. I would have preferred to call it "Baby Ford," case 0821. All babies are beautiful, even a lifeless one. Now this one had a name: Sarah.

Those in the room with the mom and Sarah said several prayers, including one asking angels to watch over the baby. Knowing the older children would not have a chance to see their little sister, they took pictures. Even though her stay was brief, she would always be a member of their family. They each said their good-byes to Sarah.

Taking the carefully wrapped infant in my arms, I found myself gently rocking her like I did my girls when they were little. With the placenta carefully wrapped and tucked beneath one arm and the body held in the other, I left as quickly as I could. Once the family had a chance to hold the baby and grieve, it was best to leave. I didn't want to have to answer any questions about what I had to do.

According to the law the coroner must *immediately* take control of and remove a deceased child for investigation, no matter the circumstances. I knew there was no way Ed would get that big white boat of a hearse up this hill, so I placed the body of little Sarah on the passenger seat of my Jeep and fastened the seat belt around her. An act my wife would not be happy with, but of which Alex, my seatbelt-monitor daughter would be proud.

The ten-mile drive to the morgue was especially long this time. I was not looking forward to the procedure at all. Little Sarah's post was scheduled at ten-thirty the following day.

For the first time since I've known him, Dr. Bilmarian entered the autopsy suite quietly, without jokes or smart-ass comments. Sullenly, he greeted me and began to quietly dictate, "Submitted for examination is the body of an infant/fetus with a stated gestational age of thirty-seven weeks. It is reported the infant was diagnosed with Down's syndrome in utero. Beginning with dissection of the placenta, its weight is within normal limits and is normal in gross appearance. The margins are smooth and symmetrical. The maternal surface shows signs of degradation and hemorrhage. Representative sections are taken for microscopic examination."

Looking up from the cutting board he was working over, he said, "I hate doing babies. Give me an old, decomposing, leprosy-ridden, syphilitic drunk any day."

"Gee, I'd never thought of that as an option, but I understand the sentiment."

Without further comment, Steve moved his attention to Sarah's little body and continued his dictation. "The body appears to be healthy and well-nourished with the appropriate weight and proportions. The infant has a small pink clip on a freshly cut umbilicus."

Without looking up, Steve abruptly ended his dictation. He laid down his scissors and picked up several small plastic containers containing the sample remains of the baby.

"I've had enough. There's no reason to continue. I have plenty of tissue. Let's call it a day, Rex." He didn't wait for a reply; he just turned and left the room hugging his precious cargo safely against his chest.

Results from the examination would not be ready for several days. In the mean time, I needed to interview the parents and Dr. Yahoo.

I reached the doctor by phone the same afternoon to discuss any prenatal care provided to Mrs. Ford. She not so politely informed me that I must be some sort of fool, as if I should know the baby was going to die anyway.

When I asked who had performed the genetic tests necessary to diagnose Down's syndrome I was informed, "Well, at three months the mother's belly was so big and all she did was get bigger."

No shit! She's pregnant, what do you expect? I thought while I chewed on my inner lip to the point of drawing blood.

"To you, this indicated Down's syndrome? Your diagnosis was based just by the size of her abdomen? What follow up tests or lab work did you have done?" I inquired.

"I didn't need any other tests. You can see I was right. The baby was dead."

No wonder Einstein, you were in charge of its care! No, I did not say it. I thought it, but I did not say it.

"When did you last examine the mother?"

"The day before the baby was born."

"Were there any abnormal findings or results that might lead you to believe the baby was in any kind of distress?"

"It was hard to hear the heartbeat, that was all."

"Did you use a stethoscope?" I hesitantly asked, afraid of what her answer would be.

"Of course, I buy a new one for each new birth."

"Was the rhythm regular even though it was difficult to auscultate?" I wasn't sure she knew what auscultate meant, but I was going to give it a try.

"Like I said before, I couldn't hear it because the baby was sleeping while I was there."

Sleeping? A baby's heartbeat stops when it sleeps? Was this what I was really hearing?

"What was the baby's pulse that day?" I asked trying to give a chance for her to correct her misspeak.

"Like I said, I couldn't really hear it."

"Let me get this clear in my mind, doctor. You didn't get a pulse, felt zero movement—yet you did nothing? Not even refer her to the emergency room?" I couldn't believe what I was hearing.

"What good would that do? The baby was just asleep."

At this point, I guess I was supposed to feel dumb or something. The longer we talked, the more I began to realize that the 'fat lady' wasn't just fat, she was nuts. No one in the western hemisphere has practiced that kind of diagnostic reasoning in eighty years. It was clear to me the only thing this conversation was going to accomplish would be to increase my blood pressure.

To prevent my inevitable stroke, I ended the conversation. I couldn't accept what I had just heard; she couldn't be that stupid. I called Mr. Ford to ask him the same questions. He confirmed what the doctor had told me with a couple of exceptions.

"What? We have plenty of money. I'm in oil. The only reason we didn't want any testing to confirm her diagnosis was, well, it wouldn't make any difference. Our religious beliefs would not allow us to terminate the pregnancy, so you see, we would take whatever God gave us. In this case, the doctor was right. The good news is the doctor told my wife she could have another one. Besides, she wasn't worried about my pocket book when she took my five thousand dollars."

"She charged you five grand?" I questioned. Is anybody else creeped out by this doctor or is it just me?

Another discrepancy was, according to Mr. Ford, the doctor never reported to the family any difficulty in finding a heartbeat.

"I would have rushed her to the hospital right away," he added.

No matter how normal this guy seemed, I did have to keep in mind the possibility it was an act. He and his wife did seem a little too calm and cool. There was a chance they killed the baby to relieve themselves of the burden of a handicapped child. I wouldn't doubt the idiot doctor planned the whole thing.

Before hanging up, I promised to advise him the moment I received any autopsy results.

Those results were ready within days.

Dr. Bilmarian called me personally to report. "I can tell you the child was not suffering from Down's Syndrome. The face was smashed down because the heart had stopped between twenty-four to thirty-six hours before delivery. Without blood pressure, the tissues compressed by the mother's pelvis could not spring back.

As for dissection of the umbilical cord, there were no vascular changes."

"What about the placenta, did it show anything?" I asked.

"Now therein lays the rub. The fetal surface was beautiful, demonstrating normal vascularization. However, the maternal surface is a different story. It shows extensive hemorrhaging and degeneration. To me that indicates placental detachment. Do you know if she has high blood pressure?"

"The way her doctor treated her, I doubt if her blood pressure was ever taken."

"Well, either way, without enough placental contact between the mother and fetus the baby would begin to suffer oxygen and nutritional deficiencies. It might not be dangerous while the fetus is small, but as it grows so does its need for oxygen and nutrition. It's called placental insufficiency." I could hear the depression in Dr. Steve's voice as he spoke.

"So, if the baby had been delivered early it would have lived?" I asked.

"There are never any guarantees in medicine. You should know that!"

"Thanks, Steve. Leave it to you to complicate my life."

*   *   *

Once again, you have all of the information available. What do you think? Was it murder, malpractice, or just a shame it didn't happen to the doctor?

Don't turn the page until you're certain.

REX'S REVIEW

Without medical care or complication, women around the world deliver babies at home every day. However, there are times when the mother has an undetected medical condition that could endanger the health or development of the baby. In this case, the baby's cause of death was due to placental insufficiency, a natural cause, and it was so ruled.

I decided to call the State Board of Medical Examiners to check up on Dr. Yahoo. To my surprise the Medical Board had never heard of her. For that matter neither had the Dental, Chiropractic, Acupuncture, nor Cosmetology boards. It turned out the good doctor's degree is in "Mongolian Folk Medicine." Gee, I'm surprised.

If Dr. Yahoo had been the average Joe on the street and tried to help Mrs. Ford deliver, she would only be held responsible for what a reasonably informed person should be expected to know. However, since she called herself "Doctor" and had accepted money for her services, the District Attorney charged Dr. Yahoo with practicing medicine without a license.

EPILOGUE

One year later, almost to the day, Mr. and Mrs. Ford delivered a beautiful, healthy baby boy. God Bless Him.

Weird note and a sign of a greater plan; my wife delivered baby Nicolas.

Blood, Blood Everywhere and Not a Drop to Drink

Lori and I were enjoying a lazy Saturday morning together. The girls woke early and went with friends to the local sledding hill. It was wonderful to sit in silence, read the paper and sip coffee. Moments like these are golden for parents. Private moments are hard to come by. For the first two years of her life, our daughter Tina *never* slept through the night, and usually slept between us in our bed when she did sleep. That is why there is a *three-year* difference between our kids. Just as we were able to claim our bed again, along came Lexi and the process started all over.

Lori kissed me softly on the neck from behind and asked, "Hey, the kids are gone and probably won't be back for an hour or two. What do you want to do?"

"What do you have in mind?" I asked without looking up from my paper.

"If you have to ask, I may have to put you on some hormone therapy," she said as she bit my ear. That got my attention. I looked up from my newspaper; she was buck-naked!

"Oh. Wow, no need for a shot. I like the way you think."

"Last one in bed has to lock the door," Lori said over her shoulder as she dashed in the direction of our bedroom.

"No fair. You're already naked," I complained as I jumped over the couch trying to catch her and not injure myself. No need for artificial hormones. Times like this make me feel nineteen again.

Our moment of passion came to a halt as the sound of my pager pierced the air, the third time. This was one time the office would just have to wait.

"I never thought I'd see the day you'd ignore your electronic umbilical cord," Lori whispered in my ear as she tried to stop me from getting out of bed to answer the call.

"Well, now you know what it takes to make me deaf. You know I'm a guy and we can only think of one thing at a time. It's just a matter of focus and priorities."

"Focus, give me a break. Looks like you're only good enough to focus for five minutes at a time," she joked.

"You'd better get your watch fixed," I said as I kissed her, pulled my Levis on, and called the office from my cell phone.

"Okay, this had better be good," I said as Betty answered.

"Well, it's about time you answered. I've been calling you for twenty minutes. Did I interrupt something?" she responded.

"Ha ha, you know we have kids and its Saturday morning. There's no time for that," lying again. I'm going to rot in hell for sure, but, I'll know people.

"Oh, good, because I think you're going to be busy for the rest of the day, at least."

"What's up, a bus crash or a mass disaster?" I asked half joking. "What is the address?" I heard myself mumble.

"One zero nine Aspen Circle," she replied.

"Is it a house or apartment?"

"It's an apartment, number 204. You know that big pink building on the right?"

"Oh yeah, my kids want me to paint our house that color. They remind me every time we pass by. I've got to get some coffee; this is going to take a few minutes."

"If you're making coffee, Detective McDonald requested that you bring him some with two sugars and no cream."

"He must be kidding if he thinks I'm going to schlep coffee," I protested. At the same time, I toyed with the idea of letting him believe I had slipped something into it. (Come on. You've thought about it once or twice in your life.)

Aspen Circle was only a few blocks away. The car was barely warmed up by the time I pulled into the driveway. Looming in front of me was a large multi-unit apartment complex three stories tall. The pink paint was peeling and somewhat faded, although in the early morning sun the building glowed a beautiful deep pink. Typically landlords do not paint unless necessary, like when it's time to sell. The building had four wings encircling a large common area. Each wing of the building had a security door requiring a separate key for entry. The main entrance opened into the center of the complex.

The sound of running water and the musty smell of damp ground attacked my senses as I entered the garden courtyard. It was a jungle with plants everywhere. An ingenious concrete stream with built-in planters meandered throughout the courtyard watering the vegetation and adding background noise, cutting down the sounds of neighbors. In the very center of the courtyard were a swimming pool and a small Jacuzzi. The water and heating bills to keep all this from freezing must be enormous. The large deck contained several picnic tables and gas barbecues.

Detective McDonald met me outside the manager's office. "Nice clothes. What'd you do, sleep in them?"

"Ted, we have to stop meeting like this, my wife is getting suspicious," I joked.

"Oh, funny Doc, you're a regular Rodney Daingerfield. After Friday's case with the floater, you are the last person I wanted to see this morning. Before you get any ideas, there is no way I'm going to breakfast with you and don't even think about going to your workshop to play."

"But Ted, you're my favorite cop. I love the way you change color. Pale green, then blue and back to green," I laughed as he gave me that go-to-hell look.

"This time I wasn't the first one here. It was Karen. Maybe you can take her for one of your famous breakfasts."

"Okay Ted, what's the story on this one?"

"Don't ask me. I know nothing. I told you this one belongs to Officer Grady, ask her," Ted grinned from ear to ear and pointed to Officer Grady who was standing in the hallway.

"Has the District Attorney been called?" I asked Officer Grady.

"Yes, he wants to hear what you think before he comes over."

Officer Grady snipped, "I don't think that he is a morning person or perhaps the bimbo who answered his phone has something to do with it."

"You sound jealous Karen," Ted said. "Just tell the Doc what you found."

Reading from her small black notebook, Karen began to relay the facts from the morning's events.

"The landlord called 911 this morning at zero two thirty reporting someone had killed one of her tenants, a Mr. Shad Williams. We were dispatched at zero two thirty six, arriving here at zero two forty hours."

"And I'm not called until 7:15? What the hell took you guys so long?" I could tell by the look on her face that Officer Grady didn't like being called a guy. She is one of very few women in a field filled with men, and just a little sensitive about her femininity. Besides, she looks as if she could beat the crap out of me.

"We always notify you when we are *sure* that there is a need for the coroner," she retorted.

"Oh no, here it comes." Ted smiled in my direction as though he knew what I was about to say.

"A need? I've got news for you officer. In this state the second a person stops breathing, they **belong** to me. My office is to be notified the moment there's notification of *any* death. It's up to me whether or not *your* presence is required. Any evidence gathered at the scene of a homicide prior to my arrival and pronunciation is inadmissible in court. Remember, they're not dead until I say they're dead."

There is an unspoken rivalry between the office of the coroner and the police departments. Departmental egos and reputations are at stake here. The police see it as their duty to investigate homicides or suicides per chance they become a homicide. The State Constitution requires the coroner of each county to determine manner and cause of death. Once so determined, the police are then authorized to apprehend the perpetrator. Somehow along the way the police have come to view my department as glorified morticians or lab rats, only to be called when their investigation is complete. The problem is two-fold:

1. This small department is not accustomed to dealing with some of the complexities of some of these cases.
2. By the time I arrive, they have moved or touched almost everything in the room. I've arrived at crime scenes two or three hours after the police began their investigation, to find an officer without gloves twirling the suicide weapon like he was in an old west movie. So much for prints and weapon placement. The legal question is, "How can you have a murder investigation before the coroner determines the manner of death?"

Karen sheepishly continued avoiding eye contact as she reported, "We entered the residence with the landlord's permission and her passkey. The body was in the bathroom; blood was everywhere. A large pool ran out into the hallway between the bath and bedroom. I felt no pulse, the body was cold and stiff, and I didn't move him. I called for backup and an ambulance, although I really doubted if it would help him. When the paramedics arrived they refused to do anything since he was cold and in full rigor."

"Did you notice any weapons?" I inquired.

"Nothing, not even a squirt gun," Ted answered wryly.

"Were there signs of forced entry or any sign of a struggle?" I asked.

"No, the house was locked with a dead bolt from the inside and not even a window was ajar. Nothing seemed out of place or obviously disturbed," Karen stated matter-of-factly.

"Had the deceased had any visitors in the past few days, or had anyone seen any strangers hanging around?"

"None, the landlord who lives across the hall says he didn't have many visitors and none at all last night that she knew of."

"When was the last time anyone reported seeing him alive?" I continued probing.

"The best we can figure, about 6:00 p.m. last night. The deceased was last seen by one of the neighbors coming home from the store. He was carrying a large shopping bag and having some difficulty with it. A neighbor offered to help, but was curtly rebuffed. The neighbor, Eric Martin, said Mr. Williams was staggering and smelled of booze," Karen said disapprovingly.

Entering the premises, we began by checking the living room and bedroom. The living room was decorated in early garage sale with accent pieces from Goodwill. The gold shag carpet desperately needed a cleaning.

"Doesn't this guy own a vacuum cleaner?" Karen asked.

Sitting on a shelf made of concrete blocks and boards the VCR blinked 12:00 and a small portable television was tuned to the Movie Channel. A lamp next to the couch was lit. Therefore, we have a clue that he was alive and active after dark. There were several cans of "Bug Be Gone" bug bombs and some newspapers spread on the floor near the sliding glass door. Is it possible that he set these off and then for some reason failed to leave the apartment? Opening the drapes revealed an apartment size patio area. A small gas barbecue, and two lawn chairs were the only furnishings. Nothing looked disturbed.

"Well, he didn't have asthma, or all of this dust would have killed him long ago," Ted determined as he sneezed.

By now, I have been in so many people's houses that I try not to judge them by their cleaning habits. It's like my mother always said, "Wear clean underwear in case you're in an accident." The deceased do not expect to die nor have strangers in their private spaces. Sometimes we find bazaar things when we respond to a call, like private video collections, books, adult toys, etc. It's our job to determine what is important and leave the rest alone, omitting mention of it in any report. Since the record is public, we want to protect the family from needless embarrassment.

The apartment was very small. Directly off the living room was a hallway leading to the bathroom and bedroom. There was a tiny linen closet at the end of the hall. Turning right at the end of the hall, we entered the bedroom. It was dark and in disarray. The bed was unmade, pillows on the floor, dirty work clothes tossed around the room.

A thick dark blood trail led from the left side of the bed to the bathroom where the body now lay. The smell of musty laundry, blood, and vomit hung heavily in the room. Moving the investigation into the kitchen and away from the wondrous smell of the bedroom, I noticed there was not much in the way of food. Not unusual for hard-core alcoholics. There were a few frozen dinners and some juice in the freezer and a pot of coffee, cold by now. (Darn, I could use another cup.)

Dishes were piled high in the sink. The smell of trash and mothballs was overpowering. The trashcan was the first place to yield anything of interest. An issue of last month's *Playboy*, a torn bus ticket to Phoenix, and three empty bottles of vodka—not the good stuff—some cheap, generic kind. Using a pen to lift bottles from the garbage, I noticed a strange aroma from their contents. One should never smell from a container at the scene of a death. What if the bottle contained poison? That would definitely a bad move.

"Let's be sure to save those for fingerprinting and send any contents for assay. Dr. Jack gets upset when we don't bring something fun for him to do," Ted suggested.

"Let's take a look at the body," I suggested.

Ted and Officer Grady led me to the bathroom. It was filthy. The shower looked as though it hadn't been cleaned in months. Mold and mildew stains painted the wall and there was a glob of hair blocking the drain. The sink had a broken faucet that dripped constantly. That would drive me crazy. The mirror was cracked with the silver eroding from the back due to years of moisture, giving a distorted image in reflection. Paint was peeling from the walls and the ceiling looked like frail stalactites. Amid this scene was the body of a man wrapped around the toilet in a pool of extremely dark almost black blood, his left arm across the seat, and hand still in the water of the commode. The blood was dried into his hair and clothes; his face held a grimaced expression.

"Looks as if he died in pain," I heard Ted whisper to Karen.

"Yes, but from what?" I interjected.

The blood appeared to be coming from his mouth and there were no apparent cuts or abrasions on or about the head or face.

"His nose looks broken," Karen commented to Ted.

"It is most likely post-mortem because there's no sign of ecchymosis (bruising). He probably hit his face on the floor when he died. If his heart had been beating it would have bruised or bled. What interests me is the color of his skin. It is really dark and ruddy. What's his nationality, Native American?"

"On his driver's license he looks white to me," Karen responded holding up the license.

Oh no, I thought, *there are only a few things that can cause a body to become dark like this and none of them are good.* First to consider is a cobra bite; it can cause discoloration of the skin like this and I've seen stranger pets at death scenes. Second might be the bite of the brown recluse spider. Within 24-48 hours if left untreated, it could cause the same kind of symptom; and brown recluse spiders are found in Colorado. Last might be a rare form of anemia, which causes the red blood cells to explode in the veins resulting in discoloration.

"Is there a poison that could account for his eternal tan?" Karen quietly asked.

"Poison, schmoisen, it was a heart attack or maybe he just puked his guts out?" Ted responded glibly.

"Good guess," I said. "He could have vomited hard enough to rupture esophageal varices (varicose veins in the throat, common in long term alcoholics). On the other hand, perhaps he suffered a cardiac arrest. However, I don't believe I've ever seen a cardiac arrest cause bleeding like this from the mouth. Perhaps it was a blood clot to the lungs? Let's see, the blood's not pink or frothy so, we can probably rule out a pulmonary embolism (blood clot in the lungs). Let's get some samples of the blood from here on the floor, in the hall, and from the toilet. We've got to make sure that it's all *his* blood. We don't want to miss it if someone else's is here too."

I asked Ted to take a sample of the toilet water.

"We might as well make Dr. Schnitz's day for him. Toxicologists love working on toilet water. Maybe we shouldn't tell him what it is. He thinks I'm crazy anyway and this might just give him the evidence to prove it. Karen, will you get the apartment manager? Have them bring the file on this unit."

Officer Grady brought the manager into the living room. In her mid-twenties, Mrs. Paqos was thin with an olive complexion and curly black hair. She was wearing a tight pair of jeans and tee shirt, clearly no bra. Okay, so I looked, but it's my job to be observant. She was visibly upset and looked as though she had been crying.

"How long have you been the manager here?" I inquired.

"It'll be six years in May," she answered.

"How long did the deceased live here?" Officer Grady asked. She seemed anxious to solve this case before anyone else.

"In this apartment, four years and one year in number 103."

"He changed apartments, why?" I asked.

"There was a problem with rodents and bugs. He hated them both."

"Were the locks changed before he moved in?" Ted inquired. "Yes, we always change the lock when a new tenant moves in." "Does that include the sliding glass door?" Officer Grady asked. "I think so," she fumbled with the file in her lap, searching for the answer.

"Is there any chance that a previous tenant would have a key?" I asked.

"I don't think so," she said pulling out receipts for the lock changes.

"Other than the tenant, who has a key to this door; maybe the janitor or the repair/maintenance man?" Ted suggested.

"The maintenance man doesn't. I let him in to the units when he needs access. The tenant can always have a copy of the key made, and in that case I don't know how many people might have a copy to the lock on this door."

"Oh, so you have a key to the unit?" Officer Grady jumped in.

"Yes, I have a pass key to all the apartments."

We already knew that since Officer Grady mentioned how the police got access upon arrival.

"Which unit do you live in?" I inquired.

"Across the hall in 202," she was looking at the door as she replied.

"How well did you know him?" I asked.

"We talked in the hall and when he paid his rent. Sometimes we spoke on the phone." There was a noticeable change in the tone of her voice as she answered.

"Are you the one who called the police?" I asked.

"Yes, I was," she admitted.

"What time was that?" Officer Grady asked sternly.

"At about 2:00 a.m. or so," she answered.

"What made you think he was dead?" Ted inquired.

"I hadn't seen him since yesterday afternoon in the laundry and he did not answer the door this morning," her eyes filled with tears as she answered.

"Was it unusual not to see him?" I asked.

"Well, not really. He does go away for several days at a time, but I knew he was supposed to be home."

Something seemed strange in this story. This woman knocks on her tenant's doors at two a.m.? She calls the police and reports a murder if you don't answer the door? Not the kind of landlord that I would want. I'm not rude; I just never hear the doorbell. She would always be calling 911 on me; I never answer the door. In this case she was right. Her tenant was dead. How did she know? Had she been in the apartment before she called the police? After all, she does have a passkey.

Realizing I could faintly hear Ted talking, I joined the real world, in time to hear him ask, "Was his car in the parking area?"

"He did not own a car," Mrs. Paqos responded, regaining her composure.

"What did he do for a living?" Ted asked from the doorway, leaning with his shoulder against the door jam.

"He was an engineer," Mrs. Paqos explained, sobbing into a handkerchief she held in her hand.

Karen jumped in trying not to be left out of the interrogation, "Electrical or mechanical?"

"Neither, he drove a train for Southern Pacific".

I thought I would laugh aloud. Instead I bit the inside of my cheek and held on. Undeterred, Karen continued taking notes like a college freshman.

"Mrs. Paqos, I get the idea there's something you're not telling us. Did you enter the apartment prior to calling the police?" I inquired.

"No," she responded defensively.

"Then, what made you suspect he was dead?" Ted asked.

"His door was locked. He didn't answer when I knocked. I tried to call him and he didn't pick up the phone either."

"OK. That makes sense, but what made you think he had been murdered? That is what you told the dispatcher wasn't it?" Officer Grady added.

"Yes, I guess that's what I said," she responded.

"I'll ask you again. Did you enter the apartment before you called?" I pressed for a straight answer.

"You won't tell my husband will you? Does this have to come out?" she asked nervously.

"Not unless it's in the official report that's public record," I tried to console her.

She continued to cry as we sat on the couch. "Shad and I had been having an affair for about two years. Several times a week we would get together. Last night I came to crawl into bed with him. I found him in the bathroom and I panicked."

"Had he been sick in the past few months? Any muscle aches, headaches, or nosebleeds?" I asked searching for symptoms that might help.

"He had the flu about three weeks ago. I made him soup."

"Did he see a doctor or take any medication?" Officer Grady inquired.

"Never, he hated doctors. He refused to go to the hospital even when he cut his hand last month, he just super glued it shut," she recalled.

"Have the two of you had a fight or disagreement lately?" Ted pressed.

"Well, I was going to Phoenix to visit my mother and we did argue about me leaving. He was just a little possessive about me," she sniffled.

That explained the ticket in the trash; he must have won that argument. It appeared to me that Mrs. Paqos was being honest about the situation. It certainly sounded like she was telling the truth. I excused her to return to her own apartment just as Bob the police photographer arrived. He went straight to work in the bathroom. Ed and Patty followed Bob in, parking the gurney in the hall outside and almost knocking down Mrs. Paqos in the process.

"Okay, I've got fresh gloves and an apron. Where's the body?" Ed whispered in my ear.

"He is in the bathroom. As soon as Bob is finished you can have him. Be careful and take viral precautions, I'm not sure what killed him, but it might be contagious."

Leaving Ed, Bob, and Patty to their tasks I turned to officer Grady. "Karen, would you like to go out for breakfast?" I asked.

Ted was making for the door by now; all I could hear was the sound of his laughter as the door slammed. Karen was a willing victim, uh, I mean guest, for breakfast. The perfect set up. She made it too easy; I almost felt guilty when I convinced her to come to the lab with me for the morning. It was clear that she did not want to admit this outing made her at all uneasy. Experience has shown me the telltale signs. First they begin to swallow hard, and then they smack their lips like a sick dog just before it ruins your carpet. So far, Karen was two for two. Oh God, do I enjoy this.

We arrived at the lab following the greasiest breakfast I could find for Karen. The post mortem was scheduled for 11:30 and we were about ten minutes early.

"It's cold in here. Do you always keep it so cold?" Karen complained.

"Trust me, when you open up a dead body, you want it as cold as possible. As the body's temperature rises, so does the smell. Besides, it helps to keep you awake," I explained.

"It's staying upright that I'm worried about," Karen stated flatly.

A loud noise precedes the operating door as it swung open, *kablam.* I thought I would have to pull Karen off of the ceiling. It was Dr. Bilmarian. "Sorry about that, I tripped on a mop bucket in the hallway. Is everybody ready?"

In his best announcer's voice he added, "Then, it's time to play our favorite game show: *Stump the Doctor* brought to you today by Sear's Hardware."

The autopsy began at 11:45 with the usual bad joke to test the dictation equipment. Those present were Jim Needy, Diener, Dr. Bilmarian, and Karen Grady, police officer. The following is a partial excerpt from the procedure:

"What did the beaver say to the tree? Give up? It was nice gnawing you." Dr. B. laughed hysterically at his own joke.

"The body of a thirty two year old white male is submitted for autopsy. He weighs 197 pounds and measures 71 inches in height. The body arrives discolored over the entire epidermal layer," Steve began the dictation.

"Wow. What happened to this guy?" he inquired.

"We are not sure. He was found lying against his toilet. There was blood everywhere. The bloody path ran a distance of about twenty feet from his bedroom to the bathroom", I explained. "With this skin discoloration I would wonder if he was under medical care for hemolytic anemia."

"Do you know if he had been sick recently?" Steve continued to query.

"His neighbor said he had the flu several weeks ago and would not go for care. He hated doctors," Karen answered.

"The flu symptoms might mimic the onset of TTP," Steve hypothesized, under his breath.

Thrombotic thrombocytopenic purpura, or TTP, is an anemia causing blood cells to become thickened and rupture in the small capillaries.

"He was a heavy drinker and the neighbors reported he was visibly intoxicated the last time he was seen alive," Karen conveyed condescendingly.

"Let's be sure to do blood alcohol and toxicology levels, Jim," Steve requested of his lab tech. "If he was a long term alcoholic, there might be liver damage. Remember that one of the signs of this type of anemia is delirium, disorientation, and uncoordinated movements. For all intents and purposes he would appear drunk to an uninformed bystander. Let's open him up, Jim."

The "Y" shaped incision revealed the contents of the thorax. The colors and orientation of the lung and cardiac tissues appeared unremarkable. As the organs were removed one at a time, the systems were reviewed. Dissection revealed the cardiopulmonary structures were within normal limits.

"The liver is removed for gross inspection." Dr. Steve continues his dictation as the large nodular organ was placed in the produce scale then transferred to the cutting board.

"The liver weighs 2200 grams and appears fatty and infiltrated." He sliced the organ like a large loaf of bread. "Multiple nodules are removed for microscopic examination."

Representative slices were placed in a small plastic container for microscopic evaluation. After completing examination of the thorax and abdomen Dr. Bilmarian announced, "There's not much of value in here. Let's open the head, Jim."

Karen smacked her lips in my ear as Jim opened the head. The smacking noise drowned out the sound of the saw.

She's at puke stage one, I thought to myself. *Next comes the hard swallowing.* Sure enough, by the time Jim had the skull loose and removed the cap with its characteristic suction sound, Karen could be heard from the trashcan practicing her bulimia impression.

Dr. B. laughed and continued to dictate, as Karen added background sound effects. "The cerebral tissue is removed for examination. Its weight was within normal limits, as is the gross appearance of the structures," Steve sang as he sliced the tissues sagitally (up and down) and coronally (side to side) exposing as much of the brain's inner structures as possible.

"There is no sign of stroke or tumor on gross examination." Steve placed a few cubes of the tissue into the plastic jar. Next he requested, "Jim, open the throat structures. Let's look for dilation of the blood vessels there. With all of this blood, he might have ruptured esophageal varices while vomiting."

Karen excused herself before we finished the examination.

"I don't think Officer Grady will be as anxious next time to go for breakfast with you," Dr. Steve noted with a broad smile on his face. "Want to go for lunch?"

"No way, I'm going fishing before anyone else dies around here," I answered.

In the days following the autopsy, more evidence was compiled as lab results became available. Blood samples revealed, indeed, the deceased was intoxicated at the time of his demise. Microscopic exam of the vessel walls indicated an increase in their thickness and the presence of fragmented red blood cells peripherally, indicating anemia. Dissection of the esophagus demonstrated several areas of hemorrhage consistent with forceful vomiting. Toxicological studies were negative for poisons or venom of any kind. Now the work is done and the only thing left to do is sign the Certificate of Death. Was it murder, suicide, or natural causes?

REX'S REVIEW

The deceased was found in his bathroom and had been dead many hours prior to his discovery. The blood on the floor was indeed due to ruptured varices, probably rupturing during an episode of forceful vomiting.

His blood alcohol levels were markedly elevated. This is not necessarily indicative of intoxication. A body creates its own ethanol in the process of decomposing. The significant findings involved the red blood cells.

Blood analysis demonstrated elevated levels of *immature* red blood cells indicating rapid loss of the mature blood cells for some reason. In this case it was determined the patient was suffering from "Thrombotic thrombocytopenia purpura"—TPP for short. This anemic disorder strikes young adults; its mechanism or cause is unknown.

This death was ruled due to **Natural Causes**. The cause of death was determined to be TTP complicated by a rupture of the blood vessels in the throat induced by long-term alcoholism.

This was a tough case. Good luck with the next one, Pop Goes the Pistol.

Pop Goes the Pistol

Twice each year, Colorado's county coroners gather for coroner's training. This is an opportunity to gather and seek help on their more difficult or most interesting cases of the past six months. In reality, it's a wonderful excuse for the morbid to gather and share their stories. As the weekend progresses and the volume of microbrew consumed increases, the nature of the tales gets more graphic. By Sunday afternoon, it's hard to believe any of the stories.

I had been asked to speak at this year's conference, only for thirty minutes. Just as a test run, I think. I was given the three-o'clock time slot on Saturday afternoon. What could possibly be worse than that? Like maybe the subject? I was told the subject was to be juvenile death or suicide. I was free to be as 'funny' as I wanted. Funny I thought to myself. Is he crazy? How could there be anything funny about the death of a child?

I sat in my office pondering what I could say and trying to think of what I had ever done to deserve this. I poured through my files looking for a lighthearted case. One where maybe the kid was a bad guy and met his end in an ironic way, maybe car thieves run over by an unmanned car . . . Nothing. Not one case that was the least bit humorous. The thought of humor was out the window.

As I searched my predecessor's files in vain, I realized I had plenty of gross cases but gross wouldn't even affect this cold-hearted crowd. I sat at my desk thinking how could I even talk about the subject. After all, my life had never been touched by the heartbreak of an adolescent death or suicide. I was sure there was a good chance someone in the audience had suffered a suicide or death of a child in their family. Therefore, I had to treat the subject with respect.

All at once, I remembered there was a time when I had been affected by a teenage death. If it was suicide or not, they'd have to decide. It was the case of a single pistol shot that devastated the world of one family. I decided to share with this cold-hearted bunch the case closest to my heart.

When the big day arrived and I walked into a packed house, I was shocked. At first, I thought I was in the wrong room.

"This is the right place, Doc," the voice behind me whispered as I turned to leave. It was Ted blocking my escape. "Got stage fright?" he jibbed.

"No. I just can't believe there are so many people."

I stood as close to the door as possible. Not for a quick escape, but to scope out the situation before going in. Was the audience armed with vegetables? Tomatoes aren't so bad, but a cabbage could leave a mark!

"Don't get a big head. It wouldn't matter if a monkey were speaking. Most of these guys are here because it's snowing like hell outside or, housekeeping is cleaning their suite and this is the only safe place to sleep in public without getting mugged."

"Thanks, now I feel much better. So, it wouldn't matter if I got up there and spoke Chinese. Is that what you're telling me?"

"Naw, I'm the one stuck to introduce you. I have to say nice things about you to the audience; I didn't want your head to get too big," Ted smiled and stepped up on stage to do the intro.

"Good afternoon, and wake up you zombies. It's time for our three o'clock speaker. I've known Rex for more than a year. In that time I've found him to be the most, how shall I put it? The biggest smart ass I've ever known. All I can say is never, and hear me now, NEVER take a call from him where an alien body or witches are involved. Moreover, no matter what the circumstance is never go to breakfast or lunch with this man. Ladies and gentlemen, I give you Dr. Rex Reedman."

Now I was nervous. The lack of applause was deafening.

"I did my best to build you up. However, half of them are asleep, and the other half are drunk. Good luck buddy. Knock 'em dead," Ted grinned, enjoying his pun and exited toward the bar. Now it was my turn.

"Good afternoon, fellow ghouls. I was asked to speak this afternoon about teenaged death and to make it funny. As hard as I tried, I couldn't find anything funny in the subject. I was hoping you all felt the same way. So instead, today I'd like to tell you a story about my first real death of a young person. You decide if it was murder, suicide or something else." I could hear chairs moving in the darkness and the definite sound of breathing, I wasn't quite sure if it was human, but there was something alive in the audience.

"In all the years I've been involved with the investigation of death, I am rarely so touched as when a young person dies. With the elderly, we understand it could be a blessing. At least they've had a chance to live. However, death in youth is a future lost and there is something inherently unjust when it happens. I would like to tell you about a case that touched my heart and was a bitch to solve."

It was a Friday around 4:30 p.m. when my pager rang disturbing my futile and halfhearted attempt at completing the previous week's patient charts.

I hate doing chart notes, so anything is a welcome break. I called dispatch, and Diane, a new trainee, answered. I could hear the shaking in her voice, something seasoned dispatchers rarely do. "Hello. Dr. Rex? There's been a shooting at 1458 Elbow Road. It's a kid."

"Okay," I sighed. "What's the family name?"

"Beckman is what was reported. Thomas Beckman," Diane echoed my sigh.

"And who are the officers on the scene now?"

"Uh, it's Patrolman Johnson, Sergeant Wills and the mortuary was called by the family," she answered.

Uh, oh, that's a bad sign, I thought. I knew Ed wouldn't touch the body until I had arrived. Nevertheless, in big cities that might not be the case, mortuaries have been known to just pick up a body and leave. Imagine what that does to your crime scene investigation?

"Diane, radio Sgt. Wills. Tell him under no circumstances should the family be allowed in the room with the deceased. Moreover, no way should the body be moved. I'm on my way."

Parents do strange things when a child dies. It's traumatic, unexpected, and could be a dangerous situation. I drove as fast as I could without lights and sirens since the county seemed reluctant to provide a set for me.

Elbow Road is not too far north of town. I've always thought that Elbow was a weird name for a road until one day I noticed that about two miles down the road, it turns west at a 90-degree angle. From a distance, it did look like an elbow.

It took me less than ten minutes to get to the Beckman's home. As I looked up the driveway there was an enormous entrance gate, at least twenty feet tall and extending far wider than necessary to accommodate the paved driveway. The sign above read "River Rock Ranch". Made of stacked river rock it was intimidating in its beauty. Washed by the late afternoon sun, the rocks were changing color when I arrived; they were looking softly purple and yellow in the waning sun. About three hundred yards up the drive; I could see a log house nestled in a large grove of aspen.

The copper roof glistened among the trees, looking like a treasure hiding in the branches. Smoke from the chimney drifted toward the sky as though it alone were the distant cloud's source. The closer I got, the bigger the house got and I realized that what appeared from a distance as just ordinary aspen trees were the largest I have ever seen, dwarfing the true size of the home. Near the base, many of the trees measured thirty to thirty-six inches in circumference and easily stood seventy feet tall. These were some really old trees. Prior to moving to Colorado, the largest aspen I'd seen was maybe six inches around and twenty feet tall.

Finally, I reached the circle drive near the main house and parked. Gardens surrounded the entrance to the house. Not the kind that one might expect, with roses and lilacs all beautifully groomed. No, this looked as if it were a tree-lined mountain path meandering to and fro with very little level ground along the way. There was a small stream bordering the path, dropping to a series of loudly announced falls. In pools created near a little wooden footbridge, I could see small trout feeding on bugs as colored sunlight bounced off the water. I crossed the footbridge near the front door and the sound of my feet echoed back to me from the rocks.

Looking up toward the door, the roof and aspens were backlit by the then setting sun. Multi-colored halos appeared around the leaves. For a moment, the scenery made me forget why I was there. The door to the house was almost as big as the gate down at the road. The river rock theme continued in the covered entrance. It felt as though I'd entered a cave, bordered outside by dense greenery and the sound of falling water, and inside by a mammoth front door made of tiny carved crystal panes set in a heavy oak frame. The clear crystal panels were offset by intricate stained glass designs. As I stepped up to the door, I could see the distorted images of people inside dancing in the crystal panels. As I rang the doorbell the housekeeper answered the door.

"Wow, you're fast. You startled me," I said.

"We saw you coming on the security monitor," she responded reservedly.

I introduced myself to the housekeeper, who told me her name was Brenda, and asked where the officers were. She directed me up the stairway to the main floor. Sergeant Wills met me when I reached the top of the stairs.

"Glad to see you Doc," he extended his hand and forced a smile.

"Hi, Charles, where are the next of kin?" I asked.

"They're making coffee with Ed and Patty. Dispatch relayed your message. So, considering the circumstances, I thought maybe someone should keep an eye on them."

"Ed's here? I didn't see the big white boat."

"He parked around in the back, in the delivery area," Charles explained.

"They have a loading dock?"

"They have everything here! I wish it were my house. You should see the home theater—and I mean *theater.*" Chuck was obviously impressed with the opulence.

"Tell me exactly what happened. Diane said a child was shot," I probed.

"His name was Thomas Jr.; he was just seventeen. This afternoon he came home from school went up to his bedroom, and somebody put a bullet in him. Parts of him are all over the room," Charles said looking at me directly in the eye, very intently, like he was trying to tell me something.

"Where is the entrance wound?" I asked, afraid to hear the answer.

"Right temple," he said, using his index finger to indicate the exact location.

Now, I know what Chuck meant by "pieces all over." Typically, gunshot wounds are neat going in but a real mess coming out. When a gun is fired, not only the bullet comes from the barrel, but expanding gases that push the projectile are also expelled at tremendous speed and with great force. When the barrel is close to the skull, those explosive gases become as deadly as the shell.

I found the bedroom by following the yards of yellow police tape stretched down the hall, like the yellow brick road. I fumbled to find the latex gloves I had hidden in my pocket as I neared the door, and I know this sounds strange, but I felt like the kid was watching me as I entered his domain.

In the corner, near an open window, I could see a red leather, wing-backed chair facing away from me. From the doorway, I could see an arm draped over the armrest and a handgun laying on the floor to his right. There was a large, visible blood spatter about fifteen inches across on the wall to the left of the chair and up the curtain. I caught myself staring at the bloodstained wall, like it's some kind of Rorschach test. I expected some explanation would suddenly jump out at me. Unfortunately, it didn't and it never has.

A faint noise in the room suddenly brought me back to the real world. The blinds were gently moving in the breeze, tapping the windowsill rhythmically. Click, click, click. There were no other sounds, and in the silence, I heard my own heart beating loudly. Looking around, I noticed a Mickey Mouse telephone off the hook and lying on the floor near the chair where he was sitting. There was a beautiful built-in study area to the right as I entered. It was built of cherry wood and set into the wall with room for the computer terminal, very well planned and obviously original construction (like I'm such a great judge of wood or architecture). The ceiling offered no obvious bullet holes, or bloodstains.

There was no sign of a struggle in the room, but with teenagers who could tell? My oldest daughter's room looks as though there has been a riot in there most of the time, and she's only seven. The bed was unmade and there were clothes lying on the floor. Several pair of tennis shoes peered out from under the dust ruffle; a soccer ball was faintly visible in the dark recesses under the bed.

While most kids would have posters of their favorite parent-hating band on the wall, young Tommy had an outstanding collection of original animation art. Disney seemed to be the theme. There were cells *from Snow White and the Seven Dwarfs* and *The Fox and the Hound.*

Judging by the wall coverings, his allowance must have been slightly more than the fifty cents per week I received at seventeen. (Oh no, I'm starting to sound like my dad, "When I was your age I had to walk to school in the snow, up hill; in both directions.")

I approached the chair to get a closer look at the body. The concussion from the muzzle caused severe bruising of the boy's face around the eyes. The exit wound had removed a portion of his face in the left temple region. Empty eyes stared blankly into space; pupils fully dilated which means no brain activity, indicating brain death, duh. Tucked into the cushion of the chair next to the body was an empty holster, presumably for the gun, which was now lying silently on the floor, giving no clue to what it had done such a short time ago.

It's not unusual to find the gun used in suicide a short distance from the body. The force of the gun going off, combined with the instantaneous loss of muscle control, results in the weapon being knocked away. In fact, I'm really suspicious when the victim is still holding the gun, a possible sign of being planted. In Tommy's lap was a wrinkled piece of notebook paper. I could see it was a girl's handwriting, "Jennifer 555-3984" with a happy face over the "i" in her name. As my grandpa would say 'Well, doesn't that add a wrinkle to the dog?'

Had he been on the phone with Jennifer? Did they have a disagreement? Break up? Good questions for parents, assuming they are in touch with their kids' lives at all. Turning to leave, I stepped and heard the frightful high-pitched "snap" that every person who wears glasses has experienced at one time or another in their lives. The sound reached my ears just as I felt the small fragile frames give way under my size-twelve shoe. Just my luck, they probably belonged to the deceased, or worse yet, the murderer, thrown from his face by the discharging gun or dropped prior to the shot. Either way they were goners now.

I was sure there'd be at least five forms to fill out for damaging evidence at a crime scene. For one panicked moment I was hoping nobody would notice. Of course, if there has been any disturbance to the crime scene it must be reported immediately, so as not to damage the investigation or potential prosecution. I placed the glasses back in their original position under the chair. Only the frame had cracked. As I looked under the chair for anything else that might be a clue, I heard breathing, *and it wasn't mine*. I looked up realizing the housekeeper had been silently standing in the doorway watching. I was busted.

"Doctor, I'm sorry to interrupt you, but Mr. Hill wants to see you in the kitchen." She was fighting back tears as she relayed the message.

"Thanks. Would you show me the way?" I asked wanting to remove her from the scene.

Brenda led me down the hall to the stairs I had come up earlier. We crossed the living room through the formal dining room to the kitchen. This was the kind of kitchen anyone who cooked would kill to have. In the center of the room was a large black granite island with rough-cut edges. The stove was commercial grade with eight burners, a grill, and a double oven. Its clean stainless steel surface glimmered in the sunlight. Standing next to the stove was a huge Sub-Zero refrigerator freezer with a matching granite facade. The window along the south wall was at least thirty feet long, covering the entire wall and offering a stunning view of Pikes Peak. I was met by

Ed who asked how long I thought it would be before he could remove the body.

"We haven't even begun the investigation; it will probably be a couple of hours before you can take him," I said. "The photographer isn't even here yet. Do you want to wait here or shall I call you back later?"

"Patty's outside with the wife. I guess we could wait for a while unless we get another call."

Twenty-four years in the funeral industry had given them a great deal of experience in handling the bereaved and I am always willing to accept their help. Those left behind are difficult to console. The deceased's problems are over, but the family's have just begun.

The mother's sobbing could be heard coming from the patio. As she and the father entered the kitchen, Patty was comforting her. Mrs. Beckman, Vicky, had flaming red, shoulder-length hair. She had been a beauty queen in her younger days; however, today she looked every bit of her forty plus years.

A third generation rancher, Mr. Thomas Beckman, Sr. cradled Vicky in his rugged arms as they sat in the window seat. His large hands were tough from years of work. It was clear; while his hands were rough and callused, his heart was not.

The Hill's cell phone rang and they excused themselves to answer another call and promised to return soon.

"Do you have any idea who might have done this to your son or what led your son to do this to himself? Has he been depressed or have any enemies?" I inquired.

Vicky's voice quivered, as she answered, "No. He has been doing well in school and sports. Everybody loves him."

Looking at Thomas, Sr. I asked, "Do you know who Jennifer is?"

"No, he didn't tell me much about his social life," he admitted.

Vicky interrupted him, "Jennifer was a classmate. They had been studying for a test together for the past two weeks."

"Was she his girlfriend?" I continued, knowing that the inability to make or maintain friendships of the opposite sex is one of the warning signs of suicidal tendencies.

"Well, they did talk on the phone for hours at a time. Occasionally they would ride horses together. Junior loved his horse," Vicky remembered fondly. She began to weep quietly with her face buried in her husband's shoulder.

"I'm sorry to ask these questions, but I need to know."

"It's okay; we want to help in any way we can. Don't we, dear?" he said as he squeezed his wife closer to him.

"Had there been any problems here at home recently?" I pressed on.

"No, he hadn't been in any trouble for the past few months," Thomas, Sr. added.

"Did he have any friends or someone with him when he came home today?" I thought that was a brilliant question. Up until that moment it hadn't entered my mind that there might have been a stranger in the house. I had just suspected the parents.

"I don't know. Thomas was at work and Brenda was at the market," Vicky explained.

"Where were you?" I asked her.

"I was at the beauty parlor. Annie Ruth was doing my hair," she stated timidly.

Such a good question and no one can answer it. Therefore, it is possible that someone else was either in the house when he returned or he invited someone in. For that matter, he could have brought someone home from school with him. My kids do that all of the time.

"Had anyone threatened him or had he seen anything that he shouldn't have on one of his horseback rides?"

"No. He never mentioned seeing anything. We've been missing a few yearlings and he's gone out looking for them, but I don't think he ever found anything or anyone. As for threats, well, Tommy kept pretty quiet about any problems at school."

"Had he seen the two of you fight or disagree in the past couple of days?" I asked as I wondered: Did he think by wounding or killing himself he could unite his parents or had he gotten in the way of their fight, in the cross-fire so to speak?

"We haven't had an argument in years," Vicky said with a beauty pageant smile. She nuzzled her head into Thomas' shoulder.

"Had he tried this before, or done anything that made you believe he was thinking about it now?" Previous attempts might mean a long-term difficulty of some kind.

"Never, he was a smart outgoing kid who loved life. He always came home with a funny story or a joke." He began to cry as he spoke.

"Where did he get the gun? Is it yours?"

"My dad gave him the pistol last week for graduation. It's entirely my fault," Tom, Sr. blurted out with pain in his voice and tears in his eyes.

"Did he ask for the weapon?" If he had it might be a clue he had *indeed* been planning this.

"No, but when I was his age my father had given me one."

"Had you told him his grandfather was giving him the weapon?"

"No, it was a surprise. I'd been keeping it in the safe at the office. I didn't bring it home until his graduation party," Thomas, Sr. explained.

"Had he ever fired a gun before?"

"Yes. We went elk hunting every fall. But he'd never fired a small hand gun." "Did he keep a journal or diary?" I asked.

"No, not that I know of," Vicky answered. "He did have his school notebook. It's hanging on the coat rack, I think," she continued.

A note of some kind would show *suicidal intent,* making the ruling clear cut. Without a note, we must proceed with caution. The chiming of the doorbell interrupted our conversation. Brenda entered.

"Investigator Craig and another man are at the door asking for Dr. Reedman," the housekeeper reported.

I excused myself, leaving the Beckman's in the kitchen. Brenda led me to the foyer where Steve Craig from the District Attorney's office, Bob the photographer, and Sergeant Wills were standing. It's a damn convention.

"So, what is this, a grave line tour?" I joked quietly.

All three smiled. Bob sheepishly nodded yes.

"Bob, the boy's body is upstairs. Be sure to get a good picture of the blood spatter on the curtains. The weapon is on the floor, and will you document its distance from the body? The housekeeper will show you the way. The pair of glasses under the chair is cracked. I did it accidentally. Make a note of it when you film them". I hoped to sound matter-of-fact so that he wouldn't taunt me about breaking the glasses.

There, it's out; I don't have to worry any more. I tried to convince myself.

"Sure, I brought plenty of film this time. I'll get lots of pictures of the broken glasses, with real film," he jabbed.

Several weeks ago, Bob arrived at a crime scene without any film in his camera. We waited for twenty minutes while Hicks Pharmacy delivered film. No one will let him forget it. Now he's known as the psychic photographer. He'll save the county a fortune on film developing; however, getting reprints are a bitch.

I turned to Investigator Craig and asked, "Why are you here?"

"Detective McDonald called and mentioned the situation. I thought I should get out here and do my investigation now while the trail is still warm and I have the chance."

The trail is still warm? Who is he kidding?

"How in the world did Ted find out so fast?" I laughed.

"Telephone, telegraph, and tell Ted," Steve answered.

"Have you spoken with the family yet?" he asked.

"Yes, they seem really broken up. He doesn't sound like the typical troubled kid, unless he totally fooled his parents." I realized that Sergeant Wills was just standing there staring into space.

"Hello, earth to Wills. Come in, Willis," I whispered.

He flinched, looking embarrassed. Smiling, he said, "Oh, sorry Doc. I was just thinking."

"Thinking a novel concept for you isn't it?" I jibed. "Have you searched the house for an intruder? It seems no one was at home when the kid came home from school this afternoon. And by the way, have you spoken with the housekeeper yet?"

"Yes. I secured the premises when I arrived. The sliding glass door was open about two inches and I couldn't find anyone in the house that didn't belong here. The alarm system and cameras weren't on for some reason. I haven't had a chance to talk with the housekeeper. Would you like me to do that now?"

"That would be a good idea. Why don't you take her outside to interview her?"

When Brenda returned from showing Bob upstairs, Wills invited her outside to talk. As soon as the front door closed Steve began to chuckle. "What's up with him? When Bob and I arrived, he was standing out front staring up at the second story windows. Is he stoned?" he joked.

"God knows people are affected strangely by the thought of death. Maybe he's preoccupied," I answered.

"That or the sixties were really good to him," Steve quipped.

"You've been in the D.A.'s office way too long," I shook my head.

"Smart-ass. Tell me what you know so far. Was he some hated rich kid?"

"No, he seemed loved by everybody if you believe the parents."

"Was he dealing drugs?"

"I don't know yet."

"Is there any sign of an intruder other than the sliding glass door being open?"

"Not that I've heard of, yet."

"Do you know anything, *yet?*"

"Not really. The boy's room is a mess. The shot went right through his temple. There are signs of powder burns."

"So, did he leave a note?" Steve inquired.

"Not that anyone has found. His mother says his backpack is hanging out here. Maybe he put something there?" I answered.

"Does he have a computer around somewhere?" Steve asked.

"In fact, he does. It's in his bedroom."

"We should check there. Now a days kids don't use paper like we did," Steve said.

What a good idea, I thought. *I probably would have forgotten to look there.* I've never found a suicide note or death threat on a computer before, but there's a first time for everything.

"Which way's the scene?" Steve asked.

"He's in his bedroom. It's up these stairs, then down the hall to the left, third door on the right. You can't miss it; just follow the yellow brick road."

A voice behind me said, "Excuse me, sir. Could I talk to you for a few minutes?" It was Mr. Beckman.

"Sure," I answered, anticipating the usual bereaved parent type questions.

He appeared composed now, unlike just moments before.

"Let's step in here," he said, pushing on a panel opening a large door that had appeared to be just a wall. "It's my quiet place," he explained.

I stepped through the door into something straight out of the movies. It was a giant secret room, every boy's dream. Directly across from me as I entered was a huge river rock fireplace, burning a six foot log. Above, adorning the mantle was a monster masquerading as a ten-point elk head. It was looking longingly toward freedom through the French pane windows to my right. The setting sun was sending little rainbows dancing around the room through the crystal panes.

In front of the roaring fireplace was an eight-foot tuck-and-roll red leather couch. Adjacent to it were two matching wingback chairs. Like the one his son's body now sat in, upstairs. On the wall to the left were more game trophies; two bighorn sheep, a pair of antelope, two pheasants and an entire school of rainbow trout in varying sizes. At least there wasn't a coroner head waiting for a mate.

"Did you shoot all of these?" I asked trying not to sound shocked.

"Oh, God, no. The elk over the fireplace was shot back in 1888 by my great grandpa, about where you're standing now. The bighorn sheep and antelope my granddad shot in Wyoming around 1930. I'm the fisherman. We eat the little ones and the big ones I mount myself." He seemed relaxed in his manner and tone.

"Please, sit by the fire. Can I get you a drink?" he politely offered as he walked to the bar.

"Just some water or a Coke would be fine."

As he brought my Coke, the crystal glass chimed when the ice struck the rim—ting, ting.

"Well," he said, handing me the glass as he sat down across from me with his elbows resting on his knees. He looked intently into my face. "I have a few questions for you, if you don't mind." His calm, slow, low-pitched tone of voice frightened me for some reason. It was sort of like being sent to the principal's office, or so I'm told. Not that I've ever been there.

"Sure, anything I can do for you," I agreed.

"Just who will determine the cause of death in this case?" he queried.

"In this state, it's the responsibility of the coroner to determine both cause and manner of death. Why do you ask?"

"What do you think you will put down for Junior's cause?" he asked tentatively.

"Well, the investigation isn't anywhere near complete. It would be at least a week until I make any kind of determination," I explained.

"A week, are you kidding? In the meantime what's going to happen to my son?" His voice went up about two octaves and he leaned forward. "Are you telling me we can't bury him for a week? His mother will lose her mind." His fists were clinched tight and I could see the tears beginning to fill his eyes.

"You don't need to wait for the paperwork; we will do the post-mortem exam tomorrow. Following that, the Hills can take him for you. I'll get the burial permit issued the same day." I attempted a soothing voice, trying to calm him.

"You don't understand. My wife's family is strict Roman Catholic. If you rule that Junior committed suicide, he can't be buried in the family plot. It's Holy Ground." His teeth clenched tight to prevent crying.

"So far, I don't have enough information to determine anything other than the cause of death to be by gunshot wound. As to whether it's self-inflected or not, that will take some investigation. What his intent was at the time he pulled the trigger will be carefully considered. We will move as quickly as possible for you," I explained.

"Look, I'm a business man and, uh, let's get to the point. What do you want? I'll pay anything. I'll never tell. Just sweep this aside. No one will notice," he begged. "For my wife, please."

Okay, where are the FBI cameras? I wondered. *This has to be a setup; doesn't he know it's a felony to even attempt to bribe an officer?*

"Mr. Beckman, I realize that you're upset about this," I reasoned. "But this isn't the way to handle it. I can't do what you ask. It's against the law, as well as the oath I took, not to mention against my ethics."

Chills were running up my back. Now I was worried. Did someone in the house shoot this boy? Were they trying to cover something up? On the other hand, did he really just want to protect his wife? I hoped it was the latter.

"Don't worry. There are other causes that might apply here. Wait until tomorrow and we'll have more information. Until then you go and take care of your wife. Make whatever plans you feel comfortable with. Ed and Patty will be great help. I'll call you tomorrow." I tried to comfort him as much as I could. I wanted out of there. I wasn't sure if I had been threatened or offered a bribe. Either one gave me the creeps. Excusing myself, I groped to find the release button for the secret panel. As I did, I entered back into the hall where I found Bob coming down the stairs.

"All done up there. What a mess. I took Polaroid's as well as thirty-five millimeter just to be sure. I put a measuring tape in the photos of the gun's distance from the body. I measured thirty-two inches. If it's okay with you I'm going home to dinner. See you tomorrow. Oh, by the way here's an extra shot of the glasses for you. I have one of my own," he said heading toward the door as he waved the Polaroid over his head.

"Not so fast. Come back here, you dog. Have you taken any pictures of the house from the outside, especially the bedroom window from below?"

"I'll do it on the way out. Good night, Doc," he said smugly as he ducked out the front door. The sound of loud footsteps on the stairs announced the arrival of both Steve Craig and Sergeant Wills.

"All finished up here. You can call Ed and Patty," Wills whispered as he headed for the front door. "I've got to go. There's been an accident out on County Road twenty-one. Somebody hit a cow. See you tomorrow." I could see his blue and red lights come on as he pulled from the drive.

"There's no note on the computer or any of the diskettes upstairs. Actually there's no sign of any note, preparations, or for that matter, intent on his part. Anybody in the house have motive or opportunity?" Steve asked.

"Oh God, don't turn this into a federal case. I'll never forgive you. I doubt that these people are child killers," I moaned. "I'm going home to my wife's idea of making dinner. The parents are in the kitchen. You interview them and I'll call Ed and Patty from my truck," I said with a laugh.

Steve escorted me to the door promising to share any information gleaned from the parents with me the next day. Halfway down the driveway, I met the big white hearse speeding straight at me in the center of the road. I swerved to avoid a head-on collision with the only person who could have hauled my body away.

Ed pulled up laughing with a cloud of choking dust right behind him. "Did I scare you? Shit, everybody gets out of my way in this. We're coming back for the body, is it okay to take him?"

"Yes, we're done. Everyone has gone except Inspector Craig. He's still with the family."

Yelling over the sound of his bad muffler, Ed leaned out the window and said, "If you want him dropped down at the county facility tonight, you know it'll cost you extra for the overtime." I could still hear him laughing as he drove away throwing rocks over my already dented Jeep. There was nothing else to do tonight so, I might as well go hug my kids and lock up my gun.

*   *   *

A call from the county morgue momentarily disturbed Saturday morning cartoons at the Reedman home. In some other house, it might be a memorable event in the life of a small child to have the coroner's office call. Not at my house. My girls think everyone's dad has dead people at their office. Lexi, my youngest daughter, held up the phone and loudly announced, as though she were working for AMTRAK, "Dad, it's those guys at your shop, the ones that can still talk."

"The post on the Beckman kid is scheduled for 1:30 this afternoon. Dr. Bilmarian won't be back from his bike ride until then," his secretary explained. To most people that mental image would be of a healthy man out riding his bicycle in the mountains. Not this time. I know it's a man on his Harley who doesn't want to be disturbed.

"They're dead; they'll wait," is one of his favorite sayings.

With the post just two hours away, I called Inspector Craig. After all, he did promise to share any information from the parents.

"Just because you work on the weekend doesn't mean the rest of the world does you know," the groggy voice mumbled.

"Okay, just tell me if you got any dirt from the parents last night after I left. Then I promise to let you get back to sleep."

"Well, according to the parents, the sun rose and set on that kid's shoulders. He was perfect, never in trouble at home or school. A little too perfect if you ask me. These parents are hiding something," he said, beginning to come to life.

"There you go again, sounding like an attorney."

"You think so? Let me tell you, those parents are sure concerned about the ruling. The dad wants it ruled an accident. I got the strong impression he was willing to pay for the results he wanted. Can you believe that?"

"Now that you mention it, he did try to influence my decision too. I just put it off as a bereaved parent."

"Let me go back to sleep, you heartless bastard," Steve whined.

I could hear a female voice in the background faintly say, "Who is it honey?"

"I have to go now, but I promise to call the kid's school counselor and talk to this girl Jennifer on Monday, Okay?" Click.

Oh, to be single again. What was I thinking? I wouldn't go through that again to save my life. I'm sure he was at that very moment, trying to explain who I was, and worse yet, *who the hell Jennifer was.*

When I radioed Wills he said, "I spoke with the housekeeper, Brenda. She told me that the boy was an angel. He never talked back and called her 'ma'am.' He sounded like the kind of kid every parent wants."

"Had he done anything different or out of the ordinary the day he died?" I asked.

"No. She said he came home from school every day, grabbed something to eat from the kitchen, dropped his stuff in the hall, and retreated to his room."

"Thanks, Chuck. If you hear anything new let me know."

As usual, I was running late and without a word to anyone, I got in the Jeep and raced to the morgue. The autopsy began, promptly, *not.*

Dr. Steve was twenty-two minutes late.

"Sorry, boys, there was traffic coming up the pass, but I knew this guy wasn't going to complain. After all, he has to wait. He has no choice. Isn't that why they call them patients?" Dr. Bilmarian said with his usual sadistic laugh.

Turning on the Dictaphone he began to test the equipment with a bad joke. "What do you call an adolescent bunny? A Pubic Hare!"

Worse than the joke was listening to it, again at high speed as he double-checked the system (Alvin and the Chipmunks telling risqué bunny jokes).

He began dictating. "Those present are Jim Simmons, Diener, Dr. Steve Bilmarian, Pathologist and Rex Reedman, Pine County Coroner."

The following is a partial transcription of the procedure:

"The body of a fourteen year old adolescent male is presented for autopsy. Weight of the body is eighty-nine pounds, measuring fifty-two inches in length. The body is normal in gross appearance. He appears well developed, well nourished, and normal in appearance for the stated age. His trunk is devoid of scars, tattoos, or areas of ecchymosis *(bruising)* as visualized at this time. However, the face shows evidence of massive trauma including severe ecchymosis around the eyes bilaterally. The stated injury being a gunshot wound to the head."

"Jim, get the powder kit. Let's make sure he does indeed have gunpowder residue on his hand," Dr. B ordered. "The entrance is on the right side measuring 2.37 centimeters in diameter. It is located 2.9 centimeters posterior to the lateral canthus of the right eye. The exit wound as noted is in the left frontal temporal region measuring 4.9 by 5.8 centimeters. The fragmented margins are consistent with the reported injury. Examination of the cerebral tissue demonstrates massive damage to the cortex bilaterally. Large fragments of osseous *(bone)* tissue are present throughout the cranial cavity."

Pulling from his pocket a small package wrapped with evidence tape, Dr. B. said, "Put this in with the kit for the FBI. It's the bullet Sgt. Wills removed from a wall at the scene. The police dropped it off earlier, in an attempt to avoid being here now."

The remainder of the post-mortem exam was uneventful. The only damage to this young man's body was the massive head injury. Initial toxicology studies revealed no foreign substances, alcohol, or drugs in the boy's circulatory system. Inspection of the gun recovered from the scene revealed the victim's fingerprints on the weapon. The chamber contained one spent cartridge."

By Monday afternoon, I had received at least ten phone calls from Mr. Beckman pleading for a ruling. I finally received the call I'd been waiting for from the D.A.'s office.

"The District Attorney is going to postpone any further investigation until after you rule," the paralegal informed me.

Things to think about before deciding this case:

1. There were indeed gunpowder residues on the young man's hands. These were consistent with him holding the weapon in his right hand and with the death scene as observed. The question is, had he fired the weapon earlier leaving the residue?

2. No note was ever found. That does not mean someone in the house did not remove or destroy it.

3. When I arrived home following the post-mortem, a brand new red Ford Explorer 4x4 was parked in my driveway. My wife reported the dealer dropped it off with no clue as to who ordered or paid for it. "Isn't it beautiful?" she cooed.

"Sorry, Dear. It has to go back, unless you'd like to visit me in prison," I explained.

"When are visiting days?" she giggled.

I was pretty sure I knew exactly who the mystery benefactor was and bribery was the wrong approach with me.

* * *

Now you know everything that we knew. Once again, it's time to make up your mind. Was it *murder, suicide, or natural causes?* On the other hand, maybe it's something else.

REX'S REVIEW

Mr. Beckman was determined to bury his son in "Holy Ground" even if it meant the risk of being jailed for bribing an officer. This was made apparent when he tried to influence the ruling with the wonderful Explorer in my driveway. Now, of course, I have to buy one or there will be no living with my wife.

Had Thomas, Sr. been aware of the law he would have known there was no reason to change the ruling. The entrance and exit wounds were offset in angle enough to prove Tom Jr. was holding the weapon himself. The gunpowder residues we recovered from his hands at the autopsy confirmed this.

We become suspicious when the angle of penetration and exit are parallel. It is difficult to hold your hand up to your head and have it be level, then shoot a gun. (Go to a mirror and try it—without the gun.)

The District Attorney had a conversation with Jennifer. She told him that she and Junior were talking on the phone while he was playing with his new gun. He held the weapon up to the phone so she could hear the spinning of the chamber. He sang, "Round and round the mulberry bush," as the chamber spun. Then he pulled the trigger, *click*.

Jennifer reported that she hung up thinking he was kidding. A few minutes later she tried to call back but the line was busy. Thomas was alone in the room at the time of the shooting. Her recollection of the incident fit with the facts as known.

Without a suicide note or stated intent, even to the girl on the phone with him, we are unable to prove "Suicidal Intent". In the state of Colorado, there must be demonstrated intent either in the form of a note, a phone call, or even E-mail, before the death can be ruled suicide.

Without any evidence of previous attempts or threats of harm to him, and due to the circumstances surrounding the death, the cause of death in this case is ruled an accident.

Manner of death: accidental, self-inflicted gunshot wound.

Are you getting better?

If you think you are, try the next case: Two for the Road.

Two For The Road

"Good things come to good people." I recall my mother's axiom anytime I meet good fortune or am rewarded for a deed well done. As I've grown older the axiom has shown itself to be quite fickle. Even the nicest most generous people have crummy things happen in their lives. Sometimes, their generosity costs them their lives. For example, billionaire John Aster was aboard a sinking ship. Even though he couldn't swim, he courageously gave his life jacket to another passenger.

Heroic acts occur every day unheralded, even unnoticed. The ladies in this story had what it took to become heroes. Maple and her identical twin sister April, now in their late seventies, had been lifelong residents of Colorado, as had the previous two generations of their family.

April noticed Maple had been feeling run down and tired lately. She needed more rest. That night's forecast said it would be the biggest snowstorm of the season. It was a good chance to sit by the fire and catch up on the rest Maple's doctor had recommended.

It was eleven-thirty p.m. when they received a call for help. Friends were stranded in the blinding snowstorm sixty-five miles away in the mountains. The young divorcee, Renée, and her eight-year-old son, Tyler, had been in the mountains all day at a church camp.

Without hesitation our two heroines warmed up their trusty old four-wheel drive Subaru. Taking proper precautions, blankets, flashlights, munchies and with map in hand, they were off to the rescue. They drove for what must have seemed like hours for two elderly women with cataracts. Finally, they neared the arranged rendezvous point, or so they thought. The blowing snow left them driving in circles for forty minutes. All the while the stranded mother and son waited patiently in their snow bound tomb half of a mile away, singing to stay awake in the bitter cold.

In subzero weather it doesn't take long for the human body to shut down. It begins with the feeling of being extremely cold, gradually feeling warmer, and then getting sleepy. At this point if you do go to sleep, chances are you won't wake again in this world.

As my grandfather was fond of saying when someone he felt incompetent managed to accomplish something, "Even a blind horse finds the trough once in a while." So it was with the two Good Samaritans blinded by the blowing snow, they ran smack into the very people they were searching for.

Damage to the Subaru amounted to a broken right headlight, while damage to the stranded pickup and its plate steel bumper was undetectable. With their precious cargo safely belted in the back seat, the sisters headed for home. Driving was even more difficult now, minus one headlight. They crept along at a snail's pace. Maple somehow managed to miss the left turn necessary to reach Interstate 25. Following April's suggestion, they backed up about eighty feet. Behind them was a blind curve, ahead a hill, and directly and across from them, their turn. Using her poorest judgment, Maple turned the car across both lanes of traffic in an effort to reach her objective.

At the very moment Maple reached midway in her unlawful traffic maneuver, the inside of the Subaru was momentarily illuminated. The beautiful white lights were quickly followed by the sound of breaking glass and screaming metal. Then silence for what must have felt like an eternity to those surviving in the back seat. It *was* eternity for the twin sisters now lying dead in the front seat. They entered and left this earth together.

Their seats had broken upon impact and now blocked exit or access to the injured in the back. The mid-sixties solid steel "hose it off and sell it again" iron dash boarded missile of a car was traveling at sixty miles an hour when it cleared the crest of the hill, just in time to end the good Samaritans lives in an instant.

It was three-thirty in the morning when my phone rang. Dispatchers are extremely polite when they call late. I think they're afraid my wife will answer the phone.

"There's a T-bone out on the highway, just past chimney rock. It's a deuce." A deuce is our slang for a double death.

Sandy advised me, "Put it in four wheel drive, Rex. There's six inches of snow on the road and the weather service is reporting it's going to get worse before it gets better."

Taking her advice, I was extremely careful driving the thirty miles to the scene. In four-wheel drive going slow is a given. Just before cresting the hill, multi-colored lights of emergency vehicles reflected off the low hanging clouds and lit the snow ahead of me. Suddenly, coming straight out of the gloom was a helicopter gaining altitude as it passed overhead, clearing my car by only about forty feet.

The officer directing traffic was quite annoyed when I refused to follow his directions and kept moving. I've got to get a light bar for my car. Angrily, looking into the driver's side window he said, "Oh, Dr. Reedman. I'm sorry I didn't recognize you, park over there."

He directed me toward the shoulder. As my headlights flashed on the scene, the twisted remnants of two cars blocked the roadway, looking like some bazaar modern sculpture. A white sheet that covered the body waved aimlessly in the wind exposing the driver's arm, which hung limply out of what was left of the driver's side door.

Seeing my car arrive, Officer Grady hurried to greet me. "The passengers from the back seat were airlifted out just a few minutes ago," she began speaking before I could close my door.

"I know. As they passed over I thought they were going to take the roof off my Jeep. I guess there were some survivors or there'd be no need to MediVac anyone," I said, trying to find something good even in a situation as tragic as this.

"The two in back of the Subaru are not in good shape. Head injuries to the young boy and the mother looked as though she had a broken back," Karen reported.

"What about the people in the other car?"

"Oh, the boat. They were shaken up a bit; the driver was negative for alcohol. He and the three passengers are about ready to be transported by ambulance now."

Karen relayed how the accident occurred. According to the highway patrol investigator, a call had been placed to the Deputy D.A., but since there were no drugs or alcohol, he decided to stay home.

I'll bet that was a hard decision to make, I thought as I felt my ears frostbiting in the wind.

As Karen led me toward the destruction, a voice from the darkness yelled, "Hey, get out of my light." It was Bob, the police photographer

For just a second I tried to get out of the way, until I realized it was almost four-thirty in the morning, there was no light and he was using a flash. I could hear him laughing, "Gotcha Doc, I'm done here. The prints will be on your desk in the morning."

As he wound his camera and disappeared into a vale of blowing snow, I could hear him say, "Doc, go look at what's in the road about thirty feet in front of the cars. You'll die."

I neared the wreckage with a slight amount of hesitance. I'm never quite sure what I'm about to see, and believe it or not, *some* things *do* bother me. If I can take just a second to compose myself, I usually do fine. I know when I arrive at the scene to view the body, every eye is watching to see if I get grossed out or worse yet, puke.

The large, primer-gray Thunderbird sitting half in the oncoming lane had a new hood ornament: a little, pale blue Subaru. The windshields in both cars were shattered. The only recognizable part of the tiny Subaru was the rear portion. The front had been converted to scrap metal, taking the occupants with it.

"They were pronounced dead by a passing dentist shortly after it happened," the voice belonged to Roman, the Colorado State Patrol investigator. "I've determined the accident was the Subaru's fault. It doesn't help to ticket a dead person, but somehow it makes me feel better."

"Well, getting killed is going a little too far to get out of a ticket, don't you think?" was the only retort I had for his comment.

While Roman left to yell at a motorist, I lifted the sheets from the bodies. Injuries were massive; both ladies had broken femurs, thighs. I palpated the abdomen of the driver; it was spongy, or felt bloated. As I pushed I could feel ribs grate. She had massive internal bleeding and most likely had broken her ribs on the steering wheel. Her pupils were fully fixed and her skin was cold. Moving my attention to the passenger, I tried to reposition the bodies to separate them. The passenger fell over like a rag doll broken at the waist. The impact had fractured her spine, probably in more than one place.

The sound of yelling drew my attention away from the sisters. It was Officer Grady screaming at a motorist, "You idiot, weren't you watching the road? If you want to see a dead body that bad I'll let you get a real close look. You don't have to run me over to get a glimpse. Maybe you would like the kids to get a better view?" She continued to berate the man as he followed Trooper Roman's directions to keep moving.

"Take five Karen, he missed you by at least six inches and wasn't going faster than twenty," Roman teased.

"If this mongo car hadn't been here, that moron would have hit me," she attempted to defend herself. I could tell she was really shaken by the near miss.

Drivers trying to get a look at blood and gore while passing an accident are a major hazard to the emergency workers at the scene. It's difficult to do your job while cars are zooming by five feet away, without the added possibility of someone rubbernecking running you over.

Remembering the photographers parting words, I walked about ten paces down the highway. There in the roadway were someone's false teeth, upside down, smiling at me. I wondered what artistic rendition of this scene would be among tomorrow's photographs. I looked down at the strange sight wondering how they could have possibly gotten there.

"Rex, you lazy bastard come give me a hand lifting these two onto a gurney." Ed Hill was standing next to the driver's door holding up an empty body bag and shaking it like it was a matador's cape.

"Not until you come and see this," I said, gesturing to the teeth.

Looking at the orthodontia on the pavement Ed asked, "Where do you think we wind them up?"

The bodies were delivered directly to the morgue; of course Ed wanted to charge double mileage for two passengers. Well, you can't blame the man for trying.

At ten-thirty the following morning, I was called from my deathbed. Okay, I just felt dead tired. It was the autopsy assistant, Jim Simmons, calling to inform me that the sisters' autopsies were scheduled for right after lunch.

I couldn't get the front door to the lab open because the locks were frozen, so I sneaked in the delivery door that leads to the loading dock, or as we call it, the "night drop." I found Dr. Bilmarian in the garage sitting on his big black Harley.

"Want to go for a spin?" he asked.

He knew I would never ride on a motorcycle, again. I rode one once and almost hit a semi-truck. I certainly wouldn't ride with a crazy man like him at the wheel. He offers me a ride each time he sees me, and each time I refuse. I think he likes the game.

Standing up he said, "If you're ready to get started so am I." He tossed the polishing rag on the floor. "Let's get going. There are two of them, and I don't want to be here all day".

The Post Mortem Examination began at three in the afternoon. Those present for the procedures were: Dr. Steve Bilmarian, Pathologist, Jim Simmons, Diener, and I, Rex Reedman, Pine County Coroner.

Dr. Steve began to adjust the dictating equipment to a comfortable height, testing the settings by singing into the microphone, "Oh, say can you see . . ."

Jim jumped in to save our eardrums saying, "I know, Roseanne Arnold, right?" He winked in my direction.

"Critics, you're all alike. Shut up and cut out the Syskel & Ebert impression." Steve then began to inspect the body of Maple first.

The following is an excerpt of the narrative:

"The body of a seventy-seven year old white female is submitted for autopsy. It is stated this overweight lady was the driver of a vehicle involved in an auto vs. auto collision. The body demonstrates obvious signs of massive trauma. They are consistent with those typically suffered in the stated manner of injury. Fracture of the femurs bilaterally is demonstrated by the aberrant motion of the lower limbs." He lifted the feet about six inches and the femurs could be seen moving half way up the thigh at the site of fracture.

"See that, this kind of fracture is caused when the knees hit the dashboard. When we get inside I'm sure the pelvis will be pulverized," he confidently stated.

"Palpation of the thorax reveals multiple costal (rib) fractures, most likely the result of impact with the steering column. Areas of ecchymosis (bruising) are noted in the left temporal and right frontal regions." The areas of bruising were consistent with the driver's side door striking her.

"The left humorous is fractured at the midpoint of the shaft. Let's open her up, Jim," Steve directed.

Jim performed the Y incision. What was left of her fractured ribs was removed. There was no evidence of hemorrhage in the fractures. The organs within the gaping cavity were floating in blood like cocktail weenies at a party.

"Oh God, this doesn't look good, get the suction in here and find out what's ruptured. I'll bet you the internal hemorrhaging killed her within seconds after impact," Dr. Steve hypothesized. Continuing to dictate, "The lung tissue appears hemorrhagic and in full collapse bilaterally. The fractured lateral margin of the T7 rib can be easily seen as the source of this pneumothorax." A pneumothorax is literally air in the chest, outside the lung tissue, between the ribs and lung. It makes it impossible to breathe.

Turning in my direction Steve noted, "The paramedics couldn't have revived this lady if they had been standing there waiting for her."

Jim removed the organs from the chest as Steve weighed, dissected, and reported his findings. "Sectioning the cardiac tissue reveals several areas of necrotic tissue representing ancient infarcts, the largest being located in the posterior inferior pole of the heart measuring 2.5 centimeters by 1.8 centimeters. Internal inspection shows a large recent infarct in the left atrium." He removed sections for microscopic examination and dropped them into the formaldehyde. When the post-mortem on Maple was complete, the following was the sum of our knowledge:

1. There were ancient and recent areas of heart damage, i.e. heart attack. One of the areas of damage showed little to no ecchymosis.
2. Her spine was fractured at T12.
3. There was a large laceration of the liver.
4. Her aorta had been torn in half. This is the major artery of the body; it is under tremendous pressure and can cause death very quickly when compromised.
5. Both lungs were punctured and collapsed due to the broken ribs.
6. There were multiple rib and leg fractures.

Following the examination of Maple, Dr. Steve began to examine April's remains. "This is the identical twin sister of case # 2337 . . ."

Findings include:

1. The spleen is ruptured. This organ destroys old aging red blood cells.
2. The liver is completely avulsed or torn away from the surrounding structures.
3. The spinal column is severed at the T10 level and again at L5.
4. The aorta was torn at spinal levels T9 and L4 consistent with the spinal fractures.
5. A severe cerebral hemorrhage is noted within the Circle of Willis. This is the major plexus of arteries feeding the brain.

This concludes the post-mortem examinations of April and Maple Ward.

It took several weeks in the hospital before Renée and her son Todd were released. They suffered emotionally almost as much as physically. Knowing the ladies who had bravely come to their rescue in the worst of conditions were dead left them heartbroken. The driver and passengers of the big boat were examined and released on the night of the accident. A trace of THC, the active ingredient in marijuana, was detected in the blood of the driver of the big car. No marijuana was found in the vehicle.

That was all the information available at the time of determination. Do you think you know the answer? Think carefully. Remember, there are two bodies.

REX'S REVIEW

The two elderly women in this story did indeed die in an automobile accident but due to drastically different causes. April, the passenger, died from injuries sustained at the scene. Her sister Maple died of totally different causes.

Remember Dr. Steve noted the damage to Maple's heart, and the fact that there was no blood in the fractures? This is because Maple, the driver, was dead at the time of impact. She died of natural causes, a cardiac arrest moments before the impact. April was in excellent health and died accidentally due to the automobile accident.

Okay, I admit this was a tough case.

Good luck in the next one: Yours, Mine and Ores.

Yours, Mine and Ores

Unlike urban real-estate sales, rural land purchases often include extras. Sometimes these gems include an old cabin, an outhouse, a barn filled with artifacts, or even a ghost.

Up in the mining districts of Colorado, the unseen additions frequently consist of abandoned mines. Many of these cave-like structures collapsed early in the last century or simply reached a dead end indicating where the veins of precious metal were no longer profitable to extract. Once in a while tales are told of gold and silver still being found in the old shafts.

Miners were an odd bunch of characters coming from across the country and all over the world in search of their fortune. Some of these adventurers found their dreams and others only found nightmares. Cave-ins and pockets of "bad air" meant the end of the search for scores of novices and seasoned miners as well.

Chipping at hard rock for fifteen hours a day with a pick and shovel sent more than one miner back home empty handed and occasionally in a box. Others changed their profession when veins became too difficult to follow or simply disappeared, becoming instead storekeepers, drunks, and gamblers.

Local history tells of more than one case of a miner finding a bonanza only to lose it in a poker game or questionable business transaction.

In the 1800s, Colorado instituted what are known as the "blue laws" hoping to curb rampant fraud in the mining camps. No liquor sales, signing of contracts, or filing of mining claims on Sundays; these laws continue to this day. However, less than scrupulous individuals occasionally found ways around these precautions. The solution was simple: kill the miner, hide his body, and wait until Monday to file a transfer of mineral rights.

Mining claims were not tied to ownership of the land in question. A neighbor who owned mineral rights could follow a vein of ore wherever it led, even if it was under another property owner's house. When purchasing land today the mineral rights don't always go with the property.

When Doug and Judy inherited a large tract of Colorado mountain property from Judy's grandfather, the real-estate attorney was thrilled to inform them that the property included the mineral rights.

"You get the land and everything on or under it," he proudly informed the new owners.

Being city dwellers from southern California the consequence of this statement was lost on Doug and Judy. However, it wouldn't take long for the family to discover the implications of the lawyer's announcement.

Doug and Judy, along with their two boys, Taylor and Zack, arrived in Colorado unprepared for what was in store for them. The boys, being typical teenagers (thirteen and fifteen), were anxious to explore the nearly six thousand acres near Broken Creek that was their legacy.

"Can we have horses?" Zack anxiously asked, even before the car had stopped.

"We'll see," Doug responded.

Judy interrupted with a typical mother's comment, "First let's get unpacked, then we'll worry about horses."

Judy had not been to the property in nearly twenty-five years. All she remembered from visiting Grandpa was that there weren't any neighbors nearby. Judy, who had grown accustomed to living in a condo, and having weekly manicures and facials, wasn't sure how long she could survive without people, or for that matter, a shopping mall down the street. Doug, on the other hand, was as anxious as his sons were to get away from the hectic pace of city life. He'd worked in the software industry for ten long years, and now looked forward to becoming a gentleman rancher.

Ah, fresh air and no one around for miles, he thought to himself as he stood on the expansive deck behind the house. "House" is probably a misnomer; actually, it was a square cut, two-story log structure surrounded by mammoth pine trees. The new home was five times the size of their four-bedroom condominium back home. Doug was thrilled with their new residence. Not only was it big enough for the family, but they owned it free and clear. Judy, on the other hand, worried how she could keep such a massive home clean, and what would they do with six bedrooms?

After the moving van left the family spent three days unpacking. The boys thought they would die before mom said they could go exploring.

Once everything had been put away to mom's satisfaction, Zack and Taylor raced outside to look around. They climbed up to the hayloft in the barn to survey their surroundings. A few trees and lots of scrub grass was all they could see from their vantage point

"Let's go hiking," Zack suggested.

It was nearly dark when the boys returned from their adventure. They were covered in dust and prickly little black stickers, but chattered about all of the neat things they'd found.

Taylor excitedly asked his mom, "Did you know we own a windmill? It's out near an old building by a stream."

"You boys stay away from that old building. It could collapse on you!" Judy warned.

"But mom, it's cool," Zack interjected, trying to get her to understand a young boy's enthusiasm.

"I know about that building. It's your Great-Grandpa Jack's stamp mill and it's dangerous," her tone was quite serious.

"Stamp mill what's a stamp mill?" Taylor asked. "Did he make stamps there?"

"A stamp mill is where mine owners crushed ore to extract the gold," Doug explained to his city slicker sons.

"Cool. Does that mean there's a gold mine out there too?" Taylor inquired.

"Yes, your great grandpa and his partner had a big mine somewhere on the mountain. However, that was a long time ago and I think it caved in before I was born," Judy explained.

If she thought that explanation would keep the boys away, she was sadly mistaken. Bright and early the next morning the boys packed a lunch, filled water bottles and disappeared over the horizon in search of "their" gold mine. Thoughts of riches had haunted their dreams all night. On their quest, they ran more than walked as they approached the dilapidated stamp mill. They thought the mine must be close by, but it took them about two hours to locate what they were sure was its opening. Piles of debris outlined the portal that darkened the cliff face.

"Cool. We found it," Zack shouted to his little brother who had fallen behind in the race for the opening. Zack being five and a half feet tall and out weighing his petite curly headed little brother by at least fifty pounds, could run faster and climb quicker than tiny Taylor.

"Wait for me," Taylor begged.

"Hurry up the.n. Zack motioned for him to climb faster as he stood atop the tailings, his shoulder length, blond hair blowing in the afternoon breeze.

Together the brothers peered into the darkness of the mine's gaping chasm. Excited by their discovery, but fearful of the blackness that lay before them, they dared one another to venture into the darkness.

"You're the oldest. You go first," Taylor implored, his large dark brown eyes resembling a sad puppy.

"Okay, but if I find gold it's mine," Zack responded to the plea from his little brother. They decided to venture in together. The midday sun only lit the entrance for about thirty feet and then it was total darkness.

"Where's the flashlight?" Taylor whispered, holding onto Zack's shirttail.

"I thought you brought it," The blame game for forgetting the flashlight continued for several minutes until it was interrupted by a loud voice coming from the tunnel.

"Hey! You boys, what are you doing here?" a deep voice boomed through the tunnel.

The boys made a mad dash for the safety of the sunlight. Each forgetting about the other in the race for the cave's opening, they nearly trampled one another as they scrambled into the sunlight. There they paused.

Again the voice boomed louder and closer than before, "I said, what are you doing in my mine?"

As they peered into the darkness behind them for the source of the voice, they thought they could see the form of an old man appear deep in the tunnel. He was dust covered with a dirty gray beard and dressed in coveralls.

"We, we were just exploring," Zack explained to the form facing them from the darkness of the shaft.

"This is my mine and you don't belong here. Get out!" the old man ordered.

Jessie Owens could not have covered ground as fast as the two young men on their race home. Frightened, dirty, and shaken, the boys reached the house only looking over their shoulders occasionally to see if the gruff old man was still chasing them.

Once safe at home, they tried to explain to their dad what had happened at the mine.

"There shouldn't be anyone there. I'm sure it was just your imagination," he calmly suggested in an attempt to comfort them. "Tomorrow I'll go back with you and we'll see, but don't tell your mom. She'd have a heart attack if she knew where you were today."

Judy went to town for supplies and a quick manicure the following morning. The men of the house anxiously loaded up the Suburban and headed toward the mine.

"There it is!" Zack exclaimed as the tailings came into view.

"Alright boys, calm down and we'll go take a look." Doug grabbed a flashlight and boldly headed to the entrance with the boys hesitantly trailing close behind.

"Be careful, Dad. That old man is probably waiting for us," Taylor pleaded fearfully.

"He might have a gun," Zack added.

With the aid of the flashlight, Doug and the boys ventured into the cavern. About fifty yards from the entrance, tunnels branched out in several directions. One went right, another left and one dropped away steeply and deeper into the abyss. Darkness surrounded the tiny beam of the flashlight. The boys stayed close to their dad and the little light. Doug decided the downward path was the one to take. They ventured deeper and deeper following the narrow railroad tracks into the tunnel, stumbling in the blackness of the mine. Doug, a six-foot-five, two hundred fifty pound former linebacker, found it difficult to stand upright or move easily in the cramped tunnel. As they reached the second level the ground under their feet leveled out. The three felt a chillingly cold breeze whisk past them. The boys wanted to run.

"Don't worry, it's just a pressure change," Dad explained.

They continued into the darkness passing side tunnels that intersected their path. The sound of small creatures scurrying as the light moved ahead of them frightened the young members of the team. Now they really wanted to get out. Thoughts of gold were not enough to overcome their growing terror. Dad, however, was having a great time. Several hundred feet in and four levels down there was no sign of the old man the boys had allegedly encountered on their previous excursion.

"Well boys, there doesn't seem to be any sign of your old man," Doug confidently reassured his sons.

That was the wrong thing to say, or, maybe it was just a little premature to mention it. No sooner had Doug announced the absence of the elderly man than a *very* cold wind blew past the group. This time it was not a change in pressure nor was it gentle. Doug nearly dropped the flashlight as a chill ran up his spine.

"OUT!" a deep voice demanded.

Doug moved the light right, left, up and down, searching for the source of the order. There was nothing to see. He urged the boys to follow him deeper into the blackness. Then suddenly from the darkness, Doug felt what he thought was a hand touching his shoulder. He almost jumped out of his skin. Shining the light in the direction he felt the contact, he strained to see. What met his eyes made him gasp. Through another intersecting tunnel leading away from the main shaft, he caught sight of an old man lying against the wall of the collapsed duct. It was a corpse dressed in overalls with a long gray beard and covered in dust. The boys yelled and turned to run. Taking about three steps, they realized abruptly that they were running into pitch darkness. They stared at the blackness before them and were almost trampled by their own father running for the surface. The time needed to exit the old mine seemed like forever to the terrified group.

Once in the safety of daylight they paused to catch their breath. "Well, I guess you boys weren't imagining anything," Dad apologized. "I think we'd better go home and call the authorities."

The phone at the Reedman house rang within twenty minutes of the discovery.

"Dr Reedman, I think you'd better put on your climbing gear and head out to the old Krider property," Judy, the dispatcher, suggested.

I've learned to follow the subtle suggestions of the dispatcher; if she says to bring specific gear with me I do. I packed my heavy coat, grabbed a rope and the helmet the fire department had given me, and I headed toward the Krider homestead. The location required no directions. It's one of the largest homesteads still in private hands;

124

the property is a local legend and well known to anyone in the county. Stories abound about the large amounts of silver and gold removed from the mines located there. Old man Krider apparently had a nose for where to dig. He was known as the 'Dutchman' of Pine County.

From my house, it took over an hour to just get to the Krider's turnoff. Then after several miles of dirt roads and traversing a narrowly steep pass, I finally arrived at the gate to the property. Even from that distance, I could see the flashing lights of emergency vehicles.

I thought I had made excellent time arriving within two hours of receiving the call for help, but I hadn't managed to beat Ted or Hank to the scene. As I parked my old piece-of-crap Jeep in the driveway, Ted jogged in my direction.

"This is great, what took you so long? Hank and I have been here for twenty minutes," Ted griped as he neared the open Jeep window.

"I moved as fast as I could, but I had to pee first. Besides, you know how hard it is to get this old piece of crap to climb even a small hill, much less a pass like that one," I explained, pointing to the summit I had just traversed.

"This is great. The family says they saw a ghost," Ted explained excitedly as he leaned on my car door, blocking my exit.

"Don't tell me I've been called way out here for a ghost sighting. Lori will kill me for missing a family dinner for a lousy ghost."

"Trust me. You're going to love this; it really was a ghost," Ted continued excitedly.

"Ted, you moron there is no such thing as ghosts." I rolled my eyes at his naiveté.

"I don't think you'll say that after you hear the story they have to tell," he retorted confidently.

"Well, unless you let me out of the car I won't hear anything they have to say. Back up and let me out of here".

"Sorry", he apologized, backing away from my door and letting me out of the vehicle.

"I see Hank's car. Why is that idiot here?" I questioned.

"He was with me; we were fishing at Twelve Mile Reservoir when the call came in. He almost caught a big rainbow using a worm."

"Almost? If he didn't land it how do you know what it was? Knowing him it was probably an old boot." I scowled.

"Never mind the fish. Come in and listen to the family tell their encounter with the ghost. It will make a great story for your Coroner's Gazette column."

"Ted, there are no such thing as ghosts. I'm certainly not going to look like an idiot by writing a spook story."

"Open your mind and follow me," he demanded.

As we approached the house, I could see a small gathering of firemen, ambulance drivers and fat Hank standing in a circle in front of the barn near the house.

"Hey, Doc. Come here. I want you to meet Doug Downey and his sons, Zack and Taylor." Hank sounded excited as he did the introductions. "They found a dead body out on their property," he continued.

"Ted said it was a ghost," I questioned.

"Ghost, cadaver, corpse what's the difference?" Hank responded.

"Or, alien," Ted mumbled.

"Well, maybe, like the existence of a *real* body. Okay, where is the corpse?" I asked.

"It's out in our mine," Zack explained.

"Yeah, he tried to chase us away from the gold!" Taylor added excitedly.

"Let me get this straight—a dead body chased you away from gold?" I asked.

"I thought they were crazy and tried to show them that they were imagining thing,s" Doug interrupted. "But when we went into the mine, I swear I felt someone grab me and tell me to leave."

"What did you do?" I asked, trying to make some sense out of the tale.

"We left!" the boys exclaimed simultaneously.

"Okay. Since we're all here, why don't you show us where the body is?" I was certain that their minds had been playing tricks on them in the dark unfamiliar surroundings of an old mine shaft. It wouldn't be the first time I'd been called out for an imaginary corpse.

The trip to the opening of the mine didn't take long. We drove for about five miles over a rut-filled goat trail. I was relieved to see the opening to the mine went horizontally into the cliff face and I wouldn't be required to climb down a rope. I hate caves, mines or any confined spaces.

The group put on their gear and Ted laid his baseball cap on a rock outside the entrance to indicate where we entered. It's an old tradition to signal any rescuers that there is someone in the mine. I took a powerful spotlight and followed Doug and his sons into the cavern. I could taste the dust as we descended the shaft, and the musty smell of bat guano filled my nostrils. I concentrated on the beam from my light and tried not to trip on debris scattered on the floor as we went deeper into the tunnel. There were old timbers, railroad tracks and rocks scattered about everywhere. It looked as though the ceiling had collapsed in several places; I didn't feel safe to be there. We followed Doug and the boys for what felt like an eternity. Deeper and deeper into the mountain it got colder as we descended into the narrow duct.

Just as I thought we should be turning back Doug announced, "It's somewhere around here that I felt the hand grab m.e" He shined his light into a collapsed passageway on our right.

"There he is!" the boys exclaimed.

As Doug's light bounced around in the tunnel we could see what looked to be an old man leaning against the back wall of the shaft.

"I'll be damned," Ted whispered from behind me. "It *is* a bod.y"

It was difficult to tell if it was a corpse or just a pile of old clothes.

"Everybody shine your lights over here," Hank ordered.

With six lights illuminating the chamber, it was clear to see the roof had collapsed filling the area with wreckage. There were timbers, rocks, and old tools almost half way to the ceiling. The bottom half of the man's remains were buried beneath the rubble.

"Somebody move this junk and let Doc in there," Hank directed.

"I don't want to go in there. I'll bet there are rats in there. You go in," I urged.

"Not me. Ted, you go take a look," Hank looked in Ted's direction.

"He's dead, let's leave him there and get the hell out of this hole. He looks like he's been there for a long time.

He's not hurting anyone, and besides, he looks comfy," Ted suggested.

"Someone has to go in, we can't just leave him there," Doug whispered as though he didn't want to wake the old gentleman.

Carefully, the group began to remove rubble from the chamber exposing the corpse.

"Okay, he's all yours," Hank was looking at me in satisfaction.

I crawled toward the body over what remained on the floor of the tunnel. I was amazed to find the corpse was mummified. The skin was dried, wrinkled, and looked like leather. In my entire career, I had only seen one or two mummies. Most cadavers are rotted, decomposed or just plain stinky. To produce a mummy requires the most extraordinary conditions: warm, dry air must flow around the corpse. Any moisture at all will begin the decomposition process. The body was so deep in the shaft that outside humidity couldn't reach him.

"Somebody hand me my Polaroid. I want to get a few pictures before you apes disturb the scene." I shot as many pictures as I could in the cramped space. I was worried once we began to remove him the rest of the roof might collapse and we'd have no evidence to help find out what had happened to him. With the photos safely in my coat pocket, we began the extraction process. Using an old support timber as a gurney, Ted and Hank carried the body back toward the surface.

"Damn, he sure doesn't weigh very much," Ted commented as they moved through the tunnel.

"He's dehydrated you fool," Hank responded.

"Just add water—instant human," Ted quipped as he clumsily stumbled on a rock.

"Instant *stinker* is more like it." I couldn't help myself.

Once the corpse was on the surface and in the light of day, his injuries were more clearly visible. The group was amazed at how well preserved the cadaver was, his empty eye sockets stared into the blue sky for the first time in many decades.

While the focus of attention by those assembled was the condition of the body, my eyes were drawn to what appeared to be a noose tightly wrapped around his neck.

"Who do you think this guy is?" Doug questioned.

"It's your mine. Who do you think he is?" Hank asked.

"Who he is isn't as important to me as who put this rope around his neck," I whispered to Ted.

"Well, maybe he did it to himself," Ted speculated.

"I think somebody else did it to him," Zack offered, looking up from the corpse.

"Who cares? Can we keep him?" Taylor asked. "I've always wanted a mummy."

"You already have a mummy . . . and a daddy, too," Zack laughed.

"Sorry boys, he belongs to the state," Ted stated flatly, as though he didn't get Zack's joke.

"Before you guys decide to auction him off to the highest bidder, I think someone should call Ed and Patty at the mortuary. He'll need a ride to the lab and I don't trust any of you to get him there safely," I remarked.

"I don't know Doc, he looks awful dry. I'll bet he could use a cold one. Why don't we stop by the Boar's Head and buy him a beer on the way to the morgue?" Ted laughed hysterically at his own joke.

"Okay, that settles it. Hank, go call Ed before Ted here takes our friend bar hopping or hires him a stripper."

Hank made the call. Returning he announced that it would take a few hours before Ed could get to the scene.

"Great, I hope it doesn't rain," Ted continued to make dehydrated man jokes.

"Well, Colorado weather can change from one second to another, and in case Dippy is right, why don't we put our friend here in the back of my jeep?" I suggested.

"Taylor and I'll do it!" Zack excitedly offered.

"Yeah, we found him, we can load him up," Taylor added enthusiastically.

"Fine with me I don't want to touch him," Hank agreed.

"While you guys pack him away, I have to go back down into the hole," I informed Ted.

"Back, are you nuts? What do you want to find? Another one?" Ted sounded amazed that anyone would voluntarily go back into the dusty, cramped tunnel.

"I need to find the other half of the ligature," I explained.

"I'll go with you Doc," Doug offered.

"You boys be careful with that mummy; don't pick at him," Doug instructed his sons.

"And you big boys don't give him any beer while I'm gone," I added.

Doug and I ventured together back down into the mine. It took much less time to reach the scene this time. Knowing where we were going made the trip a lot easier. We found the fateful shaft and went to work searching for the other half of the rotted ligature. Doug held the light and I rummaged through the debris searching for a beam or outcrop that might hold the missing rope. I moved several rocks, a shovel, and a box labeled 'Hercules dynamite.'

"Oh God, I hope this box is empty," I whispered hoping not to set it off if it wasn't.

Old dynamite is extremely unstable and can explode with the slightest disturbance. Taking the risk, I moved the wooden box revealing the broken remains of an old support beam. Tied to the beam was the remaining portion of the ligature from the mummy. With Doug's help I removed the beam. Then we found something I had never hoped to find. It was a torn, rat chewed brownish piece of paper.

"Whoa, could this be a suicide note or just a label from another box?" I asked not expecting an answer.

"The writing looks faded. Maybe it's a newspaper clipping," Doug hypothesized.

"Not a news clipping; its hand written," I noted.

I placed the paper in an evidence envelope, sticking it in my pocket with the pictures I'd taken earlier. There was nothing left at the scene of the crime that either Doug or I could find. An hour and a half had passed. We were both tired of trying to breathe guano laden air and decided it was time to leave. The mine was making groaning sounds like an exhausted old man tired of hiding a secret.

Doug looked me. "I think it's time to leave before we're the next corpses removed from this pit, don't you?" His eyes told me he was truly frightened.

The place was going to cave in any moment, so I can't say I blamed him. While I had been engrossed with what we had found and with my mind trying to put the pieces in place to make some sort of sense, I'd forgotten the danger surrounding us.

"Hell yes, let's get out of here," I readily agreed.

As we emerged into the brightness of day and fresh air, my still adjusting eyes were drawn to the horizon. I could see a plume of dust headed in our direction. It was obviously Ed, as usual, driving like Parnelli Jones in his big white death-mobile.

"It looks like Ed's here," I announced, still coughing up dust.

Moments later with a cloud of flying rock and dirt, Ed pulled up to where the group stood.

"Well, where's the stiff? I've got to get back to town for old lady Johnson's memorial by five o'clock," he shouted from the open window of his corpse-mobile. "Load 'em up."

"What do you think, this is a drive thru?" Ted responded.

"How nice of you to take time from your busy day," Hank responded. "He's in Doc's Jeep. You get him."

"We'll do it," Zack anxiously offered.

"I'm gonna make these boys my assistants," I told Doug.

"You can't have em—they're my indentured servants," Doug quipped.

"Okay boys, give old Ed a hand." Ted was glad not to handle the mummy.

"Wow, he's mummified, how cool!" Ed was impressed.

"Remember old lady Johnson? Maybe you'd better get him tied down and roll," I said.

"She's dead. She can wait a minute. I've never seen a real mummy!" Ed was intrigued.

After a few minutes of exploring the corpse, Ed allowed the boys to load the gurney.

"This will be one autopsy I've got to see. I'll deliver him after the memorial." He departed with the deceased in a whirlwind of exhaust and flying gravel.

"Well, as Porky Pig would say . . . 'Th-that's all folks!' I think it's time for us all to get out of here," Ted laughed.

As we headed for our vehicles Zack asked, "Did you guys feel that?"

Before anyone could answer or even know what he was talking about, there was a huge rumble and the mouth of the mine belched forth a cloud of dust. It had collapsed.

Doug looked at me with terror in his eyes. "Oh my God, we could have been in there."

"I hope we got all the evidence we needed, because whatever was left is gone now." I was happy we'd left when we did.

"It was like the mine waited for us to find the old man before it caved in," Taylor said prophetically.

As we drove away shaking, Zack swore he saw the old man waving good-bye from what was left of the entrance.

The mummy's autopsy was the following day. I arrived early for the procedure. I wanted to see Dr. Bilmarian's face when he opened the body bag. I even had doughnuts waiting—fresh, not day-old. He didn't seem to notice.

"Well Jim, who's first up this morning?" He asked with a Bismarck in his hand and sugar on his face.

"Doc, I'm proud to introduce you to . . . well . . . we don't really know who. Maybe we should call him . . . um . . . Dusty." He grinned in my direction realizing Steve wasn't aware his first postmortem of the day was a mummy.

With a magician's flourish Jim dramatically unzipped the rubber body bag, and in his best announcer's voice said, "Only today and directly from the depths of the earth after a long awaited return, I present to you, not Daddy, but Dusty the mummy."

"Holy cow, it's a mummy. I mean a real mummy," Steve exclaimed, dropping his doughnut on the floor and wiping the powdered sugar from his bushy black mustache. He stood speechless peering into the rubber sarcophagus. This was the first time I'd ever seen Dr. Bilmarian speechless.

"Did you guys see this? It's a real mummy," he asked, as though we didn't know what the bag contained. "Where did you get him?"

"Get him? You make it sound like he's a party favor. I guarantee you I didn't buy him at the local five and dime or steal him from the museum for your entertainment," I defended myself.

"Yeah, I know, but I've never seen a real mummy before." He sounded like a four-year-old kid on Christmas morning.

"He looks so cool perfectly preserved and so life-like. I almost expect him to rise up and demand that I take him to my leader." Steve was grinning in my direction like an idiot.

"Doc, I didn't bring the book of the dead and I swear he's not an ancient pharaoh. He's just an old miner. Some boys found him in an abandoned mine where they were playing." I was trying to be the voice of reason.

"How old was the mine? How long ago did he die? It takes a long time to make a mummy you know." For a moment he sounded like Zack or Taylor.

"I was hoping you would be the expert," I asserted. "How would I know how old the mine was? It caved in just as we were leaving. I could have been killed retrieving him and all you want to know is how old the mine was."

"Well, the conditions to make a mummy have to be perfect. Just the right humidity and airflow, not too much moisture, there must not have been any water in there or the humidity would've stopped the process. Most importantly, mummification requires time—*lots* of time," he paused. "Were there any rats?"

"Rats, why do you mention rats? You know I hate even thinking about rats." I was grossed out at the mention of rodents. "No, we didn't see rats and the family that owns the property said it was first mined by the mother's grandfather," I answered. "Maybe somewhere around the mid eighteen hundreds, no one knows for sure."

"Is he related to the current owners, maybe a distant relative?" Steve continued to quiz me as though I had some secret information I wasn't telling him.

"How did he die? Were there any clues at the scene?"

"Duh. Have you looked at his neck?" I asked.

"Oh, a rope. That doesn't mean anything. He could have liked rope jewelry." Now I knew he was pulling my chain.

"Okay Jim, put him on the table and let's tell poor ole Rex what he needs to know."

Turning on the Dictaphone, Steve began to sing, "My mummy lies over the ocean . . . my mummy lies over the sea . . ."

"You know Steve, just two more signatures and I can have you committed," I teased.

He stopped singing and looked in my direction. "Just one more—I have the first one already. However, since you're threatening to commit me, you win. Presented for autopsy this day is the mummified remains of an elderly male. He arrives clothed in overalls, boots, and appears to have a strangulating ligature wound about his cervical spine."

Steve moved with great care through the entire body examining each area of the corpse and trying to disturb as little of the remains as possible. At the conclusion of his examination, he proudly announced his findings.

"Well, Rex, this poor old fellow died due to a severe case of oxygen deprivation caused most likely due to a fracture of the dens." (A small piece of the C2 vertebra, which breaks off during hanging, and presses on the breathing centers of the brainstem, ceasing the neurologic input to the diaphragm. Death quickly follows.) "Death wasn't due to the depression fracture of the skull. That was post mortem. There's no sign of hemorrhage at the site of fracture. The fracture most likely occurred when the mine's ceiling gave way after his demise".

"Oh great, I was sure he was hanged; I could see the rope. What I want to know is did he do it himself or did somebody else do it to him?"

"Okay, Mr. Smarty Pants, did you find a note or, maybe the other half of the ligature? All I can say is how he died, not who helped him along the way. That costs extra."

"Come to mention it, we did bring in the remains of the ligature and I have a few eight by ten glossies."

"Where is it? Show it to me and I'll tell you what I can."

Jim retrieved the piece of timber containing the knot and upper half of the rope from the back room. Steve was almost as excited to see the rope, as he was to examine the corpse.

"Well, it's made of hemp, I can tell you that much," he offered.

Steve carefully examined how the knot had been tied. He looked from several directions using a magnifying glass.

"From what I can tell, this knot was either tied by a right handed person or a left handed individual facing the knot. The placement of the noose behind the right ear indicates a right-handed person. In a standard execution, the noose is typically placed behind the left ear. I'm not sure if that's due to tradition or if the state believes it breaks the neck easier. Do you know if the deceased was right handed?"

"You must be kidding. Since he died over a hundred years ago I doubt there is anyone around who knew him for me to ask."

"Did you find a note that might indicate any suicidal intent?" He didn't expect that I had such a document.

"I almost forgot. We found a piece of paper in the rubble, but the writing is so faded I couldn't tell what it had written on it. It might be just a love note." I pulled the tattered paper from the evidence envelope and gave it to him.

To my surprise, he smiled. "Jim dim the lights and bring me the woods lamp". (A woods lamp is a magnifying glass surrounded by an ultraviolet light, used to visualize fungi. In this case the ultraviolet light illuminated the faded ink, which was made of organic matter.)

Steve placed the paper under the light and to my disbelief began to read the note. "I can't tell who it is addressed to; that part is missing. It begins with 'How could you be such a thief? I trusted you to run the mill. I was aware you gambled and drank too much. I knew you weren't a God-fearing man . . . I trusted you like a brother . . . you took . . . (Another missing section) . . . without concern for her virtue . . . you lied to me and I overlooked it. However, to steal from me is unforgivable. I will kill you.' The rest of the letter has been torn or worn away."

"You're kidding. What else can you tell from it?" I couldn't believe what he was reading. It sounded like it was the smoking gun and obviously pointed the finger at old man Krider.

"I hate to burst your bubble, but it appears to have been written by a left-handed, well-educated male."

"Male? How the hell can you tell it was written by a man?" I asked.

"It's the strong deep strokes of the pen." He sounded sure of himself.

"Yes, but that's a threat to kill him and we know he's dead," I continued.

"So is everyone else from 1850. I'll take some of the hair and a tooth or two for DNA testing. You see if you can find a descendent to match the DNA to and at least I can tell you who he might be. Then we can bury him with a name on his headstone. That's the best I can do." He was clearly proud of himself for getting that far. I didn't want to admit it, but so was I.

Now I wasn't sure if I had a hundred and fifty year old suicide or murder to solve. I was certain it was not an accident. Either way the case was fruitless. If it had been a murder, the murderer was dead and there wasn't anyone to prosecute. If it had been a suicide, he was dead, and it didn't matter either. However, now I was intrigued and just couldn't let it go.

Early the following morning, I headed out to the Krider place again to ask a few questions of the only descendants of the man involved in the mystery. All I could hope was that Judy would be some kind of help and would be as interested in solving the case as I was. The family invited me in, offering to help in any way they could, even if it meant labeling their respected ancestor a murderer.

Taylor's first question was, "If you're done with him, can we have him back?"

"Sorry little buddy, we have to bury him. But I can give you the pictures we took." I hoped that would satisfy him and it did.

"Judy, I hate to ask you but I have a few questions," I continued.

"Anything I can remember I'll tell you," she offered.

"Was your grandfather right or left handed?"

"I seem to recall he was left-handed, but I'm not sure."

"Had he been to school; was he literate?"

"That I do know. My mom was proud to tell us kids that he'd been to Harvard and graduated with a degree in engineering."

"Do you know if he had a business partner? If he did, do you know his name or what happened to him?"

"I don't know that. When we moved in I found some old pictures in an album in the attic. Would you like me to get them? Maybe there are some old photos that might help."

Judy retrieved the album, and proudly began to show them to the boys and me.

"Here's Grandpa and Grandma with his sister Glenda. Great Aunt Glenda is pregnant in this one. Mom says she lost the baby and never had any other children. She moved back east and I think they said she died of consumption shortly after that. Here's one of the first ore processed at the stamp mill."

"They're all drinking beer; it must have been quite a celebration," I commentated.

"They look drunk," Zack noticed.

"Which one is your grandpa?" I asked.

"He's the one on the left."

"Mom, great grandpa has black curly hair just like you," Taylor noted.

"And he's short like you too," Zack teased with a big grin.

"Who's the guy on the right with his arm around your granddad?"

"The caption says it is a picture of Grandpa and Oren," she explained.

"Who was Oren?" I asked.

"I don't know I've never heard anyone mention him."

The rest of the pictures were of the family at picnics and church gatherings.

"I think I've seen enough. I have just one more favor to ask, Judy. Would you mind letting me have a swab from your cheek for some DNA comparisons?" I wasn't sure she'd agree.

"Sure, if you think it would help."

I took the swab and promised I'd let them know what I concluded about the identity of their mummy. Steve took the swab to do his tests. It took several weeks for him to get the results back to me, but I was sure I knew what had happened long before Steve gave me the test results.

"There is no relation between Judy and the mummy," Steve informed me. I wasn't surprised.

REX'S REVIEW

After looking at the Krider family album and receiving the results provided by Dr. Bilmarian, I was sure I had a good idea about the identity of our mummy. I was fairly certain the mummy was actually the remains of old man Krider's one time partner, Oren.

Circumstances surrounding his demise are purely an educated guess. Dr. Bilmarian said he thought a right-handed individual had tied the knot on the noose. Steve had also ruled out the mummy being a blood relative of the Krider family. Furthermore, he felt the note found in the mine had been penned by an educated left-handed male.

The only conclusion I could reach was that Mr. Krider had been distraught over the apparent sexual contact between his trusted partner Oren and Glenda, Krider's unwed sister. There also appeared to be some kind of embezzlement of ore, which led Old Man Krider to write the threatening note to Oren I found in the mine.

Mr. Krider was clearly left-handed, evidenced by his position in the photograph and the beer in his left hand. He did not tie the fatal knot. Oren, however, was holding his glass in his right hand with his left arm around Mr. Krider's shoulder indicating he was right hand dominant.

We know that Mr. Krider had attended Harvard, was left hand dominant, and upset at Oren. I could only conclude that after receiving the ominous correspondence from Old Mr. Krider and in fear of what might happen, Oren had taken his own life.

Therefore, I ruled the one hundred and fifty year old incident a suicide.

* * *

EPILOGUE

I received a visit from Judy, Doug, and the boys about one month after I had issued my findings. I rarely get any live visitors at the morgue so I was surprised to see them. The entire family was grinning like they had some big secret.

"You folks look like the cat that ate the canary. What's up?" I asked.

"Zack, you found it, you show him," Doug ordered, proudly patting his eldest son on the shoulder.

"Oh no, don't tell me you found another body?" I was certain he had by the look on his face.

Zack handed me one of the Polaroid's I'd taken and given to the boys as a souvenir.

"Yeah, it's one of the photos I took in the mine when we removed the body. So what? Did I miss something?"

Doug laughed aloud. "Did you miss something? Did you even look at the pictures?"

"Well, no. They weren't needed to make the ruling." My curiosity was growing by now.

"Since the day you gave them the pictures the boys haven't let them out of their sight. They show them to all of their friends."

"And?" I asked hesitantly.

"We were looking at them a few days ago and noticed something weird on the wall behind the mummy. Look there where the wall had collapsed. Did you see that big, silver colored streak?" Zack pointed to a spot on the photo.

"Oh my gosh don't tell me . . ."

"Yup, GOLD!" Taylor smiled proudly.

"Not just gold, the county assessor says it looked to him to be an extremely large vein of almost pure gold. We're reopening the mine. We just wanted to tell you thanks." Doug was beaming.

"Congratulations. It looks like you boys inherited your great grandpa's ability to sniff out bullion. You end up with a gold mine that really has gold in it, and all I get is an old stinky mummy."

"That's not all you get. We took a family vote and since we can't find any records of the mine ever having had a name, we decided to name it after you," Zack proudly announced.

"Yea, we're gonna call it the REX MINE," Taylor said, giving me a hug.

Well, that's the story of how I had a mine named after me. Once again, you might say I was a bride's maid and not the bride.

*   *   *

Keep Your Hands on the Wheel

When I was first learning to drive, my father was confident he could teach me. It would be 'a manly bonding thing.'

I guess the bus I turned in front of on our first outing came a little too close. I should have taken a clue when Dad's trembling, pasty white hand reached for the steering wheel and his voice cracked, "Just pull over here, Son, I'll drive home."

The next morning at breakfast he said, "We should hire Rex a driving instructor." Well, so much for manly bonding.

For the next few weeks it seemed as though the only thing I heard from the instructor was, "Keep your hands on the wheel. Keep your hands on the wheel."

Years later, when I arrived at the death scene of an elderly man seated in his pickup with his head sticking through the steering wheel, my first thought was, '*he should have kept his hands on the wheel.*'

Mr. Otto Smith was a widower in his early eighties. I'm sure it was originally, Heir Schmitt. Otto lived alone here in the mountains after coming to America forty years ago. He told people his family had been lost in the war but never explained the cause of their demise. People here respected his privacy and never asked.

His log cabin was made of hand-hewn logs; the smallest ones were eighteen inches in diameter. Don't think this is a small cabin just because each log was hand felled with an ax, dragged, cut and sawed all by one man.

Its construction was magnificent. It was oriented on the land in such a way it didn't disturb a single surrounding tree. Of course, what would you expect from the finest wood carver in the county? Otto carved little figurines and walking sticks for the children of just about everyone in town.

Otto was known for being somewhat of a recluse, so no one had missed him for several days. His medical doctor became concerned when Otto didn't show up for an appointment. Otto was punctual to a fault, never forgetting an obligation or appointment. However, not so on this occasion.

"He has been suffering from emphysema for years. Recently he has been having asthma attacks. Yesterday he was scheduled for an EKG," his physician stated to the deputy.

Dr. Wahl called the Sheriff's department when Otto neglected to show for his appointment. Now, with dusk fast approaching and the sun in my face, I was driving to Mr. Smith's house.

After turning off the highway, I was confronted with a washboard dirt road devoid of highway markers of any kind. Experience has taught me that there are a few secrets when driving on a rutted road. Actually, it wasn't so much experience as it was Ed Hill. Ed pointed out that the ruts in the road have a pattern to them. If you can match the speed of your car to the ruts in the road, it's much smoother and you have better control. Not that I ever have total control over the beast I drive anyway.

While trying to match my Jeep's speed with the rhythm of the ruts, I met an oncoming dump truck. On a small road like this somebody must give up the right of way. As a rule, and because I'm a big chicken, I will yield immediately. It is safer that way. I pulled over into the woods to let the monster dump truck pass. As the massive vehicle passed, I noticed three yearling deer spying on me from deep in the forest. They stood frozen; the only movement to betray their location was the occasional flick of an ear and swooshes of a tail. The fallen trees and heavy snow covering the underbrush made it difficult to see them.

I hesitantly backed my old Jeep down onto the road as the deer bolted across in front of me. I was hoping there wasn't another big truck headed my way.

The road to Otto's house ran along the edge of a large meadow now frozen. An antique barbed wire fence marked the boundary of the shallow valley floor and the roadway. Six miles further up the road I rounded a sharp curve and saw a string of emergency vehicles with lights flashing. I knew I'd found the right place. I parked along the road behind Detective McDonald's car. I recognized it by all the dents in the trunk; he's terrible at backing up.

Ted approached as soon as I parked, "It's a homicide. No doubt about it."

"Okay, I haven't seen the body. Have you, Ted?" I asked.

"You bet and you won't believe it. Somebody put the hit on this guy; a real pro-job."

I've known Ted for a long time and he can be excitable, jumping off the deep end once in a while. However, I have never heard him call anything a professional hit before.

"A professional hit right here in Pine Park? What makes you think such an outlandish thing?" I asked.

"Somebody broke Otto in half and stuck him through the steering wheel. Proof enough?" he asked.

"Who in the world would want to kill good old Otto? For that matter who would be big enough to break him in half? Otto was a pretty big boy. He never bothered anyone and the most radical group he belonged to was the not-so-young Republicans."

"Didn't you know? In Germany during the war he was a high-ranking officer in the S.S. He ran several death camps and only escaped at the last moment," Ted whispered.

"So, let me get this straight. You think this sweet old man was a Nazi?"

"Well, that's what the rumor is and I don't have trouble believing it."

"From what I know about the Israeli forces, they would kidnap him and return him to Israel for trial, not kill him." I tried to bring some sanity to the conversation. "Let's go take a look at the body, and then maybe this will all make sense."

We walked up the hill toward a big ditch bordering the road. An old white pickup with a broken windshield was laying half on its side in the ditch. From where I stood, there looked to be no driver.

When we reached the truck, Ted opened the passenger side door. I could clearly see old Otto. Sitting in the driver's seat, his arms hung limply at his side and, indeed his head was stuck through the steering wheel. On the floor between his feet was a small pool of blood; the source appeared to be his nose. Bob Newman, the police photographer, was just finishing up what he called a portrait session.

"Hey Rex, I got a view from the floor looking up, that'll be a keeper. Hey, have you heard, this guy was a Nazi?" Bob chattered excitedly.

"What's with all the Nazi talk? Are you looking for a reward?"

"Really, if this guy was a Nazi then this could be my big break. People from all over the world will want my pictures. They'll be in all of the papers," Bob continued to babble with a dreamy look in his eyes as he walked toward his car.

Under his breath Ted said, "I won't remind him the prints belong to the department, unless he wants to end up like the guy in Boulder who sold autopsy photos."

"The way he looks, I wouldn't burst his bubble or he might go off the deep end. God knows what blackmail pictures he has of us from the past two New Year's Eve parties," I laughed.

As Bob wandered away with dreams of fame and fortune in his head, Ted and I looked in the cab of the truck.

"Look, the key is still in the on position but the battery is dead. How long was the engine running before it ran out of gas?" Ted questioned.

"Well, if this truck is like the one my wife's cousin has, the tank holds twenty-five gallons. I know, because every time we go fishing, somehow it's always my turn to pay for gas," I complained.

"Damn, you're the cheapest person I've ever met," Ted observed.

"I'll bet I could stick a piece of coal up your butt and in a week there'd be a diamond in there," he laughed as he berated me.

I did deserve the abuse; just about every time we've been out to eat I try to stick him with the bill. It's sort of a game. I really don't mind spending money if I have to.

Ted whispered in my ear, as if anyone else was around to hear him, "I checked the CB radio and stereo; neither one was on."

I found a prescription inhaler and a wallet on the seat next to the deceased. I took out my trusty latex gloves. Just in case Ted and Bob are right, I don't want any contact poison. I picked up the wallet. Opening the soft leather pouch I could see it was empty, no cash or credit cards. In a side flap, well concealed, was a picture of a woman. She appeared youthful. However, the brown stains and tattered edges of the photograph betrayed her true age. I placed the wallet in an evidence bag and used a small test tube to take samples of blood from the floor of the truck between his feet. With my head between the deceased's feet I noticed he had not taken the time to put on socks or tie his boots.

That's strange, I thought, *for such a formal and fastidious man to leave the house dressed so poorly. Was he in a hurry?*

I shared my observations with Ted. "So, do you think he was late for the doctor's appointment?" I asked.

"From what I know about him, he wouldn't be caught dead dressed like this," Ted noted, without realizing his humorous remark. "I told you he was a Nazi. He was probably tipped off that the Israelis were coming and was trying to get away."

I think Detective McDonald wanted this guy to be a Nazi as badly as Bob did. Trying to keep my own mind in order, I reviewed what I knew. The key in the truck was in the on position. The vehicle was off the road. The deceased was not dressed as usual. The truck's lights were off so it was most likely daytime when this happened.

There was an inhaler on the seat, and he had a wallet but no credit cards or cash.

"Could someone have robbed him then done this to the body?" I asked Ted.

"There's no blood anywhere in the vehicle apart from the blood on the floor, and we can see that came from his nose," Ted rebuffed my hypothesis. "Maybe he had a stroke and that's why his nose is bleeding, or he hit his face on the steering wheel and broke his nose," he offered.

"That still doesn't explain the head in the steering wheel," I maintained.

"Let's trace the path of the truck as far back as we can. Maybe there will be a clue in the tire tracks," Ted suggested.

"Good idea. Let's do it before it gets any darker."

The two of us walked up the hill toward the Smith cabin. Following the path of the tire tracks we found he had hit a tree about one hundred yards back up the driveway. There was a really big pine along the north side of the road with a fresh gouge in the bark.

"This is probably where he lost consciousness," I said.

Following the roadway back another fifty yards we reached the cabin. The door was standing open and the stereo was playing a Roy Orbison song.

I entered the house knowing he lived alone. I expected to find nothing. From a back room I could hear a noise. Not sure what it was, I released my gun from its holster. Walking slowly up to the door I pushed it open with my foot, pointed my weapon into the room and almost shot a raccoon. I never would have lived that down. The house yielded nothing of interest or importance, other than one frightened raccoon.

Ted and I returned to the truck as Ed and Patty arrived in the big white hearse. Smiling broadly, as always, Ed went straight to the body.

"So, do I get to take the steering wheel too?" Patty looked into the cab, giggling.

"Ed, do you think it will fit in the old ambulance? It's been missing a steering wheel for years."

"No, dear, it would be too hard to steer with that head in it. Rex, how do you propose we get his head out of there?" Ed inquired.

"We? what do you mean we? Do you have a mouse in your pocket? I'm done here. You decide how to extricate him. Just don't hurt him or damage any evidence in the process."

"Hurt him? He's dead. Just how can I hurt a dead person?" Ed teased deadpan.

Ted, who had been standing silently and watching, jumped into the conversation with the suggestion, "Use bear grease on his head and just slide it out."

"It got in there without bear grease. I'm sure there's a way to remove it without it. It's like one of those Chinese puzzles," Patty noted.

"If we turn the wheel hard to the left, then the slotted space would be running up and down rather than side to side. Then his head would just lift up and out," Ed suggested.

The front wheels were jammed firmly against the ditch wall. It took three strong men (okay, two strong men and me) to turn the steering wheel. Once the steering wheel was in position things went exactly as Ed predicted. Patty lifted Otto's head from the wheel, "Ta da."

With Otto's body now dislodged and loaded into the big white boat, Ed and Patty left in a hail of flying rocks and gravel.

Ted looked in my direction to keep flying dust out of his eyes and said, "Every time he does that I expect to hear the theme to the Lone Ranger play."

Ted decided there was nothing left for him to do, so he excused himself to answer another call. I was left standing alone at the scene. Looking back up the ill-fated path of the pickup, I tried to imagine what would have caused this accident to happen. I walked the path to the cabin several times until the light was almost gone.

During my dreams that night I wondered if Ted was right. Had this been a perfect hit? Was nice, old Otto in reality a war criminal? Where would I look to get the answer? Send fingerprints to the FBI?

After tossing and turning all night, I woke with a revelation. There was no sign of forced entry, not even a footprint we couldn't account for. However, his wallet was empty. I had to consider robbery as a motive.

Otto's autopsy was scheduled for eleven-thirty; it began promptly. Those present for Otto's final procedure were the usual gang of suspects: Jim Simmons, Diener, Dr. Steve Bilmarian, Pathologist and me, Rex Reedman, Coroner.

When I arrived in the surgical suite, Dr. Steve and Jim were already there.

"Wait until you hear this," Jim said, reading from the police report submitted by Ted.

"The deceased was found with his head stuck through the steering wheel. The truck was apparently in a culvert on his own property."

"The truck's ignition was on but the engine was cold. It must have run out of gas some time earlier," I added as I entered the room.

"My question is how the hell did he get his head through that tiny space? I couldn't do it if I had all day," Steve looked at Otto as he spoke.

"Let's get started. Jim, turn on the equipment," Steve requested.

The Dictaphone showed a small red light announcing its state of readiness to proceed.

"Do you know why the blonde was fired from the M&M factory? Give up? For throwing out all of the W's," Steve laughed as always at his own joke.

"Presented for examination is the body of a man with the stated age of eighty-four, even though he looks ninety-seven. The patient measures five feet six inches and weighs in at one hundred ninety-two pounds. His hair is white in color; the body is devoid of tattoos or distinguishing marks of any kind. The patient had a history of emphysema. He has recently been under a doctor's care for seasonal allergies and asthma." Steve paused in his narration.

Turning in my direction he asked, "Do you think I should put the part about him being a Nazi in the report?" His eyes were sparkling with devilish delight at the thought. He intended to mess with Mrs. Kent, the poor lady who typed his dictation. By now, she has heard almost every gory, gruesome thing described over the past twenty years. So, maybe this little juicy tidbit might just make her day.

"Open the chest and let's get a look at the cardio-pulmonary system."

Steve was in the mood to work. Following the Y incision, he removed the lung tissue. It appeared bloated, slick, and rubbery. The normal lung surface looked like granite with all of its little black lines and white spots.

"That's disgusting." Jim looked as though he were going to lose his lunch.

"This lung shows areas of pyogenic pocketing, indicating an ongoing lung infection. Let's take sections for microscopic examination. Jim, get the heart out and prep it for me," Steve directed.

As he took the heart from Jim, he continued to dictate, "Cardiac tissue reveals atherosclerotic plaques in the descending and transverse coronary arteries. He had some pretty good blockages but there's no sign of an infarct." An infarct is an area of dead tissue caused by lack of blood flow.

"Let's get to the real meat of this. Jim, open the neck and let's see if someone helped him into the Promised Land."

Jim accessed the structures of the throat by cutting up under the skin from the chest toward the head. If done properly the structures of the neck can be removed intact. Jim did a great job and removed the throat intact. He didn't even "button hole" the skin. A buttonhole is when the scalpel cuts through the skin and leaves a hole resembling a buttonhole. Morticians hate it when you do that; it's hard to cover up for the funeral. In defense of deniers everywhere, the structures of the neck lay very close to the skin of the neck. It is extremely difficult to dissect this region without cutting through the skin.

Steve turned to Jim, "Put it up here on the cutting board," and proceeded to dissect the neck.

"There appears to be a slight amount of petechial hemorrhaging." Capillaries rupture when a force, like choking, is applied.

"There appears to be a bloodless fracture lateral to the midline of the hyoid." The hyoid bone is a horseshoe shaped bone deep in the neck under the chin.

"The bone is removed for microscopic examination. If there's blood in the surfaces of the fracture we can be sure it was anti-mortem (before death). The tongue is devoid of bite marks," Steve dictated.

Following the opening of the head, the brain was removed and dissected. There appeared to be no sign of stroke or hematoma (deep bruises), so we know he wasn't struck on the head. The balance of the autopsy revealed no further clues. I would have to wait for the microscopic test results and that might be a few days. Maybe if I walked the driveway one more time something might make sense.

It took three days for Dr. Bilmarian to call me back with any results. "Rex, I have a clue to the death, but as for the position of the body, I have no idea. The hyoid bone was fractured anti-mortem (before death). However, there isn't much hemorrhagic reaction so it must have occurred seconds before death. The good news is there are no other signs of strangulation."

"You call that good news? I was counting on it as a cause of death," I whined.

"Well, if it makes you feel better, he did die of oxygen deprivation," Steve was placating me and I knew it. Sure, if your heart stops for any reason, there is oxygen deprivation.

"There were no signs of recent cardiac arrest, although signs of past episodes were everywhere. He had eighty to ninety percent blockages throughout the heart. That's all the help I can give you. If you figure out how his head got through the steering wheel please call and tell me," Steve mockingly begged.

He wasn't much help. So, I returned to the scene of the crime just one more time. I walked the truck's fateful path three times. I pretended to be the driver and then I pretended to be the truck. Finally I just sat down in the middle of the road and stared in the direction the truck had traveled. Being six and a half feet tall, when I sit on the ground I really notice the change in perspective. In this case it made me realize that the one thing I had not pretended to be was the tire. I suddenly realized, after the truck hit the big pine tree, its tires followed the ruts in the road, right to where it now rested. Bingo. That was all I needed to put it together. Now I understood what had happened. I felt a little foolish standing alone in the woods laughing. Somehow, I had the feeling Otto was laughing too.

* * *

Did you get all of the clues? There are *two* questions to answer here.

1. What is the cause of death?
2. How the hell did his head get through the steering wheel?

Don't turn the page until you have made up your mind.

LET'S REVIEW

Remember poor. old Otto lived alone without a soul in the world to care for him, not counting the raccoon. If the doctor had not tried to check on him by contacting the Sheriff, God only knows how long he would have sat there. The inhaler on the seat and the manner in which this neat, clean man was dressed were good clues as to why he left the house and where he was going.

Otto was suffering an acute asthma attack and could not breathe. This had happened several times before and that was why his doctor prescribed the inhaler. The doctor had also told him to get in to the office as fast as he could if it ever happened again. They never dreamed this old man would try to drive himself. However, since Otto lived so far out in the woods without a phone, he had no way of summoning help. His nearest neighbor was two miles away.

Otto's death was due to **natural causes**. He died of respiratory arrest due to the severity of his asthma.

Now, I assume you would like to know the answer to the big question, "How the Hell did he get his head stuck in the steering wheel?"

This question bothered me for quite a while. The answer didn't come to me until I changed my perspective by sitting on the road. It dawned on me that after losing consciousness; Otto slumped onto the steering wheel. Since he had no control over where the truck went, the truck was free to follow the ruts in the road. Ruts in a road never go straight; instead they meander back and forth across the path. When the wheels of the truck entered the ruts without a driver in control, the truck followed right and then left then right again. As this happened, the steering wheel rotated as well. With Otto leaning unconscious against the wheel, it didn't take long for the wheel to turn far enough for his head to pass through. From that point on it was straight ahead until hitting the ditch. Between the impact of the truck hitting the wall of the culvert and the sharp turn the steering wheel made at the same time, his hyoid bone was fractured and he died. The pool of blood between his feet was his own. It was coming from small capillaries in the nose; they burst under the pressure of his hanging head.

Epilogue: Otto was not a Nazi, just an extremely nice old man grateful to be an American.

Did you get it?

If so congratulations if you didn't, better luck next time.

How do you think you will do with the next case?

Welcome to Frostbite Falls

Living in the mountains brings many surprises. Here in Colorado those surprises often involve the weather. The joke everyone tells visitors is, "If you don't like the weather, wait five minutes. It'll change." I really thought they were kidding, but it's the truth. I remember last year on the 4th of July. It was a glorious morning; the sun was shining, the birds were chirping and everything was right with the world. I went to help prepare for the local parade at about nine a.m. and it was just beginning to rain. By ten it was hailing. I mean it was coming down hard. At ten thirty there were about two inches of hail on the ground.

Someone behind me on the work crew pointed out from under his tattered umbrella it looked as though it had snowed. I love the ironies of life because at that very moment, God chose to let loose with a snowstorm that lasted twenty minutes. I couldn't believe it. I didn't want to mention that the only weather phenomenon we hadn't had yet was a tornado. To my amazement by two p.m. parade time, the sun was shining and the skies were blue. Of course, there was snow and muck along the road to help relieve the heat. At three thirty a small tornado touched ground just twelve miles west of town.

The lesson in the 4th of July from hell is: if you think you are going to live in the mountains, always be prepared. Dress in layers; have food and water in your car where you can easily get to it. Always carry something to cut wood with and something to start a fire. Never forget a coat or blanket. The most important advice is to know how all of your camping and emergency gear works. That doesn't mean just how to light them up but when and where not to.

As the seasons change so do the causes of death. In spring and summer it's the things you might expect: drowning, falls, biking and forerunner accidents. During the fall and winter, things like carbon monoxide poising, auto accidents, skiing mishaps as well as suicides are likely. People have a tendency to get depressed when the days get short, nights get longer, and deep snow keeps everyone isolated. The suicide rate seems to go up at that time of the year.

Calls to 911 operators reflect these trends. The experienced operator knows before their shift begins what type of calls to expect. It is not uncommon for worried parents to call looking for their wayward offspring. During winter, teens are often delayed returning home due to traffic or weather conditions. In the summer the causes are also traffic or weather related. In almost every case it's teenage memory loss. So when a parent calls the 911 baby-sitting service, operators usually reassure them and never hear from the panicked parent again. That is exactly how this story began.

The first call to 911 operators was at four thirty in the afternoon. Parents were reporting their sons hadn't returned from a camping trip. Dean's dad reported the boys were going up in the "peak area." He was not sure which campground they had planned to stay in, he only knew they were going hiking and were to return early that morning.

The dispatcher reassured the parents, "Most often when teens are missing, it is due to irresponsibility or minor auto problems. Don't worry; I'm sure they will come walking in any time. To set your mind at ease I'll call the forest service and ask them to search their campgrounds. I'll call you back if they find the boys."

With the parents reassured and a description of the missing vehicle in hand the dispatcher contacted the forest service. She gave the description of the missing jet-black 1990-something Ford mini truck and its custom camper shell. Once that information had been relayed, there was nothing left to do but wait while the forest rangers searched each of the fourteen campgrounds.

Three hours later my cell phone rang with the news. The boys had been located. "There are two bodies in the back of a small camper," Bobbie, the dispatcher reported.

"Oh great, my four wheel drive is on the blink. Tell me it's paved and not some back forest-service crap of a road," I moaned about having to go out.

"The truck is parked in the Frosty Falls campground, site number twenty-one. For your information, Mr. Lazy man, the road is paved the entire way," Bobbie harassed.

"Do you have a weather report for up there?" I asked, wanting to plan the proper clothes. Don't laugh. The weather here can change in a matter of minutes and without the proper layering one could freeze to death in the evening when it was eighty-five that afternoon.

"It is reported to be about fifty-seven and the skies are clear. There aren't any storms in the forecast," she continued to give me a hard time with her sarcastic attitude.

"Has the family been contacted?" I asked.

"You bet. The forest people called the State Troopers for some bizarre reason. By the time I reached the kid's house, I was told the family was already on their way," Bobbie griped.

"Let Ed and Patty know where to bring the hearse and tell the ranger it will take me about forty-five minutes to get up there."

I don't care what she says about the outside temperature. It gets cold a lot faster now that I am over forty. I bring my gloves and coat with me everywhere. I look kind of funny at the park with my kids in shorts and I looking like Nanook of the North.

The drive to Frosty Falls takes only about twenty minutes by highway. I live at almost nine thousand feet above sea level. It's three thousand feet higher in elevation. I really get winded at twelve thousand feet and so does my old jeep.

There is nothing more fun than to have friends from sea level come to visit. By the second day here they are glued to the couch trying to breathe.

Ascending the mountain in second gear was slow going for the old Jeep. Bobbie had lied about the pavement extending all of the way to the scene. It didn't require four-wheel drive, but let's say you could swim in some of the ruts. One mile of crummy road and I reached 'Frosty Falls' campground. The site was given its name back in the eighteen hundreds. When settlers arrived it was late spring and at this altitude things were still frozen, including the one hundred-foot waterfall. In the deep of winter, the falls freeze slowly at first, beginning at the banks. Ribbons of ice are added nightly as the temperature drops. Layers build upon one another until it looks as though it had been sculpted.

The real show is at sunset. The falls face due west at the head of a canyon. As the last few rays of setting sun strike the falls, they light up from within. The colors change as the beams of sun change angles. Today, however, I wasn't here for the scenery. The park ranger saw me approach, pulled his vehicle in front of mine, and turned on his light bar. These guys love their pretty lights. I don't think they get to use them very often. What do you want to bet the UFOs reported in the mountains are really rangers driving through the forest, lights blazing, just to see them work?

"You can't go any further. The campground is closed," the young man in the neatly pressed uniform, stated. As he stepped from his truck, I noticed he had his ticket book in hand.

Oh great, this ninny is going to cite me for something? I thought to myself, smiling in his direction.

He approached my window and politely informed me the falls were closed. I tried to be as nice as possible by handing him my business card and asking if he could lead me to the scene.

"I knew you were coming but I expected you to be in a county car," the young ranger apologized, looking at my beat up old primer-colored Jeep.

I followed him through the maze of tiny one-way roads. There was barely enough room for my car to fit between some of the trees. When at last we reached the scene it was surprisingly quiet. There was no one else around.

Syringe wrappers and some gauze strips littered the ground, evidence of the failed rescue attempt. Lying on the ground near the truck were two sleeping bags opened to reveal the young occupants. I knew the bodies weren't going anywhere, so I chose to investigate the contents of the camper. It looked as though the boys had been camping. Nothing unusual; there were dirty clothes, empty beer cans, a half empty bottle of schnapps, and a baggy of suspicious looking dehydrated mushrooms. Looked like the camping supplies I would have taken at their age. Food, what food? Do we have the beer?

Before totally destroying the scene, something I would rag on someone else for, I went to my Jeep for the camera. I was not about to sit around waiting for the office to locate Bob. I used my PHD (Push Here Dummy) camera, a gift from my loving father-in-law. I took pictures of the interior and exterior of the truck as well as the surrounding area.

While taking pictures of the boys' belongings stacked in the front seat, I found what looked to be freshly picked stems of marijuana. It was wrapped in newsprint and then placed in garbage bags. The entire front of the truck smelled like pot.

I heard a voice behind me say, "Wow, I'll bet I know where they got it." It was young Ranger Rick, smiling. "We've known for some time someone was growing up here. It's too difficult to look for, so we just wait until they harvest, then bust them transporting it out. If you don't mind I will take it for evidence," he said as he lifted the black bags of bounty from the truck.

What did I care? I was there to remove two bodies. However, maybe just one bud for research wouldn't hurt.

It was time to photograph the bodies; I prayed the pictures would turn out. If not, Bob the professional would never let me live it down. The boys had been moved by the local volunteer fire department in an effort to revive them. Following the failed attempt, the bodies were left on the ground in the sleeping bags. At first they looked like they had lipstick and rouge on. On closer examination it was the pallor of the skin, not makeup.

The young men looked quite peaceful, as though they would wake up any moment.

I called the dispatcher and asked, "Where are Ed and Patty?"

"They're out of town. They will be back in about two hours," Bobbie explained.

"Is anyone covering for them?" I prayed there was.

"Sure. Tony is, but he doesn't answer his pager or cell phone. I've left a message on the service."

"If he calls, tell him never mind. By the time he gets out here it will be after midnight. I'll take the bodies in my car. Boy, my wife will be thrilled," I whined. The last time I transported a body in my own car my wife refused to ride in it for a month. Of course, I did prop the cadaver up in her seat.

I opened the back of my Jeep and moved the trash and junk into one corner.

"Ranger Rick, will you give me a hand? The mortuary can't make it to get the bodies. I have to take them in my car. I'll move them in their sleeping bags," I begged for help.

We loaded the boys in the back and covered them with a blanket, the door closed without any difficulty. Once the bodies were loaded, the ranger decided it was time to go before I asked him to do something gory.

Standing alone in the woods was a little unnerving. I took the opportunity to look in the camper one more time. The windows were made of smoked plastic and could not be opened. There was a small crank-type vent in the roof; it was wide open. There was a small ice chest, space heater, and pot pipe on the tiny counter inside to the left. Everything looked normal. There was no sign of a struggle.

While I was staring into the camper, a big black Mercedes pulled up throwing dust everywhere. The doors flew open and out jumped two large men from the front seat.

"I'm Marcus, Dean's father, and this is Stephen's father, Austin. Where are our sons?" he demanded to know.

I didn't want to tell him the boys were in my car. I wasn't sure how they would take it, so I lied. "The boys are being transported to the county facility right now, you can see them tomorrow."

"What happened to them?" Austin asked, trying to hold back the tears.

"I'm not sure and won't know until the pathologist has finished his examination," I answered calmly.

"Do you have a guess or hunch?" Marcus wanted to know.

"I did see drugs in the vehicle. They may have overdosed." I tried to come up with something to tell these fathers but nothing I could say would be good.

"We both know the boys did recreational drugs, mostly pot," Austin said quietly. His eyes were swollen from crying.

"But pot doesn't kill you, does it?" Marcus asked hesitantly.

"No, not that I know of, but there was a small bag of mushrooms in their camper. Eating the wrong kind could be fatal within an hour," I explained.

"If it's okay, we've come to take the truck and their belongings home."

"I have all I need. You can take the rest. Do you need some help?" I offered.

"No, we'll do it ourselves. Maybe it will help us to understand." He began to cry.

Leaving the fathers to grieve, I tried to get the Jeep started without choking everyone with the oily exhaust. I wanted to get those bodies to the lab and out of my car as soon as possible. If they found out that I'd lied to them they'd probably kill me and take the bodies of their sons.

I dropped my cargo off at the morgue still wrapped in their sleeping bags and headed home. *That would be a surprise for Jim when he prepped them in the morning, breakfast burritos,* I thought.

The boy's autopsies were scheduled for nine in the morning. I woke early and had a quick cup of Joe out on the deck. My daughter, Tina, joined me with her hot chocolate dripping with whipped cream. She crawled up into my lap and asked, "What ya thinking about Dad?"

A psychic once told me to watch out for this daughter, "That may look like a child, but trust me; she's a fifty year old lady in that little kid's body."

I have thought many times that Tina is wise beyond her years and often I'm stunned by the quality of her advice. So, when she asks me 'what's up?' I tell her.

"I just don't know who to ask about these two young men I picked up yesterday," I explained.

"How old were they?" she inquired.

"They were high school students."

"Why not talk to their school counselor or the coach?" she suggested.

What a great idea. If anyone could give me some background on them it would be the school. I hopped in the old jeep and went to interview coach Hodge.

"Those boys were something else," he admitted. "If there was something going on, you could be sure that they were mixed up in it somehow."

"What can you tell me about their friendship that might help to sort out the cause of their deaths?" I asked.

We sat at his desk and he told me what he knew about Dean and Stephen's friendship. "Dean and Stephen had been friends for as long as either one could remember," he recounted.

As he talked, I learned that this year they would have been seniors in high school. Dean never forgot that in kindergarten Stephen wet his pants one day at naptime. He teased Stephen about it relentlessly, never loud enough for anyone else to hear but just loud enough to make him turn red. In first grade the boys moved next door to one another. From then on the two were inseparable. Their mothers called them Pete and Re-Pete.

During the school year the boys were placed in separate classes by request of the principal. It seems their second grade teacher, Mrs. Digby, resented sitting on the tack placed in her chair by, guess who?

Dean claimed in his own defense, "She had enough padding; I'll bet she didn't even feel it." The little smart-ass was righ, of course.

During vacation between ninth and tenth grades the boys were sent to summer camp in northern California. Their parents thought it would be a good idea to get them away from the "bad influences" in the neighborhood. Everyone thought a summer far from home of nature hikes, horseback riding, and swimming would make men of them.

In the mountains of northern California there are two lucrative businesses to be involved in. One is the tourist trade, including remote summer camps for rich kids. The other, a major agricultural export, is growing dope. Growers like to plant high up in the mountains where there is very little foot traffic and fewer roads nearby.

Young men from Colorado on horseback, knowing how to ride better than walk, can cover a lot of territory in the four hours of free time allowed each day at camp. With their trusty steeds saddled and ready, the boys would go "hunting" for those remote plants. Truthfully, they were lucky not to be killed by some protective grower. Instead, the young equestrians became the biggest suppliers of pot to the camp inhabitants. Three months at camp and the boys returned home with a new spirit, some great seeds and about eight hundred dollars cash in their pockets.

Suddenly coach Hodge looked at his watch. "Oh, God. I've got to go. I have a gym class right now and if I'm not there on time those boys will rip the gym apart. If there's anything else you need please call me." He shook my hand and ran toward the gymnasium. I think he gave me enough background on these two. It was almost nine and I had to get over to the lab.

I thought to myself as I walked back to the Jeep, *It is now late August in the Rocky Mountains the boy's days of summer camp ended long ago. Today, they are at the county morgue lying peacefully wrapped in their sleeping bags, smiles on their faces, dead. What a shame.*

We began the autopsies at nine a.m. Those present were Dr. Steve Bilmarian, Pathologist, the Diener, Jim Simmons, and me, Rex Reedman, Coroner.

Dr. Steve began the dictation by telling one of his stupid jokes. "Knock, knock. Who's there? Pencil, pencil who? Pencil fall down—if you don't wear a belt." He was still laughing as he began to inspect Dean's body.

"Submitted for post-mortem exam is the body of an eighteen year old male. A scar measuring 3.6 centimeters by 3 millimeters is noted in the right lower quadrant, consistent with a healed appendectomy. There are no other bruises, scars, tattoos or distinguishing marks of any kind." Steve paused. "This young man and his friend over there," he pointed to the next cadaver on the hit parade, "were camping according to the worksheet. Is this right?"

"Yes, they were found in the back of a small camper shell. When I arrived they were in sleeping bags lying on the ground. The bodies were moved by the fire department."

He looked back at the body and continued to talk, "There is a slight cherry red appearance to the skin surrounding the eyes, lips and cheeks, consistent with carbon monoxide exposure. There is no petechial hemorrhaging (these are small pinpoint bruises under the eyelids and in the mouth, they are seen in strangulation cases) within the lids of the eyes or within the orifice of the mouth. This boy wasn't choked. Were there any other clues?" Steve asked.

"I did find a big trash bag full of marijuana in the front seat. In the back where the bodies were found, there was this," I said, holding up the baggy of mushrooms.

"Whoa. Shrooms! Bring them here. Let's see what kind they are." Steve looked anxious. "These are probably psilocybin, magic mushrooms, but we should assay them to be certain they are not a deadly variety. If they are a poisonous kind, it would be the most likely cause of death."

"Open him up, Jim," Steve prompted.

The Y incision exposed the organs of the chest.

"Draw some cardiac blood for analysis," Steve directed Jim.

The organs were removed one at a time, weighed, measured and sample slices taken for further analysis. As the examination moved through the systems of the body there was nothing of significance. The young man's cardiovascular system was in perfect shape with the exception of some scaring in the lung from smoking. Cardiac blood did show signs of carbon monoxide and traces of THC (the active ingredient in marijuana.) Additionally, there were traces of alcohol and psilocybin metabolites in circulation. This meant the boys had smoked pot, consumed alcohol, and had eaten psychedelic mushrooms a short time prior to death. The autopsy on Stephen went exactly the same as Dean's; there were no other findings. Dr. Steve felt he knew the cause already. Do you?

LET'S REVIEW

Dean and Stephen were not always the best of boys. They just had a high sense of adventure. Their trip to California earlier in their lives set their minds to work. If they could just grow some dope up here in the mountains they could get rich. Typical teenage thinking, as my mom called it, "stinking thinking."

The boys were up in the mountains to check on this year's crop and to harvest just a little for themselves. They came well prepared for the task at hand, bringing trash bags and newspaper to wrap their harvest. For their own recreation they brought along some mushrooms and alcohol. The weather got extremely cold, and to keep warm the boys used a small space heater to heat the truck. In their drug-induced, alcohol-enhanced stupor, they forgot to read the label of the space heater: "Use only in well-ventilated area". The truck was closed up tight with the exception of the roof vent to keep in the heat. This allowed the carbon monoxide to build up and poison them to death. Remember the 'cherry red' complexion? This is characteristic of carbon monoxide poisoning. The open vent in the roof of the camper would do no good. Since carbon monoxide is heavier than air, it would sink.

These young men died of carbon monoxide poisoning. Their death was *accidental.*

How did you do? If you think this was too easy, try: Burning Memories

Burning Memories

A nice thing about small towns is sometimes it's easy to find background information. It's difficult to keep secrets when you've lived your entire life in the same little town. I'm lucky to live next door to a lifelong resident and a high school teacher who's taught in the local school system for the past thirty-four years. She knows everybody.

After receiving the call concerning this death, I stopped in to talk with Judy. I explained who the deceased was. She recalled having him in one of her classes. She also remembered that he had a girlfriend.

"He was devoted to that girl," she recalled.

Judy was a wealth of information. We had several cups of coffee while she related the life stories of the deceased and his wife.

Judy informed me that, while in sixth grade, Don swore he would make Connie his wife. Of course, she was only in fourth grade at the time, but that didn't bother Don. Their relationship began with bike riding and an occasional movie. By the time they were in high school everyone knew Connie belonged to Don. *Belonged,* is the operative word in this relationship. Don treated the beautiful girl as if she were his toy.

After seven years of marriage, the first of their two daughters was born. With a small baby to care for, Connie retreated into the world of motherhood. The little girl became competition for Connie's attention and Don's temper became volatile. He had been the center of his family's universe for as long as he could remember. Now all of that had changed.

Connie was miserable in the abusive relationship. Like any woman in a similar situation, she must have fantasized about killing him and ending her private hell. Ultimately, her best course of action was to leave

Don left for work earlier than usual one Friday morning and Connie seized the opportunity. She packed everything her small car could hold, leaving just enough room for her and the girls. She went to stay with her friend, Lewis, who had agreed to let her and the children stay with him in his little cabin.

Meanwhile, back at the ranch, Don arrived home Friday night and found the note informing him that Connie and the girls were gone. His anger was uncontrollable. He finally ended the evening at the Boar's Head Saloon in a fistfight with an equally drunken tourist.

Pine Park is a small town by any standard. It took Don only a short time of driving back streets to find Connie's car parked in an alley next to a small, rustic cabin.

He walked up to the house and began to bang on the door, insisting that his "woman" come out immediately.

When the door slowly opened, Don tried to force his way into the house. To his amazement he was greeted by the business end of a 12-gauge shotgun. Suddenly, this idea didn't seem so smart. Don left, feeling alone and without hope, swearing at the top of his lungs.

On August 9th at nine thirty a.m., sirens split the morning silence. Alex, my youngest daughter, came to inform me, "There's a really bad fire somewhere. The fire trucks all headed up the hill toward Elbow Road."

"Oh well, it's probably a brush fire," I told her. Brush fires are common in the mountains in the summer.

Confident the firemen would handle the situation, I went back to reading the newspaper.

The sound of the ringing phone put a halt to that endeavor.

The voice at the other end of the phone said, "Good morning, Dr. Reedman. There's been a terrible fire. The fire-chief says he thinks there is a body in the rubble. Can you get out to Elbow Road right away?"

"Yes, what's the address?" I asked.

"It's 14497, on the right after you cross the bridge. Just follow the smoke," the dispatcher explained.

"Tell Scott I'll be there by morning."

Scott has been the captain of the volunteer fire department for the past seven years.

Arriving at the scene just twenty minutes after the call, I was proud of myself for such a quick response. As I turned into the beautiful driveway, I noticed about sixty cows lined up with their heads sticking through the fence. *What an odd greeting committee*, I thought.

The driveway twisted through golden aspen trees, meadows alive with flowers and finally climbed up into the pines. As I rose in elevation the vistas became magnificent. Pikes Peak was in its full splendor. When there's snow on the summit, it's a sight to behold. I found myself slowing down to admire the view and was not concentrating on my driving. While staring at the trees, I almost ran into a cow standing in the middle of the road as if she owned it.

Cows are not known for their intelligence. That was clear in this instance. The more I honked my horn, the more interested she was in my car. Now I know why they will follow each other in single file to slaughter. If they had any brains, the first cow in line would yell back to the others, "Hey run away. They're trying to kill us up here."

I rounded the crest of the driveway and the smoldering remains of a house came into view. I could see *both* of the county's fire trucks preparing to leave. As they passed me in the narrow driveway, the driver of the first truck hit his siren and waved. His smile told me he knew just what waited for me up ahead.

What remained of the structure suggested it had been a beautiful log home. Now, all that remained was the portion of the house farthest from the garage.

"The fire must have started in the garage," I said to myself as I pulled in next to the house and parked.

Before I could get my door open, the fire chief, Scott Jones came running up. "Howdy, Doc. You have to see what we found in the rubble."

"I assume it's a body or you wouldn't have called me," I said.

"Okay, Einstein, one of these days maybe I'll just call you out for the heck of it," he chuckled.

"Good luck. You're lucky to get me out of the house at all. I could be like that previous coroner and arrive drunk and one or two hours late," I said, knowing that Scott and Mr. Plumb (an accountant and now deceased previous Coroner of Pine County) had many run-ins in the past about the lack of response from the coroner's office. It wasn't unusual at that time for the coroner to arrive hours after the initial call, leaving the law enforcement and fire personnel waiting in the snow or pouring rain. After all, according to Colorado law, they couldn't move the corpse until the coroner pronounced death.

As we walked toward the remnants of the structure, Scott stated, "The source of the fire was probably a pile of clothes on the garage floor. How it started we don't have a clue, but I suspect arson. The special determinations team will be out here tomorrow." He continued, "I'll let you know if they agree with me".

"Or not," I said with a smile.

What remained of the garage area was nothing but rubble. That's not quite correct. Actually, the cement slab was under there somewhere. Whoever said, "Ashes to ashes, dust to dust" (hmm, that might have been God) apparently never got the ashes wet. When ashes get wet they turn into a sticky yucky muck.

"Okay, I don't see a body anywhere." I said as I tried to see anything beneath the almost one foot thick layer of gunk that lay before us.

"It's right there, Dummy," Scott shouted. He pointed toward my feet and spit tobacco. "Another step and you'd have destroyed what's left of your precious evidence."

I looked closer at what I had assumed was a fallen beam laying at my feet. I knelt down carefully to avoid totally soiling my clothes. I could faintly see the traces of what was left of poor Don.

"Yummy, smells like barbeque," I said. "Hey, want some ribs?" I continued my not-so-subtle attack on Scott's ability to hold down his breakfast. "I'll teach you to mess with me," I taunted.

"You are without a doubt, the most disgusting person I know. I can't believe we're such good friends." He turned away trying to abandon me there, I was certain.

"Where do you think you're going?" I said, with just a little fear in my voice.

"Wow. You're paranoid, aren't you? I was going out to the truck. I thought you would want me to call one of your flunkies. At least notify Ed and Patty that they might need to bring the four-wheel drive out here. We wouldn't want Ed to get his big white car dirty now, would we?"

Left alone in the smoldering ashes of the building, the heavy smell of smoke filled my nose. I looked around and realized the only thing still standing on this end of the structure was the chimney, which was constructed of stacked stone. The huge, oak beams that had once supported the heavy roof were laced through the upper layers of stone. It looked like a giant scarecrow standing against the stark blue Colorado sky.

I began to dust off the remains at my feet. The deeper I dug the more of the body I could make out. Under the thick coating I could now clearly make out the charred remains of Don. You might say, "He emerged from the ashes."

Devoid of clothing and barely recognizable as human, there wasn't much evidence of Don left. I picked through the rubble near the body, trying not to disturb the scene. In the back of my mind I was hoping Scott would hurry back. It's kind of eerie to be left alone with a corpse. There's always the thought in my mind that he's going to sit up any moment and say, "Hi there Rex. What the *hell* are you doing here? Say, speaking of *hell*, have you met my friend, **Satan?**"

To keep my mind off of weird ideas like that, I stood back; actually sat back on a stump near the driveway. Far enough away that, if he did actually sit up or Satan did materialize, I had a good head start. Like that would really help.

Sitting there I tried to imagine how something like this could happen. The car wasn't in the garage, so we can rule out that this was an auto repair job gone wrong. If the Chief is right and the fire began between the victim and the door, why didn't he just open the main doors and leave? That could mean that he wasn't able to take action. (Or, maybe he was just stupid.) Was he impaired somehow, or unconscious? On the other hand, even though I know *you've* thought of it, was he *dead* when the fire started? The remains of the body will tell us some of what we want to know.

We must keep in mind that the fire could have been a diversion. Many times criminals burn the scene or the body trying to destroy evidence of their crime. Little do they know this often preserves evidence that might have otherwise been destroyed. When a corpse is lit on fire, the heat sears the skin and seals the internal organs away from the oxygen-laden world outside. This helps to slow down the rate at which the viscera (the guts and organs) decompose. If fire destroys the body leaving just the bones, they can provide information. The color of the remaining bone would indicate what temperatures the body had been exposed to. For example: at 575 to 1270 ^{F} degrees, bone is red. Above 1270 ^{F} bones turn black; while at temperatures in excess of 2000 ^{F} degrees, the bones turn white and become brittle.

Even just one or two of the cranial sutures (where the skull bones meet in the head) can help determine age. Around forty years of age, the sutures of the skull disappear. In youthful victims, there are rough surfaces in the shafts of growing bone. These growth plates are near the ends of the bone, where cartilage turns into new bone. The process continues until the child reaches maturity. During the growing years they remain highly visible.

Scott tiptoed up behind me while I was contemplating the possible causes of this fiasco. "All right," he bellowed as he grabbed me from behind. "I've called the morgue and they were already on their way."

"Oh, God," I shrieked, momentarily certain that indeed the devil had sneaked up behind me and was going to drag me into the pit. I guess I've got a guilty conscience.

"I've got to go back to the station. Lord knows what those guys do when I'm not there," Scott tried to sound sincere and innocently reached for my hand to say goodbye.

"You can't leave," I protested.

"What? I put out the fire for you and I've called for your ghoul patrol. Heck, I even showed you where the body was. Now, you want me to sit and hold your hand too? Forget it. I'm outta here," he mocked.

I don't know how long I sat there on that stump after Scott bailed out on me. I just sat waiting for the mortuary people and it was beginning to get cold. The wind was blowing off the peak and that usually means a storm is coming.

While digging in the back of my Jeep for a warmer coat, I could see a big dust cloud rising in the direction of the highway. That can mean only one thing: Ed must be driving. Sure enough, before I could get my coat from the trunk, the large white hearse came bouncing along.

Ed jumped from the big car yelling, "Howdy, Doc. Where's the crispy critter?"

"I swear you're more disgusting than I am. Don't you hate burned bodies?" I asked.

"Heck, no. They're lighter to pick up and don't smell half as bad as a floater," he said, grinning from ear to ear. "They kinda make me hungry, if you know what I mean;

nothing like the smell of a good BBQ," he continued his tirade.

"I'll never admit it in public, but I think you're the only creep who can gross me out," I responded.

I decided right then that I would never eat at his Fourth of July barbeque again. I had often wondered what his secret ingredient was, but now I wasn't sure I would want to know. "Okay, Mr. Complainer. I've got a body bag. Let's sack him up and get out of Dodge before that storm hits", he pointed at a black wall of clouds heading our way.

"The body is over here in what's left of the garage," I said, as I led him to the site.

"Wow. Look at that mess. What was he burning?" Ed asked as he scuffed through the ashy muck.

"No one knows yet. The fire investigators will be out here tomorrow," I explained.

"I've got gloves if you need some," Ed offered. He handed me a pair of really thick, blue rubber gloves. "These are better than the wimpy clear kind, they're a little more expensive, but what the heck and I'm billing the county." He laid the bag on the ground far away from the gunk and proposed, "Just lift him up and drop him in here. I'll hold the bag open for you."

"Oh no, my job's over. I pronounced him dead. Now it's your job. That's why *you* get the big bucks. I'll hold the bag for *you,*" I motioned, desperately trying to get out of handling the body at all.

"Big bucks? I get paid sixty-five dollars for each removal and I have to buy my own gas. Would you get out of bed in the middle of the night for sixty-five bucks? Oh wait, I forgot. I was asking the king of cheap. You'd get up if you thought you heard change hit the floor. How about you get the head and I'll get the feet?" Ed offered as a compromise.

"No way, the head is heavier, I'll get the feet."

As the negotiations continued the *first* bolt of lightning struck . . . the chimney. Without further discussion, he grabbed the left side and I grabbed the right. With a quick toss, the body was, as we say in the business, 'in the bag.'

"That was close enough for me. Let's go," I shouted over my shoulder as I began to sprint toward the car.

"Hey, wait for us," Ed cried. He was still trying to get the bag zipped.

"Leave him there. He's dead. If lightning strikes him, he'll never know it. In fact, a bolt of lightning is probably what he needs right about now." I tried to remind Ed that *lightning is dangerous*, while at the same time trying not to look too chicken.

When the *second* bolt, struck the hill behind the house, Ed needed no further encouragement to leave. In fact, he tried to beat me to the car.

Storms move quickly here in the mountains. A few minutes can make all of the difference in the world. Five minutes later, all evidence of the storm was gone and the sun was shining brightly. With the two of us cooperating, the body was loaded into the back of the hearse in no time.

"I'll take him to the morgue. You go down and open the door for me," Ed ordered.

"What if I give you my key and I just go home?" I was trying to sound sincere.

"That's not going to work; I need help putting him in the refrigerator," Ed smiled. He knew I couldn't argue with that. Besides, I knew darn well that he already had a key to the morgue. He won; I had to follow him to the office. It didn't take long and he was correct when he said that crispy critters were lighter than other cases.

Despite vicious gossip, I am up before noon most days. The next morning was one such morning, luckily. At eight-thirty, during breakfast, the police arrived at my door.

My daughter, Tina, yelled loudly, "The cops are here for you again, Dad." There was a time in my life those words would have sent me out the back door and over the neighbor's fence. Today however, I know I've done nothing wrong, but the immediate sense to run still surges through my body.

"Come out of the house, this is the police." The unidentified voice echoed through the hall.

I stepped into the entry to find Detective Stone holding my five-year-old daughter, Lexi, over his head and about to repeat the order.

"What are you trying to do? Give me a heart attack?" I asked, trying not to look as shaken on the outside as I felt on the inside.

"Lexi asked me how we catch the bad guys when they're hiding," Will smiled as he explained.

"The arson investigator reported his findings and I've spoken with the wife. Do you want the skinny?" he continued. He put Lexi down on the floor.

"It's only eight-thirty in the morning, how can the arson guys be done already?" I asked.

"You know, a little blue liquid and some yellow powder and—*boom*—an answer. How would I know how they do it? Besides, not everybody sleeps till noon, Doc," he teased.

"Hey, it's still early. But come on in, let's have a cup of coffee out on the deck," I suggested.

As we sat drinking our cup of mud, Will reported, "The fire department says the fire was started intentionally. They found traces of a flammable agent on the garage floor and in a pile of debris."

"Did they determine what kind of agent was used to start the fire?" I inquired.

"The chief says it's probably gasoline. They found an empty gas can, well burnt, near the door," Will explained. Then he added, "The chief sent you a package of pictures to review. He says he them wants back."

"He had them developed already? If he's that efficient, why didn't he order double prints?" I asked.

Will shrugged, "I don't know. Maybe he's as cheap as you are."

"Did they find any other clues?" I asked, trying to dodge his jest.

"I can tell you that we haven't found a suicide note or any other evidence that he intended to snuff himself," Will responded.

"What about any evidence that someone else killed him?"

"We were hoping that you'd be able to provide the answer to that," he said, with a smile. "Oh, before I forget, I was checking on next of kin for you. He was recently separated from his wife. She filed for divorce last week. I'm going to check out her alibi as soon as you can give us a rough estimate on the time of death."

"I'd say it was about the time the fire started," I said, half-jokingly.

As we finished our coffee, Will's radio blurted out that there was an accident out on Highway 42.

"That's me. I've got to run. Depending on how this call is, maybe I'll see you out there." He pulled on his jacket and headed for the door, waiving as he left.

It was about ten-thirty when the morgue called to say Dr. Bilmarian would like to begin the autopsy at three. That left most of the morning free to mow the lawn.

Arriving at the lab, I was greeted by Carol, the secretary. "The body is in autopsy room one. Steve wanted me to page him when you arrived," she said, as she paged Dr. Bilmarian.

"Hey Doc," her voice echoed over the PA system. "He's here and he brought donuts," she announced. Turning off the microphone, she smiled, "That should get him out here in a hurry."

"All that will do is get me in deep do-do for not bringing donuts," I whined.

"Donuts?" the voice echoed from the back hallway. "Did the bum bring goodies?"

"Stop right there, I *did not* bring *any* food," I yelled back. I was trying to put a stop to the feeding frenzy before it got started.

"Well then, you'd better make a call and order something for us to eat. Or, I can guarantee this post will be a stinky one," Steve threatened.

Now blackmailed, I had no choice but to call the Donut Factory and order two-dozen doughnuts to be delivered; the only way I could think of evening the score was to order "day old" ones. Somehow, to save two-fifty made me feel better. Okay, I am cheap.

The procedure began following the big doughnut drop. Those present were Dr. Steve Bilmarian, Pathologist, the Autopsy Diener, Tim, and me.

Steve activated the dictation equipment and began with a tacky joke. At least he wasn't singing today. "What does an autopsy and having sex with a gorilla have in common? Give up? Well, you can't stop until it's over for the gorilla!" He leaned on the body with his left hand as guffawed, obviously enjoying his own humor.

"You're warped," Tim laughed.

"He's warped? You're the one laughing," I said, trying to hide my smile.

"Gives you quite a visual, doesn't it?" Steve said, wiping the tears from his eyes. "I just made that up."

"That proves you need to be committed. I'm sure that joke is illegal in at least eighteen states," I said.

"Well put on your gorilla masks and let's get started," Steve ordered. "Tim, open the bag and let's see what the good doctor brought us today."

In his best announcer's voice, Tim unveiled the corpse, "Today's contestant comes to us from lovely Pine Park, Colorado . . . He's an unemployed rancher, who loves to *barbeque*. Let's give a *warm* welcome to *Don*."

Steve was in a heap on the floor, laughing hysterically. I had a feeling these two guys needed a vacation—soon. It's a good thing the doors had locks because, if anyone from the outside world saw this, we would be on "Sixty Minutes, Tonight."

"Okay Don Pardo, open the bag and let's get a look at our guest," Steve requested, trying not to lapse into laughter again.

"This is like 'Laurel and Hardy do an autopsy,'" I mumbled to myself. I admit these guys are entertaining and it tends to help break the tension about an autopsy like this one, but I think if I could get just one more signature,

I could commit them both. As Tim unzipped the bag, breaking my evidence seals, he stepped back quickly.

"Oh, my gosh! This guy is well done. Someone should have checked the thermometer sooner," he joked, but I could tell the burnt smell and sight had grossed him out.

"Lift him up here on the table so we can weigh and measure him," Steve directed.

With the corpse situated to Steve's satisfaction, he began to dictate, finally. "Submitted for post mortem exam this day, are the charred remains of a thirty-seven year old male, I think. The body weighs approximately ninety-eight pounds."

Turning off the Dictaphone Steve asked, "Is all of him here? He sure doesn't weigh as much as I would have expected."

"You have all of him," Tim responded, after looking back in the body bag.

"I'll bet he lost a lot of body fat in the fire," was Tim's hypothesis.

"You bet, burned up like a wick," Steve said, continuing his dictation.

"The body measures sixty-four inches in height. The deceased arrived well charred and devoid of clothing. The limbs are contracted, consistent with exposure to fire." Pausing, Steve looked at me like this was my entire fault saying, "I'm not looking forward to opening this guy up you know."

"Hey, I didn't set the guy a fire," I protested, as Steve inspected the surface of the body.

"He has one heck of a skull fracture," Steve noted, into his machine. "That is not so unusual. When a victim has been exposed to extreme heat, the contents of the skull sometimes boil, and since there's nowhere for the steam to go—*POP.*" He grinned at me. "From what can be observed of the charred skin, there are no visible signs scars or tattoos. Let's open him up, Tim."

I took that as a cue to step back a little. Sometimes, when they open up a case like this, things have a tendency to splatter.

"I hate crispy critters. I can't eat meat for weeks after we do one of these," Tim complained, "I used to think cigarette smoke was hard to get out of my hair and clothes, but try getting this smell out."

"Stop whining and open this guy's chest," Steve mocked Tim's whiney tone.

He continued to dictate as he probed the slimy cavity, "The cardiac orientation and vessel development appear normal. The cardiac tissue weighs 1500 grams; samples are removed for microscopic review. Lung tissue is removed and gross dissection reveals well-developed lobe structure. Tissues, when placed in water, float. Gross appearance is inconsistent with that of a fire victim. Sections are removed for micro review." Steve paused.

"Someone turn on the fan," Tim exclaimed, gasping as he retreated from the body. "I didn't think I could hold my breath that long. How can something so crisp on the outside be so slimy and yucky inside?" he questioned.

"You act like this is the first one of these you've done, you big baby," Steve chastised Tim. "It looks like everything in here is within normal limits. Let me take a few samples of the other organs and then we'll open the head. Will that make you two feel better? Tim, take a few photos of the face before we destroy it," he instructed.

Tim took photos from every possible angle before he began to remove the cranial tissues.

"Be careful with that head saw, Tim. The skull is already in pieces," Steve advised. "The neurologic tissues are severely damaged and removed for examination. There is a focal area of hemorrhage noted within the occipital lobe. It is consistent with the overlying depressed skull fracture. Examination of the osseous tissues (bone) surrounding the fracture site reveal large amounts of hemorrhagic infiltration and several small fragments of wood."

Looking over his glasses Steve added, "So much for the theory that this cranial damage was explosive in nature. This is a depression type fracture; it looks more like it was caused by a club."

The balance of the procedure was uneventful and fruitless for gaining any further information. On the following Thursday, I received the report from Will and the Fire Chief. Will reported that the wife had indeed filed for divorce and was currently seeing a coworker. "He is a big bruiser of a man; the guy looks like a biker. He had a shotgun next to him on the couch. I kept waiting for him to pull it out and shoot me," Will explained. "The only alibi they each have for the time of death was one another. It sounds suspicious to me. Did Dr. Bilmarian really say it looked like a club did the damage?" he inquired.

"At first he thought it was due to the heat. Then he said it might be something the size of a bat," I answered. "Why?"

"I recall seeing a lot of softball trophies at the boyfriend's house," Will recounted.

"If you need a search warrant, let me know and I'll call the district attorney with our findings," I offered.

"We could check his car without a warrant, if we can stop him for a traffic violation. We'll stake out his home, car, and work place. I'm sure we will come up with something on him," Will promised.

"I'm sure glad you aren't hunting me," I said nervously.

"What makes you so sure we not?" he taunted.

Not satisfied with the answers given by William, I arranged to visit the scene again with Scott. I arrived at what remained of the house twenty minutes ahead of the Chief.

Going directly to the garage area, I began to look for something that would fit the description of the possible weapon, anything that might explain the injuries sustained by the corpse. While I was on my knees digging through the ash and debris, Scott came up over the hill behind the house.

"Hey, you what do you think you're doing?" Scott's voice bellowed.

Startled, I looked up to see him grinning. "Isn't this the place with the garage sale?" I responded with mock sincerity.

"It was a fire sale and as you can see, you're too late. What we couldn't sell we burned," he said as he reached to shake my hand. "Seriously, what are you hoping to find?"

"The autopsy indicated the body received an anti-mortem blow to the head. Bilmarian thinks it was something the size of a ball bat," I explained. "I was hoping to find the weapon."

"I can guarantee that if it was in the garage, it would be gone now," he said as he joined the search.

"I was hoping you wouldn't mention that. I'd hate to have them commit the perfect murder on my watch."

"The best place to begin would be next to the body," he suggested, indicating the location where the body had been found on the day of the fire.

"The only thing here is what's left of a bicycle or the melted remnants of it, a piece of a burnt beam, and a hardened pool of aluminum," I observed.

"Maybe the pool of metal is the remains of an aluminum bat," Scott hypothesized.

"How would we prove it was ever a bat, or for that matter, how would we ever prove that it was the murder weapon?" I asked. "There are certainly no finger prints or blood stains to examine."

"I don't know. Is there some lab somewhere that could test the metal and tell us that the ABC Bat Company uses that combination of metallic components?" he asked, hoping there was such a test.

"That still wouldn't do much good. The only thing it might prove is that it was indeed a bat," I continued, trying to be sensible.

"There isn't much else here. The fire consumed almost everything," Scott noted.

"I doubt we'll find anything of consequence," I sighed.

Beginning to feel it was hopeless, Scott went to his truck and returned with a garden rake. "Let's comb the whole garage and then go through what we find," he suggested.

An hour and a half of looking through the rubble revealed several bolts, some assorted screws and nails as well as a couple of semi-melted picture frames. There was enough unburned wood to have a fair sized campfire. Most of it was sections of support beams. Scott found most of the components of a bicycle and, we think, a motorcycle or two. In the corner under something that we couldn't recognize we found an entire box of doodads, there were photographs and some old love letters.

"This looks as though it was buried at the core of whatever started the fire. There must not have been enough oxygen to burn it all," Scott informed me.

"Is that a clue?" I wondered.

"Nothing more than we already knew. The arson guys said it started in this area. They think gasoline was used to start it," he said matter of factly.

"I don't know about you, but I think its Miller time! I'll meet you at the Thunder Cloud Bar in twenty minutes," I suggested.

"I know what that means; you're stumped. I kinda enjoy this. You know I'll never pass up a free beer or the chance to see you squirm . . . but I've gotta be home before dinner or my wife will kill me," Scott protested as he quickly picked up his rake and headed toward the truck. "I'll race you," he challenged.

"No fair. You have lights and a siren, and all I have is a beat up old truck," I protested, too late. He was already pulling out with lights flashing. Well, no one ever said Scott didn't like beer. We sat for over an hour at the Cloud, trying to solve the problems of the world, beginning with who might have killed Don and how they could have done it. Scott wondered if perhaps it was a suicide. He hypothesized that the victim might have accidentally set the gas can on fire.

He wasn't happy when I pointed out that would be an accident. Besides, how would you account for the crater bashed in his skull? The more beer we consumed, the more outlandish the theories became. Before this conversation degenerated into a theory that aliens did it, we decided that a good night's sleep might help to clear the cobwebs.

At this point, I wasn't going to rule anything out—*even aliens*. Scott bid me adieu, and stumbling toward the door he assured me, "I only live two blocks away on Galley road. I can crawl home if necessary." There are some advantages to living in a small town. All it takes is a call to the police and they will come drive you home. Try to do that in a big city. As many people as I scrape up off the highway each year for driving under the influence, I vow never to be one of them.

It was Saturday, not my usual workday, but this case was driving me crazy. I decided to visit Connie and her new love without notice. An unannounced visit (flashing the badge) sometimes catches people off guard and they forget their prepared story. The cabin was quiet when I arrived eight a.m. sharp. Its best when trying this ploy to arrive early, before anyone is out of bed. At that time of day, people are somewhat disoriented and more easily tripped up.

The cabin was on Middle Street. Middle is a one-way street running north and south in the center of town. At the north end of the street lays the original part of town, dated 1886. There are numerous cabins and small houses dating from that period. Most are now just dilapidated rentals. Once a building reaches one hundred years old it becomes historic. That means it's hard to do any renovation without the permission of God himself. Connie's cabin, however, was well maintained and decorated from top to bottom in hunter green.

I knocked at the door as if I were trying to knock it down. That is something the Coroner's Association teaches. Knock hard enough to scare the heck out of whoever is in the building. Chances are they will just open the door without any struggle or debate. It doesn't always go as planned though. There was one occasion when I was met at the door at three a.m. with the clicking sound of a shotgun being loaded. That's why I don't stand directly in front of the door when knocking. After knocking twice, the door opened to reveal Connie, standing in a bathrobe.

"Excuse me. I'm Dr. Reedman, the county coroner. Could I talk to you about Don's accident?"

"Accident that was no accident," she stated softly. "Come in, please," she motioned for me to walk through the door.

We sat down on the couch and I asked, "What do you mean it was no accident?" I thought perhaps she didn't realize I was deputized and unaware that if she confessed I could arrest her. This might turn out easier than I had thought.

"Don had threatened to burn the ranch and everything we owned to the ground if it looked like the court might grant any of it to me," she explained.

Ah, I thought, *she doesn't know he was hit in the head. Let's see where this goes.*

"Did you think he meant it?" I asked.

"Don never threatened to do anything he wasn't prepared to follow up on."

"That's where the pin that holds my arm together is. He was sure I was seeing someone else."

"As tacky as it sounds, I have to ask, were you?"

"No. As much as I might have wanted to, I would never have. He'd have killed me if he thought he had any evidence."

"When was the last time you saw him alive?" I asked.

"I've only seen him in court three times and then there was the night he came over here trying to take me back home."

"Did he succeed?"

"I'm still here aren't I? If I'd have gone with him, he'd have killed me that night," she shuddered as she spoke.

"If he was so forceful, what stopped him?"

"I did." A deep, male voice coming from the darkness of the hall startled me.

"I'm Lewis, Connie's friend. This is my house." The large man entered the room clad only in blue jeans and a baseball hat and sat down between Connie and me.

"Lewis has been my savior. He offered for the girls and me to move in here about six months before I had the courage to leave," she said as she caressed his hand and smiled at him.

"That's nice," I said, noting that these two were clearly more than friends.

Seeing baseball trophies on the table I asked, "Who's the athlete?"

"I am. I play in a league." Lewis seemed proud of his trophies.

"I've never won a trophy in my life," I admitted. "However, I did get a big number one when I hit a hole in one, but that was a long time ago. By the way, where was each of you between, oh, say seven a.m. and eleven a.m. the day of the fire?" I asked.

They looked at each other and Lewis answered for them both. "We were in Continental at a baseball tournament," he said forcefully.

I nodded my understanding. "Well, I guess that's all. I just wanted to stop by and let you know I'll determine the cause of Don's death in the next few days. Then I can issue a death certificate. Once that's done, you can give it to the insurance company and claim Don's death benefits. You'll need two more copies for the Social Security Administration and for the girl's survivor benefits." I stood up to make my exit.

"Oh, I didn't even think about his insurance. I hope he didn't burn the policies along with everything else. The girls and I could sure use the money," she said.

"Isn't it clear that this was an accident? Can't you just rule it stupidity or karma and be done with it?" Lewis pushed.

"I don't think stupidity is an accepted category under cause of death, but murder is," I said, with a smile. It was about time for me to get the heck out of there. I planted the seed in his mind; now I needed to let it grow.

When I arrived back at the office I called Dr. Steve. "How big of a person would it take to do the skull damage we found?" I asked.

"A ranch hand or a pretty big dude could do it. It would take quite a heavy blow to do that kind of damage to a skull. They would need enough strength to get the bat going and the ability to control it once they did," he hypothesized.

That was all I needed to know. As I sat at my desk looking at the photos from the scene, it dawned on me how Don died. At least I'm comfortable enough that I can sign my name to it.

Do you think you know too? I've given you *every* piece of evidence. If you've read carefully, I'll bet you figured it out a long time ago, didn't you?

Was it Murder, Suicide or Natural Causes?

LET'S REVIEW

I'll admit this case drove me crazy and I it hope it has done the same to you. That is sadistic, I know, but frustration, like misery, loves company.

Several things should have caught your attention in this tale. First, was that our good buddy, Don, was an abusive jerk. He'd been abusing Connie for many years. To me, that showed insight to his personality: mean, abusive, and somewhat paranoid.

It's hard to predict what someone like that would do in any given situation. Truth told, Connie probably saved her own life and the lives of her girls by leaving when she did. Don's abuse may have eventually led to a murder-suicide. Don's abuse could have motivated Connie to kill, but as small as she was, she most likely could not swing a bat hard enough to do the cranial damage. Lewis however, was certainly big enough to do the damage and he had plenty of motivation. He was obviously in love with Connie. He *definitely* owned enough bats that had one been missing. There would be no way to tell.

Some of the other clues that should have attracted your attention were the inspection of the brain and skull. Remember the focal areas of hemorrhage underlying the skull fracture and the several small fragments of wood? If there is hemorrhage in the tissues and skull at the fracture site, it means he was alive when the fracture occurred. The wood fragments in the fracture point to the beam being the culprit.

Recall that during the post, Dr. Bilmarian noted the lungs floated and were *not* consistent with a fire victim. That's because the victim didn't die due to smoke inhalation. *He was already dead.*

The Fire Marshal determined the cause of the fire was arson. That doesn't mean that someone else started the blaze. It only means that the fire was deliberately set. In this case, the victim set it.

There was certainly enough evidence to question the wife and her boyfriend for murder, but their alibi was good. My decisive clue was Dr. Bilmarian's comment on the phone, "It would take a heavy blow."

As I looked at the photographs from the scene, I recalled that there were the remains of a heavy support beam next to the body in the debris. Now do you think you've got it?

How the evidence was assembled made the decision easy. Here is my conclusion:

Don, still very angry with Connie for leaving him, decided to get even with her by burning her most prized possessions: old photos, baby clothes, her mountain bike, etc. Using gasoline to light the big pile in the center of the garage, Don was overcome by the rapid rush of fumes and flash when he lit the gallon of gas. He immediately passed out on the floor. The very place firemen tell you to go in a fire, close to the floor where there is oxygen.

As the fire roared, he was still alive but unconscious. At some point while he lay on the floor, one of the log beams fell and hit him on the head, killing him instantly. After that, poof, human candle.

Therefore, Lewis' request that this be ruled "Karma" would have been pretty close to the truth.

The cause of death: **blunt force trauma to the head.**

Ruling on the death certificate: **Accidental death.**

Note: Within a year of Don's demise, Connie and Lewis were married. The four of them moved back to the ranch. The insurance benefits made it possible for them to build elsewhere on the property and they are now living peacefully. Connie is expecting a new baby in July.

Fore!

There are few things I enjoy in life as much as golf. However, it hasn't always been so. During my internship, the chief clinician suggested that I take up the sport.

"Rex, all doctors play golf, you need to learn the game. What else will you do with your Thursdays off?" Dr. Garrett questioned.

I thought he was nuts; the idea of hitting a little ball with a stick, then spending ten minutes trying to find it while simultaneously being berated by your companions seemed ludicrous. Nevertheless, I did as Dr. Garrett suggested. I began by spending two hundred dollars for clubs, and eighty dollars for shoes. I refused to consider the funny plaid pants and matching hat. I do have a little dignity after all.

I joined my classmates on the golf course every day during lunch breaks for a 'quick nine holes.' My friends really seemed to enjoy my attempts at swinging the club. Oh, I was good at swinging the club, but hitting the ball was a different subject.

For the first month, I had the honor of being able to loft dirt and grass chunks fifty feet. The ball was always safe from my attempted assaults. I realized just how bad I was when one day I noticed everyone hiding behind the golf cart when it was my turn. True, I had accidentally launched my club down the fairway more than once, and sent more than a few clumps of earth flying in the direction of my partner, but I'd never really hurt anyone. Lessons were clearly in order.

"Whoa, you have quite a swing," my instructor commented during my first lesson.

"You have quite a swing" was not a compliment. It was a polite way of saying, "Let me hide over here behind the cart while you try to murder that tiny, defenseless ball." Once again I realized how really awful I was at the sport when the instructor suggested, "Why don't we move way over here, so you don't kill the other students."

After ten lessons, I still wanted to quit, but I'm cheap. I had way too much money wrapped up in paraphernalia. By now, I actually had two pair of the funny plaid pants and *four* matching shirts. Therefore, I endured.

Golf taught me that God has a sense of humor. After playing just six months, and in front of witnesses I had to bribe later not to tell the exact circumstances, my day of glory had arrived. Two hundred and fifty yards away was a tiny hole in the ground, my objective. I slowly swung the club—whack. It sounded beautiful. For once, I hadn't scooped grass into orbit. I could hear the gasps of my party as the ball, at about the speed of light, sliced toward a stand of tall trees. Whack, whack it ricocheted from tree to tree and then back toward the green. To my utter amazement, it dropped into the tiny hole in the ground. Disbelief spread like a virus through my group.

"Did you see that?" Tony, the par golfer, stammered.

"I saw it but I don't believe it," Jack responded. "He must have cheated but I can't figure out how."

Yes, I shot a hole-in-one. Like I said, God has a sense of humor. I hit the hardest shot in the game of golf, proving luck is more important than skill. I have now played golf for twenty years and never again had such good fortune. That doesn't mean I don't keep trying. I practice constantly and play once a week with friends. My golf bag still has a big brass number one with my name on it signifying my achievement. It's a great intimidator, that is, until those watching see me swing. Then all they want to know where I bought it.

One Saturday evening after hitting a large bucket of balls on the driving range, I was on my way through the parking lot to my car. A scream for help distracted me. Terry, a boy who worked in the pro shop charged past me into the darkness. He never stopped to survey the situation, ask for backup, or recognize any danger to himself. He headed blind in the direction of the woman's shrieks.

A large muscular man confronted him in the blackness. I could see the man was holding a young woman by the arm. In the other hand, he wielded a golf club.

"Get out of here kid. This ain't any of your business," the man threatened Terry with the golf club.

In the confusion, the young woman escaped the gorilla's clutch and ran in my direction yelling, "Do something. That guy is crazy. He'll kill that kid!"

I couldn't believe what I was seeing. I hadn't seen two guys fight since eighth grade when Randy Thatcher beat the tar out of Jesse Wilber after school for calling him a nerd. Jessie was right, Randy was a nerd, but I didn't get in the middle of that fight either.

I thought this man would calm down and everything would be all right once the woman had escaped. I was wrong.

The kid did indeed become the focal point for the drunken man's anger. He swung the club wildly, swearing at the young man with each swipe. On the third swing, a crack echoed through the parked cars. It was the sound a golf club makes when it strikes a human skull—kind of hollow.

As I was running in the direction of the struggle, the man swung the club for a second time. I wasn't fast enough to stop him from striking the boy. I reached them in time to see the young man staggering in a daze, not quite knowing what had happened to him. Then, in slow motion, he slumped to the ground, bleeding from the head. The pool of crimson blood grew quickly in gushes with each heartbeat.

As the young man dropped to the pavement at my feet, the manager Clayton arrived with the female victim close behind. Seeing backup coming, the assailant dropped the club and staggered into the darkness.

"I've called 911," Clayton announced, as he knelt down crying next to the young man.

By then, I was using my hand towel to suppress the profuse bleeding coming from the young Terry's head.

"Oh God, its Terry," the manager exclaimed, recognizing the young man as he wiped blood from the kid's face with his hand. "He's my assistant. He was just leaving to go home for the night."

The young man was limp in my arms as we waited for the paramedics. It seemed like it took forever for them to arrive. I'm sure that's how it always seems in an emergency.

Despite heroic efforts by the paramedics and surgeons, Terry remained unconscious.

The drunken assailant was apprehended within a few hours as he foolishly returned to the golf course attempting to retrieve his car. Charged with assault with a deadly weapon, he wasn't off the hook just yet. If within six months, Terry were to die due to this assault, the man could be charged with murder.

In his vegetative state, Terry required around the clock care. He was fed through a naso-gastric tube and kept breathing with the aid of a ventilator. A ventilator requires doctors to perform a tracheotomy, cutting a hole through the neck into the trachea or windpipe and inserting a plastic tube.

For many months, Terry stared at the ceiling with the ventilator rhythmically pumping. His only movement was the occasional blinking of his eyes. Nurses came and went from his room, changing his intravenous solutions and cleaning the tracheotomy.

"Everything seemed fine until three o'clock this morning," the charge nurse told me. I had been called to the hospital to sign the death certificate.

The nurse recounted to me that a young nurse was assigned to care for Terry. She changed the IV bottles and cleaned the bed. When she was rolling him over, she noticed a small amount of blood coming from the tracheotomy. Afraid she had caused the handsome young man to bleed, she reported it to her supervisor. The head nurse then called the doctor. One hour later, the doctor arrived.

He swaggered into Terry's room, thru back the curtain, "Let's have a loo,k, he said, as he roughly tugged at the plastic tube protruding from the patient's neck.

All at once, the tube came loose, taking some of the surrounding tissue with it. Within a few seconds, the steady sucking sound of the patient breathing had been replaced by gurgling. The open crater in the patient's neck, now devoid of the tube, was bubbling with blood. The bubble became a pulsing gush within seconds. The warm fountain increased and there was nothing that could be done.

The patient bled to death as the arrogant young doctor and helpless staff looked on. When hemorrhaging occurs from the throat's vascular structures, blood fills the trachea and lungs quickly, causing rapid death. Terry's life ended within minutes of the doctor's action.

"The intern was shaking and barely able to stand as the morgue attendants arrived to remove the body", the nurse continued. "They placed Terry's body in a bottomless gurney."

This is a most ingenious device. When it is wheeled through the corridors of the hospital it looks just like an empty gurney. However, what the public does not see is a stainless-steel pan that lies under the frame of the false top. When a body is put in the pan and the cover replaced, it once again looks like an empty gurney. When I worked in the hospital morgue there was many a time I thought, *if the people in this elevator knew what was under this sheet I'd have more than one passenger.*

Luckily, most people think when a body is moved through the halls we cover them with a sheet like in the movies or try to make them look asleep. It's magic. As long as people believe, we can get away with the deception.

"We'll put him in the refer," Jacob. the morgue attendant. told the intern.

"Thanks. Will you have the pathologist call me? I want to be there for this autopsy," the intern's voice shook as he spoke.

As an intern, Dr. Anderson had not yet faced the family of a patient he'd lost. The truth is, in the six months since graduation, he had never lost a patient. Now, the reality of practicing medicine hit him like a Mac truck. It wasn't all heroics. Sometimes the good guys lose, he realized. Sometimes good guys get sued, even when they'd done their best.

As I was leaving the hospital, I ran into the golf course manager, Clayton. He invited me to share a cup of coffee. It was perfect; I wanted to talk to him anyway. This would save me a trip. However, it also meant I'd miss an opportunity to hit a bucket of balls.

We sat in the doctor's lounge with our not so fresh coffee. "Tell me about Terry," I asked as I sipped my Joe.

"He'd been hanging around the clubhouse for so long I thought I had two choices, have him arrested for loitering or just hire him." He leaned back in his chair.

"I'm certain he was happy with you deciding on the job rather that the pokey," I smiled trying to cheer him up.

"He loved golf or being around people who played the game. I remember when I first met Terry when he was six. His dad brought him for lessons."

"Golf lessons for a six-year old?" I was surprised that kids that age could even lift a club much less swing one.

"Terry was five when he picked up his dad's golf club, an act no one in his house appreciated. There were broken lamps and several cracked windows before his Dad realized Terry really wanted to play golf. He agreed to pay for the lessons; it would be cheaper than replacing houseware."

"I was twenty-five when I began lessons and I was still breaking things when I swung a club." Again, I smiled trying to lighten the mood.

"It took one lesson for me to tell Mr. Thompson his son was a natural golfer. I offered to give him a set of clubs his size and he let him keep them if he continued lessons. In just a matter of months, the six-year-old boy could clean his dad's clock on the golf course. When he swung the club, he was so smooth it was one fluid motion. Whenever Terry couldn't be found it was just a matter of calling the clubhouse. Most often he was out on the course somewhere." He smiled and his eyes twinkled as he recalled.

"Who does a six or seven year old find to play golf with?" I inquired.

"The boys (World war one Vets living in the retirement home next door) loved to play with the 'kid.' They would return from the course smiling and laughing, no sign of the arthritic old men who had teed off several hours before."

"If he was that good as a little boy, he must be quite the player now." I was jealous.

"Good? During high school, Terry was the star of the golf team; he made it look easy. He was well known for looking at the hole for several minutes, checking the wind and then telling his partner exactly what flight path the ball would take. He was rarely wrong and most times his ball stopped only inches from the cup."

"Anybody that good must have had colleges beating a path to his door."

"His future at college looked extremely bright. Princeton, Harvard and Yale all offered him full scholarships. Life was wonderful and promising for Terry. The pro circuit was most certainly in his future," he sighed.

"Until the night nearly twenty-two weeks ago, when he tried to protect a female golfer's virtue," I added.

We lost our spot in the lounge when the shift changed. I walked Clayton to the parking lot and said good night.

Thinking that was the end of the case for me, I tried to put the death out of my mind. I was surprised the next day the hospital operator called my cell phone. How she got the number beats me. (I've tried not to use it after last month's four hundred-dollar cell bill.)

The operator informed me that the autopsy was scheduled in one hour. Hospitals almost always do their own autopsies. The pathology department is in-house and the arrangement is, as the church lady would say, *very convenient*. Therefore, it is a rare occasion when I am asked to attend a *hospital* post-mortem.

The procedure started exactly on schedule. Those attending were the pathologist, Dr. Eugene Hall, his assistant, Tommy Delvecio, and myself, Rex Reedman, Coroner. The intern, Dr. Anderson, arrived late.

This procedure was missing the usual light-hearted atmosphere I had become accustomed to. The doctor began his dictation dryly. "Submitted for autopsy is the body of a white male with the stated age of eighteen. The body is devoid of tattoos, scars, or other distinguishing marks. However, there is a scar on the right temple. It appears well healed measuring 4.9 centimeters by .5 centimeters".

Blah blah blah, I thought. *This doctor could put a speed freak to sleep. He must be a riot at home.*

The examination of the thorax and abdomen were negative for contributing factors.

"Get the neck dissected Tommy, and don't slip this time," the pathologist ordered. "If you buttonhole another patient, I'm going to make you explain it to the mortician."

Button holing is when the doctor or his assistant accidentally cut a small slit-like hole in the front of a deceased patient's neck leaving a wound that looks like a buttonhole. Morticians hate it when this happens because it's very hard to close or cover up and is almost always visible at a viewing.

Close inspection of the wound showed severe dilation of the venous structures in the area of the tracheotomy. The surrounding tissue had areas of necrosis (dead tissue). When the respirator tube was removed, rotted tissue was removed as well. Dissection of the head showed signs of the subdural hematoma (a bruise between the brain tissue and the inner side of the skull) Terry suffered in the attack. However, there were no signs of recent stroke or hemorrhage.

That is all that was known at the time a decision was required. What do you think? Was the young intern responsible? After all, it did take him an hour to respond to the initial call. Had he arrived sooner would the patient have survived? Was he negligent when he yanked the tube from Terry's neck? On the other hand, perhaps it was the nurse who rolled him over, possibly dislodging the respirator tube?

Don't turn the page until you have made up your mind.

LET'S REVIEW

Poor young Terry with his natural talent for golf had such a bright future ahead of him—until one night five and a half months ago when the drunk struck him in the head with a golf club.

His life ended virtually the moment the club fractured his skull. Never again did he wake or move. The actions of the doctor were less than acceptable. When a respirator tube is placed into the trachea, it causes congestion of the local blood vessels and increases their size. This makes them extremely fragile. The doctor's removal of the tube was ignorant but not negligent.

Terry's death was due to the attack twenty-two weeks prior. Since he did not survive the mandated six months, the assailant would now face charges of murder.

Cause of death: **acute hemorrhage**, secondary to chronic insertion of a tracheal tube. Manner of death: **Death at the hands of another/ murder**.

How did you do, if you solved it *congratulations.*
Twelve down!

Old Habits Die Hard

Since I lived in a small town I knew it was inevitable that the day would come when one of my calls would lead me to the home of one of my friends. I wasn't wrong. God must have had a big laugh that day.

The call wasn't just to the home of a friend. It was to a *convent*. The nuns of this order have been hiking partners of mine for a year now. I can't tell you how much I love having them meet me at my office. Clad from head to toe in the traditional black habit the nuns make quite a sight. Not just because Mother Superior has a biting wit, which I adore and would never expect of a nun, but the reaction of other people in the office. Its classic when I give the stoic looking nun a hard time (including an occasional swear word).

About two years ago Mother Edna brought a new nun into the office. She was Sister Sophia from Romania. She didn't speak a word of English, a fact Mother Edna didn't share with me until I'd been jabbering away to the sister for a full five minutes. Who says nuns don't have a sense of humor?

Sister Sophia learned English within months of her arrival. I did my part in her education. I taught her slang. Mother Edna was not thrilled.

"Nuns do not use the word cool," she scolded. "Terms like 'bummer,' 'far out' and 'cosmic' are *not* in a *nun's* vocabulary."

Sister Sophia on the other hand, loved knowing real English. Whenever Mother Edna was out of earshot, she would use her forbidden language. Once she really had a grasp of American humor (sorry Mother), I found her to be extremely funny. Sarcasm became her favorite. She can sound sweet and innocent while ripping your throat out.

During the course of our friendship, she told me about Romania, her family, and growing up. One day I asked her what it was like to grow up in a communist country. What she told me gave me chills—**God bless America**.

* * *

Winters in Ukraine are harsh. The days are short and the nights are cold. Sophia didn't mind the cold as much as she dreaded the darkness. In the summer, she could lie with the window open and watch stars all night. However, in the deep of winter, the shutters were bolted tight, leaving the young girl trapped—a feeling with which she was very familiar. Growing up in a communist state brings such feelings to many a freethinking youngster.

Sophia's way to escape from the feeling of oppression was to hike. Her idea of hiking was to trek out into the pathless forests surrounding her village. Some days she walked ten miles in the rough terrain. Alone, she was free to think and pray without distraction. However, walking where she did had hazards beyond the wild beasts, dangers anyone born in the freedom of the west can only imagine. The best way to survive was to avoid contact with humans and avoid being seen. A good rule was not to look at anything very closely or for too long.

With the woods no longer feeling safe as they had been, Sophia turned more and more to the Church for escape. At the age of sixteen, she entered a convent as a novice.

When she turned twenty, the Bishop decided that for her dedicated service the young nun should be sent to the United States. Her assignment was to help start a convent in the mountains of Colorado.

When she arrived at the airport in New York, she spoke no English. The local Bishop had been informed of this and dispatched a young priest to meet her at the airport. Father Simon had been practicing his Ukrainian for weeks in excited anticipation of her arrival. Now was his chance to practice his skill. He was confident. He rushed through the airport and toward the gate, late as usual. The plane from London had already arrived and passengers were coming up the causeway toward him. He felt like a salmon swimming upstream, but living in New York had taught him how to navigate in a crowd without being trampled. At only five foot four, he'd had nightmares about just that. As the sea of humanity streamed in his direction, he scanned the crowd for a nun.

It wasn't hard for Father Simon to pick out the Sister. Sophia was a stately woman standing almost six feet tall, beautiful, and clad from head to toe in an old-fashioned black habit. She was surprised and embarrassed by the priest's enthusiastic greeting.

"Hello, Sister. Welcome to America," he began yelling over the crowd the moment he saw her.

Coming from an extremely small convent in rural Ukraine, Sophia was not accustomed to large groups of people or loud noises. She felt as though every eye in the place was trained on her.

"This can't be a priest," she muttered to herself. "Oh God, are all priests in America so undignified?" America would hold many surprises for the young nun.

Father Simon instructed her, in his best Ukrainian, "Have a seat," while he claimed her baggage. He didn't notice the quizzical look on her face. Of course, he also didn't realize that he had actually told her, "Help yourself to the furniture."

She knew America was rich, but *free furniture*, right in the airport? This truly was a wonderful place.

* * *

Things became more routine once Sophia had settled in Colorado. With Mother Superior as her only companion and translator, her misadventures began.

Six months later in late summer, while hiking in the mountains near the convent, Sister Sophia noticed what appeared to be a truck parked in the forest. The little voice in her head told her to keep moving and not to look. So following her intuition, she trekked into the woods in another direction. Returning to the convent snuggled in the woods, she reported her sighting to mother superior.

"It's probably just a hunter parked there or someone who was out cutting wood. Don't worry," Mother Superior tried to alleviate her fears. These explanations made Sister feel much better—for about three and a half weeks—until once again she came to the same spot while walking. There it was again. This time she stood behind a big pine tree and looked a little more carefully. It was a multi-colored, green camouflaged, four-wheel drive pickup. As she looked closer she noticed a piece of tubing running from the cab to the bed of the truck.

Oh Lord, it's a big gun, she thought to herself.

Now she was sure this was a military vehicle. Her heart pounded so loudly she was certain it would betray her presence. She ducked closer to the tree and tried not to panic. Remembering encounters with Soviet troops, the young nun ran back to the convent without stopping or even looking back. It was two miles to the safety of the convent. Out of breath she ran inside slamming the heavy carved door behind her. She bolted it, just to be sure. Feeling safe, she sat against the door and tried to gather her thoughts.

Mother Superior heard the door close and came up from the basement. "Sister, are you okay? You look like you've seen a ghost."

In her best broken English (*That's unfair, her English is ten thousand times better than my Ukrainian.*), Sophia explained that the truck was still out there in the forest and had not been moved in weeks.

Mother Edna tried to calm her by explaining once again, "It's probably someone who broke down and hasn't come back for the truck, that's all."

Sister Sophia protested, "It's an army truck, with a big gun on it." Her eyes widened as she spoke.

"Okay Sister, tomorrow we will *both* go out and look. Will that make you feel better?"

It had now been one full month since Sophia first reported the abandoned truck. Can you guess where this is going?

At what seemed like the crack of dawn, young sister Sophia woke Mother Edna with tea and toast. "Get up Mother, it's time to get going," the Sister ordered without raising her eyes for fear of "that look."

"That look" was the one that the older nun used when the two of them were in public and sister committed a misstep. Sister dreaded that look.

It had been raining off and on for the past two days and the aroma of the wet forest filled the air with that wonderful clean smell. The hike was strenuous to say the least. They traversed two miles up hill through deep pine needles and low hanging branches. The dense forest was dark in places, but when the light streamed through the branches, it looked like a painting.

As they walked, Mother found herself humming "Amazing Grace." It was her way of coping with the altitude. If she didn't think about it she wouldn't be so tired. As Mother Superior trudged along lost in her own world, the young sister sprinted ahead.

"Yes, yes I'm coming Sister," was all the older woman could pant out. As expected, Sister Sophia arrived at the mystery truck minutes ahead of the now exhausted Mother Superior.

"Why are you hiding behind the tree, sister?" Mother Edna asked as she collapsed under the same tree. "Are we there yet?"

The young girl held her fingers up to Mother Superior's mouth. "Shhh. Don't be so loud. They will hear us," she whispered.

"I can hardly breathe after being dragged halfway up this mountain. Moreover, when I get here you try to suffocate me. This is not the way to move ahead in the Church, Sister."

"Oh, I'm sorry Mother," Sophia whispered. "I was just worried that someone would hear us and we'd get in trouble," she continued to grovel quietly.

"Who will hear us, Sister? We own this land and there aren't any neighbors for five miles," Mother Edna tried to reassure the young nun.

After catching her breath, the Mother slowly stood and looked through the branches. Sure enough, there was a small truck with a camouflage paint job.

"Yes, yes I see it, Sister," Mother Superior whispered in response to the nun's tugging at her habit.

"Let's go over and get a closer look," she continued to speak softly, partly to keep the younger nun calm and partly because at this point her heart was pounding in fear. From where she had stepped from behind the tree, the elder nun could clearly see someone sitting in the driver's seat.

"You stay here, Sister, and I'll go get a better look," she sternly instructed the sister.

"If you're going, I'm going," Sister Sophia said with a firm tone the older nun had never heard before. "I'm not staying here alone!" she continued.

"Okay, I didn't know you would feel so strongly about it. Let's go."

The two approached the truck, with the younger nun clinging to and hiding behind her mentor. About eight feet from the vehicle Mother inhaled a fly.

"Yuck. What was that?" she exclaimed as she spit out the bug.

It was almost at the same moment, the two realized they were standing in a fly storm that surrounded the truck. The few neighbors the nuns have told me a loud screaming noise emanated from the depths of the woods and two black streaks were sighted heading toward the convent that morning.

*   *   *

At eleven thirty a.m. both my phone and pager sounded at the same time. Oh well, I didn't have any plans for my Monday, yet.

"Okay Doc, are you up and around?" The voice on the phone giggled. It was Betty at the Sheriff's office.

"What? Do I have some bad reputation for staying in bed?" I asked.

"Sure do. Every time I call and your daughter Tina answers, the first thing she says is, 'I'll check to see if he's sleeping,'" she retorted.

"I'm going to have a talk with that girl about what she tells people. Well, at least she isn't saying I'm on the john. I'd rather have a reputation for being sleepy, if you know what I mean," I said in my own defense.

"Well, put on your hiking shoes, get out your compass, find your slicker, and be sure to bring your nose plugs. This one sounds bad," Betty warned.

"Are you sure this is in our county?" I asked, hoping it might fall in the neighboring jurisdiction.

"You'd get the call no matter what. Don't you remember Jackson County's Coroner is in the hospital?" I could hear her sadistic tone coming through loud and clear.

"Tell me what you know, you mean old woman," I laughed.

"The nuns at Our Lady of the Mountains Convent just called and they have found a dead body. They're requesting that we send an ambulance or something."

"An ambulance? Then why are you calling me?" I asked, sure that I'd found my way out of this.

"I asked them when they found the injured. They said it had been a month. Now, the way I think, if these ladies found him a month ago, I'm sure his condition hasn't improved any. Would you think differently?" Betty was clearly enjoying this.

"You must know something I don't, so spill," I begged.

"Okay. The nuns report the vehicle is engulfed in a swarm of flies. Yuck. So, I assume the occupant must either be dead or wearing really bad cologne." Now she didn't even try to hide her laughter.

"You know, Betty, I have the authority to deputize people if I feel like it. I'm beginning to think you would make a great deputy coroner. Maybe you would like to go on this call with me, or maybe you could handle it alone and I could go fishing." I had her now and she knew it.

"Truce, truce you win Doc. I never want to go out with you for anything."

"Hey, I'll buy lunch," I offered.

"Definitely not to eat ever, if you let me out of this discussion I'll tell you the shortest way to the scene," her tone had changed.

"Chicken, okay where do I go? I didn't even know there was a convent around here."

"You were right in the beginning. It's just over the border in Jackson County. Since their coroner is laid up with a kidney stone, guess who gets to booney bash seven miles up a logging road?"

"Not another rut-fest. You know my old Jeep hates hills." I knew I was begging.

"Stop whining Mister Cheapo and take this down. I'm only going to say it once. Take Highway 42 west from town. Go through the town of Continental, keep going until you pass the back entrance to Twelve Mile Reservoir, about six miles after that you will pass through Lake Edward. Just about two miles after you cross the county line look to the left. There will be a *blue toilet seat* nailed to the fence. Turn in there. The nuns say the road forks about two miles up. Be sure to take the right fork or you will end up at what they called the 'drop off.' Mother Superior says you won't be able to miss the convent."

"I think I'd rather have the kidney stone than do this," I said, as I hung up the phone.

I followed Betty's advice. I found my waterproof coat and bottle of cinnamon oil. Just a dab of cinnamon on a toothpick and a little under the nose and you can bear almost any noxious odor. As usual, my old Jeep just didn't want to start, but a shot of ether in the carburetor and, *vroom,* I was off.

Following the vague directions, I stayed on highway 42 for almost an hour. In that time I almost hit three elk, two deer and a fox. It must have been animal rush hour. I passed through Lake Edward, which consists of a small store with one gas pump and an elementary school. That's it; if you blink, you miss it. There are a lot of tiny towns like that in Colorado. I have no idea why it's named Lake Edward. There isn't a lake for more than ten miles.

Now, according to my directions, I should find a blue toilet seat nailed to a fence somewhere. I just love directions like this. At sixty miles an hour I'm supposed to be able to find a subtle landmark. It reminds me of the time I had to find a dead deer next to the road as my only landmark. Is it too much to hope for a big flashing neon sign saying, "Convent this way. Turn here, Dummy?" I guess that's out of the question.

A gentle mist was falling as I crossed from Pine to Jackson County. The road began to rise more steeply and wind more tightly as the summit of Bilkerton Pass neared. With the wiper blades slapping out an irregular beat I tried to keep one eye out for the dreaded blue toilet seat. About a mile over the summit, and—there it was. A bright, *blue tractor seat* nailed to a fence that looked as though it had been in place for a hundred years. Every other fence post was weathered and falling over in a different direction.

As I turned onto the rutted path that passed itself off as a road, the thought crossed my mind, *What if a mile down the way there is another driveway with a toilet seat, and I'm turning up the tractor seat road?*

I hate these back roads. I told myself to quit grumbling and stopped to try (emphasis on the word *try*) to lock the hubs in four-wheel drive. This task has at times taken several minutes and more than one hammer. My brother-in-law refuses to even get out and try anymore.

I admit this old beast can be stubborn at times, but I kind of take it that the universe is giving me a message. You know, if it's hard to get the thing in gear and it slows me down, well, maybe I miss an accident that I might not have otherwise. That kind of thinking drives my wife crazy.

The poor old heap struggles, but once she gets up a little speed the ruts are easy to drive in. Once in a while I do get turned around and have saved myself by following the deepest ruts when I come to a fork in the road. This was just such a time.

When I got to the T in the road, the road to the right looked easier, but the path leading left was better traveled. Ah. Let's see, Betty said to turn right at the fork in the road . . . no that's not right. She said to take the right path or you will end in a drop off. The choice to take the path better worn seemed best. Left was the "right" path. I later found that the road to the right had been washed out three years earlier in a heavy spring runoff.

As I came around what seemed to be the tenth switch back, I finally saw my goal. About a half mile away in the trees sat what looked like a castle. A bell tower with a slate looking roof was clearly visible through the aspen trees. As I pulled up in front of the big stone building I was impressed at its enormity. The stones were quarried granite from the local mountains. It was easy to tell because the local stone has a pink hue to it.

I knocked on the huge oak door but was not sure anyone inside could hear my feeble attempt. The door was so big and my hand so small. I tried again, using my flashlight. The huge door finally moved, revealing a tiny woman with a big smile.

"Hi Doc, it's nice to see you. The others are in the chapel," the tiny woman motioned for me to enter. She led me through the gigantic halls lined with solid oak floors and beautiful carpets.

"These rugs are beautiful," I marveled aloud as we crossed another hallway.

"Sister Sophia makes them here in our workshop," she replied.

"I can't believe you put them on the floor. They should be framed and on the wall as art."

"We have to keep the floors warm in the winter, so they wouldn't do much good on the walls now would they?"

Okay, now I felt small.

As we entered the narthex, I saw Detective Will Stone talking with Sister Sophia, who looked shaky and a little pale. The young nun peered at the floor as she softly greeted me.

"Hey Doc, can I talk to you outside?" Will asked as he gestured to the main door. "I haven't been able to get much information from the nun. She says the body is about two miles up the hill at the end of the meadow," he said, pointing to one of the biggest mountains I'd ever seen.

"Hill, that's no hill. It's a mountain! Where is the road?"

"There is no road, just a footpath," Mother Edna said as she joined us on the steps.

"We have to hike?" I asked.

"Well, if you can fly that might be an option," Mother added with a smirk.

"I'm not looking forward to schlepping the body all the way down the side of that mountain by hand," I grumbled.

Now, Detective Stone clearly works out every day and probably runs ten miles when he's done. The idea of hiking uphill for miles didn't seem to bother him at all. I, on the other hand, am old, out of shape and, let me be honest, lazy.

"Has anyone called Ed and Patty from the mortuary?" I asked.

"The dispatcher said she'd call them after she found you," Mother Edna explained.

"Well then, they should be here anytime now", I said hopefully. "Mother, what did you see when you found the body?"

"We didn't get too close. There were flies everywhere. I saw what appeared to be a man sitting in the driver's seat. The windows were rolled up, I think. The truck is painted green with black swirl lines on it. We didn't stay too long, if you know what I mean," she said with a sweet smile.

Will tapped me on the shoulder and pointed up the driveway. "Is that the morgue people?"

Coming over the rise was a big Ford Bronco with a large roof rack and pulling a trailer.

"Look at all that dust. He's hauling ass," exclaimed Will.

He suddenly realized he was standing next to the Reverend Mother and said with the most horrid expression, "Sorry Mother."

"We prefer carrying donkey," she smiled broadly.

Ed and Patty pulled up with dust flying everywhere and the sound of screeching breaks just in time to save Will from further embarrassment.

"Wow, what a road. I turned right at the fork back there," Ed's voice boomed.

"I thought we were gonna die for sure," Patty added.

"The directions were a little confusing to me too," I said.

Ed reached out to shake my hand. "I hear from Betty that the body is up in the hills a little way."

"A little way are you kidding? It's two miles straight up hill." Oh no, I was whining again.

"All right," Ed exclaimed. "I was right."

"Right about what? Why do you seem so happy about going eight thousand miles up hill into the boonies?" I thought he was nuts.

"That's why I brought these," he said, pulling the tarp that covered the trailer. There, to my amazement, were four all-terrain vehicles, gassed up and ready to go.

"We were on our way to Lake Anderson for a fishing trip with the kids," Ed explained with a smile of satisfaction.

I think I was the happiest to see the lazy man's answer to hiking. It took about ten minutes to unload the vehicles. Patty opted to stay behind with the young nun, but Mother Edna insisted on going along for the ride. She stated that she wouldn't reveal the body's location unless she could go along. To witness a fifty-year-old nun in full black habit, astride a big ATV, driving (pardon the expression) *like a bat out of Hell,* made me laugh so hard I almost fell off my vehicle. I'm sure I'll rot in hell for that evil thought.

With Mother Edna as our guide, Will, Ed, and I headed off into the forest. We were an odd looking caravan I'm sure. Mother Edna yelled with delight as she jumped her four-wheel drive over bumps and roots kicking up the golden Aspen leaves behind her.

"The convent has to get one of these!" she yelled over her shoulder as she raced through the dense forest.

It didn't take long to arrive at the scene on the mini four-wheelers. We reached the very top of the knoll and from a small clearing of big ponderosa pines you could see forever. On the far side of the clearing was the camouflaged four-wheel drive.

"How in the world did they get this way up here?" Ed asked as he removed a blue plastic body bag from his pack. "I didn't see any roads."

"He must have worked his way between trees from the highway," Will suggested pointing in the direction of the highway.

"That would be seven miles," Mother Edna offered as she stepped hesitantly toward the truck. She held a white handkerchief over her face as she approached. Standing in front of the vehicle, Mother Edna removed a small black Bible from her pocket and began to read quietly.

"Should we tell her it's a crime scene and she's standing on evidence?" Will asked in a whisper.

"If I were you I wouldn't try to tell that woman anything. Did you see the way she drove that ATV?" Ed asked.

As the nun counted her beads, Will looked into the cab of the truck. "Oh. my gosh. Put on your protective gear, this guy looks horrible," he warned as he backed away from the truck covering his mouth.

Time for a cinnamon stick, I thought to myself.

As I looked in the window I could see the remains of a man seated at the wheel. His hands were at his sides and his head was tilted back. He was wearing a plaid shirt, a bright orange reflective vest, and a hunter's hat. I opened my backpack for my rubber gloves and camera. Bob, the county photographer, was on vacation, so this one was on me. Hoping that I don't get a glare from the windows, I took outside pictures of the truck. What Sister Sophia thought was a gun turned out to be a large piece of PVC pipe, used by sportsmen to hold their fishing poles.

"Time to open up the truck," I announced, hoping someone would volunteer.

At times like this people have a tendency to stand back and watch to see if the coroner is going to puke. To tell you the truth, knowing that keeps me from losing my lunch sometimes. Just call it peer pressure. I opened the vehicle, praying the body wouldn't fall out on me. My nose was engulfed in a cloud of a noxious, foul stench. This guy had been locked in the truck, dead—for probably a month. At this point I doubted that an entire jar of cinnamon would help remove the odor. Gasping for clean air I closed the door and begged for Ed to give me a hand.

"If I have to," Ed mumbled.

He placed a vintage WWII gas mask over his face. "MMMoNN on grrommnd," Ed ordered as he dug in his pack.

"Where the hell did you get that thing? I can't understand a word you're saying."

Lifting the mask from his face Ed repeated his order, "Let's spread a tarp on the ground so we have something to put the body on."

"Oh, I *thought* that was what you said," I lied as I helped him spread the tarp on the ground.

With Ed's help and the nun looking on, we reopened the vehicle. I took as many Polaroid pictures as possible between breaths.

"Will you hurry? I can't hold him up much longer," Ed mumbled from under his mask.

"You've got the gas mask and you're fussing at me?" Oh no, wrong thing to do, having expelled my air I was forced to take a deep breath of the green cloud.

"Let's lay him down, quick," I begged.

I hoped I wouldn't hurl. I could taste the death stench. Tasting it is the only thing worse than being forced to breathe it.

With the body on the tarp, I realized we'd left part of him still on the seat.

"What do you say we leave that there for the tow truck driver?" Ed teased, pointing to the remains on the truck seat.

"Hey, where's Will?" he asked.

Hearing his name called and thinking the worst was over, Detective Stone stepped out from behind the truck. "Oh you guys need me?" he asked sheepishly.

"Yeah, will you get the rest of this guy off of the seat?" Ed was obviously smiling under that ridiculous gas mask.

"Are you kidding?" Will grimaced and looked at Ed as though he was going to soil the scene with his breakfast. "I don't do dead very well," he continued, thinking that if he just kept talking we would forget the request.

"Never mind, just stay up wind. Doc, and I will handle it, but you owe us one," Ed jibed.

"Free speeding ticket, anything you want," Will promised as he ran from the scene.

"Yeah, you go keep the nun company," Ed said under his breath.

As Ed and I went through the truck there were a few things that caught our attention. First, the truck wasn't closed tightly as we had first assumed and the driver's side window was rolled down about four inches. Second, Ed found a hand written suicide note on the floor near the gearshift. Third, a loaded handgun, a hunting rifle, and a knife were found lying on the floor under the glove box. The dashboard was covered with pictures. There were photos of a dog, a horse and several of those family pictures from Sears. Lastly, an empty bottle of "Yukon Jack" was at his feet.

"Okay, we'd better slow down and look at this carefully," I said, hoping Ed could hear me under that fixture attached to his face. "My gut's telling me something's wrong here."

Ed just stood there nodding his head as if in agreement. I still wasn't sure he could understand me or even hear me.

"I think the first thing to do is make sure we get the rest of this guy out of the truck," I continued.

Ed stood there continuing to nod as I removed the tissue still adhering to the seat cover. I know it sounds bad, but I try to remember there is a rubber glove between the gunk and me. Once in a while gloves do break, but let's not think about that now. Once everything and everybody had been removed from the cab, Ed and I had a better view of the truck's interior.

"Hey, look what I found," Ed mumbled as he held up a small nap sack he'd found under the driver's seat. He laid it on the tarp next to the body. Returning to the search he moved the seat, looking behind and finding nothing except the car jack.

"There's nothing in the glove box, not even registration for the truck," I noticed.

Standing back we looked at the fruits of our search. Ed removed his protective gear.

"Let's see, there sure isn't much here: guns, booze and a note. It looks like this guy did himself in," Ed hypothesized. "But knowing you the way I do, you're going to try to tell me it was a murder, aren't you?"

"Everything is murder until proven otherwise," I responded.

Will returned with Mother Edna just as Ed and I got the body bag closed. "Do you want the Mother and me to put up some evidence tape around the truck?" Will asked.

The look I gave Ed sent him into tears trying to contain his laughter.

"Let's see, we're fifty miles out in the woods on an unmarked trail on private land . . . If putting up tape would make you feel better, go right ahead." I felt the need to patronize his apparent ignorance.

"Don't leave the keys in it," the nun offered.

Now Ed was on his knees in a full guffaw. "I'm sure she's right, but wouldn't it be funny to see someone come across the truck, keys and all. Wouldn't it serve a thief right?" Ed was holding his stomach now.

I could tell by her look that Mother Edna didn't understand our gales of laughter. However, in this line of work sometimes our sense of humor is the only defense against depression.

"I think I have seen enough. I'll take the Mother down to the convent and then I have to get going. I'm sure my Chief thinks I died by now," Will smiled as he offered his excuses.

"It's okay, Will, we understand. I'll make certain you get a copy of the autopsy report, unless you'd like to attend the post. You know I like to buy lunch for the crew on autopsy day." My grin betrayed the underhanded kindness of my offer.

"I think I can get by on a copy of the report. Pictures aren't even necessary," Will said as he and Mother Edna started up their ATVs.

Ed tossed me the keys to the truck still smiling broadly, as Mother Edna and Will disappeared into the depths of the forest. The sound of Mother Superior's motor screaming and her voice yelling encouragement to Detective Stone could be heard echoing throughout the forest.

"Now that all of the help is gone, what do you say we pack him up and follow their lead?" Ed asked.

"Have we got everything?" I wondered aloud.

"It's all packed and wrapped up. All we have to do is zip up the body bag and we're outta here." Ed sounded anxious.

We loaded the body on the back of Ed's ATV, tying it down with twine. Hey you use what's at hand. The only other option was to drag it down the hill and I don't think the next of kin would be too happy with us if we chose that option. Going down the hill was a little slower than coming up. Ed was extremely cautious with the body bouncing around.

When we arrived back at the convent, I placed a call to a towing company, instructing them to remove and impound the vehicle. I just provided them with the address and billing authority, the driver would have to figure out how he was going to get that thing out of there. (Sometimes it's easier not to provide *too* much information.)

Ed and Patty called on their cell phone to say the body was at the morgue and "on ice." They were going out of town fishing, so if I needed to do a removal, I was on my own. My wife hates that kind of news. It means I have to use the family van. I still don't understand her upset. After all, the bag was zipped tightly, and it's not like something leaked out.

The next day the evidence that had been gathered at the scene was ready for review. Thank God, the pictures turned out great. Not one red pupil or flash glare. Of course, it's pretty hard to get a retinal flash from a dead person. The truck had been placed in our evidence lot. I'm still not sure how the tow truck managed to get it out of the woods. Of course, I'm not about to ask him, but maybe the nuns will tell me.

As I reviewed the photos prior to autopsy time, I was struck by what I saw. The weapons were lying on the floor of the passenger side of the truck, seemingly out of the driver's reach. The photos further revealed blood spatters on the passenger side of the cab and window, as well as seat area.

"Dr. Reedman, please report to necropsy," the paging system announced. That's a nice, clinical way of saying, "Hey, we're about to start the autopsy so get your lazy butt to the morgue."

As I neared the morgue I could hear the distinctive voice of Dr. Bilmarian singing, "Trailers for sale or rent . . ."

Oh no, he thinks he's Roger Miller, I thought as I opened the morgue door.

"Hey there, Rex, it's nice of you to show up. We were just about to start without you," Dr. Bilmarian interrupted his song just long enough to harass me. He continued to hum as his eyes moved to the still closed body bag on the autopsy table. "I know how much you love decomposed bodies, so we were going to wait for you no matter how long it took. I had a heck of a time getting a diener to help do this post mortem. For a minute I thought it would be just you and me," he flashed a full grin in my direction.

Just then Ted came into the morgue still pulling on his gloves. "Does anybody have any mint or cinnamon oil? If I have to do a stinker I'd sure like to avoid smelling it," he said as he moved to the body bag and began opening it.

"At least he's been in the freezer overnight. That ought to help," Steve noted. The colder the body is, the less volatile the fumes are.

"Do you think we could freeze him first?" I asked.

"Come on, let's get started," Dr. Bilmarian ordered as he turned on the dictation equipment. With the Dictaphone running he began with his usual tacky joke.

"How many Chiropractors does it take to change a light bulb?" he asked. "Give up? Only one, but it takes ten visits." His own gales of laughter prevented him from continuing.

"Very funny, That joke is as old as dirt. Do you want me to start with the AMA jokes?" I threatened.

"I quit, I quit," he said still smiling at his dig.

"Okay, I'm ready Ted. Open the bag and let's see what the quack brought us today."

"You're pushing it, buddy," I said, as I backed away from the body bag, fearful of what would come puffing out when it was opened.

Dr. Steve began to dictate in earnest, "Submitted for examination is a Caucasian male with an approximated age of forty-two years. The body arrives sealed in a county issued body bag with evidence seals intact. Removing the body bag reveals a well-decomposed, male body, showing severe signs of skin slippage. The body is clad in blue jeans; a plaid long sleeved shirt, a blaze-orange vest and hat. Several generations of maggots are noted as well as some form of beetle. Samples are taken for review."

"What did you guys do to this body?" Steve asked. "He's falling apart on the table."

"A month locked in a hot car in the woods has a tendency to do that to a person. Of course, the ride off the mountain strapped to the luggage rack of an ATV probably didn't help the situation," I answered.

"That must have been Ed Hill's idea, it sounds like him anyway," Ted observed.

"I was just glad I didn't have to carry him out on my back," I commented.

Steve asked Ted to remove the clothing and save it for evidence. Then he continued his dictation, "The body weighs approximately 187 pounds and measures 68 inches. Gross examination revealed an apparent entrance wound in the left temple measuring 2.0 centimeters by 1.9 centimeters. This wound was approximately 2.9 centimeters posterior to the lateral canthus of the eye. There is severe distortion of the normal facial features, consistent with a GSW (gunshot wound) to the head."

Steve squeezed the head between his hands; the crunching sound demonstrated the fragmentation of the skull.

"The right parietal region exhibits an apparent exit wound measuring 4.9 centimeters by 6.9 centimeters. The tissue in either area is devoid of stippling (little pieces of gunpowder that get under the skin when a weapon is fired at close range) or signs of burning."

Looking up from the foul cadaver, Dr. Steve asked, "Do you think this guy intended to do this to himself?"

"Well, the suicide note found in the truck states he couldn't continue to live with the knowledge that his wife was having an affair."

"I guess that might lead to offing oneself, if anything would," Ted editorialized.

"You're single, what would you know about it?" Steve jibed.

"Has anyone asked where the wife or boyfriend was when this happened?" Steve inquired as he poked and prodded at the body, trying his best to avoid the wafting aroma.

"Since we weren't sure just when it happened, I thought it would be best to wait. A time frame of some sort would help," I answered.

"Let's see if we can determine approximately when it took place," Steve suggested as he motioned for Ted to hand him a fresh scalpel. He continued the postmortem dictation. "Opening the chest and removing the costal tissue reveals the lungs of an apparent smoker. When removed they show no sign of tumor or infarction. A sample of representative tissue is placed in formaldehyde for microscopic review . . ." Steve paused his dictation.

"Rex, judging by what's left of the organs and the number of bugs in here, it looks to me like he probably died about forty days ago."

"Oh, that makes it easy. 'Mrs. Jones, where were you and your boyfriend, say, about forty days ago?' I'll bet the cops will pin 'em down easy on their alibi," I said sarcastically.

Ted smiled and Steve ignored me completely, choosing to continue with his dictation. "Inspection of the thorax and abdomen reveal no signs of tumor, infection or any disease process."

Blood was drawn from the heart and vitreous fluid taken from the eye for further laboratory analysis. Blood will show any recent drug or alcohol use, while the fluid from the eye, due to the near absence of blood flow, retains contaminants for a much longer period of time.

"Since it looks like the cause of death isn't down here," Steve said pointing to the abdomen, "Let's look at the head. It seems as though there might be a cause there. Oh, look it's a gaping gunshot wound to the head," Steve said cynically as he pulled the remaining scalp tissue from the skull fragments.

"And my friends call *me* weird?" I questioned.

"I'm staying out of this one," Ted giggled under his mask.

"Okay, look here," Steve, pointed to the skull which he had placed back together as best as he could. "This hole in the left temple is smaller and better defined than this one in the right side. The bone fragments appear to be blown inward. The left side, however, is nearly completely gone. Did you find a bullet at the scene?" he asked.

"Not a thing, but we haven't checked the vehicle yet. I thought for sure it would be in the body somewhere," I explained.

Steve smiled and removed his gloves saying, "Good luck finding it. If you do, we can weigh it to check for caliber. I'm sure there's not much left of it judging by the damage to the victim's head. Close him up, Ted. I'm outta here."

The autopsy concluded with no further information available. Immediately following the autopsy, Steve took off on his Harley. I had to go over the truck with a fine-toothed comb, but the effort was worth it. Lodged in the side panel between the passenger's window and the windshield was a bullet. It was smashed almost flat but there it was.

Details came together two days later. Detective Stone called to let me know he had received the preliminary autopsy report and had visited with the wife of the deceased. The wife claimed that at the time of the death, she was out of the state at her mother's house. She had tried calling but he never answered the phone. She assumed he had packed up and left, as he had done on several previous occasions. According to her, the idea that she had a boyfriend was pure fiction.

"Sorry, Doc, but I think her story checks out. I wish I could do more. How are you going to rule?" Will inquired.

"I have no idea. So far, I know the guy was shot and I have a flat bullet the size of a quarter, which is no good for ballistics. I think I'm going to sleep on it—the evidence, not the bullet. I'll call you when I figure it out," I promised.

Well, there you go. I've given you all of the facts and several big clues. Just how did this poor schlock die? Have you figured it out?

Was it *murder, suicide, or natural causes?* Don't turn the page until you think you have the answer or you've given up.

LET'S REVIEW

I'm pleased to tell you that the wife didn't do it. For that matter, neither did the victim. Oh, he had the best of intentions; tortured by the thought that his wife was being unfaithful, he intended suicide. However, every once in a while God steps in with a small dose of irony, and here he was—at it again.

Remember what the deceased was wearing? The color called blaze orange? Hunters wear it for visibility. Deer can't see it, but most people can. One month before discovery of the body, it had been rifle season for deer, which was the first clue. The second clue was the direction of the fatal shot. It hit him from the left side, where his window was rolled down about four inches.

The third hint was that his weapons were on the passenger's side on the floor and still loaded. In my experience it's hard to reload a gun with half of your head gone.

What really happened? He went hunting and became depressed. Deciding to commit suicide, he wrote a note and surrounded himself with wallet pictures of his loved ones. Then he consumed a great deal of 100 proof whiskey. However, before he could do the deed, a stray bullet from another hunter, a distance off, passed through the driver's side window. It struck him in the left side of his head.

The cause of death: Accident . . .

Note:

Following the final disposition, our local priest, Father Timothy, who is short, fat and smokes two packs of unfiltered Camels a day, was contacted by the nuns. Sister Sophia noticed the spot where the truck sat for a month was devoid of grass. It was just dirt. The sisters believed if the Father would bless the ground with Holy water, everything would be okay. The nuns dragged the breathless old priest up the hill to the dreaded spot. Reluctantly, he went with the nuns. Not satisfied with the usual sprinkle, the sisters insisted he carry one whole gallon of Holy Water up the mountain.

"Jesus, Joseph and Mary, where in the world are those ATV's you told me about? I thought you said, 'we only had to walk up a hill behind the convent'. You didn't tell me it was a blasted *mountain*. I'm not Moses, you know. I don't climb mountains," he complained constantly as they ascended the peak.

When the group finally reached the location, the priest used the entire gallon, not just to make the sisters happy, but he didn't want to carry it back down the hill.

The truth known, I returned with the nuns to the spot on the hill a short time later. The ground was covered with snow, except for the spot where the truck had been sitting. It was covered with wildflowers.

Ring Around the Rosie;
A Pocket Full of Powder Burns

One afternoon in late August, I was trimming trees on our property. When you live in the forest this is an annual "Y" chromosomal ritual. I was happily involved with this manly endeavor, when I felt the faint vibration of my pager. This was not good. Maybe it was Lori calling me for lunch by beeper, because I'm deaf and she's tired of screaming like a banshee. Or maybe something not nearly as appetizing was waiting at work.

It wasn't lunch.

I anxiously called the county's new computerized message center to pick up my first hi-tech message. I was hoping someone had called to invite me fishing. My arms were tired from sawing and a fishing rod would provide just the therapy I needed. I was greeted by a sweet sounding almost sexy digital voice.

"Welcome to the Pine Park message center."

Cool, I thought. No more gravelly throated Betty giving me a hard time.

"Enter your pin number NOW," the computer prompted.

I complied obediently and waited for my message to play. Several solar systems collapsed as I listened to the sweet voice repeatedly urge me, "Please be patient. All operators are currently busy helping other callers."

Other callers, I thought. Who's she kidding; it's the morgue for Gods-sake.

Finally, the sweet, impersonal, unsympathetic, unaffected, mechanical voice insisted that I "reenter your pin number, please."

Once again, I entered the three-digit code. Another star system collapsed as I waited for clearance to enter this cyber-Hell.

"The pin number you have entered is invalid. Please try again," it ordered, now sounding sarcastic.

Great, now this computer thinks I'm the village idiot. With my luck it's keeping track of the number of attempts I make to access the system. I'm sure I'll be listed somewhere in next month's newsletter. I mean, really how hard can it be? My code is 000. I tried one more time, in vain.

This time, 'the voice' curtly demanded I contact my systems administrator for access. Because, this automated witch now thinks I am obviously some sort of mental midget.

I found myself asking the dial tone, "What's a system administrator?"

Never thought I'd hear myself say this, but give me demented, warped, gravel throated old Betty any day!

Giving up on the new hi-tech system, I called Betty directly in the dispatch center. I took great delight in berating the new system.

"So, just who and what's a system administrator?" I inquired.

"Well, love bucket, I am the one and only goddess of communications and system administrator. Is my pinheaded little coroner having a hard time adapting to the twenty-first century? You know we installed an automated system just so I wouldn't have to deal with people like you all day, don't you?"

"If your fancy system could remember my access code I think I could muddle thru," I jibbed back. "My code is 000 and your machine can't even remember that. Isn't computer language based on ones and zeros?"

"You know the only reason we keep you around is for the laughs don't you? Your pin number is not 000 it's OOO. Check out the letters on your key pad, I'll wait."

"You mean the letter 'O' not the number zero?" I asked, to be sure I understood.

"The letter 'O'," she reiterated, waiting for me to realize O's numerical counterpart on the phone dial.

"Are you kidding me? I have to dial 666 to pick up my messages?" I could hear faint laughter from the earpiece.

"You gave me that number deliberately, didn't you?"

"I thought it was fitting. The Chaplin has 777 and no one else wanted 666. Besides, for a ghoul like you it's easy to remember."

"I give up. Tell 666 what's so urgent."

"Okay, I'll help you out this time, Beelzebub. There has been a death at 13265 Highway 46 North. The name is Frank Lubing. It's a gunshot wound to the head. That's all I know. Now will you get out there before the officer on scene calls me for the fifth time wondering where you are?"

Being coroner in Colorado's smallest county, I knew sooner or later death would call on friend. It comes with the territory. When I first took this job, it was easy. I was new in town and didn't have any friends. As time passed, odds shifted.

I'd known Frank casually for at least five years. He seemed so happy-go-lucky. I couldn't imagine he would ever pop himself. My mind was spinning as I drove. Did my friend really shoot himself? If things were that bad why didn't he call me for support? Was it possible he didn't think of me as a friend, or didn't I hear his plea for help? Wow, guilt over a death. This is a first; it's always been just another dead body to me. I have to put up a hard façade. I call it 'my doctor's face.' If I let my emotions become involved, I wouldn't be help to anyone. I'd be known as 'Rex the crying coroner.' Of course, I feel terrible for the relatives. To lose a family member is traumatic to say the least.

I arrived at the scene finding Deputy Ken Kelly anxiously waiting beside his patrol car.

"Thank God, you're here, I just hate being around stiffs. Your dear departed is out back with Detective McDonald. Just follow the brick path, I'm out of here," he said, as he pulled away spraying dust in my face.

I always get little nervous just before I enter a scene. There is this moment of self-doubt and paranoia; will I remember what to do? Or, will I forget to put film in the camera again, and ruin the case?

"I have to warn you, Doc; he did a pretty good job. His brain is scattered for twenty feet. The crows were at it when we arrived. So, he might not be all there." It was Detective Newman razzing me as I cleared a hedge surrounding the back yard.

"You're telling me, I have to trap crows and pump their stomachs to recover evidence you and your men couldn't protect?"

"Nice to see you too, Doc," he smiled and pointed me toward Frank's resting place.

"Well Ted, you'd best fill me in on what you know so far."

"It looks pretty clear to me he shot himself. What really happened, that's why you're here, and I'm just a cop."

"Sure, pull the cop bit and ditch me here to do the dirty work!"

"That's bull and you know it. All you have to do is use what the 'sixties' left of your little gray cells; Ed and Patty do the entire cleanup."

"Speaking of them; Ed and Patty, not the volume of my functioning gray cells . . ."

"Yes, they were called about the time we paged you. Their big, white, death mobile should come rolling in any minute."

Ted reported that Bob the photographer had finished his photo session, and 'I was free to trample any evidence I came across.' A clear reference to the time I stepped on a deceased's glasses, compromising a crime scene.

Moving around the corner of the house, I could see Frank's body about fifty-feet away, lying limply against a giant Ponderosa pine.

I approached cautiously. If not for the small hole oozing blood in his left temple, I'd half expect him to jump up and yell, "Surprise!" However, from the sizable hole in the right side of his skull, this was not likely.

When someone decides to opt out of this mortal existence using a firearm, there are several telltale signs as to whether they actually did the deed themselves, or had a little help.

So, I began looking for clues to exonerate my friend.

I immediately wrapped his hands in brown paper bags, sealing them with red evidence labels. This would protect any gunpowder residue or foreign material, which might remain on his hands. I was still examining the scene around the body when Ted announced the arrival of Ed and his big death wagon.

"Well, here comes Ed and Patty. I can see their dust cloud coming up the driveway. You know, as fast as that man drives, I should write him a ticket."

"You'll be sorry if you do! Next time you call him to come rescue you from a corpse, he just might drive the speed limit and leave you waiting in knee-deep snow. I can see the headline now 'Local cop freezes to death waiting for mortuary recovery team.'"

"You're right; he does have us at his mercy doesn't he?"

"Us? Don't include me in this. I don't even get a red light on my car. I have to obey the speed limit. The county commissioners say, "You don't need a light. They're dead they'll wait for you." Personally, I don't mind his habitual speeding, as long as I'm not in front of him. Anyway, he's usually on his way to rescue me from a cadaver or two. Don't get me wrong, I'd never want to be a passenger with him at the wheel."

"You wouldn't have too much to say if you were the one in the back. On second thought; you'll probably still be complaining as we lower you into the hole," Ted teased.

"Unless of course, you go first with a fatal case of frostbite."

As Ted looked for the gun I could hear Ed coming around the hedge, singing, "Hi ho, hi ho, a body here must go . . ."

"That is one sick man," Ted whispered. "I think he enjoys his job a little too much."

"Oh, my friend, you're mistaking his facade. When you deal with death every day, the mind develops ways to cope with the depressive nature. I think I'd rather have him singing than show up in a shroud dragging one leg behind him, sounding like the Bella Lugosi."

"I remember . . ."

"Oh, Doc, not another 'I remember' story. Can't you just tell it to Frank? He has a lot of time on his hands now and I'm sure he'd love to hear all about it."

"As I was saying before I was so rudely interrupted. When I was an intern in Los Angeles, we did so many violence related autopsies, I became slightly paranoid and started carrying a gun. If you think Ed's nuts, you don't know the meaning of the word. I've worked with certifiable nuts."

"You're going to tell me anyway, aren't you?"

"Like I was saying, California's autopsy suite had eight tables all operating at the same time twenty-four hours a day, seven days week. Occasionally, to break the boredom someone would yell 'INCOMING!' At that point you'd better duck. It meant someone on the other side of the room had just lobbed a spleen in your direction. The spleen being a blood filled organ, it splattered hemoglobin everywhere when it landed. It was a sick kind of water balloon fight."

"Forget Ed. You're the sick one."

"Telling him about the spleen toss? That's a trade secret. You could be disciplined for it," Ed smiled.

Ted, now grossed out by the visual image of a spleen fight, retreated to search elsewhere for the missing gun. Ed knelt next to me by the body as Ted made his escape.

"Wow, it looks like Frank did quite a job on himself."

"That's putting it mildly, if he did it himself. The main problem here is there seems to be no gun. That makes shooting yourself kind of difficult doesn't it?"

"Ah, you can't fool me. You know as well as I do, when the bullet passes through the brain, a victim loses motor control and can't hold the gun; not to mention the gasses throwing it out of his hand. Wouldn't you be more suspicious if the gun was still in his hand? Gotcha, don't I? You think someone else killed him. I know you so well. 'Every death is murder until proven otherwise,'" Ed was grinning from his pseudo victory.

"Well, buddy who knows me so well. You're right. I've seen suicide weapons tossed quite a distance. Now, in this case there's gray matter spread twenty feet over the lawn. I still see no gun. I find it difficult to believe the heavy metal gun flew further than his brain did. Don't you?"

"Have I told you lately just how much I hate you?" Ed said, mocking a serious expression.

"I'm happy to bring you sleuths a body bag and some rubber gloves. But, if you think for one minute I'm the one getting stuck picking up brain pieces, you have another thing coming." It was Patty protesting as she brought a body bag from the wagon. I noticed she bore only two pair of extra-large latex gloves.

"Don't worry, dear. Frank didn't have much in that head of his . . . it won't be difficult," Ed chuckled.

"It'll be easy," Ted stated sardonically, as he pretend to look for the gun. "The crows carried away most of it for you. If you wait any longer they'll have the job done completely."

The scene did seem to be getting a lot of attention from ravens in the nearby trees. I think they were just waiting for us to leave so they could finish their afternoon buffet.

"Great, it'll be fun trying to explain to Dr. Bilmarian why there's no brain tissue left to examine," I mumbled. "He thinks I'm nuts now; wait until I try and explain how a crazed flock of crows descend on us, as if sent by Satan himself. There were thousands of them and they consumed of the evidence."

"Yeah, use that one. I'm sure he'll buy it," Patty chuckled as she relented and gingerly began picking up remains from the lawn.

"The entrance wound is perfect. Anyone want to join me in a chorus of ring around the Rosie?" Ed joked as he began to help Patty retrieve what was left of Frank's gray matter from the grass. They placed the tissue in small evidence bags.

"'Ring around the Rosie?' I told you he was demented," Ted mumbled as he continued looking for the gun.

*   *   *

I should explain. The term 'Ring around the Rosie' refers to the appearance of a close gunshot wound. When the muzzle of a weapon is held in contact with the skin it makes a pretty little hole surrounded by a distinctive speckled pattern of unburned gunpowder, bone and blood. Remember, not only the bullet comes out of the barrel, so do the explosive gasses and bits of gunpowder.

Since the skull is a sealed unit, gasses from a gun firing into it have nowhere to go as they expand. The result is bruising around the eyes and a large exit wound somewhere on the skull, often on the opposite side. Unless of course, they use a small caliber weapon, in which case the projectile has a tendency to just rattle around in there.

On first sight, the entrance hole looks a lot like a rose in partial bloom, thus our slang term.

The Rosie's size is a big help in determining how far away the muzzle was from the point of entrance. The farther away the business end of the weapon is, the more dispersed the burn pattern. However, at distances beyond two or three feet, there are no powder burns.

Since Frank had what Ed referred to as 'quite a Rosie,' we can assume the barrel was in close contact with his skin. The question: was Frank holding the illusive firearm or did someone else hold it for him? If we could find the gun, fingerprints would make the job easy.

*   *   *

"Okay, we've picked up the big pieces. There were sixty-eight of them, if you're keeping count. As for the rest, it's mostly syrup and it will just have to be hosed into the grass. I'll bet this will be a really green lawn next year," Patty joked.

"You're all sick!" Ted observed aloud.

"Since the scene looks pretty clear of evidence, including of course the gun, and Bob has photographed everything, why don't we just bag him up and get out of here?" I suggested. No one argued.

Patty put the evidence bags into a sealed cooler while Ted and Ed placed Frank into the black body bag. Ed wheeled the gurney to the wagon threatening to leave Patty if she didn't hurry up.

"If they're leaving, so am I. Something about this place gives me the creeps." Ted escaped by offering to carry the cooler for Patty.

I took a good look around for the gun before leaving. The crows hovered waiting for me to finish whatever stupid human thing I was doing. I looked everywhere thinking the person who shot Frank had dropped it in their escape. The attempt was futile. There was just no gun. I was certain the police would be back later with a metal detector to try again. Well, at least I hoped so. They left enough evidence tape around the scene to choke a horse.

Patty and Ed delivered the human sized 'Zip Lock' containing Frank to the morgue within an hour. They placed him in the cooler, knowing his post mortem wouldn't be until Monday. There was no way Dr. Bilmarian would start so late in the day. He was golfing.

The following morning at seven o'clock sharp my home phone rang. Now, one must keep in mind in my world there is no such thing as seven a.m. I stumbled from bed to answer it. Anything to stop its incessant ringing; I tried my best to sound perky and awake. Not wanting whomever this inconsiderate bastard was to know they had waken me. My new friend, "the mechanical voice," greeted my fraudulently polite, perky hello.

"Doctor Reedman, your postmortem examination has been scheduled for today at two o'clock." Without another word, the system disconnected. Hanging up the receiver, I realized I'd just received a robotic phone call informing me of my own apparent autopsy today at two. I hope this computer doesn't know something I don't. I guarantee Betty is going to hear from good-ole 666 about this.

While I spent the night sleeping, Ted had the late shift. He wasted no time in beginning his investigation.

I arrived at the office, late as always. On the way to my cubicle, I stole a Styrofoam cup of lukewarm coffee from the micro lab. Suddenly it dawned on me as I guzzled my java just why it's called the microbiology lab . . . they grow bad things in there. Maybe, I should reconsider and bring my own coffee from home tomorrow.

Looking at my desk I couldn't believe the number of notes from Ted. There was a pile bigger than I wanted to read. I knew if I didn't at least read through them Ted would be insulted. He had apparently been back to Frank's house with a metal detector and found no sign of the gun. He did report however, finding 'twenty-three bottle caps, one rusted pocketknife, what was left of a Vote for Eisenhower button, and a dollar-eighty-three in assorted coinage. Oh, and near the body's location one 45 shell casing.'

His second memo noted he had 'called out a dog team to search for the gun. It, too, was unsuccessful.'

The third of his Post-It notes informed me 'the dogs were of no use, and apparently were more interested in the area around the crows buffet zone.'

I was afraid to read any further. Had this mad man called out a psychic in the middle of the night? Had I missed a séance? Eh, it wouldn't matter. Frank wasn't much of a talker in life; somehow I doubt he'd be any more vocal in death.

Ted's litany of notations seemed endless. Didn't this guy have anything else to do last night but sit and fill my desk with Post-It notes? Overall, he seemed to discover Frank was a lifelong bachelor. (Duh, everyone knew that!) Sherlock also uncovered the fact the deceased owned two companies along with his partner, Jack Hinkle. The businesses were profitable and well insured.

There didn't seem to be any strife between the owners. His employees all appeared to love him, 'he was always there and knew your name.' As far as Ted could gather, Frank had a pretty ordinary life. 'He didn't belong to any clubs or organizations. It seemed this guy just went to work, came home and occasionally went shooting.'

Now, the first thing to enter my mind when hearing somebody is as squeaky clean as he seemed to be is, there's more going on here than anyone knows. Everyone has the dark or secret side they rarely show the world. Sometimes it's a secret or two hidden somewhere in their belongings or past. After death we find a lot about people and their lives. Somewhat like going through your ninety-year-old grandma's steamer trunk after her funeral, only to find she once lived in Paris and was a can-can dancer. It's seems strange to me how well we get to know someone after they're dead. In this case, we would have to find what drove Frank to do this to himself. Was there a dark secret someone held over him? Had he done something he just couldn't live with? Or, was this a case of cold-blooded murder staged to look like a self-termination? I was feeling a bit weird digging into the personal life of a friend. I was afraid of what I might discover and if it would change my opinion of him. It would be hard to keep a straight face at the funeral knowing the deceased had a fetish for rubber chickens or something weird.

Somewhere in my mind it seemed there was a link between Frank's current room temperature condition and some business endeavor. The crime scene didn't reflect any excessive hatred as one might expect to see in a lovers' quarrel. You know, like eighty-nine stab wounds to the chest. This was a single, well-placed shot. Was this really a suicide or had someone placed a perfect shot into the side of his head, making it look like he did it himself?

Before I knew it, two o'clock arrived and it was time to open Frank up.

"Dr. Reedman, report to suite one," Betty announced over the intercom.

I hurried because I didn't want to miss the unveiling. Opening a sealed body bag is something of a ritual. It's a mix of Christmas, because everyone in the room is anxious to see what we've got and Halloween, when you're not entirely sure the thing isn't going to jump out at you screaming while trying to sink its long fangs into your neck.

Entering the autopsy suite, I was of course late. Dr. Bilmarian looked at me and began to quote, "Once upon a midnight dreary, while I pondered weak and weary."

"Okay, so you're either a big fan of Poe or someone ratted to you about the crow problems we had."

"Now, what would make you think a thing like that?" he smiled.

"Look, it really wasn't my fault. It was Ted and his bunch they couldn't keep the damn birds away," I explained.

"Ugly as you are, you couldn't give them a hand and frighten away at least one crow?"

"Now, that's not fair," I protested. "Frank looks much scarier than I do."

Bilmarian continued his harassment as Ted entered the room.

"Hey, I helped toss him in there and I guarantee right now, Frank's no 'Beauty Queen.' Anyone breathing in this room looks better than he does. Trust me," Ted answered.

"I think a few of the ones not breathing look better than he does," I added.

"Well then, there's nothing left to do but open up this oversized baggie so we can find out what which of you is the real winner," Dr. Bilmarian suggested.

Unzipping the black rubber coated container, we moved Frank to the autopsy table where we could begin the external examination. Ted stood back as Dr. Bilmarian began his dictation. Me, I've got my face right in the middle of it, forgetting for the moment this is one of my friends.

"The deceased arrives clothed in a flannel hunting jacket in a red and black checkered pattern, blue jeans, western shirt and cowboy boots. His hands are bagged and sealed with red evidence tape bearing Rex's signature," he began his dictation.

"I didn't do a gunshot residue on his hands. I just bagged them," I admitted.

"Let's do it now before we screw up and forget."

While continuing to dictate, he unwrapped the seals and collected samples from both hands,

"The deceased shows large raccoon-like bruising surrounding the eyes bilaterally." He paused his microphone. "I guess it's time to play strip the cadaver, if I can get this arm out of the jacket sleeve," Dr. 'B' continued his examination by disrobing the body. "Judging by his state of rigor mortis he died sometime Saturday morning."

As he pulled the left arm from the jacket sleeve the room reverberated with the oddest sound. Strangely enough, it sounded like a handgun hitting a tile floor. The three of us stared at the 45-ca. revolver now resting on the floor against Ted's boot. I could see Ted was relieved it hadn't gone off and at the same time feeling a lot like the new village idiot. He'd had men and dogs looking over hundreds of square yards in search of a weapon, the very one which just dropped from the victims jacket pocket. Ted hadn't searched the body assuming I would do it and I didn't do it because I thought he already had.

"Well, it looks as if we've found the gun," Dr. Bilmarian noted. "Outstanding detective work, officer. You should be commended on your fine abilities!"

"You mean committed, don't you?" I added.

Ted just stood there blankly looking down at the gun. Its barrel was pointed directly at a very sensitive male place.

I could tell Dr. Bilmarian was smiling broadly behind his blue surgical mask.

"I'm surprised it didn't fall out when we bagged him," Ted feebly attempted to regain his composure. "I'll just run it down the hall for a quick print check. Ted carefully slid the gun into a manila folder, being cautious not to touch it. "I'll let be right back."

"Oh sure, he'll be right back, just about the time we're finished here," Doc chuckled.

He knew Ted hated autopsies and would do anything to get out of one.

"I'll bet he stays to personally supervise the process," he continued his abuse of the now absent Ted.

Dr. Bilmarian resumed dictating while continuing his examination of the corpse.

". . . The left of the cranium exhibits a small rose shaped entrance wound consistent with that of a close contact gunshot wound. Moving to the right side of the patient's head, we find an explosive exit wound. This is consistent with the use of a large caliber weapon, similar to the one which has now been recovered for analysis." This time I could see the smile thru the corner of his mask.

Doc began measuring the entrance and exit wounds. He diagramed and photographed them from every angle, direction and all at different distances. It was my job to hold the ruler type scale in the each photo. I have a photogenic thumb.

Our next step was to place a steel rod in through the entrance wound, and out of what we could reconstruct as the point of exit.

*   *   *

Using a rod in this way allows for a bullet's trajectory to be analyzed. In most suicides, the entrance point is lower than the exit. This seems to hold true no matter what hand dominant the deceased was. There appear to be two ways in which there are exceptions to the rule.

Men who have served in the military have a tendency when shooting themselves to do it standing and prefer a single shot to the temple. They also have the unique tendency of turning their thumb toward the floor. Now, the handgun is upside-down. This results in flatter trajectory, thus the entrance and exit wounds are more level. Of course, this is also a pattern we see in murder made-to-look like suicide.

When the average Joe decides to do 'the deed,' there are two favorite ways. The first method is in the mouth. This ends up taking out most of the occipital region (back) of the skull. If our hypothetical victim decides he is 'just going to blow his brains out,' he will typically lean the barrel of the gun upward against his temple and 'bang.' The result here is what we see most often, an entrance wound lower than the corresponding exit injury. Of course, there is third possibility if a midget shot you!

* * *

"Well, Rex, my best estimate based on the lividity patterns is that he was in a seated position when he died. In that position these head wounds line up parallel to the floor. That shot went straight across through his temples, and I might add, at close range."

"A level shot, straight thru and at close range, eh?"

"I know where your mind is going. You think someone snuck up behind him and blasted a shot level thru his head," Dr. Bilmarian teased.

"Don't forget, after completing the task, they put the gun in his jacket pocket. Oh, yeah, then they escaped unseen," I had to add my peace.

"Unseen? Let's see here, the man lives miles out of town, has no lighting, virtually no neighbors and you're amazed your villain escaped undetected. That is, if he existed in the first place. Can't anybody ever just simply die around you or is everything murder?"

"You know, you and Ted are beginning to sound alike. There're tests to do yet."

"Speaking of which, why don't you give me a hand here and finish up Frank's final probing. My trustworthy ghoul called in sick today."

Wonderful Ted is down the hall drinking coffee. He gets to eat doughnuts while he waits for the fingerprint, blood trace, and gunpowder residue tests. That should take most of the day. If we ever find the bullet we can do ballistics' and he can waste more time supervising. At least we have a gun and we can use it to match chamber marks with the shell casings Ted recovered from the crime scene.

Me, on the other hand, I get to help wade through what remains of the corpse. Continuing our exploration, we drew ocular fluid and cardiac blood for analysis.

*   *   *

Fluid from within the eye is often compared with blood from the heart. The heart has a high number of blood vessels; this blood would reflect conditions closer to the time of death.

The eye on the other hand has very small, narrow vessels, so circulation to the fluid within the eye takes much longer. A poison or a toxin found within the ocular (eye) fluids would lead one to assume long-term exposure, while a poison or toxin found within the circulatory system might only have been there for a short time. Of course, there's always hair analysis.

*   *   *

Next came the sectioning and sampling of all of Frank's internal organs. He even took a piece of what the crows left. Once Doc was satisfied he'd seen everything there was to see, and he had a little piece of it, he thought we should close.

His demeanor reminded me of a demented tourist, 'Just picking up a knick-knack for the kids back at home.'

In this case, it was liver and lungs. My children received no souvenirs that day.

In the following few days some of the forensic evidence came in. Hank Boren, our in-house genius, took great delight in torturing me with the results.

"Hey, doctor death. Want to see some interesting readouts?" he said, poking his head over my cubicle wall.

"Can I stop you?"

"I think you're going to like what I have to show you." He held up a folder about an inch thick.

"Okay, what has the mad scientist found?"

He opened the folder to show me computer printouts. "See, can you believe it?"

"It what? I have no idea what you are showing me. It looks like an EKG and I know he shouldn't have one of those."

"These are the blood gasses! See here where the red line goes way up?"

"Sure, now I understand," I mocked.

"This is his alcohol level. See the blue one? That's his barbiturate titer."

"So, what you're telling me is, Frank was drunk and stoned at the time of his demise?"

"Stoned and drunk would be like saying 'the Titanic made a short stop to take on ice!' I would be amazed if he could walk, or for that matter, even aim a gun in his state. His blood levels are almost off of the chart. If he'd waited an hour or so, he'd probably have died of cardiac arrest or alcohol poisoning."

"Well, your charts sure make me think more about murder than suicide."

Hank retreated to his lab satisfied he'd thrown me a curve. How can someone blind drunk hold up a heavy gun and pull the trigger? I guess hitting a target at point blank range wouldn't be too hard.

The real curve I didn't see coming. Ted showed up about an hour after Hank had dropped his bombshell. He had a couple of 'problems' with the evidence in his little folder.

"Okay, I have good news and bad news what would you like to hear first?" He held a folder to his chest.

"Don't toy with me. I know, it's all bad news so, just get on with it."

"Wow, what put you in this mood?"

"Sorry, Hank just let me know that Frank was stoned on barbiturates and blind drunk at the time he died. You're here to tell me that it's not Frank, right?"

"Pessimist, I'm here to tell you that Frank had no gunshot residue on his hands, but interestingly enough there were powder burns in the pocket lining".

"That could mean someone else held the gun inside his pocket and pulled the trigger," I hypothesized aloud.

"Oh, I have better news. You are the luckiest man alive. It turns out the prints on the gun belong to his business partner!"

"Who by now has douched his hands in everything from Windex to gasoline."

"Don't worry. I sent a team to meet with the partner yesterday. I had them print him and do a GSR test. The fool didn't even want a lawyer," Ted gloated at his efficient work.

"Well, are you going to tell me the results of the tests?"

"Sure, they were positive!"

"You mean, he'd fired a gun before you interviewed him?" Could it be this easy?

"Oh, it's not him. He has an airtight alibi. It seems he'd been out target shooting the same morning."

"Alone I expect."

"Nope, he was with Bob Riggers, the manager of the produce department at Town Market."

"Let me get this straight; the dead guy with the gun in his pocket has no residue on his hands, but the business partner does?" I asked just to be sure I hadn't gone insane.

"That's pretty much it for now. Oh wait, there was one more thing," he said, sounding like Colombo. "Dr. Bilmarian found a letter to the deceased in the jeans pocket. It was from his business partner to Frank questioning a recent personal purchase with company funds. He also found a second shell casing in the jacket pocket. Apparently, there was a rip in the lining".

"Wow, maybe things weren't all milk and honey between the two. Sounds like the one who could benefit most might want to take care of his financial drain, personally."

"There's nothing worse than a scorned woman or cheated business partner," Ted observed.

"I've had both; trust me I'll take the ex-wife over the business partner any day. With the wife, she only wants everything you own, all the money you'll ever earn and any external evidence of your 'Y' chromosome. A partner, on the other hand, wants his money and your hide. In this case, it's looking like someone wanted the hide."

My workday ended at five-thirty. Home to my big chair was all I could think of. As with most things in life, the thought is always better than reality. My recliner brought me no solace. My mind kept scanning for a solution by running the facts over and over again.

Frank was highly intoxicated to say the least. He had a note in his pocket, which might be viewed as bad news, therefore driving him to suicide. On the other hand, it wasn't a suicide note. This meant we'd have to assume it was not self-inflicted, for now.

He had a close contact shot to his head and yet no gunshot residue on his hands. Did that mean the note should be viewed as a threat? Was he murdered? How could that be? The scene showed no apparent struggle. However, someone could have snuck up from behind him while he was napping.

Now, Ted tells me there are two shell casings. Who takes two shots to kill himself? I wondered about the high levels of alcohol and especially the barbiturates. Had Frank been doing a drug deal and the dealer did him in? Was one a practice shot or did he miss the first time? Of course, there was the possibility the one found in the pocket could be from a previous use of the gun? The questions were still racing in my head as I slipped to sleep.

The next day brought no great revelation about Frank. Just the persistent question of how Frank's prints weren't on the gun and his buddies were? It was going to be up to Ted and his crew to find the links in this case. Ted just loves doing what he calls the footwork. I think he has a sadistic side that loves to see the person he's questioning sweat and squirm. He makes his own friends nervous when he begins to ask questions at parties.

*   *   *

Ted's inquisition process began with the partner, his prime suspect. He took no time in arranging a face-to-face meeting. It was held on neutral ground to keep the victim off guard. The choice was Mama's Kitchen, a favorite breakfast spot in town. As usual, Ted would arrive early. He'd get a booth in the rear with his back to the wall. This allowed him to observe his victim before they knew they were being watched. Also, there's a psychological effect on the victim. When he can't see who's behind him, he becomes uneasy. This uneasiness makes it a breeze for Ted to trip someone in a lie.

* * *

Ted didn't want to be out gamed so, twenty minutes before the arranged time, he arrived and secured his favorite booth. He sipped coffee waiting for his prey to enter the web.

Jack Hinkle, local businessman and part time real-estate investor, slowly scanned the restaurant looking for Ted. It didn't take long for Jack to find Ted's table tucked in the corner. As he sat down, he ordered a cup of coffee.

"I thought I'd be your first suspect," Jack said, as he calmly added cream to his coffee.

"Good morning to you, too," Ted sarcastically replied. He drank from his cup and looked directly at Jack over the rim.

"Well, I thought we'd cut through the soft sell and get right to the point. He didn't have any relatives and I'm his business partner. I'm the one to profit. Therefore, I'm the guy to look at first."

"Gee, you've convinced me. You must be my man. Finish your coffee and we can take a ride down to my office. This was the easiest case I've ever had."

"You know I don't think that's funny, don't you?" Jack was not smiling. He didn't mind pointing out the obvious himself, but didn't really want to be under scrutiny. He'd thought if he pointed out the fact he would gain from Frank's demise; Ted would reassure him he wasn't under suspicion. After all, it was just a suicide.

"Just kidding, you'll have to take your own car," Ted's cup hid his smile.

"No really, I didn't have anything to do with that idiot taking his own life! I was miles away at the time."

"What time was that?"

"I don't know exactly, but whenever he was killed."

"'Killed?' You said, killed. You didn't say committed suicide. Why?"

Ted was now completely enjoying himself. He could see Jack begin to shake slightly and his voice was cracking. These were signs of being nervous, but about what aspect of the questioning. Was he just worried Ted might find out he was with his mistress or, had he shot his partner?

"I don't know when he died, so I can't tell you where I was. All I know is I wasn't there and I didn't do it," Jack was adamant about his own innocence.

"You still haven't answered my question. Why did you say killed instead of suicide?" Ted tightened the screws.

"I meant to say suicide but it's so hard to believe much less say when a friend dies."

"Just a minute ago you referred to the recently deceased as an 'idiot' or is my mind slipping?" Ted was not going to let one misspeak get by him.

267

"I meant an idiot for shooting himself. He was a nice guy in real life." Jack forced a smile.

"Well Jack, here's the problem," Ted paused to slowly sip his coffee.

"Your good buddy and business partner died of a 'gunshot to the head'. Are you with me so far?"

"Yes, so what?" Jack readjusted his position in his chair.

"The funny thing is, he didn't have any gunshot residue on his hands."

"And?"

"It's kind of hard to shoot yourself and then clean your hands, isn't it? An even funnier thing is, at the time my deputy tested your hands, you did test positive for gunshot residue. You see how it makes me wonder."

Jack sat back in his chair. "It was Saturday, right? Well, I had gone shooting in the morning. That would explain the residue on my hands and since newer automatic weapons blow back very little if any gasses that would explain the lack of gunshot residue on Frank." The muscles in his face twitched unconsciously as he offered his alibi.

"Shooting in the morning. Was it a human target?" Ted coldly watched Jack's pupils for a reaction. There was none.

"Paper targets."

"I suppose you had company on this safari, someone who could back up your tale?"

"It's not a tale. It's the truth. You can ask Bob Riggers from the market. He was with me." Jack hoped having a witness would take the heat off of him.

"I'll make a call to Bob and verify your story. I have just one more question, then we can order something to eat. I'm starving."

"What now?" Jack was getting agitated and slightly paranoid.

"Can you tell me how your fingerprints were found on the gun and poor old Frank's weren't? You know it just strikes me as kind of strange that you have the residue and your prints are the only ones on the gun."

The blood drained from his face. "Oh God, he used the 45 didn't he?"

"45, interesting you mention that. I don't think we've told anyone. How did you know the caliber of the weapon?" Ted couldn't believe his ears. This guy was just digging himself deeper with every word. However, as long as Jack wasn't under arrest, Ted wasn't required to provide a lawyer or tell him to keep quiet.

"It was my gun," Jack sheepishly admitted.

"This is looking better and better for you here, Jack. Partner dead, gunshot residue, your prints, and now your gun." Ted smiled, he was sure he had his man.

"I loaned him the gun three months ago. He was thinking about buying one for himself."

"It sounds like it wasn't your best decision. I'll check your alibi. I'm sure Bob will clear this up for you. Let's eat, I'm starved," Ted grinned broadly, which completely unnerved Jack.

Jack excused himself. "I'm not that hungry. I think I'll just go to the office."

Ted enjoyed a big farmer's plate and three more cups of coffee before returning to work.

It took no time for Ted to locate Bob. 'Town Market' isn't that big.

"Bob, I'm looking into Frank Lubing's death. Could you answer a few questions?" Ted asked quietly.

"Sure, anything I know," Bob looked up from the ground beef he was stocking.

"Where were you on Saturday morning?"

"It's my day off. I was out at the crack of dawn target shooting."

"Were you alone?" Ted inquired.

"I was until about ten o'clock when Jack Hinkle showed up. We stayed until about twelve-thirty. Jack's a lousy shot but I've got to give him credit. He keeps trying."

"How is he at close range?"

"Close range?" Bob looked puzzled.

"Oh, nothing, I was just thinking aloud. Thanks, Bob. You've confirmed what Jack said. That's all I needed to know."

Ted returned to the office with his hot information.

"Hey, Doctor Death, I just had breakfast with Jack Hinkle and a quick chat with Bob from the market. Want to hear some juicy info?"

"Don't tell me, the coffee was cold and there's a special on frozen chicken."

"No, but my breakfast companion was pretty cool," Ted leaned against my cubicle wall almost knocking it down. "He sat there and calmly informed me Frank's 45 was on loan. It seems the weapon belongs to Jack!"

"I know that. The serial number came back this morning showing Jack Hinkle as the registered owner." Now, I was the one smiling. I had beaten him to the information and didn't even leave the office.

"Well then, Dr. Smarty Pants, did you know Bob Riggers confirmed Jack's alibi? He joined Bob about ten o'clock and they shot until around noon."

"So, Jack really was shooting at the time of Frank's death. You know, I just didn't believe him for some reason. Maybe it was the note in Frank's pocket. It sounded ominous. What did he have to say about the note?" I asked.

"Oh, God, the note! I forgot to ask him. I'll have to track him down and inquire about it." Ted looked slightly embarrassed he'd forgotten the letter.

"Ted, good buddy, I'd go back and ask about it. For some reason Jack thought Frank was stealing money from the company, probably for his drug habit."

"Drug use and embezzlement of company funds, now there's motive for murder," Ted appeared uplifted by the thought.

"Or, a great reason to off yourself if you thought you'd been discovered," I added.

"Spoilsport, you know murder is much more fun than plain old suicide."

Ted left to find Jack and quiz him for the second time today.

In a small town it doesn't take long to find someone, or for that matter, be found. Jack was easy to locate. He has personalized license plates on his Mercedes, 'HOTSHOT.'

"Sorry to interrupt," Ted said, poking his head into Jack's office.

"You, again. I thought you'd asked me everything at breakfast." Jack was annoyed about being questioned at work.

"There was just one more thing. I forgot to mention your letter to Frank. We found it in his pocket." Ted sat down near Jack's desk.

"Okay, the accountant discovered fifty-thousand dollars missing from our books. He thought it looked like Frank had stolen it. I just wrote him officially, as required by the Securities and Exchange Commission, to inform him we would be doing an investigation." Jack pulled a copy of the letter from his desk drawer and handed it to Ted. "Here, keep it."

"Did you know Frank was ripping off the company?"

"I had a good idea he was getting extra money somewhere, judging by his spending habits. Embezzling from the company, I had no idea."

"What was he buying that made you suspicious?" Ted took out his little black notebook and began scribbling.

"It wasn't so much what he bought. It was more about how he began acting. He seemed nervous and jumpy for the past six months. There were days we couldn't reach him. He was angry when we had business to do. It was like it was interfering with his life." Jack rocked back in his chair.

"Did you have any idea of what was bothering him?" Ted inquired.

"I thought he felt overworked and suggested he take a vacation or even retire. It wasn't like he needed the money."

"What was his reaction?"

"He got angry, accusing me of trying to take control of the company. That was two weeks ago."

As Ted was interviewing Jack, the mail arrived. Jack sifted through the bundle of letters as he listened to Ted jabber on.

"Well, I guess you have control now, don't you?"

"I didn't want control. That's too much work. I wanted to retire and play." He opened one of the letters as he spoke. "Oh my God, it's a letter from Frank." He turned gray in the face as he read.

"Well, what does a dead man have to say?" Ted could hardly control himself. He wanted to rip the document from Jack's hands and read it for himself.

"It's in response to my letter about the investigation. Here you read it," Jack said, as he handed the letter to Ted.

> *Memo: Mr. Jack Hinkle*
> *From: Mr. Frank Lubing*
> *Re: Company control*
>
> *Jack, you dirty bastard,*
> *How dare you accuse me of theft? One half of that company is mine and I can take whatever I want. If you want control of the company, it's yours. Just send me a cashier's check for two million dollars for my half and you can have it all.*
> *I will get even with you for this even if it kills me!*
>
> > *Sincerely*
> > *Frank*

"It sounds like he was just a little pissed at you," Ted commented. "Will you copy this for me? I'd like one for the files."

Ted returned to the office, letter in hand.

"Well, it sounds like there was a power struggle going on between Jack and room temperature Frank," Ted whispered over my cubicle wall.

"Power over what?" I whispered back over the divider.

"The company. While I was there Jack received a letter from the corpse. Read it, I already have a copy."

A letter sized piece of paper floated over the cubicle wall, landing on my desk.

"Well, as my grandpa would say 'doesn't that put a wrinkle on the dog?' I had been considering Frank took his own life somehow but if he was planning on doing himself in, why would he request two million dollars? He wouldn't be able to spend it."

"And, if it was about control of the company, why kill yourself? Kill your partner," Ted suggested.

"You know, I was thinking that, too. There was profit and power for each of them if the other one were to die."

Ted and I spent several days pondering the evidence we'd gathered. By Friday we were ready to make a ruling in the "Lubing" case.

Don't turn the page until you have reviewed all of the evidence. Was Frank's death due to murder, suicide, or maybe just an accident?

REX RULES

This was a complex case and not a simple one to rule on. There were several potential scenarios and none of them were good. In a situation like poor room temperature Frank's, how the case is ruled could affect the living profoundly.

If I ruled this a homicide, Jack Hinkle could go to jail for life or get the needle. If Bob Riggers was lying to help Jack, he would be facing some time in the big house as well. If I were to rule this suicide or an accident, Jack stood to gain financially from the insurance as well as inheriting the company outright.

In Colorado, one of the primary requirements for ruling a suicide is some form of notification of intent. In the old days this meant a note or perhaps witness. Now, in the age of modern technology notification, it could be in the form of an e-mail or voice message.

In this case, notification could have been the letter Frank sent to Jack via U.S. Mail. Frank did threaten to make Jack pay even if it 'killed' him. I had to consider that Frank had set this up to look like Jack did it. Sure he'd be dead, but Frank would be in prison for the rest of his life. Revenge does not always make sense to the stable minded.

In this case there are a few loose threads, five of them to be exact.

The first thing to consider was the lack of gunpowder residue on ambient temperature Frank's hands. The rip in the jacket lining explained this. When the weapon was placed in the pocket, it was put in the hole between the coat lining and the pocket. When the gun was fired the lining trapped the residue, while his hand in the pocket was protected from exposure.

The second complicating factor was the gunshot residue on partner Jack's hands. We had to entertain the idea that Jack was being truthful with his explanation about target practice. He did have a witness. However, since the exact time of death could not be determined, we must consider Jack had opportunity to do the deed and then join Bob at target practice.

Next to consider was the flat trajectory of the projectile. This sent me back to the jacket looking for an answer. As repulsive as it might seem, I tried on Frank's coat in an attempt to reenact the scene. I found it imposable to lift my hand to my head without inverting my grip on the gun. Therefore, when Frank placed his hand in the coat pocket, the only way he could put the gun to his head was to turn his hand upside down, thereby creating the straight across shot.

The fourth complication to think about was the two casings. Since one of the casings was found in the jacket pocket, we can be fairly certain it was the shell that killed Frank. The other casing was most likely from a previous testing of the gun. However, we must consider a killer could have left it behind as well.

Lastly, Frank's reported behavior. Frank exhibited classic symptoms of depression. He withdrew from friends and associates. He displayed a total disinterest in daily activities or business endeavors. People who suffer depression tend to 'self-medicate'. Often, this is done with the use of alcohol or drugs. In this case, Frank chose a combination of alcohol and barbiturates.

After reviewing these facts, I came to the conclusion Frank did indeed off himself. I was certain he staged this to frame his partner for the death. Circumstances led me to believe this show was planned far ahead of time. He had the foresight to borrow his partner's gun and protected the fingerprints that came with it.

The letter Jack received met the qualifications of a suicide threat. As for the coat lining, I found it extremely hard to believe Frank placed the gun there by accident. By putting the gun within the coat, Frank brilliantly protected his partner's fingerprints on the gun and at the same time kept gunpowder residue off his hands. Placing the weapon in the pocket also kept the gun in place after it was fired. Most often the weapon is thrown from the hand as the fatal shot is fired due to the force of the explosion and simultaneous loss of muscle control as the brain is liquefied, We are always suspicious when the gun is still in the deceased's hand, a sure sign it was placed there. With the gun in the jacket lining, as his hand was thrown from the gun, the lining retained it. This would lead investigators to believe he had not shot himself, brilliant!

Ruling: Suicide. Cause of death: Self-inflicted gunshot to the head.

The Lady of the Lake

To me, Colorado is beautiful any time of year. I enjoy the fall snow when it comes down like powder and only requires a broom to be removed. I even revel in the spring snow when it's so heavy, deep and clogs my snow blower every two feet.

Summer, however, is my absolute favorite. The days are warm, sunny and afternoon thunderstorms can be counted on to cool the evening off.

I am obviously not alone in my admiration for the pleasures of Colorado summers. About mid-May motor homes, trucks hauling boats and pop-up tents begin flooding into town. Some are here for the entire season; others are headed up to numerous alpine lakes, big boats tightly in tow.

We enjoy keeping a small secret from our visitors in Pine Park. 'Sometimes it snows in June or even July.' Shopkeepers smile at the tourist in his plaid shorts, sandals and black socks, knowing in about an hour temperatures will drop thirty degrees and then snow ten inches.

Our search and rescue groups are often called out to find some poor unprepared hiker or camper missing in a surprise June blizzard.

Between high altitude and almost nightly sub-freezing temperatures, there are places here in the mountains where snow never melts. This makes for a lovely sight, fishing where the temperature is in the seventies looking up at snowcapped peaks and high valleys.

At high altitude something else rarely warms up, the water in those lovely deep blue lakes. By deep blue I do not mean just their deep azure color, I mean depth. Most are so deep the average temperature swing from winter to the heat of summer may be only one or two degrees. That makes for a cold swim, no matter what the air temperature is. Can anyone say soprano?

Every few years some poor idiot, often intoxicated on something, tries to swim across one of these gems to a scenic point or outcropping.

"Honest Martha, it's not that far. I was a champion swimmer in high school. I can make it. Just watch how easy it is."

The problem is it does not need to be far away when the water temperature is forty degrees.

People just don't realize how fast the human body loses heat in near freezing dihydroxide (okay, water). In fact, one can die of hypothermia in slightly cool water if you are submerged long enough. The human body is poorly equipped to resist internal heat loss to water. The hair we have is designed to rise up when we are cold, trapping a small layer of escaping body heat to keep us warm. This doesn't work in water. Unlike other mammals such as whales and seals, humans lack a heavy layer of fat to insulate us . . . at least most of us do (. . . but I have an aunt I'm sure could survive a long, cold winter in the arctic sea just fine).

*   *   *

Many times our victim is observed swimming along like Mark Spitz, and then suddenly, onlookers are witness to their hero simply disappearing under the surface as his muscles seize up from loss of body heat. Occasionally, an onlooker or friend tries to go to the rescue and while attempting, suffers the same fate.

"One little, two little, three little idiots . . ."

I don't worry, though. We're aware that within a day or two the gasses of decomposition begin to form within the corpse. They become human corks and pop to the surface.

However, I've heard legends from the old boys of times where the body sank deep enough the extremely cold water kept it from decomposing and never coming up. That is until some shocked fisherman snags what he thinks is a record-sized trout only to find a body dressed in a roaring twenties tuxedo on the end of their line. "Gee, and only on eight pound test!"

* * *

June sixth had been a wonderful day. Our oldest daughter graduated the eighth grade and was off for a two-week tour of Europe. It pays to have two doctors for parents. She was 'really interested in the art galleries,' and would be well chaperoned by trusted friends who travel the world every summer. I justify it by thinking she will return home with a greater appreciation of America, its advantages and freedoms. I want her to realize there are places in the world where these benefits are not available to the masses and there is no hope to achieve. The truth, all justification aside, she is fourteen. I want her to be aware there is a big world to explore and our small town is not the universe. In short, do not marry your hick, high school sweetheart until you have explored other lands.

On the other hand, if you really love the schmuck, marry him and know what you are giving up.

Our youngest one was at summer camp for a week; for her . . . a good time, no deep life lessons.

Lori and I spent our first day alone grilling steaks and planning our romantic evening. A slow dinner, then maybe a DVD we had not or could not watch with the girls around. This could turn into a fun night. To my surprise, it actually worked out exactly as we planned—great food and even better company.

Evenings like that are rare. Most times, I can count on receiving a late night call informing me someone has gone to meet his or her maker. Why people decide to die at night is beyond me. Night calls make Lori nutty. She claims once awakened, she can't go back to sleep until I return home safely. Me, on the other hand, pure excitement; a mystery to solve makes my day or sometimes my night. I know it is somewhat sick but I will admit death intrigues me anytime day or night no matter how much I protest at the time.

Today's call came at the fortuitous hour of eleven o'clock and involved a female body washed up on the shore at Tree Line Lake. Eleven thousand feet above sea level and up a dangerous one and a half lane pass with, might I add, no guardrails. Not the way I was looking forward to spending the day.

I hate taking the drive up this pass so much I have only done it once in ten years. The hour-long drive to the snake pass cut-off leading to the lake gave me plenty of time to build up a bit of anxiety. It had something to do with the several turns with thousand-foot straight drops to the canyon bottom. I have watched too many Hollywood movies as the car plummets to the valley floor bursting into flames as it bounces off the canyon walls ending in a great explosion. I ascended the pass at a snail's pace and was happy to see pull outs, just in case of oncoming traffic. My palms sweated on the steering wheel, making it slippery. "Great, I'm going to die," I thought.

As I neared the last switchback, I knew I was in the clear and had made it safely. That was just before a large buck deer and his friends decided it was a good time to cross the road. Apparently, my moving vehicle provided the perfect challenge for this endeavor since they chose to cross just in front of my bumper. It is amazing how fast you can stop a car without a heartbeat. After I regained my composure and dried my seat cushion, I idled the last mile toward the summit, for fear this was some kind of demented deer game and they'd be back for round two.

I reached the summit and could see down to the lake. It was not difficult to spot the death scene, flashing red and blue lights on the far side of the lake. This must be a slow crime day or something really big must be happening to have so many cars respond to a simple drowning.

I pulled to the shoreline as close as possible. I did not want to have to trip over too many rocks to get to the body. I fumbled under the passenger seat trying to find my kit of goodies I had under the seat. I knew it was there. I had seen it roll off the seat as I stopped to play deer games.

"Well, are you just going to hide in your jeep all day or are you going to come give us a hand with this human bobber?" It was Ted Newman with his face deformed as he pressed it against my windshield.

"Good God, man! That makes the second time today I've almost lost bladder control. You know this game of 'make the coroner jump out of his skin' is going to give me a heart attack someday. Then where will you be?"

"The question is where you will be."

"Hopefully, somewhere out of your jurisdiction!" I was lying, of course, but it was the best comeback I had at the time. Ted is a great cop and would find exactly how my wife had killed me I'm certain.

"Sorry man, but you're such an easy target. So, are you napping or looking for monsters under the seat?"

"I lost my tool kit under here and I can't seem to find it," I explained. "Here it is." I grabbed my bag and opened the door, bumping him out of the way.

"About time; follow me," Ted ordered, ignoring the fact I'd just tried to knock him to the ground with my door.

As we neared the cadaver's resting place, we tripped more than walked over slippery rocks. As I approached the body, every cop near the body was standing in a semicircle staring at the cadaver as it bounced against the rocks with every ripple.

"Gee guys, why hasn't anybody pulled her out of the water?" I asked, somewhat shocked they would just stand there and watch her bob against the shore.

"We know better than to touch one of your bodies until you arrive," Officer Karen O'Hara explained with a smart-ass look.

"Besides, she just keeps splashing there in the rocks. We figured she wasn't going anywhere." Ted sounded somewhat cold hearted.

"Has anyone taken pictures or interviewed any witnesses?" I asked.

"The photo session has already been done. Karen took some real beauty shots of us all," Ted sarcastically explained.

"I mean of the body, nitwit."

"Oh, the body. She got a few nice ones of her as well," Ted grinned.

"Ted, will you get the water temperature and Karen, can you take the air temp and wind direction?"

I took out my trusty Polaroid and snapped off a few shots of the body. Not that I don't trust Karen, but I've seen film screwed up too many times to stake my investigation on someone else's photographic skills without a few back up shots of my own.

"Okay, you guys give me a hand and let's pull her out of the water." I was begging, but tried to make it sound like an order. I was hoping they would just jump in the water, which Ted was loudly announcing to all assembled was "a warm 45 degrees." To my surprise, two highway patrolmen stepped up and lifted the body onto shore, rolling her onto her back as they did.

Her body was a pale bluish white and had the appearance of a plucked chicken, covered by more goose bumps than one could count. The officers thought this was quite funny and got a subdued chuckle from almost everyone. However, I recognized the significance of her plucked appearance and felt I had my first good clue in this macabre puzzle.

*   *   *

Erector papillae muscles are tiny; they raise the hair on your neck when you're frightened or cold. Once dead, the nervous system ceases to provide input to those or any other muscles resulting in stasis. In other words, if they were erect at the time of death, they remain that way forever.

* * *

The fact this woman was covered in goose bumps indicated to me she died cold. The question is, how did she get cold? Was she cold, killed and then dumped into the water, or was she alive when she went into the water? I questioned if she had gone into the cold lake voluntarily or had someone given her a little help? What seemed strangest to me, more than the goose bumps was her odd dress, was that she was clad in nothing but a nightgown and socks. Granted, it was a thick flannel nightgown, but somehow I thought it totally inappropriate for swimming.

"I hate to ask this, but have you called Ed and Patty at the morgue or are we going to have to wait two more hours for them to come?" I whined to Ted.

"I tried to call them before you were paged but couldn't get a cell site from here. Too many high peaks blocking the signal. So, I drove to the top of the pass to call. They said they 'didn't do floaters and you were on your own with this one.' He kept a straight face as he relayed their message.

"I hope you reminded them they have a contract. It says twenty-four hours a day, seven days a week in rain, sleet, snow they are to provide for the recovery of bodies." I was upset feeling they meant it. Ted seemed so serious. How would I explain to Lori the odor of a floater in my car? If you think cigarette smell is hard to get rid of . . .

"Just kidding, they should be here any time. You know Ed. He loves this dead stuff as much as you do. I think you're both sick."

"Hey mister, you're the one who keeps finding dead bodies. I just come when you call me. Besides, I prefer the term eccentric!"

"You have to have money to be eccentric, until then you're just crazy to me."

As we stood debating who was the more demented one, Ed arrived with his purple suburban/body wagon or, as he refers to it, the 'rural rigor mortis recovery rover.'

He bounded over the rocks like a mountain goat. Looking at the body he immediately radioed Patty, who was wisely waiting in the car where it was safe and warm.

"Sweetie, bring a thick bag and some duct tape so we can seal her up tight." Looking at Ted he smiled, "I don't want her to leak since we don't have a divider between the cargo area and the driver's seat. I don't want her to begin warming and smell up the suburban either."

"I don't want to even think about it. You are two warped people." Ted walked away to direct the investigation. His men were putting out evidence tape and searching for anything they could find.

Patty brought Ed the bag and tape he had requested. I took the opportunity to walk away from all of the action. Walking along the lakeside a few yards, I looked to see if there were any boats moored near the scene. Even with the bright sunlight, the opposite shore was out of view and there was not a boat in sight.

Kneeling at the water's edge I reached into my little kit and retrieved a Champaign cork in its little wire basket, tossing it into the water about ten feet from shore. I watched as it bobbed slowly back toward me. When it reached shore, I retrieved it and pulled a little orange ping pong ball from my pocket. This time I tossed them both at the same time. They landed next to one another about five yards out. I sat down to watch. Actually, it was quite relaxing having a quick smoke and watching my instruments bob around in the water. I almost forgot why I was there.

"Sit around, is that all you do?"

"Damn Ted, quit sneaking up behind me!"

"What are you doing? Everyone else is working and you're over here smoking. Just what is that you're smoking anyway?"

"Nothing unlawful, officer. I have a note from my doctor. I was just watching my experiment."

"Experiment? A cork and a small ball? Those are called toys."

"Yup, just watch." I pointed to the cork, which by now had drifted back toward me by at least five feet. Then we searched for the ball. It had moved out toward the opposite shore a good twenty feet from where I'd thrown it in.

"Wonderful, corks don't float as well as balls do. Where did you go to school for this? Larry and Moe's school of investigation? I'll bet it was a correspondence course," Ted harassed. "Did the signed diploma cost extra?" he continued.

"Okay, I'll try to explain it so even you can understand. See the cork?"

"Yes, I see the cork. Where did you hide the bottle when you finished it?"

Totally ignoring his insinuation about my being intoxicated, I tried to make him understand why I was playing in the water.

"I threw it into the water over there," I said, pointing to the entry spot. "See where it is now?"

"Sure, it's bouncing in the rocks."

"Alright, I threw the ball in the same place at the exact same time and see where it is?"

"Drifting out to sea; just like your mind," he answered still looking confused by why this game was so important.

"Let me put it this way. The cork with the wire cage floats low in the water and is subject to the movement of the lakes current and wave action. The ping pong ball on the other hand has almost no draft in the water and is subject to the wind direction to move. Since the ball is floating away and the cork is drifting back to shore I can assume the current and winds are moving in opposite directions."

"And this will help your syphilitic brain decide she drowned how?"

"The body obviously didn't enter the water where we found her. There's not a boat or campsite in sight, so she must have floated in from somewhere else. Maybe knowing the direction of the wind and current we might be able track her movement in the water. Of course, there will be the fish bites and organic matter from the corpse to examine. That might be a big help in showing where she's been."

"You are a sick man to even think of this shit. I saw the body. I don't even want to think about being eaten by fish. Uck!"

"You know, it's the eyes they go after first." I knew I had him and now was my chance to turn the knife for making me jump at every opportunity. "Then, it's usually the ears followed by any other soft parts. You don't have to worry. They only take little bites, a lot of them, but just little ones." I thought he was going to puke on the spot.

I was enjoying Detective Newman turn three shades of green when he was rescued. A patrolman radioed. He'd found a small dingy about twenty yards up the beach. Ted had the officer photograph it before pulling it onto the shore.

"Wear gloves and don't disturb anything in it," he ordered over his walkie-talkie.

As we passed Ed and the body (Patty had returned to the heater in the car), he joined our jog toward the boat.

"We didn't have to touch it," the officer reported to Ted. "It was just floating here against the rocks, so we just left it."

"The oars are stowed," Ted observed, "so no one's been out for a midnight row."

"This is a Zodiac. They're made of thick rubber with a low draft and look in the stern. There's a motor back there. These things are made to really get up and move." Ed was suddenly some kind of expert in high-speed rubber boats, an odd expertise to acquire (sarcasm a bitter form of humor). He continued to educate us. "These are the kind used by the Marines and Navy Seal teams. You can run them right up onto shore and not damage them in the least." Ed had obviously acquired a vast knowledge of the subject; God knows where.

"We get the idea, Cliff Calvin's," Ted stopped Ed in mid-sentence. "I'll have it covered and put into one of the bigger vehicles. I don't want to leave it out here all day. One of you guys pull the motor up and figure out how to move it without destroying it."

"Good idea, but you can't fool me. You just want to get out of helping Ed load up the body."

"I don't need his help, I have you!" Ed stated sardonically with a Boris Karloff laugh.

"Wonderful, I thought I'd get out of having to handle this one. Floaters are hard to hold on to," I complained.

"Don't worry, I don't think she'll complain if you slip and drop her," Ed said, looking at me with an 'I know you've done it before' look.

"We'll wrap it up if you guys get her moved far away from here. She looks bad and I can't get the eye thing out of my mind. Besides, I'm worried she'll begin to stink soon," Ted bargained.

We could not believe our ears. All we had to do was remove the victim? Ed and I loaded up the slippery pre-chilled corpse quickly before Ted reconsidered his foolish offer.

We knew this left the poor deputies to seek out witnesses and inventory every occupant of every boat, tent or cabin on the lake. It seemed to me I got the best end of the stick for once. After all, Ed and Patty had the bloated corpse and all that went with her. All I had to do was make it home safely down the pass without encountering a second round of the deer dashing game.

Ed, being well known countywide as a speeder and tailgater, followed me down the pass. Now, I am in a rickety old Jeep devoid of power steering, power brakes or for that matter power anything. Hell, my wheels are hardly round and are balder than my uncle Frank. Behind me are eight thousand pounds of rolling steel, containing one certifiable maniac at the wheel, his terrified wife and an occupant already dead!

This goliath was four feet off my bumper and had aircraft landing lights, which Ed calls 'emergency lights,' flashing directly into every mirror in my car. Blinded by the light, my pupils retreated into my skull from the shock. It reminded me of my college days when I went into the 7-11 at three in the morning for the Twinkie I just couldn't live without for some odd reason.

I could hardly see the road ahead of me and was certain I would end in a fiery crash down a quarter of a mile of sheer rock face.

Thinking fast, I used one of the little pullouts, letting Ed rapidly pass by. Sneaky I know, but I am ugly, not dumb. I was not about to let him push me to my demise and then charge the county for retrieving my charred remains. Now I was the one on his bumper.

Of course, I had not thought this through completely. I didn't realize with him now in the lead it meant I was going to be eating his dust as we descended death canyon. We made it without me ending the trip as a cinder.

Thanks to modern technology, the next morning my slumber and hopes of snuggling was interrupted by a polite computer voice informing me the 'cork's postmortem would be at 10:15, thank you,' click. Great, I would get to spend my morning digging inside a rotting day-old floater while Lori could lounge in bed.

I've found many times in my career, the way to get what you want from a pathologist or forensic technician, is to arrive bearing food. The species 'pathologist—gobilist' prefers a pastry diet. Anything gooey, sticky and/or covered in powdered sugar is a winner. If it were filled with some other equally sweet mixture, they'd willingly sign a blank death certificate.

I arrived at the lab with two boxes of the stickiest, most frosting drenched doughnuts the doughnut factory could provide. Passing through the staff lounge where the techs and office staff take their breaks, I dropped the first box in the center of the table. They moved in like the infantry on D-Day. I moved my plan of bribery into full gear with the doctor's lounge. As I placed the box on the table, a voice came over the loudspeaker . . . "Reedman is in the building and has doughnuts! That is all." It was gravely throated Betty with a mouthful of a jelly filled.

The lounge doors suddenly swung open. In rushed every doctor within six blocks. I was pushed aside as hands groped for a pastry. These well-educated healers descended on the poor defenseless container of sweets like a ravenous herd of leaches attacking a hemophiliac.

"If Reedman spent money on doughnuts we all know why," Dr. Steve mumbled as he devoured his first sweet roll.

"He's trying to bribe us, as usual," Dr. Higgins added.

"That's for sure, but what do you think the scheming bastard is wanting?" Steve replied.

"Probably wants us to come out to a scene again. Remember when he thought he'd found an alien body?"

"Oh, yeah, you mean the decomposed cow," Dr. Dillon added.

These three continued to harass me to my face as though I weren't there.

"This is the kind of treatment I get when I do something nice for you guys. You automatically assume I'm here to bribe you or try to manipulate you to do something for me?" I tried to sound insulted and hurt by the allegations.

"Well? You are aren't you?" Steve smiled.

"That's beside the point. I just can't believe it was your first thought."

"You are trying to bribe us aren't you? I know every time you show up with doughnuts, especially fresh ones and not day olds, you are after something. You know even a rat is aware he's being conditioned." Steve reached for another sweet roll.

"You're right. I want something."

"Well, spit it out. Depending what it is you might be buying lunch too," Dr. Dillon threatened.

"I just want to stay as far away as I can from this floater case. I do not want to hear 'come here and get a close look at this or hey Rex, smell this!' I hate floaters," Well there it is. If it cost me burritos for lunch I would be willing to pay the price.

"Let me make sure I'm hearing right. The grossest foulest man I know who can stand at my autopsy table while I do a burned body and eat a BBQ sandwich is afraid of a little floating girly body. Hell, she hasn't even warmed up enough to begin to smell." Steve just couldn't believe I was hesitant to attend.

"It's not the fact it's a girl and you know I'm not bothered by rank smells. My first post mortem was a floater. Ever since then I just don't like doing them. They feel like rubber and reek like rotting fish."

"Well, a couple of glazed pastries aren't getting you out of going in there. If I have to go so do you," Dr Steve smiled but I knew he meant it.

The autopsy began promptly. Dr. Steve began to test the equipment before the denier even had the body in the room.

"She's just been bob bobbin along . . ." He was singing into the Dictaphone, amused by his own wit.

The doors from the freezer section swung open with a resounding bang as the assistant Larry wheeled in the corpse.

"Thanks for the eats, doc. I loved the sweet rolls. Here's your morning project." He moved the body bag to the table.

"I guess there's no putting this off. We might as well open the bag and see what we've got." Steve directed Larry to unzip the body bag.

Reading from the toe tag (Yes, we really do tag the toe,) Larry used his best announcer's voice, "Ladies and gentlemen, let's hear round of applause for our first contestant on today's 'name their demise.' She is the lovely Rita McCall. It says here Rita enjoys late night swims and deep diving. Her favorite hobby is feeding the fish!"

"Give up, Larry. 'The Price is Right' has an announcer. Just unzip the baggie and let's have a look at our cork."

I was shocked by what it contained. She was without a doubt the most beautiful woman I'd ever seen. Really, even as a corpse I would have gladly been seen out to dinner with her. Up at the lake I really hadn't looked at her. Not as a human being anyway, just as another dead body. Her nails were perfect and the autopsy lights gave her skin a movie star glow.

"Wow, she's beautiful!" Larry stated my own thoughts aloud.

"Don't you recognize her? It's Rita McCall, the famous model." Steve sounded amazed he had a celebrity on his slab. "Get the beauty queen out of the bag and let's have a closer look." Steve stood back as Larry and I removed the body bag.

"Okay, let's get going. The body arrives clad in a flannel nightgown and slipper like socks. Cut them off boys so we can get down to some tissue." Steve was getting serious now. I think the celebrity thing was freaking him out a little.

Ignoring the order to cut off the clothing, Larry reverently removed the outer clothing and placed them in a brown bag for exam later by the lab team.

"Oh, my God, she isn't wearing anything else!" Larry exclaimed.

"What's wrong with you, boy? Haven't you seen a naked female body before? Maybe we have been working you too many hours. You should take some time off to discover what a warm, live woman is. They move you know," Steve harassed about Larry's virginity. "Really, if you're getting excited about a cold dead woman you need help. I don't want to find you in the refrigerator someday checking out the new babes!"

"Wait a minute here. She is pretty good looking. Check out her manicure. Look at the detail. That's not easy and it looks as though it has been done recently. There isn't much nail growth and it doesn't look like they've been on long enough to have been filled," Larry observed.

"Now I'm really worried about you, Larry. How do you know so much about women's manicures and what does filled mean?" Steve continued his harassment of Larry as he prepped the tools.

"I was raised with three sisters. I know all about nails, hair and menstrual cycles. I even know how to French braid hair. By the way about every two weeks they have to go back to the manicurist to have some kind of putty put in where the nail has grown out. Then they are buffed and new polish is applied. Sometimes little decals are put on, but look at her nails. These little bluebirds are painted on with a very small brush; that's not cheap."

"You know Larry, sometimes you really frighten me." Steve was impressed with Larry's breadth of knowledge about 'woman things,' but wasn't about to admit it.

Steve began to externally inspect the cadaver. "The body arrives covered with contracted erector papillae muscles, giving her a plucked goose appearance. Her pallor is a light bluish white in appearance. She is cold to the touch and has an advanced degree of rigor at this time while fixed. The body is devoid of lividity. The skin is intact with no sign of skin slippage. Her pupils are equal and fixed," Steve paused.

"She died really cold but wasn't in the lake too long, less than twelve hours. There isn't much evidence of the fish feeding on her. You know fish love fresh meat. A body floating in the water is like using power bait. Rotting flesh is a fish magnet."

"Is that what those marks on her legs are?" Larry asked, looking grossed out by the thought of being fed on by fish.

* * *

Fish bites are easy to imagine. However, skin slippage is a very strange thing to see for the first time. My first experience observing the symptom was during my initial autopsy. He was a large black man who'd drowned three days earlier in Lake Tahoe. As I moved the body to the exam table his skin began to slide off revealing the sub dermal layer, which appeared snowy white. I remember thinking, wow, we really are all the same under our skin. The pathologist explained after a body has been submerged or left long enough to decompose, interstitial fluids begin to pool between the epidermis and the deeper sub dermal layers. This results in the epidermis becoming fragile and easily separating from the layers below. Disgusting no matter the scientific explanation, trust me on this one.

* * *

Steve palpated the skull for any signs of fracture. "I feel some give to her skull. She might have a fracture. We will be able to see it better from the inside when we cap her. It looks like there is a small cut on the back of her skull just below the crown of her head."

Larry moved in, combing the hair aside to measure and photograph the wound. It had been hidden in the hairline and there was little blood in the cut. I didn't notice any bruising around the surrounding tissue as I peered over Larry's shoulder while he tried to work.

"Has she been x-rayed yet?" Steve directed his question to Larry.

"Full body films were done when she arrived," Larry answered proudly.

"Good, we'll take a look at them when we're done here."

Next, Steve turned his attention to the face checking her mouth for foreign objects. He removed a small piece of food and some kind of algae looking substance placing it gently into a sterile container. Then he checked her eyelids and lips for any indication she'd been strangled. "Well, there's no sign of any petechial hemorrhaging around her lips or eyes to indicate she was strangled. I guess we should open her up." Steve picked up a scalpel and began making the 'Y' shaped incision across her chest, exposing her ribs as he pealed back the overlying tissues. Larry removed the ribs with the aid of a large pair of tree trimming shears.

* * *

It might sound weird, but we prefer 'Craftsman' tools from the hardware department at Sears. Of course, we never tell the sales person what we plan to use them for and they come with a <u>lifetime</u> guarantee. Somehow, it strikes me as ironic considering where we use them.

*   *   *

"Well, she sure looks healthy on the inside. Her lungs are nice and pink so we can assume she didn't smoke or live in Los Angeles. Let's remove one part at a time, boys."

Larry began by removing the lungs and heart as a single unit placing it on Steve's dissection board. He began checking the blood vessels to be certain she hadn't had a stroke or heart attack. He then removed the heart and dissected it checking the internal structures.

"I can tell you she was an athletic person. Her heart is beautiful. I wish mine looked as good". Inspecting her lungs, "They are pink and healthy looking but somewhat spongy when touched. Larry, fill the sink and let's see if they float."

Steve tied each bronchi tightly closed and gently placed first the left, then the right lung into the warm water. They sank like rocks. He gingerly lifted them from the sink and drew fluid from the each lung, then took several sections adding them to his little bottle.

*   *   *

A healthy lung when placed in water will normally float. The alveoli are still filled with air making them buoyant. A lung from a victim of pulmonary disease or drowning has fewer air sacs functioning either due to

298

body fluids such as puss, tar or water filling them. They sink like rocks.

This woman drowned.

* * *

"Sure looks like these are filled with fluid. We will examine them microscopically as well as submit them for chemical analysis later." Steve set them aside.

"So far, the heart looks good and the lungs act like a drowning case. Where do you want to look next?" Larry inquired.

"Let's check her stomach for any pills or anything that shouldn't be there."

Larry began by tying a string around the base of the esophagus and at the duodenum (where the stomach empties into the small intestine). He then tied two knots at the base of the stomach, one to keep the small intestine from leaking and another to contain the stomach gunk. Steve carefully cut open the stomach only to find it empty with the exception of some red sediment, most likely from a bottle of wine, some spaghetti and a little water. He took samples for analysis. "We'd better find something good here soon or this is just looking more and more like a simple drowning. Open her head and let's see if we can find a fracture or see if she stroked out on us. Judging by the cut on her scalp, I'll bet we find a nice hematoma on her occipital lobe," Steve hypothesized.

I could see his mind at work. He was sure she had been hit in the head suffering a brain injury, which caused her demise. Larry retrieved a scalpel and the bone saw. He began to scalp and remove the top of the skull.

* * *

This is probably more than anyone would ever want to know, but the process begins by a cut made from behind one ear, over the top of the head, to the other ear. The scalp is then peeled back to the base of the skull. (It makes a strange but hauntingly familiar sound. It took several procedures for me to identify it as sounding like ripping a pair of blue jeans, slowly.) The front half is then folded down to the chin. An incision in this manner allows the mortician to suture it back in place within the hairline, hiding the cut.

With the bone saw a notch is placed at each temple. This stops the top of the skull from sliding backward during viewing at the funeral. Without the notch, morticians get mad. They don't want to hear half way through an open casket service, "Gee. I don't remember Uncle Willy having that ridge on his forehead."

* * *

"Larry, hand me the gray matter and let's take a slice or two."

Larry removed the skullcap and it made the same ripping cloth sound. Before Steve could even reach for the bone, Larry flipped it over to check for a sign it had indeed been fractured.

"I'll be damned. Sure enough, here is a fracture. Just where you said it would be."

"Now that you've made your brilliant diagnosis, would you give it to me so I can see for myself? You know it's that doctor thing. Something about you not being qualified to diagnose?" Steve teased.

"Trust me. I recognize a fracture when I see one, especially one as big as this one," Larry barbed back as he relinquished the bone to Steve.

"Good call, doctor-ette. It's a fracture alright," Steve backhandedly complemented Larry's observation. "Okay, mister smart ass, do you think you can get her brain out in one piece this time?"

"A little silence while I undo some of God's handiwork," Larry smiled, recognizing the complement and began the intricate procedure of removing the cerebral cortex, cerebellum, brainstem and as much of the spinal cord as possible.

*   *   *

Removing a brain begins by severing its connections to the skull. These tough ligaments are difficult to cut and at the same time not injure the delicate brain. The brain has the consistency of a bowl of Jell-O. It is easy to tear or puncture. Removal of the brainstem, which descends into the upper spine, is even more difficult. While carefully cradling the brain, the technician must use a long handled scalpel and reach past the brainstem to the spinal cord. This is a tricky task. The brain stem is loosely attached and can come apart in your hands.

*   *   *

"Well, here you are sir. Please note the entire structure is intact and has suffered no nicks or cuts." Larry proudly handed the woman's central nervous system or most of its controlling parts to Steve.

Inspecting the outer surface of the brain, Steve noted, "Here on the occipital lobe is an area of bruising. Somebody get a picture of it."

I used my handy pocket Polaroid to get a few close-ups.

Steve began by weighing the brain, then slicing it up like a fresh loaf of bread. "No signs of a stroke or any indication of a tumor. However, this section of the visual cortex has a distinct hematoma. It looks as though it lines up with the fracture and the cut on her head. Whatever hit her, hit hard enough to fracture her skull and bruise the brain." Steve made certain to take selected samples for microscopic examination after they hardened in a formaldehyde solution. "The brainstem exhibits a depression like ridge where it exits the skull. Her brain swelled at some point for this to happen. While we're here, let's take a closer look at the cut in her scalp," Steve suggested.

Larry replaced the skull and put the scalp back in place. He shaved the hair from around the wound, allowing a clear view and then photographed it from several differing angles. Steve moved in to look up close and personal.

"Well, it's a crescent shaped cut measuring 2 cm x 1.5 cm. The apex of the crescent is in the inferior position. Larry, excise that portion of the scalp and put it in solution."

* * *

This is a significant finding. The widest portion of the cut was at the top. This indicates an upward blow to the head or a downward one depending on the position of the victim's head when struck. The point of initial contact will be the smallest, with the wound widening as the blow continues.

Once removed from the skull there is no way of orienting the piece later when it's examined. Therefore, the technician places sutures indicating the inferior and superior points before cutting it away. You can't trust the direction of hair growth for orientation since hair grows in all different directions.

*   *   *

"Only one last thing to do, Larry, you lucky dog. I think we should do a full rape kit and let's see if we come up with any genetic material. Also don't forget to send some of her blood and hair for DNA profiling." Steve removed his latex gloves, signaling to me that he was finished with the physical examination.

"So, what do you think? Any signs of foul play or shall I just sign this one off as a tragic accident?" I asked, tongue in cheek.

"Judging on what I've seen, her death lacks any signs of intrigue to me, so I'd be inclined to see it as an accident," he jousted back.

"Accident. A ruling of accident simplifies my life tremendously. There's so much paperwork with a homicide or suicide," I mocked his sarcasm.

"Don't warm up your word processor just yet. Remember something could have fallen and hit her in the head causing the injuries, or someone could have struck her from behind with a hammer. I have done my part. Now you have to take it from here."

"I've been at this long enough to know better than make a ruling until I've seen lab results, had a chance to chat with the sheriff's deputies and maybe even interview a witness or two."

I returned to my office and found one of Ted's infamous series of post-it-notes on my desk lamp.

"My guys located a yacht this morning. The occupants said one of their party was missing. It was a young woman named Rita." Ted, using only his badge number, signed the note. Of course, I had to call him immediately to get the dirt.

Once he finally answered his home phone I pleaded, "Tell me what you found out with the boat people."

"Why are you calling me? Do you know the sun is up? I'm on the night shift you know. What's so important?" I'd woken him from a really deep sleep. I didn't mind disturbing him. He gleefully calls me in the middle of the night, insisting I bring fresh coffee to some horrific scene and it doesn't seem to bother him.

"You left me a note about a missing woman and some people on a boat. Tell me what you found out."

"There were two men in their forties and a two year-old boy on the boat. They said, "The female was the last one on the deck and wasn't noticed missing until breakfast time." I put a full report in your mailbox. Now can I go back to sleep?" For a moment I felt bad for waking him. I hadn't looked in my inbox yet.

According to Ted's notes in my mailbox, there were two other large boats anchored near the victim's vessel. They were several hundred yards away in opposite directions. Ted and his men had already interviewed each of the occupants. He included copies of each officer's notes from their interviews.

Now, all I had to do was spend the rest of the morning reading each officer's individual notes and constructing a timeline of their observations, and then I would have to add in the autopsy findings. I hate this part of the job. To me, it's just needless paperwork. However, the district attorney seems to like it when I follow through. He claims it makes his job easier when he has to prosecute someone.

I reviewed interview notes from the first boat anchored about two hundred yards from the victims yacht and in the neighboring cove. According to the three people on board it had been a quite night on the lake until about seven PM when they all heard some yelling coming from somewhere on the lake. "It didn't sound like a fight or anything; it was more of an excited sound. Maybe like people partying and getting a little out of hand," the man on board reported.

The owner stated, "Sound travels in weird ways and echoes on this lake. It must be the steep canyon walls. Sometimes you can hear every sound on the lake as clear as a bell and other times you can't hear the boat anchored fifty yards away. So we just ignored it and went to bed."

The wife reported the same course of events. "We had no idea anything might be wrong."

The second group of officers reported four people onboard a luxury motor yacht. It was anchored almost in the center of the lake. This afforded those aboard a unique opportunity to hear sound coming from almost every anchorage on the water. Due to the position of this oversized motorboat, these passengers had the best chance to identify the direction of any disturbance and at the same time could most likely hear any conversation most clearly.

Interviewed separately they all reported a similar story.

"They said they'd heard some yelling coming from the direction of the victim's boat," the patrolman wrote.

"It sounded like people having a quarrel of some kind. It lasted about fifteen minutes. Then it was quiet for a short time. I'm not sure what time it was but the loud noise began again a little later," the owner George continued to explain. "I couldn't hear clearly but I remember something about 'we are coming and don't worry.' There was a name mentioned but I can't recall what it was."

The officer noted he believed this witness but was concerned about their lack of recall about times. According to the notes, the deputy asked each member of the party and they recalled going up on deck to see if they could hear the conversation more clearly. Everyone agreed the second round of noise was 'sometime after we'd had dinner and were enjoying a drink in the salon.'

Alcohol consumption most likely accounted for the collective lack of recollection about any kind of time.

The last of the reports came from the officers who'd been to the victim's vessel.

They interviewed the child first. Of course, he had no idea of anything other than the fact he'd been fishing earlier in the day with his dad and had eaten a hotdog for dinner.

Children make difficult witnesses. They recall information in relationship to other activities. Such as, 'it happened while I was taking a bath.' God only knows what time they bathed. They certainly don't know.

The next interviewed was a man referred in the report as 'the owner of the boat,' Quinton McCall. When asked what happened to his wife, he claimed as far as he knew everyone was in bed, safe. "We all crashed at about eight o'clock."

The officer indicated he had some doubts about the going to bed by eight. He noted if his wife were missing from bed for long he would certainly be aware of it. Reading his entry, I had to agree. If my wife got up in the middle of the night I'd definitely notice it. Of course, I am a light sleeper and would be aware if my wife went for a midnight walk around the deck.

As I reviewed statements from occupants of the other yachts, I began to wonder. There were several discrepancies. The neighboring yachtsmen report several 'episodes of somebody calling to someone apparently in the water.' This did not match the report from the victim's spouse. If he really didn't know she had gone overboard during the night, why did the witnesses report hearing someone promising for 'her not to worry? He was coming.' Why did he claim he 'hadn't missed her until morning?' I wondered if he actually knew some tragic accident had occurred. Of course, there was the possibility he killed her and was afraid to report the real facts, for fear of incriminating himself. After all, in the absence of a butler, the husband had to be the guilty party.

By reviewing the cryptic notations it was apparent to me I would have to return to the scene and interview him myself. I would also need to check out the victim's boat for a hammer with blood or hair on it, assuming it ever existed or had not been consigned to the depths of the lake. I needed to get myself psyched for the harrowing drive back up to the lake.

Dr. Steve poked his head into my office. He was smiling as though he had some fantastic secret or was about to pull a practical joke on me.

"Boy, do I have some intrigue for you. I just don't know where to start! This is the best thing I have found to ruin your day in months. I can't tell you how happy it makes me to do this to you."

"I know you're a sadistic prick. I have seen you work. There aren't many job openings for sadists these days but pathologist is definitely one occupation still accepting applicants, isn't it? What mystifying data do you have that could possibly ruin my day?"

"This is wonderful. Let me begin with the fact your beauty queen was on cocaine. She also chose to consume an entire bottle of fine, and I do mean fine, bottle of Bordeaux. We analyzed the sediments in her stomach. Give us enough time and we'll be able to tell you which vineyard and vintage it was. Her blood gas tests show a high level of alcohol, more than a single bottle of wine would account for. Cool, eh?"

"What's so great? We see the combination of drugs and alcohol ending up being lethal all of the time. So far, your attempt at crashing my mood is not working too well, you know. The blow to the head was enough evidence for me to think about murder."

"Oh, that's not the good stuff. I was just setting the stage for your few remaining gray cells to begin fusing together."

"Now, you have me worried. What are you trying to hint at? I'm obviously not picking up your clues or psychic message here."

"Remember her lungs didn't float? Guess why." It was obvious Steve was going to torture me

"Uh, duh, they were filled with water," I mocked.

"Ding, ding. Give the man a cupie doll."

"Your big surprise is the woman's lungs were filled with water? She drowned you know. You are aware we found her in a lake. You semi-functional brainstem idiot, did you expected to find sand in there?"

"Ah, now you're on tract, you neuron impaired rectal genius. Filled with what? Pure crystal clear, alpine runoff you say. I think not." He was smiling in satisfaction. He had me and knew it. "Guess what I found."

"Puss, tar, liquid propane?"

"You schmuck, I thought you would get it right away. Okay, her lungs were filled with water."

"I said water. Why did you make me try to sound like an idiot?"

"Uh, because you stopped at water. You didn't say what kind of water."

"H_2O, you know water? Filled with fishes and other creepy little microscopic slimy creatures, kind of water?"

"Close, but no cigar. Water containing a fair concentration of chlorine. Like pool water." He was almost satisfied with his cerebral knife twisting at this point.

"Oh, my God. She died in the Jacuzzi. I have my case now."

"Don't get to confident. You haven't heard the good part yet."

"More? Don't tell me there's a small rodent involved in this somewhere?"

"Nothing so exotic, but remember Larry's rape scan?"

"A thrill he won't forget and one which will require some lengthy form of counseling I'm certain," I prophesied.

"Forget Larry for the moment, Mr. mono-neuron man. Guess what he found?"

"Oh, let me take a wild guess here. Could it have been semen?"

"A cigar for the mental midget. Of course semen, in several orifices. Kinky, eh?" He was grinning. I could tell he was imagining how such a thing could happen. By the look in his eyes, he was enjoying each option just a little too much.

"So, they enjoyed an active and varied sex life. What impact does it have on her death?"

"I'm fine with whatever two consenting adults want to do in the privacy of their bedroom. There is only one problem, the key word here is two. The sample from orifice number one is A+ and the one from the other orifice is B-. It gives you something to think about, doesn't it?" He seemed happy parceling out the information slowly, like a Chinese water torture.

"I think it's more information than I wanted to hear. It gives me a mental image and now I'll be joining Larry in therapy. I think you're a sick pervert to enjoy imparting such graphic information."

"I resemble, I mean, resent that remark and take great offence to it. Have a nice day!" he mockingly stated.

'Have a nice day.' Is he kidding? Why couldn't this be a simple drowning? I could explain away each clue individually. However, when I started to add them up I just couldn't get the reports to coincide with the lab findings. This meant there was no choice I had to go visit the victim's family at the lake.

*   *   *

When I arrived at the water's edge I realized I had no way to get to the boat. I had not thought about bringing my own. For some reason, even though I knew better, my mind pictured these mini ships at a dock like cruise ships would be. Without a launch there to meet me I was stuck. If I called the victim's boat, they would know I was coming and would have a chance to destroy or clean up any remaining evidence. Therefore, I tried to be clever and call the foursome anchored in the middle of the lake. If they would give me a lift, I could still surprise the husband and maybe catch him of guard.

I dialed the yacht using my cell phone. I found, despite what the man on TV says, no one 'could hear me now!' Without cell service from my location, I had two choices. I could see if my spare tire floated and paddle out, or I could drive back to the summit hoping to get a cell site. Having a college degree and a lousy spare tire, I chose the latter.

The owner of the yacht, 'Queen Bea,' was extremely happy to help me. He said he realized I did not want to announce my arrival and would come pick me up in his dingy. A few minutes later, a sleek looking speedboat arrived and pulled right up onto the sand.

"This doesn't have wheels so I can't get any closer. If you're Doctor Reedman, hop aboard." The man piloting the boat smiled broadly and introduced himself. "I'm George Peterson, welcome aboard. I thought you might want to come out to my boat first. It would give you a chance to check out their boat with my binoculars before you went calling. Besides it would look less suspicious if we went there first."

"Good thinking, George," came out of my mouth. However, my mind was thinking, this was weird. Had he hatched some covert mission between his boat and the shore?

"I have been watching their boat since the police left. Of course, I make sure they cannot see me. I have a pair of navy surplus binoculars. They work great," my new friend explained.

"George, you've thought this out haven't you?"

"Well, I read a lot of murder mysteries and detective novels. You can learn from those books you know. I read a lot of books by an author who goes by the name of Reason. I'm sure it's a pseudonym but I learn a lot."

Captain George docked the 'dingy' on the port side of the 'Queen Bea' away from any prying eyes on the victim's boat. There was no ladder to climb. A stairway emerged from the side of the yacht as we approached.

He was a man of his word. He introduced me to his wife Bea, thus the name of the vessel. Then, he took me directly to the bridge where he had the biggest set of binoculars I had ever seen. They required a mounting bracket to secure them to the railing. George focused the spy device toward the dead woman's boat.

"Here you go. Now you can see her boat. It's the only one in the cove to the west."

As I peered thru the eyepiece I could see the other vessel close up. My eyes adjusted and the vessel's name came into focus. I began to chuckle. The boats name was boldly emblazoned in big gold letters across its stern.

It was named, 'The Lady of the Lake.'

"What's so funny?" George asked.

"Look for yourself. Can you make out the name of the boat?" I was still giggling.

"The Lady of the Lake. Ha, I get it. You found her in the lake. I wonder if he had it in mind when he christened her."

"I hadn't gone to the 'he planned it' place in my head yet, George. I was thinking about King Arthur and the Lady of the Lake. You know, kind of romantic."

"You need to read more murder mysteries. I have read a ton of them. Trust me when a man names his boat like that and then his wife is found floating in a lake. I begin to think about my uncle."

"I know I shouldn't ask, but what about this reminds you of your uncle?"

"My uncle Jerry was a magician. He always said, 'the best way to hide something from the audience is to hide it in plain sight.'"

"So, you think he planned to kill his wife at the time he bought the boat and then just waited for the right time to throw her overboard?" I asked.

"It just makes me somewhat suspicious," his eyes sparkled.

"You know, the poor guy could be a college history professor and just happens to like medieval lore."

"Well, if I'd named this boat 'the killer Bea or the Bea killer,' I'm sure my wife would question my motives."

"You may be right, George. Do you think you can give me a lift over to their boat? I'll see what I can find out."

"Sure, but first take one of these." He handed me a small two-way radio. "If you need help or a lift back, just call me. I've set them both to channel three."

"Are you a spy? Where do you get this neat stuff?" I was amazed at the tiny transmitter.

"I buy stuff online. You'd be blown away by the things you can find. These have a four-mile range and can be voice activated. Do you want me to record the conversation from here? I can do it digitally and burn you a copy."

"I don't think it will be necessary. Just give me a lift and I'll take it from there."

We bounced over the waves at what George referred to as, "Just the right speed to catch the tops. It gives a smoother ride."

As with most boat owners showing off their toy, we took the long way to allow me to fully appreciate the full performance of the eight trillion horsepower engine.

"See, smooth isn't it?" he screamed in my direction, hoping I could hear him over the roar of the jet we were strapped to. As for being a smooth ride, my kidneys disagree.

I thanked God the demo ride only consisted of once around the lake at slightly below the sound barrier. I was shaken and relieved to arrive at the victim's yacht. George, the speed demon, had not helped my composure. I asked permission to board as George sped away, leaving me hanging onto a ladder, no retractable staircase here.

"Come aboard before we have to fish you out of the drink," the unseen voice ordered.

"Thank you," I replied, as I clambered over the rail onto the deck. "I'm Rex Reedman, the coroner."

"I see you've met George. You can hear his boat all the way around the lake when he opens it up. My name is Quinton McCall. Rita and I own this floating hole in the water. Welcome aboard," he smiled and invited me into the salon.

The living room was bigger than the one at our house. It was obvious no expense had been spared. Not only was the furniture plush, it had every electronic gadget anyone could ever want. There was a large flat screen plasma TV at each side of the room. The stereo cabinet was taller than I could reach. As I entered the room, it was evident he had a top of the line surround sound system. It vibrated the deck.

"Cool system, eh?" he said turning down the Tina Turner special on MTV.

"Wow, I wish I had this at home. Of course, with my luck it would shatter my windows. Is the concert you're watching on DVD?" I asked.

"Hell, no. We have a full satellite network on board. We use it for the GPS navigation, Internet access and it lets me do some day trading from vacation."

"You do have all of the toys, don't you?"

"I'm lucky. My grandpa made a bunch of money and my only job is to spend it. Its tough work but somebody's gotta do it," he smiled. "What can I do to help you? I know you're here because of Rita's death. Do you need something, a drink maybe?"

"No, thanks. I would like to look around and maybe ask you a couple of questions if I could."

"I have some E-Mails to respond to. You can look around all you want," Quinton said with what appeared to be a sincere smile.

Okay, now I'm feeling somewhat strange. Does he really want me to have a free hand to examine the scene or, is he using this time to hide evidence?

"Before you go, I just have one quick question. According to the report I received from the officers there was another man and a little boy here. Where are they now?"

"Oh, Tom and his son, Jackson. They left after the police were here. Tom thought it would be a good idea to get Jackson home before he started asking questions about Auntie Rita."

The explanation made sense to me. If I had a small child at a death scene, I think I would remove them as well. I was disappointed I had missed the opportunity to interview the two. Nevertheless, I was most interested in the person still on board.

I walked the deck and found a huge Jacuzzi hot tub outside the master suite door at the bough of the ship. I removed the cover and checked for signs of blood. I found two plastic wine glasses floating in the filter and nothing more.

I thought if I were in the pool and got out, where would I walk and what would I do. With a preconceived notion of her actions, I began to retrace her path from the tub to the master cabin.

Slipping on the deck in my slick dress shoes, I grabbed the handrail and noticed a few strands of hair lodged in the rail coupling. They were about ten feet stern of the tub. Placing them in an evidence bag, I swiped the rail for occult bold. As I continued to check around, I noticed a brownish patch on the water rail nearby. It looked as though the fiberglass had been scuffed. I could see small fiberglass fibers poking up, but not much else. I'm sure in the darkness this wasn't seen by the officers on the scene. Again, I took samples. I also checked the on deck storage areas for a hammer as Dr. Steve suggested. There were no hammers or blunt type objects to be found. I wondered if they had all been thrown overboard. I paced the deck and inspected every accessible space and surface. Other than the hair fibers, there was nothing to find.

"Did you find what you were looking for?" Quinton said, making me jump, since I hadn't heard him come up behind me.

"Oh yes. Now I just have a few questions about the night she passed."

"I don't know much about what happened."

I took out my little notebook so I wouldn't forget his answers. Age is affecting my memory.

"My first question is about your blood type?"

"Me? I think I'm 'A' something, why?"

"Just a standard question. Can I take a scraping from your cheek for DNA scanning? We want to clear any evidence we find. Having your profile will help rule you out, since finding your DNA would be a normal occurrence," I explained, hoping this would assure him he was not a suspect and make it easier to collect the sample without having to obtain a subpoena.

"I don't have any objection. I'm sure my genes are scattered all around here."

This was certainly not the response I had expected from him. He seemed extremely cooperative. However, I was hesitant to voice several questions I had on my mind. Like, how was it he could seem so calm and unaffected by his wife's death only hours ago? In addition, was he unaware of the second semen finding? Had there been a threesome and he was okay with it or, did he have no idea his wife had been with another man?

"I wonder if you could lead me thru the events of the evening," I asked, notebook in hand.

"Well, we had a BBQ and listened to music on the deck in the late afternoon. I think Jackson went in to watch a Sponge Bob marathon on TV. While he was entertained, the grownups had a few drinks. We enjoyed the Jacuzzi for a while and as far as I can recall, we all went to bed somewhere around eight o'clock."

"Everyone on board went to bed at eight?"

"Eight or eight thirty, I'm almost certain of it."

"Did you or your wife get up sometime in the night? Maybe to the bathroom or back out on deck?"

"Sorry, I can't recall. I noticed she was not in bed with me when I woke in the morning. I thought she'd gone on deck to read or have an early morning cup of coffee."

"Can you tell me what you did when you found she wasn't on board?"

"I looked and found the dingy rope cut. I assumed she had taken it to shore for some reason."

"And when she didn't return? What did you do then?" I was writing as fast as I could in my little book.

"I tried to call her on the cell phone but couldn't get a signal. So Tom took the Jet Ski to shore and walked up to the summit where he could get a connection. When he couldn't reach her, he called the police."

"I couldn't get a cell site either. I had to do the same thing," I commented. "I have just a few more questions if you have the time, then I'll get out of your way."

"What do you want to know?" he asked.

"What is the relationship between you and your guests yesterday?"

"Tom is an old friend of Rita's and mine from college. Jackson is his two-year-old son. Tom's wife left them destitute about a year ago. Rita tries to include them in some of our outings. She says they need a woman's influence in their lives. They come out for a week or so when we come to the lake. Jackson has a great time. Since we don't have any children of our own, she spoils Jackson at every opportunity."

"I have just one more strange question, but I need to know if you are aware of Tom or his son's blood types. We'd like to rule them out as well."

"I have no idea. No one ever needed a transfusion, but I know Rita is type 'O+,' but for anyone else you'd have to ask them."

"You have been a great help, thank you. I know this is not an easy time for you. If there's anything my department or I can do to help you please call me anytime," I handed him my card.

I said goodbye and using the tiny spymaster transmitter called George. Surprisingly, he arrived to pick me up within seconds. He'd been waiting for my call with the motor running.

"Just in case you needed out of there in a hurry. I was listening to your conversation over the radio," George reassured me. I'd had back up whether I'd wanted it or not.

"I told you not to do that!" I protested.

"No, you said 'not to record it.' You didn't say anything about not listening."

"George, you have to keep your mouth shut about anything you overheard and remember I did not tell you nor was I aware you were doing it! You need to stop reading detective novels and start reading romances instead, I'm sure it would make Bea happier."

"Don't worry. I know how to keep a secret," he said, as he dropped me back at the beach, almost throwing me out of the boat as he struck the sand at ten knots.

"I'll keep an eye on him in case he does anything strange. I'll call you immediately if there's anything suspicious," he promised as he sped away.

God help me. Somehow, I have acquired a wealthy middle aged James Bond wanna be as an unpaid assistant. I hope he does not do something stupid to compromise this case. As far as I was concerned, he knew way too much confidential information for a civilian. He might inadvertently do something to tip off my suspect or worse, acquire illegal evidence, barring me from using it. This made finding the truth as soon as possible imperative, before anything had a chance to go wrong.

I returned to the office and gave the samples I'd acquired to Steve for the forensic team to analyze. It would be several days before the final genotype profiles would be ready. I could use this time to track down Tom and have a chat.

*   *   *

Thanks to the Colorado criminal database, I found our good friend Tom listed. I was able to find his criminal record for 'sexual assault.' Hence, it was my lucky day since Colorado takes a DNA sample from all felons. Good ole Tom's was right there for me to download. With a huge feeling of pride in my ingenuity, I took the readout to Steve for comparison with his findings when they were ready.

When he finally had the results, the samples of the mystery lover were no longer a secret. They appeared to be a perfect match to Tom. Furthermore, the hair samples were from the victim's husband and the trace blood found on the water gutter type "O+." Now the quest was on. How did his hair get on the railing and how was her blood impregnated into the water rail? Someone was not being honest and had a few hard questions to answer. Just whom it was with the secret to hide had yet to be determined.

It did not take long to find good ole Tom once I turned Ted and his bloodhounds loose. Within a day of mentioning to Ted I needed to talk to him, he was in my waiting room, not voluntarily.

"We found him at his sister's house. Not a very well thought out strategy for hiding," Ted dropped the handcuff key on my desk. "He's all yours, but when you're finished don't let him go. We have a few outstanding DUI warrants on him. I think the judge will be happy to see him again."

"Do I have to leave him cuffed while I talk to him?" I asked in total ignorance.

"I gave you the key. What do you think. They're only traffic warrants. It's not like he's James Mason or some other mad killer."

"You mean Charles Manson, don't you? James Mason was a famous movie star."

"What do you think, you're on 'Jeopardy?' Mason, Manson, what's the difference? I got the guy you wanted, who cares what alias he is using."

"You're ability to discern between a movie actor and a serial killer gives me great comfort about my family's safety and just a little concern about who you have in my waiting room."

"Don't worry; it's not 'Dirty Harry,'" he smiled.

"That's Clint Eastwood, you moron," I grinned back.

"Well, whoever he is, he's yours for the next half an hour. Do what you like with him, but don't leave any marks," Ted escorted the prisoner into my office and unshackled him. "Dr. Reedman, this is Thomas Fox, the second man onboard the 'Lady of the Lake.' Have fun boys. I'll wait outside."

I could tell being brought to my office in cuffs freaked out Mr. Fox. He was not sure just what was going on.

He was aware Rita had died. Somewhere in his mind, he had to be thinking he was suspected of committing her murder.

"Relax, I just have a few questions about your night on the boat."

"Sure, she was my friend. If there's anything I can do to help, let me know." He seemed nervous.

"Well, what can you tell me about Rita and how she went overboard?" I asked looking him directly in the eyes, just in case he had a subconscious reaction to my inquiry.

"We had a great weekend. We did a little fishing and had a BBQ on the deck."

"When was the last time you saw Rita alive?" I pressed.

"It was around eight o'clock when we all went to bed," he was bouncing his foot under the table. This was a certain sign he was not telling the truth or that the line of questioning was making him nervous.

"Let me put it another way. What time did you and the deceased have sex?" He stopped breathing for a moment.

"Sex, what are you talking about? She was my best friend's wife," he stated adamantly.

"You know, I almost want to believe you. However, we have one small problem."

"What problem? I didn't kill her." He was visibly shaking as he responded.

"The problem of your genetics. We found a sample in the deceased's body. Do you want me to tell you exactly where in her body?" He was shaking his leg so hard now the table between us began to vibrate.

"How do you know it's mine? It could be someone else's."

"We have your genetic profile from the corrections department. They took a sample of your blood when you were incarcerated for sexual assault. It's a perfect match."

"Oh God, no. It was supposed to remain a secret." Tears began to trickle down his face.

"Oh, so you do recall an encounter with the deceased?" I almost felt sorry probing any further, but I had to know the truth.

"Does Quinton know what you've found?" he asked with an understandable unsteadiness in his voice.

"Not unless you've said something. Of course, if the three of you were having a group interlude, it would explain the presence of your genomes. There is nothing to be ashamed of. Things go on in bedrooms you would not believe. I have seen it all. So, there's nothing you can tell me that will shock me. I promise not to judge you."

"I knew it was wrong at the time. I had a bad feeling in the pit of my stomach. He doesn't know anything about it. Please don't tell him until I've had a chance to move to the South Pole."

"I don't think you have to worry about moving. The District Attorney will put you somewhere really safe for the next fifty years."

"Whoa, wait a second here. I did not kill her. I just took advantage an opportunity presented to me. Sure, I had thought about taking her for years. I loved her I wouldn't hurt her."

"Judging by where we found your genetics, hurting her didn't seem to be on your mind at the time."

"Listen to me. I went back out to the tub at around midnight. Suddenly, she shows up with a bottle of thirty-year-old scotch and a sad story of how Quinton spends more time on the computer than her. She began to feed me shots and kiss my neck. I couldn't help myself. She offered and I went for it. I knew it was wrong but I couldn't resist."

After Larry's lustful display toward her corpse, I could only imagine what the live thing was like. I questioned if I could have resisted the temptation of ravaging her. I kept in mind the fact this unfaithful dip was going to face the husband eventually. I would not want to be there. I am sure it will involve a homicide.

"So, after you had this hot time, what did you do?"

"She was drunk and began to feel guilty. She wanted to wake Quinton and confess to him she'd just had sex with me."

"Did that make you mad?" I questioned.

"No, not mad, frightened. I told her to forget it. There was no way she'd get pregnant and we'd never do it again. She insisted on confessing. We quietly argued for a while. She started to get dressed and then just passed out alongside the Jacuzzi. I went to bed hoping she wouldn't remember it in the morning." He was crying openly as he answered.

"She passed out on the deck?" I asked just to set him up for my next question.

"Out like a light."

"How do you know she was alive when you ran?"

"I didn't run. I just went to my cabin. I was hoping it was all just a bad dream and I'd wake up."

"You didn't answer my question. How did you know she wasn't dead?"

"Because she was breathing and as I entered the salon, I could hear her throwing up over the side. Hard liquor and a steady swell will make you seasick quickly."

Ted returned promptly to collect his bounty. "Time's up. We have to be running along now. I hope you got what you wanted, doc." He was smiling as he left holding his shackled prey by the arm. "If not, I'm sure you'll be able to reach him at the county jail for the next few days."

As my office door closed with a bang, I began to laugh aloud. I know it must have sounded like I had lost my mind. I just couldn't help feeling a great sense of relief I wasn't that poor bastard. Really, the best thing he had to hope for was a long jail sentence for the DUI charges. It was the either jail or face the husband in a dark alley somewhere, sometime.

I did not want to make the drive back up the pass again. I had been lucky enough to do it twice and survive. I just knew the third time would be the charm and I would die for sure. However, I really wanted to talk to the husband. Should I tell him what we'd found? After all, he was the next of kin and had a right to know or should I hold it back and see what he knows first.

I sat at my desk planning some brilliant strategy to interview the husband. I was interested to hear his side of the story. The intercom interrupted my attempt at deep thought. It was Betty calling to inform me "the husband is on his way to your office and wants a copy of his wife's death certificate."

Wonderful, how do I tell a grieving relative I cannot rule on a cause of death without tipping my hand? If he'd found out about the tryst, he may have hit her on the head and thrown her body overboard.

"Dr. Reedman?" Quinton McCall asked as he stepped through the door.

"Mr. McCall, have a seat. I would like to ask you a couple of questions before I can sign Rita's death certificate."

"What else do you want to know? I've told you everything I can remember." He didn't sound the least bit intimidated by my inquiry.

"Well, Mr. McCall, I just wondered about your zodiac. How long had it been missing before you noticed it?"

"It was gone when I woke up in the morning." Now, he looked taken aback.

"So far, I'm having a little difficulty making the evidence match up with the autopsy findings. I hope you can help me out."

"Okay." I could tell by the look on his face he thought I had some secret knowledge.

"Here's the first place I'm having some problems. I have two sets of witnesses who swear they heard fighting coming from your boat, early in the evening she disappeared."

"We weren't fighting. We were yelling to be heard over the stereo."

"One witness clearly heard someone say 'don't worry, we're coming.' How do you explain it?"

"Rita wanted the deli tray brought up from the galley and I was yelling to her not to worry, I was on my way. There was not anything sinister in the conversation. What nosey neighbors we have. I thought I had anchored far enough away from everybody else to get a little privacy. I guess I didn't go far enough."

"Well then, the second round of yelling later in the evening?"

"We just had a discussion about being on vacation. She was angry about how much I was working and loosing on stocks. Maybe we got a little loud. Rita gets upset when I do day trading when we're taking a break from the rat race."

"What happened following the 'discussion? Did you resolve it?"

"I answered one last e-mail and she went nuts. She threatened to leave. I knew she was too drunk to go anywhere. She'd had almost an entire bottle of wine by then."

I was beginning to think I was on the wrong path. Maybe the clues were pointing in a different direction and I wasn't seeing what was right in front of my eyes. The husband's explanations made perfect sense. However, somewhere in my gut I felt there was more here than met the eye.

"She just went down to the bar and had a drink."

"Did you join her?"

"No, she gets abusive when she's had too much to drink and has a tendency to throw heavy objects. I've found the best thing to do is just stay out of her way until the next day." He smiled tightly. "I took a sleeping pill and went to bed."

"Sitting at the bar was the last time you saw her alive?" I asked.

"Absolutely, I didn't see when or if she came to bed I was knocked out by the pill."

"Thanks for your help. With what you've told me, I think we can get everything signed sealed and delivered in the next few days."

"Thank you so much. I have to go arrange for her memorial service."

"I hate to sound like 'Colombo,' but I have just one more question. Did you have any life insurance on your wife?"

"I think we do. I know her agency has a policy on her and I think we have a couple of our own on each other. Is that all?"

"Yes, sorry to have kept you so long. I'll call you when the documents are completed."

Now I was really in a fix. I had to try and decide whom I was to believe: her husband, the lover, or my evidence.

Just as I was ready to leave for the day, Dr. Steve appeared at my door holding a computer readout.

"I have some raw data for you. Do you want it or would you rather think about it until morning?"

"You know I'll never sleep if you don't tell me what you know."

"I have good news. The hair sample you gave me had some roots attached. I ran them through the rapid sequencer. I can tell you with an eighty percent certainty the hair was the victim's husband's and was fresh."

"So, it was his hair on the underside of the rail." The gears in my head were running full speed.

"I have one more piece for you. The brown stain sample you gave me was her blood. There were microscopic filaments mixed in with the blood. I checked and they were fiberglass. Larry went back to the body and checked for matching material." He dramatically paused, waiting for me to ask what he found.

"Okay, you win, what did you find?"

"Tiny shards of fiberglass in her hair around the wound. Now, do you think you'll sleep any better?" It was a rhetorical question. He knew damn well I wouldn't sleep until I had thought this all out.

I spent the evening running scenarios thru my head and vodka martinis thru my GI tract.

I ruled out a falling object due to the fact everything on the boat seemed well secured to the superstructure and nothing appeared missing. I also ruled the two-year-old out as a suspect for obvious reasons.

With two suspects eliminated, I felt I had made great progress. However, it meant another fifty options.

No one could deny the fact she had sex with Tom and Quinton. Their DNA was there to prove it. However, there would be no way to guarantee the act was consensual or even simultaneous. I wondered had the three of them been having a group encounter in the hot tub. If it were true, the question had to be asked. Was it possible she didn't want to be involved. If some kind of struggle occurred, it could account for her going into the drink.

Another possibility was she having an affair under her husband's nose. Maybe it was in an effort to get even for him overworking and not paying attention to her. Sleeping with your husband's best friend would be a good way to settle the score.

An affair being discovered or confessed to might have enraged the husband enough to knock her on the head. Maybe he threw something back at her during one of her reported fits of anger. He had admitted to having an argument with her.

Another option I did not want to overlook was the distinct possibility she had committed suicide. If she were truly remorseful over her encounter with Tom or something else, she could easily have thrown herself into the lake in a moment of despair, hitting her head on the way overboard.

There was one more thing I had difficulty getting to make sense. It involved the dingy. Why had it been found so close to her body? Remembering the data I'd found by floating the ball and cork contradicted the boats relationship to her body. They should have ended up on opposite sides of the lake.

In my increasingly intoxicated state, I tried to think if I had missed anyone who might have done this. Who had knowledge of the victim's movements, habits and have opportunity. Then George entered my mind. He mentioned watching the victim's yacht. Who knows how long he had been observing her. He certainly possessed enough spy gadgetry to keep a close eye on her. Now I was prepared to blame a nice old man. It was time to quit the martinis.

Setting aside my wild scenarios, I began to think about the autopsy and my trip to the boat. The answer had to be found there. People lie to cover their butts all of the time, but I've never had physical evidence lie to me. I have misinterpreted it on occasion, but the facts reveal themselves if you look hard enough.

As I thought about the lies and half-truths related to me by all parties involved it occurred what had really happened. To prove it, I had the physical evidence, DNA, and had used good old listening skills.

I know what happened. Do you?

REX REVIEWS

This case had me stumped for days. However, when I looked with an unimpaired mind, it wasn't difficult to hypothesize what happened.

My mother always said 'the way to make a decision was to write each option down and then simply eliminate one at a time.' I sat with a pen and paper and made a list.

I began with suicide. I ruled this out due to the fracture in her skull and any trace of a note or reported threat to do harm to herself. Even intoxicated or judgment impaired there had to be some sign of intent or previous threat. In this case there was none.

It seemed everyone had an opportunity to kill poor plucked Rita, with of course, the exception of the kid. George had to be eliminated because he had witnesses as to his whereabouts at the time of Rita's demise.

The husband wasn't about to kill his wife. He waited on her and put up with her throwing things at him. If he were going to kill her, I think he would have done it long ago. I had the feeling he would have been glad to have Tom take her off of his hands. If he was as rich as he'd indicated, he certainly didn't need her money.

As I reflected, I kept coming back to the lovers account. It seemed to be confirmed by most of the evidence.

The boyfriend said 'she wanted to confess' about their interlude. He even admitted to arguing with her about it. I only have his word she was alive when he left her.

The key to this mystery came early. When interviewed, Tom, the lover, related Rita had initiated the encounter and later regretted it. He said when she got up to get dressed, she passed out alongside the Jacuzzi and he went to bed. His statement about her condition as he departed gave a big clue.

"Because she was breathing and as I entered the salon I could hear her throwing up over the side. Hard liquor and a steady swell will make you seasick quickly," he alleged.

The vomiting was confirmed by the food particles found in her mouth at the autopsy, giving his story creditability. The only thing wrong with his diagnosis of alcohol induced seasickness. It was wrong.

The skull fracture and corresponding hematoma, or area of bruising on the brain, brought the signs together.

When a trauma to the head severe enough to cause such injuries occurs, the brain begins to swell and bleed. Since it is encased within a sealed unit, the tissue has nowhere to go, forcing the brainstem down into the foramen magnum or opening to the spinal cord. This edema is what causes the depression around the brainstem we found during the exam. As swelling progresses, neurological centers for respiration, located in the brainstem are affected and breathing ceases.

One of the first physical symptoms is the victim begins vomiting. Another possible sign of a traumatic brain injury is a high-pitched cry or noise. During his interview, Tom reported Rita exhibited both symptoms.

Now, we have the essential signs and symptoms. It's time to put them all together and explain how they occurred.

Tom indeed enjoyed a brief encounter with the intoxicated source of his desires. Their tryst was unknown by Quinton. However, Rita had plans to remedy the situation. Once this act of infidelity had been committed, she was going to inform him of the sordid details.

Tom was faced with a terrible choice. He could let her tell Quinton, which would certainly end a twenty-year brotherhood or worse. On the other hand, he could try to talk some sense into Rita, stopping her from causing irreparable damage to their friendship.

The evidence indicated Tom's story was not quite as he had related it. When Rita was dressed and still insisted on informing her husband, Tom pushed her in an attempt to stop her. As Tom said, she did fall backward onto the deck alongside the Jacuzzi. He left the part out about her striking her head on the deck. She appeared to be passed out and shortly began throwing up, he reported.

Her vomiting was due to the fact his push caused her head to strike on the deck's water gutter. Tom caused a fatal brain injury and wasn't even aware of it.

He went to bed thinking she would never remember. Well, he was right. She would never regain consciousness to remember anything. As she lay dying on the deck, he lay sleeping.

How to prove it?

Simply falling couldn't produce the force necessary to cause the injury to her skull and brain. She just wasn't tall enough to generate the gravitational forces necessary to create the fracture. She had to have been pushed or fallen from a greater distance than reported to accelerate hard enough to produce such an impact. We know by the shape of the cut on her scalp, the fatal blow was in an upward direction. The only explanation is she was facing him at the time he shoved her backward. She struck the back of her head on the gutter, causing the upward appearing blow.

The big question to answer is how she ended up in the water.

Her husband gave a clue to this during his interview with the police and again with me later. He claimed to have gone to bed after taking a sedative and not missing her until morning. He also claimed to know nothing about the missing dingy. Both were lies.

He betrayed himself when he said he hadn't missed her. The argument between Rita and Tom was loud enough for the neighboring yachts to hear. Quinton had to be disturbed by it. The disagreement took place just outside the master suites deck access to the hot tub.

At some point after Tom left Rita on the deck, Quinton went looking for her. He admitted he thought she was going to take the dingy and leave him. In the silence following Tom's departure, he was sure she'd done just that.

When he found what he thought was her dead body on the deck, he was certain he'd be blamed due to the earlier yell fest and didn't want any suspicion cast in his direction. If she were found in the water, people would think she drowned and his problems were solved. The beauty was it would appear as though she had drunkenly fallen overboard while trying to depart in the zodiac. With no witnesses, all he had to do was push her body overboard.

In his haste to set the scene, instead of untying the intricate knot, he cut the zodiac's tether with a knife. Since the motor and propeller were submerged, they made the boat move under the influence of the current and not the wind direction, ultimately ending up within yards of her cadaver.

The forensic clue, which supports this scenario, was Quinton's own hair found on the railing where Tom reported Rita's fall. He scraped his head when he shoved Rita overboard leaving his genetic fingerprint behind.

I thought it was suspicious when he showed so little grief over his wife's untimely, bizarre death. All he was interested in was getting a copy of her death certificate. You see, a death certificate is required to collect any life insurance, and more importantly, have the deceased disposed of.

Now we know how and why it was done. There's just one twist left to address. The ruling:

Drowning was her cause of death. However, her manner of death had to be listed as death at the hands of another. The courts would call this some degree of homicide.

Just who was to be held responsible by the District Attorney might surprise you.

It wasn't Tom. He had no idea he'd injured Rita nor did he have any plan to do so, therefore, his actions were an accident.

The husband, on the other hand, was culpable. This was proven by his fresh hair sample and the goose bumps on the deceased. They indicated Quinton dropped her in the water while she was still alive. He obviously had not tried to revive her or even look to see if she was still breathing. If he had checked and still dumped her into the lake, his crime was even more heinous.

Birds on a Wire and Fish Can't Swim

I love Colorado. If you squint just right when the snow falls, it looks like lace coming from the sky. So beautiful and delicate, I almost forget I'm freezing my manhood off.

About the time I realize we've gone through two cords of wood to keep warm, its mid-March and I begin to look forward to July. Summer and its daily thunderstorms bring fond memories to mind: fishing, wearing shorts and getting really burnt by the sun. At nine thousand feet we have less of the atmosphere to protect us, thus one can count on an annual scorching by our solar friend.

With winter a distant memory, Pine Park enjoyed the Fourth of July festivities. In a small town, the Fourth has a special meaning. Not that we are more patriotic than larger populations, but I think we enjoy showing it more. I recently had a newcomer to town describe our Independence Day celebration as 'the Fourth of July in Mayberry'.

His observation struck me as a complement to our community. True, we do have a small lake in the center of town with a fountain in the center. A large white gazebo sits at the western edge of the water. Fishing is restricted to those under ten and over seventy years old. The catch and release policy is strictly enforced.

This is the setting for the July celebration. Before dawn, groups begin to assemble their tents and booths for the party. Hot dogs, hamburgers and any kind of sweet, slurpy drinks are available. Cotton candy and popcorn vendors really clean up. At dusk fireworks begin, followed by a local orchestra playing the eighteen-twelve overture (with cannons) set to fireworks; it's an impressive show for such a small community.

Lori, the girls, and I enjoyed the night's festivities. By the time we returned home to participate in our neighborhood ritual, fireworks in our driveway with the neighbors, it was well past one in the morning.

In years past our night ended much earlier due to the lack of pyrotechnics available to the aging men of the neighborhood. However, the little boys we were accustomed to terrifying with our fiery displays are now in college (I hate growing older; I remember the day when the dads introduced them to potato cannons). Somehow, these same young men, students of the mining college in Bolder; have a unique understanding of explosives. They also are in close proximity to the Wyoming border where a mining student can acquire a myriad of luminescent explosives, to the delight of their pyromaniac fathers.

Going to bed at one or two in the morning is difficult on the aging body. There were times I could stay up and party for two or three days at a time. Those days disappeared by the age of forty. Therefore, the seven a.m. call from our automated system was an unwelcome wake-up to say the least.

"There has been a dead body found at the Shore of Chessman Lake. Respond immediately code three, police are waiting." The computer disconnected before I could even try to reply. Code three requires flashing red and blue lights or at least flashing alternating bright lights. I don't even have bright headlights on my jeep much less a light bar. They would have to wait until I could get there by obeying the speed limit. If they wanted me to arrive any faster then the county would have to provide a police escort for me.

With explosions still echoing in my ears, I dressed and left for the reservoir. While the drive isn't far, I still hate going there. The road is winding, narrow and with very few pullouts. I made it to the scene within thirty minutes of the call. The daily storm clouds were building as I arrived.

"Let's take what evidence we need and get the hell out of here!" Detective Newman suggested as I stepped from my Jeep.

"Are you afraid of a little rain?" I asked.

"No, but it's dangerous to be out here," he defended in his hurry to depart.

"Before we run for our lives, would you mind telling me why I'm here?"

"Okay, a local found a tourist dead alongside the road."

"Show me the body, let's take a few pictures and go home. I need a nap."

Ted showed me the corpse. It was a man in his early twenties. He was just lying on the ground, dead.

"Hey Rex, look what I have for dinner." Returning from the lake, Officer Rodgers held up two big trout.

"I told you to stop taking your pocket fisherman on patrol with you," Ted disciplined his subordinate.

"I didn't need a fishing pole. I just reached down and grabbed them."

"I've heard you tell fishing stories before but this one beats them all," Ted smiled.

"Honest. There were about ten of them over on the far side. They were just swimming up against the shore. All I had to do was grab the two biggest ones."

"Take your photos and let's get out of here," Ted grumbled, "Oh yeah, be sure to take a picture of the big fisherman and his trophies."

"Take your photos and let's get out of here," Ted reiterated.

I took pictures of the body and the surrounding area. I thought the scene might help later in determining the body's location in relation to the surroundings. As I inspected the cadaver it seemed perfectly normal. It looked as though this young man just dropped dead on the spot. He was wearing khaki pants, tennis shoes and a matching plaid shirt. A fancy 35mm camera was strung around his neck.

While Ed and Patty were removing the body, something I avoid at all costs, I admired the scenic beauty. The body was located beneath a stand of gorgeous Ponderosa Pines. Running along the property line was a barbed wire fence to keep intruders out. This boundary extended along the highway through a small pond and off into the distance. It looked like a postcard setting with Pikes Peak reflecting off the water and aspen trees on the far side of the pond. I thought, now that's what people come to see, nature at its most spectacular. The only thing missing to make it perfect was a herd of elk.

Ted exhibited initiative and had the deceased's photographs developed before the autopsy had been scheduled. The sheriff's department has a secure photo-processing lab on site. The photos showed the scene in great focus. I noticed in the pictures something I hadn't observed at the scene. There were three dead birds on the ground about ten feet from the corpse.

I rushed to arrive by the time the autopsy was scheduled, arriving to the procedure loaded down with doughnuts. There's no sense taking a chance on ruining all of my conditioning of the staff at this point.

Dr. Steve began the post mortem a few minutes late. It seemed he had missed breakfast and was wolfing down on long johns.

"Sorry I'm late but Reedman brought food and I couldn't begin until I'd had my fill in the lounge." There was still frosting in his mustache as Steve explained his tardiness.

He began the procedure as always. He sang into the Dictaphone, "Rain drops keep falling on my head . . ."

"Raindrops? What are you singing about?" Larry the denier questioned.

"He was found after the rain yesterday, wasn't he? I think the song is appropriate."

"Your taste in music leaves something to be desired and I won't even comment on your delivery. If I were Simon, I'd ridicule you and toss you off American Idol," Larry harassed Steve.

"Critic, undress this guy and let's get started," Steve grinned in Larry's direction.

Larry obeyed, cutting the victim's clothing from the body and placing it gently into an evidence container.

"Wow, even stone cold dead this guy has some abs. Look at those muscles," Larry observed aloud.

"Has anyone told you how strange you are?" Steve commented.

"Look, hard abs and he's been dead for at least a day," Larry defended himself, trying not to sound like an admirer of the male physique.

Steve began to seriously dictate his observations.

"The distinctly male corpse has had his external wardrobe removed, revealing a fit male physique." He didn't note Larry's admiration of the corpse's physical condition.

"Larry, you idiot, don't you recognize rigor mortis when you see it?" Steve questioned.

"You mean his stomach muscles aren't as taught as they appear?" Larry questioned.

"No, you idiot. The tight muscles are due to rigor mortis. Hadn't you noticed the tension in the rest of his muscles?" Steve inquired.

"Sure, but he's just buffed," Larry answered.

"Larry, you brain stem. He's just thin and his rigor is just more prominent. He's no more physically fit than you or I. We'll leave Rex out of this since he's old and decrepit."

Steve continued to dictate. "The external abdomen exhibits a fern like pattern of burns across the epidermis radiating from the waist to the sternal region and neck. Open him up and let's have a look inside."

Larry did the Y shaped incision, opening the chest and bowel. Steve inspected the organs one at a time.

"Well, he looks fine in here, but I wonder about his heart. It looks as though he might have suffered some damage there. As for the brain it looks like he had a stroke judging by the damage to the gray matter."

The balance of the autopsy was uneventful. While it looked as though our corpse just reached his expiration date and died, the postmortem findings were insignificant.

The following day, Ted delivered photographs from the victim's camera. The deceased had an eye for photography judging by his pictures. He could have placed them in a gallery without resistance. The first three pictures were of the pond and the reflected scenery. The next five photos were of the same pond with the storm clouds in the background. The dark gray storm appeared ominous. The last two pictures were of the storm and were close up. Suddenly the rest of the pictures appeared blurred and out of focus and then there were none.

As I examined the photographic evidence I realized how the deceased arrived in his current state of rigor.

My evidence could prove without a doubt how this man died.

Have you picked up the hints?

If so, you know what caused his demise.

REX REVEALS

If you missed the obvious hints and clues, I'll enlighten you.

The deceased was found alongside the road. The scene was a beautiful one of the Colorado countryside.

Our corpse forgot something known by all high country residents. Stay away from windows and any form of metal during lightning storms. Lightning can penetrate glass easily and is attracted by metal, tall trees or bodies of water.

Lightning frequently causes the death of flat-landers trapped in open fields during thunderstorms. However, in this case, the deceased had taken an opportunity a local would never take, being out in a lightning storm and unprotected, pure stupidity.

The victim's death was due to a close lightning strike. When lightning struck the pond it was transmitted though the wire fence to the victim who had been leaning against it taking his memorable photographs.

This explained the pattern of burns on his chest and indicated his death was due to electrocution. The presence of the dead birds gave me the first clue as to what led to his demise. They were sitting on the fence at the time of a lightning strike in the pond and were all electrocuted as the current passed thru the wire fence. Lightning hitting the pond also accounted for the ease with which the officer was able to catch fish. The electric charge caused the fish to become disoriented and dazed.

The fern pattern of burns on his abdomen and chest are most frequently found in electrocutions such as lightning strikes. The burns extended from the spot he was leaning against the fence up toward his head. They look just like the lightning bolt we all observe in the stormy sky, branching out like the limbs of a tree.

Ruling: death due to electrocution; cause of death, accident.

Schizophrenics are Never Lonely

A week, even a month may go by without a death in Pine County. At first the lack of fatalities is a relief, a welcome break. There's time to spend with the family and get a few things done around the house.

However, the more time that passes without what my daughter Lexi refers to as 'a creepy crawly corpse call' passes, I begin to get nervous. Not that I'll no longer be needed and lose my job.

I get the feeling God is saving up for me, lulling me into a false sense of security. Just about the time I begin to think we may be able to go camping, God is saying, "Let's just see how many bodies Rex can handle at one time. Maybe we should throw a good bus accident at him . . . Hey grim reaper, gather up a group of sinners ready to cross over and get them on a gambling bus up to Reedman's area! Camping, who does he think he's fooling?"

Lesson number one; never let God know what you have planned. Just quietly go about your business and hope he doesn't notice. Unless you need help, then scream as loudly as possible. Of course he'll probably be too busy messing with my life to ever hear you.

I had just completed packing the bare necessities for a night in the woods with my loving wife: a bottle of wine, some cheese and a sleeping bag. Before we could leave the house my pager and cell phone went of simultaneously. Thanks to modern technology and the county's new phone system, it can call multiple numbers concurrently. Lucky me.

"Answer it and you're dead." Lori looked serious.

"Look, I'm sure it's just the guys letting me know everything's under control," I assured her. "Nothing is going to interfere with our plans."

"If we don't sleep together under the stars tonight, I guarantee you will be sleeping there alone."

"Okay, it's just a quick trip out to Green Valley Falls to sign a death certificate and we can get on our way," I explained as I hung up the phone.

"You have one hour. Any longer and you'd better bring a locksmith with you." She wasn't smiling.

*   *   *

It didn't take long to reach the scene. It was only about five miles from our house. It is a short distance by car but a world away when it comes to construction. This area is part of the old mining district. In the late eighteen hundreds building codes were nonexistent. Miners arriving to seek their fortunes in the goldfields were not met by construction companies or realtors ready to sell them a lovely home. Each man took his ax and saw into the forest near his claim and began building his home. Those with more time before the bitter Colorado winter rolled in used stone as well as lumber. Others were not much more than lean-to's. Many cabins were place in front of or over the entrance to the mine shaft, not only for security, but it made it easier to get to the mine in the depths of winter.

As I arrived fire trucks were still on the scene, putting out hot spots. Ted and several police cadet's greeted me at what remained of the front door of the rustic cabin. It was still smoldering as I passed through.

"Be careful in here. The fire chief said it could collapse any moment," Ted warned as he gingerly traversed the charred wooden floor like an overweight ballerina.

"Careful is my middle name," I bragged.

Once again, I'd forgotten my own axiom: never let God know what you're up to.

I pensively stepped out onto the floor and it felt secure enough to relieve my fear of it falling out from under me. I took my less hesitant second step, followed by a confidant third. It was at that moment I knew God was giving me some special attention.

The floor beneath my feet began to emanate the most pitiful groan followed quickly by the sounds of individual wood fibers splitting. I knew what was to come next. I could tell by their faces so did the onlookers, now standing safely across the room. Without endangering themselves, no one could move to help as the floorboards began to give way beneath me. By adding their body weight to the already unstable flooring, they would ensure all of our deaths.

"Hold on, I'll get a rope!" Ted promised excitedly.

"Oh thank God, I'm saved! I'm not going anywhere, you know. I hope. Hurry just the same, please!" I was afraid to talk too loudly for fear the sound of my own voice would send me crashing.

"Don't move," the Fire Chief wisely advised me from his point of safety in the doorway.

"Sage advice. Thanks, you rectal genius. I hate to bring this up, but does this place have a basement or am I worried about falling two feet?" I was looking for some reassurance from those assembled. I'd feel like a real moron if the ground under the floor were only inches away and here I stood like a cigar store Indian afraid to move.

"Basement is an understatement. There are two levels below we know of. You know old Dirk was a miner. You never can be sure of what might be down there." The Chief's comments made me feel so much better.

"I'm sorry I asked. Don't you people have a ladder or something to get me out of here?" I demanded, sounding I thought somewhat calm, considering my present predicament.

"A ladder might knock down the rest of the structure," the chief confidently informed me.

"Wonderful. If I hit the lottery, I swear here and now I'll donate it to your department for rescue training." Agitated, I responded somewhat above a whisper, big mistake.

The floor made another deep moan followed by a high-pitched creak. The entire structure shook. The last thing I remembered as I passed through the floor was the sight of my friends running like rabbits and the sound of splitting timber fracturing around me.

I have been told I plummeted through what turned out to be three levels of tunneling. Ending up in a pile of freshly excavated soil, I was saved from a broken neck by the soft dirt. However, I hadn't avoided the inevitable concussion.

I awoke three days later in the hospital, semi coherent with Lori sitting next to my bed looking as though she hadn't slept in days.

"Good morning, mister sleepyhead." She was smiling a nervous kind of smile. "The next time you don't want to go camping, just say so. You don't need to go to all of this trouble."

"Sure, let's go camping," I could hear myself say, even though I couldn't move to lift my head.

My paralysis was not due to injuries, but rather the massive doses of intravenous drugs being pumped into me. I just floated in my bed.

Lori kissed me softly on the cheek and left to tell the nurse I had regained consciousness.

"She's beautiful. I don't blame you for wanting to stay with her," a voice from the other bed whispered over the room divider.

"I feel lucky to be here at all. I thought I had said my last goodbye as I fell," I answered my unseen roommate.

"Oh, it would have been your swan song if you hadn't been lucky enough to land in that dirt pile."

"Did I really hit something soft? My head sure doesn't feel like it. The last thing I recall was a loud crack."

"You fell right through the floor and into a deep mine shaft where the fresh tailings were dumped."

My roommate had obviously been eavesdropping on conversations regarding my condition and circumstance for the past few days. As with most people he seemed more than willing to share his acquired knowledge, no matter its source.

Lori and the nurse returned, followed by my neurologist and orthopedic surgeon.

"Gee, I've never had my own medical staff before." I tried to be my smart-ass self.

"We're here to answer a few of your questions and ask a few of our own, if you feel up to it," the neurosurgeon, Dr. Powell, asked softly.

"What do you want to know? Who's the president?"

"Well, what do you recall about the accident?" he asked as he looked into my eyes like a bad hypnotist.

"I remember hearing the floor grunt and seeing my friends butts as they retreated, in a valiant effort to save me. However, I understand I was extremely lucky to fall down an open chute and land in a pile of soft dirt."

"If falling through the floor is the last thing you can remember, how do you know what you landed in?" Dr. Powell seemed puzzled. As I looked at Lori and the nurse they had the same look.

I confidently and somewhat curtly told them of my conversation with my roommate. Their expressions changed from puzzled to concern.

"Sweetheart, are you telling us someone here told you about what happened?" Lori asked hesitantly.

"Sure, when you left to get the nurse. My roommate told me everything he'd overheard about my accident."

"Are you sure you aren't just recalling flashes and putting them together. It's a common way to deal with amnesia. The brain tries to fill in the blank spots," Doctor Powell explained, as though I had some kind of brain damage.

"Just ask the guy in the next bed. He'll tell you what he said," I confidently squeezed Lori's hand.

"Rex, there's something we should tell you." He pulled back the curtain around my bed. "You have a private room. You don't have any roommates and you haven't since you arrived. I think you have a closed head injury and are hearing things that aren't there. This might continue for the next few days. In the meantime enjoy the good food, soft bed and hourly blood checks."

Lori kissed me goodnight and, following the staff, left me alone in my private room for the night.

"You know they are out in the hall discussing how badly you're injured." The voice returned from the direction of the drape.

"Oh, I'm sure they think I've lost my mind," I answered my injury-induced companion.

"Don't listen to them. No matter what they think, when you wake you'll be better than before."

As my IV drugs began to kick in the curtain slowly closed around me and the lights dimmed.

My comfortable night consisted of being awakened hourly by the outline of a white clad, badge-wearing vampire, who for some reason wanted more hemoglobin from me. I seem to recall asking exactly what might have changed in the past twenty minutes requiring such close monitoring. I recall the answer clearly.

"Blah, blah, umdiddle tisk chumble blah blah."

Thanks to the morphine pump, it made perfect sense to me.

Daylight broke and the vampire retreated to darker locations within the hospital. My morning nurse threw back the blackout drapes and cheerfully asked if I'd slept well. For a moment I felt like the witch when Dorothy spilled the water on her . . . 'Help me I'm melting . . .' I've never wanted to kill a caregiver before, but this angel of mercy was testing my brain injury. I realized as coroner I could sign her death certificate as an unfortunate accident.

"Your honor, she choked to death after becoming entangled in the drapery cord. I helplessly had to watch her die, since my IV prevented me from coming to her aid."

*   *   *

"The doctor took you off most of your medications overnight and said you could have a full breakfast. Oh and I'm to tell you your CAT scans were normal, at least for you, whatever that means." She gave the schoolgirl giggle and retreated, taking the tray of food with her.

"Didn't I tell you everything would be alright?"

"Alright, that nitwit just took my food with her and I'm going to starve."

I looked toward the foot of my bed and the hair on my neck stood on end. I was obviously suffering an episode the doctor had warned me about. I knew what I was seeing wasn't real. Never-the-less, his lips moved as he spoke and he was looking directly at me. I was trying to ignore the fact he was some kind of Native American clad in white buckskin adorned with fine iridescent beadwork. In his hair he wore five feathers in a leather lanyard.

"Child, do not make heavy your heart. You have not gone with the crazy one."

"Oh yeah, I'm perfectly sane. I just see Indians that aren't here."

Under the blanket I clandestinely pushed the morphine button hoping it would put me back to sleep.

"Even now, as you summon more drugs, I am here and so are you. Do not be frightened; it is the brave warrior who ventures into the world of shadows alone. Everyone around you suffers the closed eye." He gently smiled, comforting my spirit. As I looked in his direction, he faded slowly before my eyes.

I wondered how long these drugs would take to wear off. I don't mind a mild high, maybe four martinis. This, on the other hand, was a little more than I was at ease with. Maybe I should have pushed the plunger only once.

I wasn't about to mention his presence to anyone for fear they'd keep me in a locked ward, indefinitely.

Three days in the hospital and I was beginning to feel like a pincushion. Every phlebotomist seemed to marvel at the size of my veins. One commented 'you have veins like a horse.' This observation sent my mind in several directions. Like, just how did she know how big horses veins were and did that mean she could use a bigger needle than before.

When the staff was certain I could function fully and had no risk of suffering a stroke, they released me to finish recuperating at home. They obviously had harvested sufficient hemoglobin from me to keep themselves in business for some time and felt I was of no further use to them.

*　　*　　*

Returning to my office I was greeted with the typical 'good thing you landed on your head' comment. In response, I proudly exhibited the external cerebral evidence of my brush with death.

"A lump on your head. It isn't even discolored," Ted seemed disappointed by my lack of severe injuries. "I expected to see at least a few sutures or maybe a large gash or two and all you have to show is a lump on your skull!"

"It really hurts. Does that make you feel better?" I asked still hoping for even a slight hint of sympathy.

"Oh yeah, by the enormous size of it you must be dying. I can't believe you're able to stand upright with such a severe injury."

"I should be at home resting in bed you know. The doctors want me to take a little time off to recuperate," I defended my bump.

"You're the biggest crybaby I know. You get a tiny lump on your head and you want to go home to bed. Go ahead and leave, wimp," his eyes sparkled as he berated me.

"Maybe just a nap and I'll be back in a day or so."

"Nap, eh? Is that some kind of code for fishing?"

"Hey, I've suffered a huge emotional as well as physical trauma here, I could have died you know."

"Landing on their head might have killed anyone else on the spot. However, I can't think of a safer place for you to hit. Your head is empty to begin with and your skull is harder than most rocks."

"This is entirely your fault. I followed you across the floor. Maybe if your enormous weight hadn't weakened the substructure I wouldn't be in this condition," I responded to his mocking.

"I warned you the fire chief said it might collapse. We already know you are off work for the next week. Your doctors faxed over a disability request. So, go enjoy your fishing, I mean napping, guilt free," he smiled, waving the fax in my direction.

"I may be neuron impaired but I recognize an opportunity when I see one," I started toward the nearest exit.

"Yeah, don't worry about us. We have plenty of time to work on your case. It won't take more than a day or so of our valuable time to find the origin of the fire and why the old man's body was already showing signs of decomposition at the time of his autopsy."

"I forgot, you wouldn't know about that. You missed the postmortem. You were enjoying that Craft-o-matic bed and its eighteen comfortable settings while we opened him up. You go home and get some rest now. Remember its doctor's orders," he waived the fax in my direction once more.

I left feeling guilty, abandoning Ted with the task of finishing this case. As I drove home, his admonishment echoed in my head. Gradually, I realized the source of my guilt. It wasn't the work, it was the fact he sounded just like my mother.

". . . No go ahead and go to the movie without me. I'll just rest here on the couch. I have all of my medications and the phone near me on the table. If anything happens, God forbid . . . I'll call 911. They can be here in fifteen minutes. They will have the equipment to break down the door. I'm sure they'll have enough time to revive me . . . cough, cough. Go and enjoy yourself. I'll be fine; don't even think about me here alone."

*　　*　　*

Ted knew I'd go home and think about what could start a fire in a cabin with an occupant who had obviously been deceased for some time prior to its ignition. I knew, during my hospital stay, Ted had acquired much more evidence than he'd hinted at. After all, he had attended the autopsy and had obviously received the pathology report as well as the fire investigation forms.

For once in my life I did as I was told and went home to bed. I had a moment of temptation as I passed over the South Platte River on my way to the house, but resisted.

I took the pills the doctors had given me and slipped between the sheets. As I floated off to sleep I realized my television shut its self-off. I didn't remember setting the timer. It didn't matter. The medications made it impossible for me to move or even care how my appliances were working on their own.

The next thing I remember was the sensation of a violent earthquake as my bed shook. Growing up in California I can tell you the feeling of ground moving will wake even coma patients. I sat bolt upright in bed eyes wide open prepared to run for my life. Instead of a 6.5 quake, I found my Indian friend bouncing on the foot of my bed.

"I thought you would never wake up," he stated flatly. "You sleep like an old bear in winter."

"These are some powerful drugs," I said looking at the hallucination seated next to me.

"Do not be distracted by the white man's medicine. You should be thinking about the man in the flames."

"You woke me up to think about work? I'm on sick leave."

I was clearly injured worse than I had realized or I've lost my mind. There is a difference between hearing voices in your head and arguing with one aloud. By having a disagreement with a nonexistent companion, I fit the definition of truly being demented. This is what syphilitic drunks do, not sane members of society. I'm certain I'm not syphilitic and confidant I'm not drunk. However, as for being stoned, the medications made that difficult to rule out.

Still, I found myself being reminded of my duties by an apparition. No wonder these drugs cost so much.

"Fly in sleep young vulture, picker of bones. See times past. Your answer lays in history, not in ashes. The solution to your problem is simple. It can come from flesh and is older than the dust." My ghostly friend faded with a smile.

The medication made it difficult for me to remain upright, or for that matter, conscious any longer. I laid my head on the pillow. When I woke from my pharmaceutical coma, my strange guest had gone but I kept thinking about what he'd said.

My week of confinement passed slowly, I think. However, Lori claimed I slept eighteen hours a day. Monday finally arrived and I could hardly wait to get to work. I was certain Ted had the case of the burned man solved by now and maybe, without the drugs, my friend would leave me alone.

"Well, tell me what you know about the crispy critter in the cabin?" I asked Ted.

"We were waiting for you to get back to wrap that one up," he smiled impishly.

"It's been more than a week. You must have some information to report by now, at least some lab results."

"Lab reports, let me see. I seem to recall something about a lack of accelerants, or was it flammable substances. I just can't remember at the moment. I think my blood sugar is low. I missed breakfast you know."

"He wants you to give him doughnuts. Until then, he speaks like the crow, enjoying the sound of his own voice, making noise but no sense." My hallucinogenic friend had returned, standing behind Ted and offering unneeded council.

"I know he wants me to get him food, I'm not stupid. I'll run and bring back some pastries to loosen his tongue," I answered without thinking.

"Loosen whose tongue and who are you talking to?" Ted looked as though he was going for his handcuffs just in case I was looney and might need to be restrained.

"Just speaking hypothetically. Do you see anyone standing behind you?" I asked, faking a smile.

"No, do you?" Ted looked at me strangely and nervously glanced around just in case someone was there. "If you see someone there maybe we should stop by the doughnut factory to increase your blood sugar then drive by the hospital. I'm sure they still have your old room available."

"He still wants doughnuts. Do not be deceived this one is concerned about his stomach, not your brain. He is like a small chipmunk filling his cheeks for winter. Feed him to shut him up."

"Make up your mind. Is he a crow or a chipmunk?" I berated our unseen companion.

"I'd like to think I'm more the gentle stud type." Ted looked at me as though I belonged in a seventy-two hour lock up for observation.

"I'm just kidding. Ever since the hit on the head, you know it's affected my sense of humor. I'm a little slow." I tried to get out of sounding completely insane.

Arguing with people no one else could see or hear was not about to make me friends or influence people.

"Let's go out and get Danishes my treat," I offered.

"I'll drive. I wouldn't trust you with my kid's bike much less behind the wheel of a County car." Ted grabbed his keys and we were off.

I like riding in a police cruiser. Drivers look straight ahead as you pass and if you are behind them they immediately slow down to the speed limit. Most of all I like the lights and siren. Of course, there is the added benefit. No one is going to pull you over no matter how you drive. It's a wonderful feeling of power.

'Make him turn on the lights and noise thing," a voice demanded from the backseat.

"Shut up, they're not toys," I answered.

"What aren't toys and why should I shut up? I didn't say anything." Ted took his eyes from traffic and looked at his new insane friend, me.

"Sorry, ever since my fall I keep hearing a little voice in my head. I didn't know I was talking aloud," I explained.

"God, as if you weren't weird enough before."

After receiving his bribe of glazed coronary disease, Ted's memory improved dramatically. I learned the man from the fire was named Dirk and he'd been mining that claim for seventy years. Apparently he filed a mining claim and began digging at the age of fifteen. The old man staked his entire life on the fact he could 'feel gold in the ground beneath his feet. Ted further stated the old boy worked alone digging tunnels in search of the illusive treasure. Apparently there were several more levels below my landing spot. Investigators found tunnels leading in all directions; some just came to dead ends while others seemed to go on forever, occasionally ending in large caverns. Obviously old Dirk had been a busy man for a long time.

Once back at the scene Ted continued eating one of the giant cinnamon rolls he'd conned me into buying him at the doughnut factory. Between bites he filled me in on what he knew so far.

"He lived alone, had no relatives and I can't find any bank records relating to his life at all."

"How did he survive, I mean how did he pay for food and supplies? Didn't he go shopping for the past seventy years?" I asked.

"The grocer said he paid for his food and mining supplies with gold. The county clerk said he paid his taxes promptly every year with fresh bank notes." Ted slurped his Starbucks coffee and continued to relay his findings.

"During the autopsy Dr. Steve found areas of necrosis throughout the corpse. He had something called syderosis. The fire helped preserve what remained of the old boy by searing his skin and stopping much of the decay. The thing doc found interesting was there was no sign of smoke damage in the lung tissue. He said it meant the old guy was already dead when the fire started, or he would have inhaled smoke and soot from the fire. The only thing the lab could find in his lungs was granite residue and other kinds of assorted dust."

"Sounds to me he had what miners call 'rocks in the box'. He must have had quite a raspy cough. I doubt any soot could have penetrated his petrified lungs," I hypothesized.

"Rocks in the head is more like it. He lived his life in a hole chasing treasure he never found, what a waste."

"Ted, you surprise me. You are getting prophetic in your old age and somewhat cynical as well."

"Age has nothing to do with it. If you had fallen onto a big pile of gold nuggets, I'd think you were an eccentric genius but, you landed in a pile of plain dirt . . . I rest my case, you are a nut."

"You greedy bastard; if I had hit pay dirt in my descent you'd have been right there digging it out of my fractured and bleeding skull. I would have died while you filled your pockets."

"The point is, you landed in sandy soil. There was nothing to dig from your head and I do mean nothing,"

"Empty head or not, I do realize one thing you've overlooked. How could an unsuccessful miner survive almost a century, paying for his existence with cash and gold nuggets if he hadn't hit something?"

"Maybe he had another source of money, like an inheritance or even a social security check."

"Buddy, you've already said he had no bank accounts and do you really think a stipend from Uncle Sam could have supported him? Social security does not come in the form of gold dust."

"If you're right, it would mean he had a strike hidden away somewhere in the mine." A greedy smile came across his face as he spoke.

"Well, if he did have a secret stash it isn't going to do him any good now. He's dead and it's lost. How do you account for the fact that he was already decomposing when the fire started?" Ted inquired.

"I suppose we can rule out the idea he started it since he was already lifeless."

"Dr. Steve ordered a closer look at the fireplace. He thinks a fire could have smoldered for some time and ignited after his demise, or perhaps the chimney was blocked and he was overcome by carbon monoxide," Ted explained.

"I suppose it's possible. It would be difficult to tell about carbon monoxide poisoning by his skin color (it would have turned cherry red if CO were the cause) but you didn't find any in his blood gasses, did you?"

"Well no, but the toxicology boys found cyanide in his system."

"Did anyone observe any signs of frothing in his mouth or lungs or signs he'd had a pulmonary bleed?"

"No, just traces of cyanide in his brain, blood and in the fluid taken from his eyes."

Cyanide is what they use in the gas chamber to kill prisoners. It is also used to extract gold from the rock it is found in. Extreme caution is needed in the process or it will kill faster than you can say Jack Robinson.

"Okay, it was present in his system but obviously not enough to cause his demise," I noted.

"Maybe someone was slowly trying to poison him and the fire just beat them to it," Ted surmised as he kicked at the ashes on the ground.

"Let's see, he was a hermit, so we can assume he didn't have a chef. Therefore we can rule out the cook. Do you honestly think he had a butler? You know in most murder mysteries the butler almost always did it."

Ted didn't find my sarcastic scenarios helpful or even funny. He just stared at me as though I might really be brain damaged.

"You chatter like the squirrels. Standing here on sacred ground and laughing about the death of a great spirit, you dishonor your ancestors." Oh God, my friend was back.

"Holy ground, Great Spirit; what are you talking about?" I asked my hallucinogenic companion.

"Who said anything about Holy ground or spirits?" Ted asked looking at me as though he was certain I had lost my mind.

This was beginning to really drive me insane and if I was going to resume my career, I had to tell someone about my new buddy. Ted and I had been friends for quite a long time. I knew he could keep a secret. I just hoped he would understand my predicament.

"Ted, you and I have been friends for a long time and I trust you."

"Sure, you can trust me to the end. I consider you my best friend; however, it doesn't say much for my selection of friends."

"Quit teasing. I have something serious to tell you and I hope you will keep it a secret."

"Don't tell him. He's just going to have you locked up. If he thinks you see ghosts, he'll never want to be alone with you again. He already thinks you're a loon," the chief warned.

"I really don't care if he thinks I'm certifiable. I can't take this any longer."

"Who thinks you're certifiable and who do you keep talking to?" Ted, of course thought I was talking into empty space, as any insane person would do while visiting with their imaginary friends. "Do you need to go home and rest" Ted seemed genuinely concerned about my wellbeing or, maybe just for his own safety.

"I mean it. Ever since I woke in the hospital I keep seeing this Indian guy and he's continually badgering me with advice and information he thinks I need to know."

"You mean an Indian like Gandhi? Is he wearing a diaper? Ask him the meaning of life for me will you," Ted mercilessly mocked.

"I really mean it. He's been following me around making cryptic remarks. I keep blaming it on the medications I'm on but there is part of me that wants to listen to him and follow what he tells me to do."

"Don't worry. My cousin Luther swore he saw pixies for three months after he tried to fly off of the garage roof in the third grade. Just ignore it and it will go away," he tried to assure me I was still sane in his opinion.

"Pixies, I'll show him pixies!"

Suddenly a strong wind blew Ted's hat from his head.

"Ted, if I were you, I wouldn't piss off my hallucination. He might get mad and do more than blow off your hat next time."

"That was just a freak gust of air. I think you need to take your medication."

"What proof does this white man wish?" the chief asked.

"Ted, the chief wants to know what you need as proof he's really standing behind you."

"Quit trying to scare me. You know I don't like this creepy crawly stuff. Let's just go back to the office and look at the photos from the autopsy."

The chief reached out and hit Ted in the back of his head.

"Ouch! Something just hit me." Ted exclaimed.

"Bone picker, tell the mouse I know he has six-hundred dollars in his mother's teapot in the closet,"

"Okay, I'll try. Ted, the chief says you have six-hundred dollars stashed in a teapot in your closet." Ted turned pale and grinned sheepishly.

"Impossible! No one knows about my cash stash. I must have told you while I was drunk or something."

"Ask him if he wants me to tell him where he keeps his dirty images. You know, he has all twelve additions of something called 'Girls Gone Mad.'"

"Well then, the chief wants to know if you'd like him to tell you where all your dirty movies are hidden. He says you have all twelve editions of 'Girls Gone Mad.'"

"Oh my God, you really do see a ghost, don't you?" Ted looked at me in total amazement.

"You really do have money and porn stashed?" I asked just as amazed. Ted always seemed so straight-laced to me.

"Forget that. This is cool. What is the chief's name?"

"Oh, now you believe me. You know, I've never believed he was really there myself so I've never bothered to ask."

"You speak as if I am a log. I'm dead, not deaf you know," the chief answered.

"I know you're standing there, but now I wonder why you haven't told me what to call you, since you seem willing to tell me everything else."

"First lesson from the ancestors; never answer a question which has not been asked," the chief calmly explained.

"Well, what did he say?" Ted, now a total believer anxiously inquired.

"He says, 'I never asked so there was no need to tell me.'"

"So ask, damn it! If I'm standing next to a ghost I'd feel better if I knew his name and if he is going to follow me into the bathroom . . ."

"You may tell he who sits to pee, I will not follow and I am called 'Walks In Rain.'"

"He wants me to tell 'he who sits to pee' and by that, I think he means you he has no interest in joining you while you perform any bodily functions."

"Hey! I have a prolix kidney and I have to sit or I get an infection," Ted stated defending his seated posture.

"You mean a prolapsed bladder, don't you?" I asked, knowing fully well there is no such thing as a 'prolix kidney.'

"Kidney, bladder what's the difference. This is wonderful. The problem is if we tell anyone about our phantom friend here they'll throw us both out of office and probably lock us up. We have to keep him a secret. Do you agree?" Ted looked more serious than I'd ever seen him in my life.

"Do you actually think I'm going to admit to anyone else I have an Indian following me around? The only reason I told you is I had to say something to someone. My wife is a medical doctor trained in psychology, one word from her and I'm in the locked ward and she inherits my entire estate."

"Estate? You own a house, two cars and three storage units filled with junk. Who are you kidding?" Ted smiled.

"One man's estate is another man's garage sale," I retorted.

"Rex, you know we're here to solve the old man's death. Does our friend have any insight as to what happened to him, or are his skills limited to what I have hidden in my closet and under my bed?"

"Ah, a question asked. The Great Spirit requires an answer be given, understood or not."

"What does he say? Can he help us or not?" Ted asked anxiously.

"Well, he says you've asked a question and he is obligated to give you an answer; whether you understand it or not. If you expect a straight answer from him you are sadly mistaken. Are you good at puzzles?"

"Every Sunday I do the crossword puzzle in ink. I think I have a good chance of deciphering his silly little riddle."

"I told you, the answer you seek can come from flesh and is more ancient than the dust. From here you must find your own solution. Look around, the explanation you seek is before your eyes and beneath your feet."

"Okay mister 'New York Times,' he says the solution is under your feet, it can come from flesh and is more ancient than the dust. I'm really looking forward to hearing your genius solution."

"That's it? He can't say I saw a wild man run in and set fire to the cabin? All he can do is say the answer is more ancient than flesh? Hell man, my mother-in-law is that old."

"Somehow, I don't think he's referring to your mother-in-law, sits to pee. Think, what can come from flesh and is older than dust?"

"Rocks, of course. I don't see how that helps. There are rocks everywhere; we're standing on a mine for God's sake!"

"Excuse me? What rock comes from flesh?"

"Kidney stones of course," he smugly answered.

"Maybe he means a special rock or gold ore. I don't think there are any Kidney stones scattered around here. You're the self-proclaimed riddle master, go ahead. What do you think he's trying to hint at?"

"I want to know why he just can't tell us what to look for or even where to begin to search. Is there some kind of spirit rule that says he can't just give us the answer?"

"He probably wants to see how good you really are at solving silly riddles."

"Hey, I got the rock part."

"Oh yeah, real hard, we're in the Rocky Mountains. Rocks were a real difficult answer to come up with."

"There must be something special about a rock here. Maybe the old man left a will stashed under a stone. It might give us a clue about possible heirs." Ted was grasping at straws if he thought we were going to find a fading document down here that would solve this case for us.

"The only special kind of rock I can think of is gold. Maybe the clue refers to a hidden vein of precious metal," I hypothesized.

"Well, the only way to know is to go back down into the mine." Ted was not thrilled at the prospect.

We climbed down into the shaft via the opening I had provided when I fell the last time I was here.

This time I descended somewhat slower using the ladder left behind by my rescuers.

"Please tell me you brought your big policeman flashlight, I only have a small one." I asked.

"Flashlight, mace, stun gun, handcuffs and silver bullets for my gun. I was an Eagle Scout, you know"

"A slightly over prepared type A, paranoid Eagle Scout I'd say."

We reached the bottom of the ladder and after a few steps were glad we had a flashlight. The darkness engulfed us as the light from the portal we'd descended rapidly disappeared behind us.

"Rex, the old miners were a strange group. They had odd superstitious habits like carving bizarre things into the walls of these shafts. I've been told there have been booby traps and curses found in some mines."

"Well, let's try to avoid those mines."

"I was thinking, perhaps the Indian is referring to a glyph hidden somewhere on the walls."

"I think the air must be getting thin. You're actually making sense. I've heard of salt miners carving entire churches inside mines."

"If we find a cathedral down here, let's say I'll be the next corpse."

"Ted, it's more likely we'll find he carved his own crypt somewhere down here."

"A grave down here. If we do find some coffin thing down here, I'm 'Casper,' gone, out of here, history. In fact the more I think about it, we should leave now and call somebody from the bureau of mines or mummies."

"Good Lord man, what are you afraid of? The corpse is back at the morgue and there's nobody else around. Would you really want to miss out on telling everyone about the big gold strike you found?"

I knew I'd get him by greed or ego, either way he wasn't leaving.

"Are you kidding me? You think I'm going to risk my life with you and your transparent friend for the glory of gold?"

"Well, we were sort of counting on it."

"You know of course, I hate you."

"Ask him if that means he's in," Walks in rain asked.

"The wet one wants to know if that means 'you're in.'"

"Both of you, shut up and somebody lead the way," Ted begrudgingly surrendered.

"Go down the tunnel leading east, as far as it goes," the Chief instructed.

"He says go down the tunnel to the east," I interpreted.

"East, west, all I can tell is up and down. I guarantee down is not my preferred direction," Ted complained. "Get out your trusty compass and let's go."

"Me? You're captain marvel Boy Scout. Are you telling me that with all that crap you listed off, you don't have a compass?"

"Hey, I have the manly Maglite two thousand, equipped with the lightning on feature."

For a moment I was impressed, in fact almost intimidated. But then, God gave Ted 'a little special attention'. His special issue waterproof, bullet-proof flashlight made with the deluxe Kryptonite case began to flicker, followed quickly by pitch blackness. Ted shook it, banged on the wall and spoke several magic words that one should not use in mixed company. It was still dark.

"I hate this thing," Ted kept repeating as he switched it off and back on in some hopeless delusion that the thing would miraculously come back to life. It was still dark. As a matter of fact, I would swear it was getting darker.

"Ted, when was the last time you checked the batteries in that thing?" It was a simple question.

"Never. They just gave it to me last month and I've never used it."

"Did you put new ones in it when you got it?"

"Don't you think it would come with good batteries in it?"

"Where is your flashlight? Or, are we going to stand here in the dark discussing me?"

"At the risk of totally freaking you out, I didn't bring batteries for the flashlight either."

"We're going to die. I knew it. You and your ghost buddy will somehow survive but, I'm dead. I know it. I'm the guy on 'Star Trek' who beams down wearing the red tunic; everybody knows he's a dead man," Ted continued to babble to himself.

"Wow, quite freaking out. We are not going to die. I brought one of those new flashlights, the kind you shake and you have light forever, guaranteed."

"You have the only defective one ever made. I just know it."

"Lord, you are more tightly wound than I thought. Here, if it will make you feel any better, take this box of matches."

"Sure, as soon as I strike one to find my way out, I'll be in the midst of a methane cloud and blow up!"

"Ted, look at it this way, I'll be right here with you."

"You can't fool me. Your ghost will find a way to save you. I'll just be bits and pieces and you'll be on Oprah explaining the freak accident."

"Ted, have you checked into medication?"

"The only time I need medicated is when I'm around you for more than an hour."

"Well, there's your sign. We should work together in fifty-five minute bursts, and then you'll be safe."

"Squaws go down this tunnel," the chief sternly instructed.

"The wet one says go down this tunnel. It must go east."

"Is he back? I'll bet it was him that killed my flashlight. I read once ghosts drain the batteries in your equipment."

"Bone Picker, tell tiny humming bird I cannot hear his buzzing, I am old and hard of hearing."

I laughed to myself and turned in the direction Walks pointed. We crept down the passage expecting to fall to our deaths with each step. Our little light was true to the advertisement. It recharged with each shake. The thing the marketing company failed to mention in its infomercial was the beam only lit about five feet in front of us. I became alarmed by a scratching sound that seemed to be following us. Each time we stopped, so did the strange noise. Maybe we had more than one phantom with us on this quest.

"Ted, hear that scratching noise following us?"

"Yes?"

"What do you think it is?"

"Sorry, I was marking our path by etching a line in the wall as we go."

"With what? That just sounds wrong somehow."

"My flashlight," he replied sheepishly.

"Well, as much as I'd like to give you grief, that is probably a good idea."

Just as I was beginning to believe we were lost, the tunnel narrowed and came to an end.

"Well, here is the end of this tunnel." I lifted my flashlight and couldn't believe the carving before me. "Oh my God, there is an 'all seeing eye' carved into the wall."

"All Seeing Eye. What the Hell is that?" Ted whispered.

"It's a Masonic symbol."

"Masonic, you mean like 'National Treasure'?"

I have been a Free Mason and member of the Shrine for about six years. As my grandpa lay dying his last request was that I join the craft. Men of his generation and many in our family had been Masons for the past two-hundred years. Of course, I resisted joining for nearly twenty-years. I just could not understand why he wanted me to join a club consisting of ninety-year old men. Once I was fifty, I realized if I didn't join I never would, besides now they didn't seem so old.

"If you had listened to me when I invited you to join the Mason's, you wouldn't be asking dumb questions now and you would have enjoyed the 'National Treasure' movie even more."

"I may not be a Mason, but, my dad belonged to the rotary. Does that help?"

"As a Master Mason I understand the glyphs but I can only tell you so much. Some of the information refers to Masonic mysteries I can't explain to you."

"You a master, they must let anyone in."

"Be nice or I won't tell you what the eye means." I threatened.

"I don't care what any of this means. Just follow whatever your ghost or secret symbols tell you to go and, let's get out of here. I'm beginning to get the creeps."

"Well, the eye is the watchful eye of God it is found in the east looking toward the west watching over all worthy and unfinished works. So, I think we should follow the tunnels going west. If I am right somewhere we should find a pillar. If he really was a Mason and wanted to leave a clue he just might use Masonic symbolism."

"Wind up your little light Moses and lead the way. I won't even ask about the pillar."

"The ledged of King Solomon's pillars is no secret. Don't you read the bible?"

"The people of Israel hid their most valuable treasures within the pillars of King Solomon's temple."

"You are going to turn me into a crazy DaVinci code nut and then sacrifice me, aren't you?"

"Oh yeah Ted, me and the other fourteen guys at the lodge are out to eliminate you. Then without you to resist us we can take over the world. Did I mention I'm fifty and known as the 'kid.' Most of the brothers are over eighty. I don't think they are much of a threat. It would probably take them all to hold you down to drink the Kool-Aid."

"Here's the end of the tunnel and I don't see any pillar. So much for your theory. Let's go now," Ted confidently exclaimed.

"Oh ye of little faith," I held up my tiny lamp.

Ted looked toward the ceiling as the beam fell on two large pillars.

"Wow, two pillars and a big room," Ted said, sounding amazed.

"The one on the left is named Boaz and the one on the right is called Jachin. Well, that's what the bible says."

"I don't care what they are called. They look as if they grew directly from the bedrock. I can't see a tool mark on them anywhere."

"Well, it looks like old Dirk didn't spend all of his time looking for riches. From the fine work on this monument he spent years carving. I promise if he has engraved the all Seeing Eye, Jachin and Boaz, there are more hidden Masonic clues here than we have seen so far."

"Okay, now I'm beginning to believe you," Ted continued to lovingly caress the finely carved pillars.

"Ted, old buddy, I think you are right. The air down here is affecting our thinking. Why don't we go back to the office and look at a few autopsy pictures. After all, we are here to solve a death, not go on a treasure hunt." I hoped I sounded interested in the death and not the Masonic clues. What I really needed to do was recruit a few detectives who were Master Masons.

"At last, I've been waiting to hear you say let's go. I hate it down here. Last one to the surface is a rotten egg." Ted started for the exit. It took about five seconds for poor Ted to realize he had no light and was charging into pitch blackness.

"Okay, you lead the way. God, the only thing I hate more than being down here with you and your buddy is being in the dark."

Ted was clearly relieved as we emerged from the labyrinth into the bright mid-day sun. I must admit I was just as thankful. For all of his whining, I was certain Ted had forgotten. I was the one who had fallen and almost died in these tunnels. True, I had luckily avoided an appointment with the grim reaper. However, I was also the one now stuck with an ethereal friend.

Several days passed before I was able to locate a detective who was also a master mason. Jack Schnitz was a "Worshipful Master" of the lodge in Pebble, Colorado.

Jack arrived somewhat dismayed about my statewide search for a detective that fit the bill.

"I've been called out for a lot of weird reasons, but a request for a Mason? My captain was asking questions I didn't know how to answer. When I saw the communiqué I wasn't sure about the request myself. After all, you are known statewide as some kind of kook, you know."

"Kook is putting it mildly. I'm aware of my reputation, one which I might mention I am proud of. How shall I put it? This case involves Jachin, Boaz and an all seeing eye." I waited for a reaction.

His pupils dilated and then quickly constricted; a sure sign of understanding.

"You're kidding, right?"

"I wish I were. Would I have put out an APB for a brother if it weren't serious?"

"Not unless you were looking for a severe punishment, since it would be a clear violation of your Masonic oath."

"I really wasn't seeking the ultimate penalty."

"How shall I know you as a master?" Jack wisely inquired.

"Do you want the oath or the points?" I responded.

He made me do both. Satisfied I was indeed a brother he asked the details of the case. I filled the bewildered detective in about my observations and the facts of record.

"Holy dodo, take me to the scene. This I've got to see for myself."

"Wouldn't you like to eat first?"

"Food? You are kidding? Let's see what you have then we'll eat."

It took the better part of an hour to reach the scene and descend five stories down to the level of interest.

"Oh my God . . ."

"Stop before you say anything you might regret," I smiled with a certain degree of satisfaction.

"Now I see why you sent out the message. These pillars are obviously the pillars of Solomon."

"When I saw them I knew I needed the help of another who had been raised."

"This may be more than I can help with. We may need the assistance of someone more enlightened than either of us!"

"Before you give up, what do you think we are looking at?"

"I'm really not sure. These are obviously meant to be Solomon's pillars. But, do you think he has hidden a treasure inside?"

"No, I think he left them as a clue as to where to go next."

"Next. Just what are you thinking?"

"Well, I don't know. He obviously was well versed in tradition. What if we follow King Solomon's order to the apprentices?"

"Go to sea, down here?"

"No let's go in the direction they found the body, maybe the next clue is to the north."

"Lead the way."

"What Great Spirit do you chatter about? I know nothing of this king and I give my word there are no bodies down here," Walks in Rain responded.

"The king was the king of the Jews and he sent men to find his top mason when he was missing." I answered, forgetting I was responding to someone Jack was unaware of.

"I know who Solomon was. Why are you telling me the story?"

"Oh God, I forgot. You haven't met my specter friend. Jack, meet 'He Who Walks In Rain.' Walks meet Jack."

"Damn, you are nuts! You talk to invisible people? Let me out of here. I'm missing my son's little league game."

"Trust me Jack. When I woke after a fall down here I've had a companion no one else seems to see. I thought I had lost my mind but, he seems to be real and has helped guide me toward the clues we've found so far."

"If my captain finds out I've come all this way to help a crackpot chase a ghost around in the dark he's going to be pissed."

"GHOST, who is he calling a ghost? I am a spirit!" Walks was angered by the term and seemed to take it personally.

"Jack, don't say that. He'll get upset."

"Upset, who are you kidding? There is no such thing as ghosts."

"He prefers to be referred to as a spirit."

"Oh God, I'm trapped with a psycho and didn't bring a gun." Jack sounded freaked out a bit.

"Please, don't go crazy on me. He really exists no matter what you think. At first I didn't believe it either."

"I'm leaving you and your friend here, I'm going home." Jack moved toward the exit.

He was stopped by a strong foul smelling wind. In fact he was almost knocked to the ground by the blast.

"What the hell was that? It stinks, did you fart?" Jack exclaimed.

"I told you don't make him mad. He can really scare you if you persist."

"If you think a downdraft is going to change my mind about your sanity, you're crazier than I thought," Jack quipped.

"Are all of the white eyes as doubtful as this?" Walks responded. "If he needs to see more I will teach this young willow." Walks was not happy.

"Jack! Please listen to me; don't aggravate my phantom, whether you believe or not, just indulge me or I can't guarantee your safety," I pleaded.

"You are a nut job."

"Don't say I didn't warn you. Okay Chief, do that voodoo you do so well."

With that I unleashed a power I truly had not seen, or expected.

From the depths of the westward tunnel came a scream. It frightened even me and I was expecting some strange event.

"Jesus what was that?" Jack was terrified.

"I warned you; don't anger my guardian 'Chief, Walks in Rain.'"

"You mean there really is a 'spirit' you can talk to?"

"Just trust me . . . If you don't, I'm sure he will try to convince you with another demonstration."

"No, I'm good. I believe you. Let's look for any other clues and solve this case. I just want to go home."

"Okay Chief, you heard him, tell us where to go next."

"The answer you seek is deep in the breast of mother earth where two paths meet in a cross." The chief advised.

"Jack, we have to go down."

"Just how far down? Does your friend have any idea?"

"Nope he just said to go down."

"Of course we do. It couldn't be up that would be too easy. Stop passing gas and shake that little flashlight and let's go."

"I don't have gas. The Chief may, but it's not me. My kids would say the one that smelt it dealt it so, it must be you."

As we stepped over fallen beams and piles of crushed rock, Jack hit his head on the partially collapsed ceiling, twice.

"Damn chicken little, would you mind warning me if you see the roof is falling in?"

"Sorry, it is difficult to see with this small light."

"Why didn't you bring a bigger light?"

"Ted brought a big light the last time we were here. The batteries died. I'll keep this one thank you very much. I really thought it would be easier than this, you know I assumed we would just look at the pillars and that would be it. Why didn't you bring your big policeman flashlight?"

"To tell you the truth, I didn't think you would drag me on a trip to the center of the earth. How far down does this thing go?"

"I have no idea. We've gone down four levels and it seems to just keep going. It's hard to believe the old man did this all by himself."

"He did? Are you sure? I mean who told you that he did?"

'Well, Ted said that was what he was told."

"I wonder who told him that. You know the first rule of law enforcement is to double check the facts."

"Now you make me think I might have missed something, like maybe the old man had someone helping him. If that's true then there is somebody out there who would have a motive to kill him."

"Someone he might have told about where the ore was the most promising. Or, who might have found it themselves and wanted him out of the way so they could claim it for themselves," Jack hypothesized.

"Oh great, if there is a killer out there how do I find them? The old boy was good at keeping secrets I wonder if he told anyone else about his helper. If not, we may never find out who it was."

"If you hadn't considered there was someone with a motiv,; what were you thinking happened to him?" Jack seemed truly interested now. I guess every cop has some point they begin to question all aspects of a mystery. When the clues get under their skin, solving the case becomes all consuming.

"I was going with the idea it was a natural death and the fire was just a fluke. You know he had a fire burning and died of carbon monoxide poisoning then lightning struck the house and it burned to the ground with him in it."

"Did the autopsy show evidence of carbon monoxide poisoning?"

"Not really. It just seemed like the most likely scenario."

"I was just thinking who did he sell his ore to? They would at least know there was gold on his property. Maybe they could have snuffed the old boy," Jack continued to brainstorm.

"He did use gold to pay the grocer. But he is older than Dirk. I doubt he could have even hiked up to the cabin much less climbed down here to mine gold."

We climbed down one more ladder to the fifth level as Jack continued to offer other solutions to this mystery. We were so busy offering each other theories I had forgotten how deep we were or for that matter how bad it smelt.

"There are no relatives that might want him dead?"

"Not one, I guess he out lived them all."

As we crawled along the tunnel in almost pitch darkness covered in dust, we found the intersection the chief mentioned. Once again there was a glyph skillfully carved into a niche on the wall.

"Rex, shine your light up here so I can see it a little better."

"It looks like a leaf. Well, you know what that means."

"Probably time to dig, eh?" Jack guessed.

With our bare hands and a piece of fallen timber we began to move the dirt at our feet. We had only gone down a few inches when we found something that made a clunking sound as we hit it. It was an old strong box. Jack strained to lift it and we started toward the surface dragging our bounty as we went. All thoughts of who killed poor old Dirk were gone. In almost total silence we slowly made our way to the surface.

Once we were safely above ground we anxiously pried the iron box open.

"At last, something that might actually solve this mystery," I said as I opened the rusted lid.

The box contained a folded piece of paper and under the parchment to our surprise GOLD, lots and lots of gold.

"No wonder the damned thing weighed so much," Jack observed. "I thought I was going to get a hernia carrying it up here."

"I've never seen so many nuggets in my life," I was amazed.

"It is beautiful." Jack observed. "Read the note."

"It looks like a last will and testament." As I began to read, another document fell from the will and landed at Jacks feet. He scooped it up as I read the one I held.

"This says, 'I bequeath all of my worldly possessions to the benevolent uses of the Shrine for the benefit of handicapped children. Oh my God, he wasn't only a mason, but a Shriner as well. It looks to me as if the shrine hospitals will not need to do fund raising for a long time. They'll need to name a wing or two after this old guy"

"Wing; try a hospital or two." Jacks voice was shaking as he read his piece of the puzzle.

"What do you have there?" I asked.

"It looks like a map to a treasure room and if it is right, there is enough cached to fund twenty more hospitals."

"Let me see. I've never seen a treasure map before."

"You know, this has been a terrible waste of your time. After all I'm really crazy and I talk to people who don't exist. This whole thing has been a gross waste of your valuable time. We really wouldn't want to upset your Captain. So, why don't you just write this off as a total waste of time, forget about what you have seen here and go home, like you threatened." I smiled, knowing he was an honorable man and would not leave. However, part of me was hoping he would take me up on the offer. No such luck.

Jack's parchment was a map locating the old miners stash. It wasn't concealed in the pillars. It was buried behind the 'All Seeing Eye'. All we would have to do was break through the wall to find the treasury.

Reluctantly, we called the County Sherriff for help and to turn the box, map and gold over to him. I must admit, for a few minutes as we waited for reinforcements to arrive, the thought of keeping just a few of the nuggets was discussed. It was only natural to consider the idea, but in the end we both realized we were not good crooks and would most likely be discovered. It was fun to consider what we could do with just a few pieces of gold.

The Sherriff posted several guards at the cabin to protect the mine until the proper authorities could come and remove the treasuries hoard. I think he posted more than one deputy just so they could keep an eye on each other, more than to keep off thieves. Within a day, the

Colorado Department of Mines had found and recovered the bullion. There were several million dollars in nuggets and gold dust. Jack and I were glad we didn't have to carry it all out ourselves. However, for a percentage, we would have gladly tried.

With the gold safely removed and Jack back on the job in Pebble there was just one thing left for me to do. Solve the mystery of what or who killed old Dirk. I took all of the autopsy pictures as well as the toxicology reports home to review. There was not much to see in the photos, just a dead old man partly decomposed. His charred skin made it imposable to determine by looking if he had been poisoned by carbon monoxide since the classic cherry red appearance was not visible. I read and reread the toxicology report there was no trace of poison other than traces of cyanide. The levels did not seem high enough to have killed him. But each person would have different sensitivity to the toxin. The post mortem report showed no evidence of any recent fracture or sign of a concussion so I could rule out a hit on the head. There was no indication of a hyoid fracture so strangulation was out as a cause. There just seemed to be no answer to the question of what had done him in. Maybe it was just a natural death caused by the rock dust in his lungs. People do die of asthma attacks. That did not account for the fire and what caused it. The fire department said there were no signs of arson or any accelerant to spread the fire. Pardon the pun, but I was at a dead end. When there is nothing left to do, I usually find a nap helps. So, I curled up on the sofa and went to sleep. I was awakened by a smack on the top of my head. It was Walks in Rain standing over me.

"You sleep more than the cat. Do you waste your life dreaming?"

"I was thinking. Sometimes it helps to let the subconscious mind do the work."

"Bone picker, what troubles keep you sleeping?"

"Well, I just can't figure out what killed the old miner." Great, I've become accustomed to having a spirit around. Now I just carry on conversations with my imaginary friend and don't even worry that someone thinks I'm off my rocker.

"Why do you try so hard? I told you how he died."

"You did not!"

"Your head is harder than the rock. I told you look in the past. Your answer can come from flesh and can be more ancient than the dust.

"Oh. The solution just gets easier and easier each time you tell me that."

"Send for the chipmunk. He thinks he is a riddle master."

"Oh yeah, he's got rocks. Tough challenge there."

"Eh, go back to sleep and remember your journey."

He smiled and faded, leaving behind the echo of his condescending laugh. When I woke in the morning I had the answer. He was right. It was my conversation with Jack that gave me the clue.

Do you have it? It is so simple . . . .

REX REVEALS

The clinical reports had no clue to the cause of death. There were no fractures, bruises, contusions or signs of poisoning. There were no suspects for a murder. In most cases that would leave only natural causes as a ruling but, not in this case.

All it took was a good meal and some deep sleep to bring the conversation with Jack back to mind. Actually, it was Lori accusing me of being as she put it "a cover fanning fart monster" and moving to the sofa that clued me in.

The memory which popped into my head was of poor Jack, when he kept complaining I was passing gas. Honest, I wasn't. However, there was a cause for the foul smell Jack had attributed to my bodily functions: Methane and a little sulfur.

Methane gas occurs naturally, not only from the gastro intestinal tract, but also from the decay of organic material and volcanic activity. This concoction of toxic and explosive gasses is often found while deep rock mining, in the pursuit of precious minerals. Old timers call it 'bad air.'

Here is the solution: Methane gas had been building up in the mine. Most likely Dirk hit a large pocket while digging. The gas seeped up from the shaft into the cabin and had a sufficient concentration to suffocate Dirk in his sleep. (Yes, you could die from your dads farts.) He died several days before the volume of gas became explosive. Once the concentration of methane reached critical mass all it needed was a spark or flame to set it off. It ignited due to an unknown cause, most likely an ember in the fireplace. Following the fire, the levels of gas dropped due to the fact it had been consumed by the flames.

Testing for methane is not done at the time of autopsy and leaves no outward sign to detect unlike carbon monoxide which turns the skin red.

So the clue that Walks in Rain kept referring to was the gas, "It can come from flesh and is more ancient than the dust."

So, the cause of death was ruled accidental.

Official Grading Scale

Correct	solutions Grade
Zero	You are a Corpse
One	You should be a corpse
Two	You should be embalmed
Three	You qualify to dig graves or occupy one
Four	You could be an autopsy technician
Five	Mortuary school is in your future
Six	You are an average sleuth
Seven	You would be a good detective
Eight	You read the solutions first
Nine	You have cheated somehow
Ten	You should be a coroner
Eleven	You are a coroner
Twelve	You could be a pathologist
Thirteen	You know the author!
Fourteen	You are psychic.
Fifteen	You exaggerate more than the author.
Sixteen	You've read the book before
Seventeen	Call the author; I need your help!

Good luck with the next book;
Murder, Mayhem or Just a Damn Shame.